BLACK

Also by Christopher Whitcomb

Cold Zero: Inside the FBI Hostage Rescue Team

BLACK

A Novel

Christopher Whitcomb

LITTLE, BROWN AND COMPANY

NEW YORK   BOSTON

To Mick and Jake.
It's all about the journey.

Little, Brown and Company
Time Warner Book Group
1271 Avenue of the Americas, New York, NY 10020
Visit our Web site at www.twbookmark.com

First Edition

Library of Congress Cataloging-in-Publication Data
Whitcomb, Christopher.
    Black / Christopher Whitcomb — 1st ed.
        p. cm.
    ISBN 0-316-60101-2
    1. Government investigators — Fiction. 2. Terrorism — Prevention — Fiction.
3. Undercover operations — Fiction. 4. Women legislators — Fiction. I. Title.
PS3623.H564B56 2004
813'.6 — dc22

                                                              2003060805

        10 9 8 7 6 5 4 3 2 1

                Q-MART

        Design by Bernard Klein
        Printed in the United States of America

BLACK

PROLOGUE

―――――

Presidents' Day

THE PLATFORM CLOCK in Washington DC's Union Station read 23:37 as Jeremy Waller walked into a quiet, almost empty terminal. Thirteen haggard-looking passengers followed him without words. None of them carried luggage or newspapers or books. They wore close-cropped hair and plain street clothes, trying to hide the rabid intensity of men consigned to a mission.

Waller pulled the hood of his sweatshirt over his head, then pushed his hands into his pockets, straining his eyes left and right for signs of countersurveillance. He noted an off-duty conductor flirting with a woman at the information desk and a group of European backpackers sleeping in chairs near the D portal, but nothing stood out as suspicious.

Deep breath, he told himself. *Just let 'em go.* Jeremy slowed his steps, allowing some of the other men to hurry past. Hunger gnawed at his stomach and sleep deprivation clouded his thinking, but there was no point in rushing. Something deep down told him that this night would end better with caution than with speed.

Halfway through the station, Jeremy stopped at a souvenir shop, feigning interest in a display of White House paperweights and CIA T-shirts. He waited patiently as the last of the stragglers disappeared behind him; their reflections faded across the shop's tinted plate-glass window. Jeremy had been sent to work alone tonight, independent of his otherwise closely knit team.

Good, he thought. The people who sent him did not tolerate mistakes. Success would depend on attention to detail, creativity, and design, three things he had never really trusted in others.

Once he was sure everyone had gone, Jeremy found his way to the historic train station's front door and emerged into a grand, shadowed portico. The midnight air spit out something that felt more like snow than rain, sending chills through his six-foot-four, 185-pound frame. Though Jeremy was fit and muscular, his low body fat worked against him here, offering little insulation against the cold. It didn't help that days without sleep and food had stripped away clarity of thought and made it hard to remember even basic tradecraft.

Jeremy backed himself into a dark corner, trying to hide while he assessed his surroundings. The parking circle looked abandoned except for its ring of sodden flags hanging lifelessly at parade rest and an occasional beggar shuffling by in search of warmth. Two DC Metro cops sat quietly drinking coffee in a radio car off to the left. A taxi driver shuffled in his seat, working a crossword. With Congress out for winter recess and the president in Texas, the city felt dead.

The quiet traveler hunched up his shoulders and stomped his feet, trying to stop the shivering long enough to concentrate on his mission. He had just over an hour to move from Union Station to the Egyptian embassy. Sometime after 1:00 AM, a smoke-gray Cadillac STS bearing DC tags would pull up to the embassy gate and flash its lights. All he had to do was record the license plate number, document the embassy's security response, and return to the train station undetected.

Simple, he decided, rubbing his hands against the cold. Simple except that they'd given him nothing to accomplish the task. He had no money, no map, no car. With the exception of the calling card

PIN he'd memorized and his wedding ring, they'd stripped him of all identity.

The following is an individual event of indeterminate duration, the selection coordinator had instructed. *Your objective is to move surreptitiously to an observation post and gather essential elements of intelligence without getting compromised. Under no circumstances will you divulge your identity to anyone other than HRT personnel.*

The orders came with no directions to the objective, no address or route reconnaissance. None of this surprised him. This was *selection,* after all, to the FBI's Hostage Rescue Team, an organization that picked just a handful of new operators each year. Jeremy had waited his whole life for a night like this.

"Thirty-five twenty-one International Court," he whispered under his breath. The selectee shifted his weight, trying to stay warm. He looked around, scanning for evaluators. HRT personnel drove SUVs, mostly — big Suburbans, Explorers, and Dakotas. If they were out there, he couldn't see them.

"Thirty-five twenty-one."

He mumbled the address, which he'd obtained through directory assistance from a pay phone on the train. Memorizing the street number would have been simple under normal circumstances, but physical exhaustion had hampered even basic mental tasks. Each day of HRT tryouts started well before dawn and stretched long past dark in an endless marathon of ten-mile runs, high-angle obstacle courses, and full-contact fighting. Each night, some nameless operator would wake the selectees with a flashbang grenade or a siren's yelp. Within moments, they'd be thrown into a live-fire shooting situation in a place HRT called the "Kill House." By dawn, they'd be back in the mud, racing against their own ability to survive.

Half the selection pool had already dropped out or fallen to injuries. The survivors couldn't remember their own names.

Jeremy waited at the edge of the portico until a black Town Car pulled up to the curb; then he folded a discarded *Post* over his head and ran out to meet it. The Egyptian embassy lay somewhere out there in the rain — a six-mile trudge in better weather, but Jeremy had no intention of walking. Going hypothermic in a winter downpour proved nothing but stupidity. HRT wanted thinkers; that's what they'd get.

Waller smiled at his own cleverness as he ran. After a quick call home from the train's pay phone, his wife, Caroline, had contacted a limo company and hired a car. The solution seemed so obvious, he wondered if he'd overlooked something.

Jeremy reached the door just as the driver opened it for him. "Good evening, sir." It was midnight, but the Pakistani driver seemed strangely alert.

"Thirty-five twenty-one International Court, Northwest," Jeremy said when they were both inside. "I'm in a hurry."

The driver nodded, sensing from Jeremy's tone that this passenger preferred no conversation. He probably thought it strange that this man carried no luggage and wore only light clothing in such awful weather, but everything had been paid in advance and the driver was glad not to have to get out and open the trunk. This was just another passenger, a fare on a miserable night.

The driver checked his rearview mirror and pulled away from Columbus Circle as Jeremy tried to warm himself in the back. The car looked pretty good for its mileage. Glass tumblers rested on dark red napkins. Evergreen air freshener. Coltrane at low volume. Caroline had specified something anonymous, and Washington was full of black Town Cars with tinted windows. They looked understated, every bit as common as a Joseph Bank worsted.

Waller slumped back into the leather seat and closed his eyes. Just a moment's rest, he thought. Five minutes of sleep for a thirty-one-year-old FBI agent caught far from home. Surely they were following him, wondering what in hell he was doing, but that didn't matter now. They couldn't see in through the tinted windows, and by the time they figured it out, he'd be safely back on the train to Quantico.

▌▐

"WE ARE TO here, sir, please," the driver said some indeterminable time later.

Jeremy flinched in his seat and sat bolt upright as the small man smiled and pointed toward an imposing stone structure. He rubbed his eyes and cursed himself for falling asleep.

"You would like me to pull up to the gate?" the driver asked.

"No . . . no, just park over there." Jeremy pointed to an open spot across the street. HRT wouldn't want to cause any real-world alarm with this little exercise, so when the Cadillac passed, it would probably stop only briefly. He'd have a small window of opportunity to meet his objective.

The embassy looked eerily still in the early morning mist. Tall gates opened inward from a guardhouse. Two uniformed security officers sat inside watching monitors and looking bored. An eight-foot stone wall ran left and right into trees that blocked Jeremy's view of the sides and back. He began to sketch on a pad of paper from the courtesy basket, making little arrows to indicate cameras and countermeasures — stick figures for guards.

"This car behind us. Is someone you know?" the driver inquired after a few minutes.

Jeremy glanced over his shoulder as a car slowed and pulled to the side of the road. All he could see through the rain were headlights, but they flashed twice. This had to be the *mark*.

"I think they are doing signal to us, sir. You want I should back up?"

The car stopped fifty yards behind them, too far for Jeremy to distinguish color and make.

"No, stay here until . . ." He leaned onto the armrest, careful not to expose his face in the window, and watched as a smoke-gray Cadillac STS accelerated past them, close enough to touch.

JNG445. The license plate glowed as brightly as neon.

Jeremy wrote the number on his notepad as the taillights drifted down toward Massachusetts Avenue and disappeared. He looked back toward the embassy in hope of seeing some activity worth noting, but there was no movement. No lights flickered. The guards never even noticed.

"OK, bud," he said when he felt sure he had fulfilled his mission. "Take me back to the train station." There was no reason to explain. The chauffeur was paid to drive, not ask questions.

Jeremy fell back into the luxurious seat and smiled broadly. Finally, he could really sleep. Fifteen minutes in the car, an hour back to Quantico, maybe a little shut-eye before dawn. The tension flowed from his body as if a giant spring had been uncoiled within him.

The driver started the car, and his high beams flashed on, cutting through the drizzle like houselights after a captivating show. Jeremy started to lean forward to ask the driver to put on some different music, when his eyes seized open in astonishment.

Out of nowhere, a tall, angular man appeared between the headlights and crouched down behind the distinctive front sight of an AK-74.

The driver screamed, threw open his door, and launched from the front seat.

What the hell? Jeremy wondered. He instinctively reached to his right hip before remembering that HRT had taken his Bureau-issued Glock 23 prior to selection. Glare from the dome light made him squint as he turned back toward the embassy for some kind of reference. But it was too late. Both rear doors flew open at the same time. Guns appeared out of the darkness.

"Freeze, asshole!" someone yelled. The cold steel barrel of a 9mm Uzi settled, rock steady, three inches from the tip of Jeremy's nose.

The rest happened so quickly, his sleep-deprived mind could barely keep up. Someone climbed in behind him and shoved his face down into the seat. Well-trained hands wrenched his arms behind his back and ratcheted steel cuffs onto his wrists, high up behind the metacarpal vestige. They'd done this before.

The man with the Uzi forced Jeremy down onto the limo floor as his partner twisted the cuffs, using steel-on-bone leverage to move him. One of the men stomped his heavy boot into Jeremy's spine as the other screwed the weapon's flash suppressor into his temple. Three doors slammed shut in rapid succession. The engine raced. The dome light faded. Jeremy felt the sharp prick of a hypodermic needle, then the car shuddered beneath him as his captors stole him away.

❚❚❚

"WHAT IS YOUR name?"

Jeremy awoke in a narcotic haze and blinked his eyes, trying to adjust to the brilliant light around him. There were no windows. One door. Cinder-block walls, stained dark at the margins. Water flowed across the concrete floor. He sat in a steel chair, the sort he'd

seen in government office buildings. This one was bent so badly he
had to balance to keep from falling backward.

He might have thought this a drug-induced hallucination if not
for the pain. His hands had gone numb from lack of circulation. His
shoulders throbbed from the way they'd tied him. The thin, metallic
taste of blood stuck to his tongue. He remembered Roger Glover
sucker punching him in the eighth grade. These knuckles were
smarter; sharp enough to cut without breaking teeth.

"What is your name?"

Jeremy heard the voice as if through a tunnel, distant and mono-
tone. His head fell forward, but someone sprayed him with water so
cold it straightened his back. A garden hose snaked in through the
door. His shirt lay in rags on the floor.

What the hell? he wondered. Anger rose up in his gut, overpower-
ing the fear and the pain and the complete incomprehension of
what had happened.

"What's your name?"

Caroline's face appeared in front of him. They hit him with another blast of icy water. Then the kids. Maddy, Chris, Patrick. He
shivered against the cold.

Whack! Another blow, heavy and blunt, hit him somewhere in the
front of his face.

He dropped his head and blew mucus out of his nose, onto his
chest. He started to retch, but there was nothing in his stomach to
vomit. His eyes welled up uncontrollably as a clot of blood loosened
behind his lower lip and spilled out of his swollen mouth.

Who are they? he wondered when the fog cleared long enough for
rational thought. Egyptians? Why the hell would they care about
some guy in a rented car? Americans? Who? Couldn't be the FBI.
They didn't work like this.

Wait a minute, Jeremy thought. He carried no credentials, no
badge, no ID of any kind. Maybe they didn't know who he was. The
revelation prompted Jeremy to open his eyes and lift his head. These
people had simply made a terrible mistake.

"Stop . . ." His voice seemed to lose itself. "Stop. My name is . . ."

But the words caught in his throat. Maybe it was the convulsive
shaking from the ice water, or the way his tongue stuck between his

broken lips. Something froze in his wandering mind long enough to keep him from announcing his identity. Maybe that's what they wanted — for him to admit he was . . .

ZZZEEEEEEEE!

A high-frequency wail shot him bolt upright in his chair. It raged in his ears, loud as the flashbangs HRT threw, only sustained, like a tooth drill, undulating and burning in his skull. He tried to shake it out of his ears, but it stuck to him.

"What is your name?" someone yelled, point-blank.

My God, what is happening? Jeremy's mind started to run from him.

"He ain't talkin'," one voice said. Boston accent. "Give him the water board."

There was movement, then hands, a table, and he was lying flat on his back with his head over the edge. Two men held him as another clamped a thick leather strap over his forehead. They pulled it taut, wrenching his head backward, almost perpendicular to his body.

"Last time. Who are you?"

Jeremy's eyes darted back and forth, searching for reference, as a short, dark figure emerged from the other room. The man stepped in from the right and stood over him a moment. He wore a green T-shirt and had long hair. His eyes stared down through Jeremy's exhaustion and pain and fear to a place reserved for nightmares.

"My name is George," he said, almost endearingly. "I need to know yours."

Jeremy tried to call out, but the leather strap stretched his neck at a cruel angle, making it almost impossible to talk. He tore at the restraints, uttering unintelligible grunts. No one else spoke. The room fell so quiet, Jeremy could hear water flowing out of the hose and into the drain.

The dark man placed a towel over Jeremy's eyes, and all light faded to a vague gray pall. He waited for the pain, rigid as a child in a dentist's chair, but there were no blows. Someone pressed a cloth against his face while another poured some kind of fluid down his throat.

Jeremy choked, completely bewildered at the sensation. The fluid erupted in his nostrils as he seized against the tonic, bucking, lurching, helplessly sucking more of it down his windpipe into his searing lungs. His body started to spasm, tearing at the restraints as the liquid raged in his chest, stealing the air, shutting out the voices, all sound, the light.

Images of his family flashed through the agony as he choked. He remembered strange things: a Slinky moving down stairs, the smell of honeysuckle, Cap'n Crunch for breakfast . . .

The whole room glistened steel white, then disappeared. Into black.

▮

WHEN HE AWOKE, Jeremy found himself fully clothed, cleaned, and free of all restraints. He sat in an overstuffed parlor chair with his arms out beside him. An Art Deco chandelier hung from the center of the room, filling the space with warm, diffuse light. A television blared next to him: Pat Sajak introducing a *Wheel of Fortune* contestant from Ojai.

Jeremy looked around, trying to recover his bearings. Walls covered in brocade fabric and marked by ogee moldings and brass sconces rose to tall ceilings. *Hotel, probably,* he thought. Expensive.

Closer, seven of the thirteen other HRT selectees rested quietly on couches and comfortable chairs, staring blankly at the floor. They looked broken, devoid of personality and ambition. Two other men stood near the door: Jeremy's Pakistani driver and the man with the AK-74.

Jeremy licked the inside of his swollen lip to make sure his mind was not playing tricks on him. Every instinct urged him to get up and run, but something in the look of his fellow selectees stilled his legs. None of them seemed intent on leaving. Maybe they knew something he didn't.

"Give me an *R!*" one of the contestants said. Vanna moved to turn three letter cubes.

The Pakistani driver chuckled. "They love that friggin' *R*, don't they?" he asked no one in particular.

Suddenly, two HRT operators entered the room. They spoke briefly to the doorkeepers; then the selection coordinator, a thick man named Quinn, moved to the center of the room. He spoke benignly, as if the faces staring back in amazement were nothing more than furniture.

"The following is an individual event of indeterminate duration," he announced. "Your next objective . . ."

You thought you had proven yourself, but you never had.

PHASE I

Alice started to her feet, for it flashed across her mind that she had never before seen a rabbit with either a waistcoat-pocket, or a watch to take out of it, and burning with curiosity, she ran across the field after it, and was just in time to see it pop down a large rabbit-hole under the hedge.

In another moment down went Alice after it, never once considering how in the world she was to get out again.

— *Lewis Carroll,* Alice's Adventures in Wonderland

I

Four Months Later

"THE COMMITTEE WILL come to order."

United States Senator Elizabeth Beechum, a Democrat from South Carolina, tapped a wooden gavel and stared out over S-407, a Capitol hearing room reserved for top secret briefings. The space felt typically quiet this morning, barren of the reporters, pool cameras, and curious tourists common to other congressional forums.

"Good morning, gentlemen," she said, noting that of the twenty-odd people in the room, she was once again the only woman. *Typical,* she thought. She'd seen progress during her twenty-three years in Washington, but Congress remained the world's most powerful boys' club. The fact that a Republican Senate had elected her to a third consecutive term as committee chair — the only such cross-party vote in anyone's memory — had little to do with gender. She was a consummate professional in a world that spoke its own language, handed out secrets grudgingly, and demanded uncompromising allegiance to rules. Even the Republicans knew they needed her.

"Before we get started, I want to read into record that this is the United States Senate Select Committee on Intelligence." The four-term senator spoke loudly and with a refined Southern lilt. "Today's session is a closed hearing on technology matters. All minutes, conversations, and proceedings are classified top secret, in their entirety."

Beechum read in the date, the time, and a list of the witnesses seated in front of her. There were two representatives from CIA and one each from the National Security Agency, the Defense Intelligence Agency, the FBI, and the Department of Homeland Security. She called out the names quickly, like a homeroom teacher reciting the roll. This was rote process, an administrative speed bump she'd bounced over a thousand times before.

"I want to thank you all for coming today," Beechum added, slightly distracted. The committee's six other members settled into their seats as she glanced down at the morning's *Washington Post*, which lay discreetly propped against her knees.

BEECHUM AND VENABLE LOCKED IN DEAD HEAT, the top headline proclaimed. Despite Democratic efforts to pick a presidential nominee by the end of March, the race still looked too close to call. Connecticut governor David Ray Venable held on to a four-delegate lead, but party officials from California to New Hampshire were vowing to vote their conscience and Washington was awash in speculation. With a month to go before the Democratic National Convention, Beechum knew that the slightest turn in momentum — just one decent news cycle — could make her the first woman ever to lead a major party's bid for the White House.

"Let me say that we are particularly honored to have a special guest with us this morning," she said, trying to concentrate on the matters at hand. "Mr. Jordan Mitchell."

She nodded toward an elegantly dressed executive perched at a witness table directly across from her. Mitchell's perfectly groomed shock of white hair, John Dean glasses, and bespoke suit stood out in bold contrast to the lineup of military uniforms and drab, government-grade polyester.

"Welcome, Mr. Mitchell," the senator said. "It's nice of you to join us."

Jordan Mitchell needed no further introduction. As chief executive officer and majority stockholder of Borders Atlantic, the world's largest telecommunications company, he rivaled Bill Gates as the best known of America's billionaires. His How to Succeed in Business books often ranked among the year's bestsellers; his high-profile acquisitions filled financial pages around the world. Magazines often fawned over his triumphs. He'd been profiled by *60 Minutes*. Twice.

"Good morning, Madam Chair," he said, smiling. "I want to tell you what an honor it is to testify before your committee. I've long admired your objectivity and foresight in safeguarding this great nation. And I want to add that you look even more . . . engaging in person than on TV."

Charmer, Beechum noted in the margins of her agenda. Fortunately, he wasn't her type. Men like Jordan Mitchell condescended to women, rebuffed oversight, and largely ignored any authority greater than their own. He lived for himself in a secular world of bottom lines, balance sheets, and cost-benefit analyses. She'd seen enough of his kind during her two decades in Congress. His money and power singled him out in the business world, but it would serve him poorly in here.

"Thank you, I'm sure," Beechum replied, trying to sound flattered. "This committee certainly appreciates your cooperation. I understand you canceled a trip to Dubai so you could join us."

Mitchell nodded his head. He saw no need to elaborate.

"I want to assure you, as I said before," Beechum continued, "that our discussions are classified in their entirety and will not leave this room. We all understand the sensitivities of this issue and want to make you feel comfortable being completely candid."

Mitchell smiled politely. He felt comfortable in Washington, but only while clinging to two steadfast tenets: (1) *never trust a politician* and (2) *never say anything you don't want to hear on CNN two hours later.* Jordan Mitchell had billions of dollars resting on the new initiative they'd invited him in to discuss, and there was no way he was going to tell Beechum or her cronies anything that would place it in jeopardy.

"If I may . . . ," a voice interrupted.

Oh, hell, here it comes. Beechum winced. She turned toward Marcellus Parsons, the senior Republican from Montana. The tall, lanky cattleman adjusted his bolo tie, cleared his throat, and fired up his Big Sky hubris.

"I want to tell you, sir," Parsons said, "what a distinct honor it is to have a man of your singular accomplishment before this committee. The new Secure Burst Transmission — or *SBT* — phones that your company has developed will reestablish the United States as the preeminent leader in the worldwide telecommunications industry. We're honored by your presence."

Beechum tried not to choke on Parsons's kowtow. He was right, of course, about the technology. That's why they were here: Mitchell's company had developed a totally secure, low-cost encryption system that would allow virtually any subscriber to communicate without fear of interception. It worked as well on cell phones and landlines as it did in cyberspace and would be a boon to businesspeople, Internet marketers, and personal privacy advocates.

Unfortunately, terrorists, criminals, foreign governments — anyone capable of shelling out $59.99 a month — would enjoy the same protections. Unless Mitchell shared his secrets with U.S. intelligence agencies, Borders Atlantic would set back signals interception efforts by twenty-five years.

"Why don't we get started, then," Beechum suggested. "Mr. Mitchell, I believe you understand our concerns about this new Secure Burst Transmission technology. The United States government spends tens of billions of dollars each year gathering information on offensive foreign powers. As the rest of our witnesses will attest, signals intelligence accounts for almost eighty percent of our overall information-gathering capability. It's a vital part of our national defense."

The committee's witnesses — all government scientists and intelligence program managers — suddenly straightened to bent-leg attention, hoping Beechum would call on them for support. Each of them knew that these hearings carried real consequence. They all wanted to contribute.

"I would like to point out," Parsons fumed, "that not all statements by the chair represent the intentions or opinions of the committee." He cleared his throat again and nodded directly at Mitchell.

"I, for one, hold dear the First, Fourth, and Fifth Amendment protections guaranteed in our Constitution and want to remind everyone of this country's proud traditions of innovation and enterprise."

Beechum tossed down her pen and shook her head. She poorly tolerated attempts to grandstand, especially when they implied any lack of respect for the Constitution.

"Senator, this is not about the Bill of Rights . . . ," she replied, but Parsons interrupted.

"Then what is it? How does the United States Senate drag in one of this nation's most prominent businessmen and accuse him of —"

"I accused him of nothing, Senator," Beechum barked. "I simply —"

"Please, Madam Chair . . . Senator Parsons." Jordan Mitchell raised his hands like a referee stepping in to break up a clinch. These legislators hadn't even made opening statements yet, and they were already starting to kidney punch and bite.

"I understand both sides of this issue," he said with the same avuncular confidence he used to sell books and cell phones, "but I think it is important to point out that these same objections have been raised with each major communications advance since the telegraph. Every time private industry comes up with something new, the government cries out that it will stymie their efforts to protect the greater good of the people. You cannot expect the technology sector to maintain superiority over foreign competitors then rein us in when our efforts exceed your ability to manage them."

"We are at war, Mr. Mitchell," Beechum chided. "With terrorism. I can't show you the actual intelligence, but the FBI and CIA have credible and specific evidence of plans to strike a major American financial institution within the next few months. These SBT phones you are looking to introduce would give terrorists free lines of communication and make our job much more difficult. It could cost lives."

Parsons bristled at her preaching. Like others on the House and Senate intelligence committees, he had received classified briefings about what was now known informally in Washington as "Matrix 1016" — an SCI, or Secure Compartmented Information, report regarding efforts by a little-known Saudi fundamentalist cell to attack or disrupt the Federal Reserve. Nothing in what Parsons had read pointed to specific dates, times, or methods for this long-lead plot, and nothing in that report gave Elizabeth Beechum the right to give one of America's leading entrepreneurs a civics lesson.

"This committee's primary concern is oversight, not regulation," Parsons argued. "One of our most important functions is to prevent abuses of power, to make sure this government never oversteps its authority. I see no correlation between any classified intelligence reports and Mr. Mitchell's new phone system."

"Senators, if I may," Mitchell interjected. "I fully understand that we are at war with terrorism and that we all have individual responsibilities. The problem is that we can't stop technological advancement in the name of security. Private industry would never have developed the Internet, microwave-based communications, satellites . . . hundreds of remarkable inventions, if scientists were held to some government-administered litmus test."

"This is different," Beechum argued. She had worked her entire career in the intelligence community and knew its back alleys and mirrored hallways better than anyone else on the Hill. "Signals intelligence is our most effective weapon against terrorism, and you are rendering it obsolete."

"Please," Mitchell said incredulously. "Intelligence agencies have always found ways to defeat sophisticated encryption. Look at the FBI's Carnivore program and the NSA's Echelon system. Both were created to eavesdrop on otherwise secure communications, and both have been very effective. Yet, people have a reasonable expectation of privacy on their phones and computers, and fortunately for the consumer, my company has come up with a way to restore it. That's not treason . . . that's good business."

"We're not trying to infringe on America's right to privacy," Beechum huffed. Two decades on the Hill had given her a rock-steady sense of national security and a keen eye for bull. "We're protecting our responsibility to investigate and gather intelligence."

"I understand that," he said. "But you are an elected public servant, and Borders Atlantic is a private business with shareholders, a board of directors, market analysts, and lawyers — all of whom tell us that we have the legal and ethical right to develop this technology." He paused for effect. "If you feel it necessary to try to dissect our new SBT technology, jump right in line with our competitors, but please don't make Borders Atlantic a campaign slogan for this year's elections. Do not vilify us for political gain."

Beechum rocked back in her chair, stunned at his strident arrogance. She planned to challenge an increasingly vulnerable president in the fall. Mitchell was taking one hell of a chance in goading her.

"You don't really believe that, do you?" she asked. "You don't really think that the right to make a dollar should override the government's right to protect itself."

"I'm a businessman, Senator, not a spy." Mitchell looked Beechum straight in the eye when he said it, and she felt his power. This man had $47 billion in personal wealth and a huge multinational company behind him. He bowed to no one.

"Mr. Mitchell has a valid point," Parsons interjected. "This new encryption technology will mean thousands of new jobs, billions of dollars in revenue, trade parity, market share . . ."

"And two new factories in your district!" The words jumped from Beechum's mouth before she could gather them back.

Parsons stared at her, as did the other sixteen members of the committee. Politicians often threw mud, but not over pork. Everyone in politics knew that constituents voted their pocketbooks. There wasn't an elected official alive who wouldn't have welcomed factories like Mitchell's into their district.

"I would think," Parsons growled, "that the esteemed senator from South Carolina might consider her advocacy and protection of the tobacco industry before casting stones about factories in Montana."

What had started as a quiet hearing was fast degenerating into a slugfest.

"Borders Atlantic is proud to bring nearly fifteen hundred new jobs to an economically challenged region of the United States." Mitchell nodded, ever the tactician. "We could have built additional plants in Thailand or Mexico or even China, but we chose to stay with the world's most productive workforce. In fact, we pledge to keep all new high-paying technology jobs inside the United States, where they belong."

Bravo, Beechum thought. He had prepared well.

"It's not the factories I object to, Mr. Mitchell; it's the technology behind them. None of these jobs will matter much if the Americans working there have to live in constant fear of terrorism."

She stopped herself short of proselytizing. "Before we nominate Mr. Mitchell for sainthood," Beechum said, "there are still some questions the committee and I would like to ask."

"I have all morning, Senator," Mitchell answered. He nodded to Parsons and the rest of the committee, professional yet almost shamelessly nonchalant.

Beechum's legislative assistant, a Harvard man in a club tie and a wrinkled Lands' End button-down, leaned toward her with a stack of briefing papers, statistics, facts, and accusations. One of the folders — a top secret national security assessment — offered her all the ammunition necessary to knock Mitchell right onto the seat of his hand-tailored pants, but there was no point in playing her trump card yet. Without television cameras and politically savvy reporters, these hearings amounted to nothing more than a backroom pose-down.

Senator Beechum laid down her pen and took a drink of water. She was a Democrat in a land ruled by Republicans, and now they were declaring war on her authority. *So what?* she thought. This bastard was good, but she was better.

▮

"BEEF! BEEF! BEEF!"

Jeremy Waller pushed his way through a crowd of men, trying to find a better view. Fifty HRT operators huddled near a kids' swing set outside a split-level rambler in a Virginia subdivision called Hampton Oaks. All HRT personnel were required to live near the team's training compound on the Quantico Marine Corps Base, facilitating quick response, and this was close enough to walk. Jeremy had just moved his family into a similar house down the street.

"You got 'em, Big Man!" someone yelled.

The focus of everyone's attention seemed to be Albert Devroux, a Charlie Team assaulter, better known among HRT operators as "Beef." At six foot three, 268 pounds, he still looked more like the kid in his Naval Academy football team photo than an FBI agent.

His flattop haircut glistened in the withering afternoon sun. Sweat flowed in streams down the back of his pockmarked neck. Dirt and grass stained the knees of his khaki pants. He'd tried this once already.

"What's the course, and what's the record?" one of his teammates demanded.

Beef stared back into the man's eyes, breathing heavily, trying to match his intensity. It was a rhetorical question, of course — the kind of thing men say to each other when they don't want to admit they're scared.

The "course" looked pretty straightforward. Beef stood behind a starting gate fashioned from croquet wickets and a garden rake. A well-worn path led across his back lawn, between the swing set and the trampoline, to an old hula hoop and a white plastic patio chair. Right in the middle of the seat rested a clear plastic cup filled to the rim with ice-cold Michelob.

The rules were simple: each competitor would get two attempts to run out to the hula hoop, complete a single push-up, then sit in the chair and chug the beer. Each run would be timed. The fastest time would win.

The problem — and there was always a problem in HRT contests — amounted to the location of the hoop and the chair. Albert had just recently installed an invisible dog fence around his yard, and the hoop lay dead center atop the underground shock cord.

Everyone would still be eating burgers and corn if one of the wives hadn't complained that electric shock training seemed like a cruel way to treat the family pet. Albert pointed out that he had already tried it on himself and found the shock only mildly uncomfortable. That claim led to challenge. Challenge led to rules. Rules led to competition, and within twenty minutes, every man at the party had poured outside to test himself against the invisible fence.

Jeremy knew that participation in this contest put him in a tough position. As a probationary member of HRT's New Operator Training School (or NOTS), he still hadn't earned full membership in the elite club. The veteran agents standing around him would expect full effort, but they would not appreciate being upstaged by one of the "fucking new guys." With graduation just three days away,

Jeremy had to find a way to do his best without antagonizing the men who would control his fate for the next five or six years.

"Come on, baby, you can do it!"

Albert's wife, Priscilla, hollered down to him from the back deck. Most HRT wives wouldn't have interfered at a moment like this, but she stood above the fray like a battle warden, waving a barbecue spatula with one hand and tending Beef Jr. with the other. She couldn't have cared less about decorum; this was a matter of pride.

Jeremy found a place at the edge of the crowd and shook his head. Whatever the contest, HRT operators wielded their survival-of-the-fittest mentality like a broadsword. Perhaps it made sense on some level. Only one person comes in first at a gunfight. Second place rarely matters.

"Are . . . you . . . ready?"

Beef rolled his head around on his broad shoulders, clapped his hands together, and nodded. The smell of crab cakes and pork barbecue floated out over the back lawn. Small packs of kids dashed in and out of the crowd, oblivious to the war brewing around them.

"On your mark . . ."

Quinny, a navy grad himself, stood next to the starter's box with one hand on Albert's shoulder and the other on a stopwatch.

"Get set . . ."

The crowd quieted. Priscilla Devroux lowered her spatula.

"Go!"

The place went nuts. Fifty men and assorted sons called out like spectators at a rock fight. "Beef! Beef! Beef!" they yelled, waving their fists in the air and laughing at his misery.

He moved slowly at first, measuring himself. The first eight or ten steps were easy, but as he got closer, the collar started to growl down low beneath his ears. After that, every step got harder. The growl turned to shock. A steady current of pain shot through his body, overriding natural electric impulses, turning muscles against themselves.

Beef tried to pick up speed. He knew that the big muscle groups would fail first. The legs. The back. They would cramp up and make it tough to continue, no matter how hard his mind pressed him forward.

He leaned all 268 pounds of muscle and bone into the contest. This was it, he told himself. Priscilla was watching. His fellow assaulters were cheering. Hell, all of HRT was counting on him. If Albert didn't make it into the chair, a NOThead might actually lay claim to the Top Dog trophy. In the twenty-one-year history of HRT, that had never happened.

Beef crossed the lawn, dived into the circle, struggled to his knees, and managed to get both hands flat on the ground.

Just one push-up, he coached himself. *Just one.* The beer drinking would be easy.

▐

TWO HUNDRED THIRTY-FOUR miles south of Quantico, outside Raleigh, North Carolina, seven corporate executives gathered in a professional park for a little game of their own. The D'Artagnon Center looked like a thousand other office parks, a half dozen single-story pods with shingled roofs, big windows, and lots of parking. Dentists and pediatricians liked them for their relaxed atmosphere and easy access. In fact, suite 411 had been leased just a week earlier to Dr. Hernandez and Associates, general practitioners. The sign on the door still smelled of wet paint.

Inside, six men and a woman sat quietly in a sparsely furnished waiting room. Sunlight peeked in through cheap venetian blinds. Crumpled magazines lay on simulated wood grain. Wal-Mart prints hung in black lacquer frames on the walls.

"Cheap damned HMOs," one of the executives groused under his breath. "I've seen better decorated whorehouses." A couple of people nodded and smiled. No one else talked.

Shortly after they arrived, a door opened, and a homely nurse with reading glasses and field-hockey ankles stood in the doorway. The name tag on her uniform read "Debbie."

"Good afternoon," she said. "Dr. Hernandez will be right with you, but in order to expedite things, we need you to strip to your underwear."

"Strip to our underwear!" one of them exclaimed. These were powerful executives from one of the world's top corporations. Who the hell was she to ask them to take off their clothes? Besides, this group included a woman — a very *attractive* woman. Things like this didn't happen in corporate America. Not in an era when a casual glance could end up in sexual harassment litigation.

"Please, do as I ask," Nurse Debbie said. "I'll be back shortly." With that, she turned and left.

No one moved at first, but after a couple of tentative glances, a doughy, bespectacled corporate security executive named Dieter Planck self-consciously unfastened his Hermès tie, unbuttoned his shirt, and slipped off his Ferragamo loafers. While five other men and a woman sat in their chairs trying to decide if they really wanted to relinquish their pinstripe armor, this man dropped his pants and folded everything in a neat pile on the carpeted floor.

He sat back down in his chair with rolls of perfectly hairless gut hanging like milky bratwurst into his lap. Silver-rimmed glasses shimmied down his sweaty nose.

After a few moments, the door opened, and Nurse Debbie reappeared.

"The doctor will see . . ."

She stopped in her tracks, obviously perturbed that her patients had failed to follow instructions. "Excuse me," she huffed, "but the doctor has a very busy schedule today, and we won't get through this unless you do as I ask."

Her tone left no room for misunderstanding. These junior scions of American enterprise made ten times her salary, but the first step toward this company's new executive vice presidency passed through the door behind her. She held the key.

"I see you're ready, sir." She nodded toward the German. "This way, please."

With that, Dieter scooped up his neatly folded clothing and waddled after her in bare feet. The door closed behind him with a firm thump.

"Screw it," one of the men said after a moment. He shed his Hugo Boss three-piece and sat down in a bright red thong. A human resources consultant from Orlando stared a moment too long, then grudgingly shed his togs, too. Within a few moments, all of them had stripped. In a corporate world where the color of a designer label could differentiate between strength and vulnerability, these people had just rendered themselves impotent.

∎

WHILE JEREMY WALLER and his mates swam outside in the testosterone pool, Jeremy's wife, Caroline, sat in the house trying to stay cool with the rest of the HRT wives. Patrick, their ten-month-old, had missed his nap and wasn't happy. Maddy and Christopher were running around with all the other kids. She had a presentation due at the office on Monday and no time to take the afternoon off for foolishness like this.

But today had been marked for HRT. No arguments. No excuses. The team's initiation process included a formal graduation ceremony for incoming NOTS graduates, but that was a private affair. Today was for the families. All were expected to attend.

"What a beautiful little boy!" A refined-looking woman reached out to wipe a dribble of formula off the baby's chin. "You must be Caroline Waller. And this must be Patrick."

Patrick started to fuss again. *Perfect timing*, Caroline thought.

"Louise Cannell, dear," she said, offering a Junior League smile. "I just wanted to take this opportunity to welcome you aboard."

Caroline recognized the name. Her husband, Steve, was one of the assault team leaders.

"Nice to meet you." Caroline smiled. It was the only thing she could think of. How does one thank the wife of a man who sent Jeremy home bleeding, bruised, and exhausted every night?

"You call me any time you need something, OK? We have to stick together while these boys are out doing whatever it is that they do." Louise offered a kind smile and disappeared among the casserole warmers. She didn't strike Caroline as someone she'd confide her deepest secrets to, but then again, any port in this storm might be worth hanging on to.

This sudden change in lifestyle had come as a bit of a surprise to the Waller clan. Their first four years of Bureau life had been wonderful. Springfield, Missouri, was a vibrant, affordable city that allowed them a nice standard of living on an entry salary of $41,370.

Northern Virginia, on the other hand, seemed like one boundless subdivision with no sense of community. Housing was much more expensive here, and she'd stayed home with the baby for a year, creating a gap in her résumé that made job hunting tougher than she'd hoped. Even with a master's degree in psychology, she'd had to settle for a low-paying position on a community services board.

Fortunately, Maddy and Chris liked their new school and had found plenty of friends in the neighborhood. The other NOTS wives had formed a close support network, sharing everything from baby-sitting to an occasional girls' night out. Jeremy seemed genuinely happy in this new job, despite the long hours and sometimes brutal work. This was Jeremy's dream, but she'd get used to it, too.

"Mommy, Mommy, Daddy's up nextht!"

Maddy flashed by, covered in Fudgsicle. Her tongue poked through the hole where two front teeth should have been, translating common English into the second-grade lisp.

Patrick stared up at her from beneath his bottle, sensing that quiet time had ended.

"Caroline!" someone yelled. Priscilla Devroux shuffled in with Beef Jr. dangling from her mansard hip. "Your man's out there thinking he's gonna put all these other boys down. Ain't you even going to watch?"

The thought hadn't occurred to her. But with all the other wives looking on, Caroline didn't really have much choice. HRT wives supported HRT husbands. She knew the rule like a marriage vow.

"Go ahead on out, sweetie," Melissa Tovar said. She reached for Patrick and nodded toward the back deck. "You go and cheer him on."

▮

BY THE TIME Nurse Debbie returned to the waiting room an hour and ten minutes later, the six remaining executives had begun to fume. They sat in their underwear, with no laptops, PDAs, or cell phones to occupy their time. The man in the red thong slumped in his chair with his jacket pulled over his shoulders, withdrawn into embarrassment. The lone woman sat quietly at the end of the line in a frilly bra-and-panty set of Italian design, ignoring the glances.

"OK, look," the nurse said, leaning through the half-open door. "I hate to do this to you, but Dr. Hernandez just got called to an emergency at the hospital. I'm afraid we're going to have to let you go and reschedule for later in the week."

The groans and deep breaths told her everything she needed to know about their feelings. These people wasted time on nothing, particularly while in their underwear.

"If you could just check in with the receptionist on your way out, she'll get you signed up." With that, Nurse Debbie turned and disappeared someplace behind the door.

"You've got to be shitting me!" the man in the thong exclaimed. He stood up, snatched his clothing off the floor, and hopped into his pants. "We sit here all morning for some stupid physical and get treated like a bunch of management trainees? I don't have time for this crap."

"Who do they think they are?" another man asked no one in particular. The others dressed quietly, as if this were just another day at the office. When they were done, the door opened again, and the nurse entered with her clipboard.

"I hate to inconvenience you," she said, "but we just located another doctor to conduct your physicals. If you could just slip out of your clothes, we'll try this again."

"I'm out of here," the man in the red thong announced. One of the other executives followed him out the door. The other four quietly stripped off their clothes again, just as directed.

"I thought I was done with this sort of thing when I processed out of the Navy," one of the men said after a while. He didn't look upset. He was simply trying to make conversation.

The Hispanic lawyer beside him offered a hand and a tentative smile. "Joel Garcia. Office of General Council in New York," he said. "You here for the Quantis gig?"

The navy man nodded. "Fred Hastings. Portland office."

"Mark Den Ouden," the next man said. "I run the Bangkok motherboard plant."

The last candidate, a tall athletic-looking woman of Middle Eastern extract, sat with her knees vised together, hands neatly folded in her lap. Her evenly tanned, well-conditioned body almost glowed at the margins of her expensive lingerie, making it hard for the others not to stare.

The woman could have introduced herself as Sirad Malneaux, vice president of the company's IT division in Atlanta. She might have bragged about her meteoric rise up the corporate ladder or mentioned that corporate in New York had called personally to recruit her for this new position. But she didn't. The quiet, beautiful woman at the end of the row stared straight ahead and said nothing at all.

JEREMY WAITED UNTIL all the veteran operators had tried their luck with the course before moving up to toe the line himself. Everyone crowded around him as Quinny held his hand on Jeremy's shoulder and set the stopwatch for official time. Fritz Lottspeich and the rest of his NOTS class stood three feet off to the side offering various thumbs-ups and winks of encouragement. Everyone knew that Jeremy had the last and only chance of beating Beef's run. Though HRT's big man hadn't actually downed the beer, he had been the first to make it into the hula hoop and complete a push-up. Despite all the bravado, it had been the best effort anyone could muster.

"Are you ready?" Quinny asked. Jeremy leaned forward onto his left leg, held his hands out in front of him, and concentrated on the chair across the lawn.

"On your mark . . . get set . . ."

"Hoo-ah!" Lottspeich yelled, drawing more than a few scowls. New guys were supposed to keep their mouths shut.

"Go!" Quinny yelled.

Jeremy pushed off from the starting line and moved fast, jogging toward the hoop, picking up speed like a long jumper searching for stride. If the men yelled after him, he couldn't hear. The bright afternoon light dimmed around him. Smells of barbecue disappeared. Even Maddy's beautiful little voice faded into distraction.

Unlike most minds, which narrow at times like this to a single focus, Jeremy's began to unfold with possibility. Instead of fixating on a single approach to the problem, his consciousness swelled with variability.

HRT evaluators had noticed it during selection. While most candidates bulled their way through challenges, Jeremy relied on creativity and enterprise. In one hostage scenario, he had avoided violent confrontation by assuming the role of a drunken street person and sneaking in the back door while role-playing HRT evaluators waited for the typical frontal assault. In another he won a twenty-mile overland race by stealing a bicycle from the FBI Academy garage and peddling his way past the rest of the crowd.

What rules? he'd asked when other selectees complained about cheating. He had been given an objective and Global Positioning System coordinates for the finish line. No one said anything about how he was supposed to get there.

HRT's front office agreed and watched him each day with greater interest. Whether planning arrest scenarios, running shooting drills in the Kill House, role-playing, or competing in physical contests, Jeremy distinguished himself with ingenuity. He wasn't always the fastest or the strongest, but he never failed to achieve clarity of thought.

The industrial psychologists that HRT had contracted to evaluate selection detailed this in their test results. *Extraordinary,* their reports read. *Remarkable.* HRT's selection coordinators agreed. Team records listed a couple other candidates who came close to Jeremy in terms of IQ, but none of them possessed his psychological profile. With regard to originality, intuitive intelligence, and emotional maturity — key traits in an HRT operator — this man stood out as a singularity. He looked perfect.

Jeremy cared nothing about IQ scores or personality types as he closed on the hoop, though. Caroline smiled down at him from the deck. Maddy floated down the slide. The whole team stared on with varying degrees of expectation, but he concentrated on the problem at hand. The only things that stood between him and a cold mouthful of beer were a couple hundred volts of DC current and a gut check.

Jeremy crossed the lawn and started his dive five feet from the hoop. Both hands landed in the circle on the first bounce. He struggled to his knees and propped himself in a forward lean, but his muscles fought back in wrenching spasms. A thick, jagged pain shot up into his skull, then down his spine. Strange sensations stuck in his mind: the smell of marzipan, the taste of lime, a hollow ringing in his ears.

Just one push-up, he thought. He bent his arms, reflex took over, and by the time he pushed himself up and rocked back on his knees, he knew he'd won. Even trembling now under a high-frequency shiver, he started to smile. All he had to do was sit in the chair and drink the beer.

Jeremy slowly climbed to his feet and stood in the circle. He cupped the beer between his paralyzed hands, turned to sit, and lifted his feet off the ground.

And then it was over. Suddenly the pain subsided. Shapes and noises filtered back into his conscious mind. Parts of his body still ached, but only out of recollection. Maddy waved at him from the top of the slide.

Jeremy looked back at the crowd of HRT operators just a stone's-throw away. His NOTS class stood there, hoping he had the will to finish the job. Fritz Lottspeich, his closest friend among them, nodded his head, urging him to chug the damned thing and get it over with.

But it wasn't as simple as that. This was about legacy. Jeremy had a chance to define himself among the operators. Maybe they'd never figure out that once he lifted his feet off the grass and sat in the plastic chair, all the voltage lost its ground. It was high school physics — the reason birds can roost on power lines. The moment he raised his feet off the well-worn turf, that damned collar became just another piece of leather. Maddy could have worn it herself without bothering her pretty little neck.

The crowd stared at Jeremy as if he were an apparition sitting there in the middle of the circle with his legs crossed beneath him. Twenty seconds had passed, maybe more.

"Holy shit," Beef mumbled. "What's up with this guy?"

When Jeremy had recovered enough for the taste of marzipan to leave his tongue, he raised the cup to the crowd. "To NOTS," he toasted. Anything more would have been a taunt.

█▋

NURSE DEBBIE RETURNED to the waiting room after another hour and a half.

"You're not going to believe this," she said. "But the doctor we found had a personal emergency and had to leave. I'm very sorry, but we're going to have to reschedule after all."

Garcia laughed out loud. Hastings shook his head and immediately reached for his pants. "What the hell is up with you people, anyway?" he asked the nurse as she turned to leave.

"I'm just doing my job," Nurse Debbie snipped before storming out.

The Bangkok plant manager buttoned his shirt. "I don't give a damn either way," he said. "As long as I'm on the company dime . . ."

The woman dressed as dutifully as she had disrobed. First the skirt, then the white linen blouse and waistcoat. She buttoned the garments quickly, precisely, turning away from the others to prevent the process from becoming a strip show.

"Can you believe this?" Hastings asked her. He looked a bit put out that she hadn't said a word all morning. "I have two reports waiting on my desk to finish. If I had known that we . . ."

Suddenly the door opened again, and Nurse Debbie reappeared. She stared at the floor and gripped the clipboard tightly against her chest beneath crossed arms.

"Headquarters just called and said they are sending the program director over to conduct your physicals." Her voice began to shake. "They want you to undress again."

"Right." Hastings laughed. "Tell your program director to kiss my ass."

Garcia finished tying his shoes. Den Ouden buckled his belt.

"Come on," the plant manager said, motioning to the woman. "You gonna let these idiots jerk you around like this?"

Nurse Debbie watched as the three men marched out. Only the close-lipped woman stayed behind. She slipped off her jacket and started to undress again, just as directed.

"Actually, that won't be necessary, ma'am," the nurse said, once the others had gone. "The doctor will see you now."

With that, she waited for Sirad to gather herself, then led her out of the waiting room and down a hallway. Nurse Debbie walked quickly, still holding the clipboard to her chest like a shield. "Thank you for your cooperation," she said, stopping at a closed door. "You've been very sweet to put up with all of that."

She knocked twice, then opened the door to reveal a stark white room furnished with nothing but a glass-topped conference table and six low-rent chairs. A handful of men sat quietly around the table, jotting notes on legal pads.

"Congratulations, Ms. Malneaux," the man at the end of the table said. "You've just passed the first hurdle in this application process."

Sirad shook her head in dismay, unable to say a thing. This was no doctor's office. The men sitting in front of her were not giving physicals; they were the same six colleagues who had waited outside with her all afternoon. The man offering congratulations was Dieter.

II

ROOM 3171 IN New York's Albemarle Building was known throughout the business world as the "War Room." Every corporation had
one, that sanctum sanctorum in which top executives hunkered
down against hostile takeovers and proxy skirmishes, but this chamber had become legend.

Originally designed by Edward H. Clark during the waning years
of the Gilded Age, this sumptuous space had seen little renovation in
more than a century. Who would dare change a thing about a room
that allegedly hosted a fistfight between a young President Theodore
Roosevelt and an impertinent railroad executive? Rumor held that
the first man to commit suicide on Black Thursday in 1929 launched
himself from the room's vaulted Tiffany windows, falling thirty-one
stories and smashing into a double-parked Wills Sainte Claire. The
massive red-oak conference table at its center still bore the mark of
a .45 caliber bullet that supposedly bounced off a Paulding Farnham
candlestick after a former CEO fired his gun in a fit of jealous rage.

While most boardrooms came with teleconference technology, Internet connections, and electronic jamming devices, the War Room
carried the Empire swagger of another era. From its claro walnut

paneling to the black bile tones of its palace-sized Oushak carpet, room 3171 looked like a space bred for conflict.

Jordan Mitchell liked it that way. He believed that men perform better when surrounded by consequence. That's why he lined three walls with select pieces from his renowned collection of Henry rifles and Luddite truncheons. Though corporate wars are fought with cell phones and frequent-flyer miles, Jordan Mitchell never let his people forget the time-proven utility of blunt-force trauma.

"How are her polls?" he said, leading an assistant into the War Room. Mitchell wore a gray Savile Row suit and a Charvet oxford so tightly woven it shimmered like mica. He marched to his customary place at the head of the conference table, where a breakfast of three-minute eggs, grapefruit juice, and dry baguettes waited on antique bone china. He stood to eat.

"CNN/*Time*/Gallup puts Venable up by three points," answered his chief of staff, a tall former marine named Trask. "That's a statistical tie, but Beechum has gained four points in the past week and outperforms Venable among those most likely to vote. *Newsweek* has her on next week's cover. *USA Today* is running a big profile tomorrow. She definitely has momentum."

"For now." Mitchell nodded. He snatched up one of the eggs and began to pace.

"The president fears her more than anyone else in the field," Trask ventured. "She has name recognition, charisma, a squeaky clean background. I don't know, boss — lots of people think this country might finally be ready for a female commander in chief."

"Perhaps. But it's not because she's female; it's because she's the only one in the race with any balls." Mitchell began to tap the egg with the edge of a fork. "She's going to try and turn us into a campaign slogan, you know — a breakout issue. If she can define SBT as a threat to national security, she might be able to stop us through the FCC."

"It won't work," Trask said. He rarely offered such bold speculation, but this seemed obvious. "People vote their pocketbooks, their consciences, their values. I don't see anyone voting their cell phones."

"This isn't about cell phones!" Mitchell barked. "It's about fear. Congress last year spent more money on terrorism than on all social programs combined — education, health and human services, transportation, all of it — and we still see threat advisories. We've invaded two countries, rearranged the law enforcement and intelligence communities, plowed two hundred billion dollars into the war effort despite a failing economy. And what have we gotten with all this? Nothing. No weapons of mass destruction; no ties between Saddam Hussein and al Qaeda. The American people have had enough of terrorism and know that this president's policies simply don't guarantee protection."

Mitchell put down his fork and rubbed his temples. He hated to start the day with a headache.

"If she can find a way to link SBT with terrorism through this . . . Matrix 1016, we're going to face significant problems," he said. "Do we have the report yet?"

Trask reached into a pile of folders and briefing papers.

"Right here, sir," he said, handing his boss a thirty-four-page document bearing Defense Intelligence Agency letterhead and a blue-ink SCI stamp in the top right corner. "Most of the language is typical military intelligence, but check page seven."

Mitchell flipped through the document, quietly gloating over the fact that his wealth and connections had brought him information so secret, members of the House and Senate intelligence communities had only seen heavily redacted executive summaries. He stopped at a passage highlighted in yellow.

"Looks like they've got some signals intercepts . . . phone conversations, Internet-based wire transfers," Mitchell said. "So what?"

"Read on," Trask advised.

"'Sole source HUMINT inside Riyadh and a highly positioned operative in New York indicates significant contact between known al Qaeda sympathizers and a major American corporation,'" Mitchell read aloud. "'Frequency analysis, corroborating information detailed in FBI file 315A-WF-17753 and FISA trap and trace logs (BA-799, BA-811) suggest . . .'"

Mitchell froze midsentence.

"That's right," Trask said. "They know about our relationship with the Saudis."

"Which means they've tracked our communications, but they can't decipher our traffic." Mitchell smiled, thumbing through the document, searching for more of Trask's highlights. All phone-based interactions between New York and Riyadh had been handled through SBT prototypes. "That's why Beechum is so nervous. She's obviously seen more of this report than the rest of the committee. How close are we?"

"Riyadh signed the memorandum of understanding last night," Trask answered. "The new ARVIS satellite launches next Tuesday from the Svobodnyy cosmodrome. Our magnetic resonance and microwave targeting packages ship tomorrow; country clearance and visas for our crews in Dubai should be ready by . . ."

"Should be?" Mitchell interrupted. "What do you mean *should be?*"

"Will be," Trask corrected himself. "This is nailed down, Mr. Mitchell, from wire authority on all monetary transfers to medical evacuation drills into Qatar. By the end of this summer, Quantis will be the hottest product on four continents. Everything is moving right on schedule."

Mitchell's expression turned from consternation to pride in the time it took him to put down the report and resume his breakfast. Like most telecommunications companies, Borders Atlantic had suffered in recent years because of stagnant U.S. markets, but while competitors wrote off debt and hid their troubles in accounting magic, Mitchell had doubled R&D. The result, his scientists told him, was a new algorithmic encryption model based on something called "stochastic wave generation theory." Program managers assured him that this encryption rubric was so advanced, it would take NSA's mainframe computers more than a year just to map it.

Two months from now, Mitchell planned to introduce the world to a new SBT cell phone called Quantis. It was smaller, lighter, and more attractive than anything else on the market, and it could transmit gigabytes of information, including full-stream video, in encrypted microbursts. The days of traditional long-distance charges and by-the-minute fees were over. For a modest buy-in and $59.99 per month, consumers could enjoy the world's first completely private, Internet-compatible cell phone — and do so in style. The wafer-thin phones weighed just two ounces, ran off a watch battery, and easily fit into a jacket pocket without even creating a lump. It would revolutionize the market.

"All right, what about sales?" he asked, turning to other matters. "Give me some figures." He shoveled a piece of baguette into his mouth while pushing a manicured finger through the folders.

Trask watched Mitchell's finger as it flipped through the pile and paused almost imperceptibly on the green-tabbed file marked *Publishing*.

"Number two, sir. You sold thirty thousand copies, domestic, last week. Those are last night's quotes from our source at the *Times*."

Mitchell opened the folder to a collection of newspaper reviews, magazine articles, and in-house sales projections. His latest book, *The Trade*, burned blue-hot on the *New York Times* bestseller list but hadn't yet reached the coveted #1 slot.

"Good." Mitchell sipped his juice. "Very good indeed."

He smiled broadly, not at the book's success but at the speed with which his chief aide had assessed his intentions. Having sources at the *New York Times* was expected, but having executives like Trask who could virtually read his mind meant validation. In an era when personnel management often revolved around eldercare, flextime, and self-actualization retreats, Borders Atlantic built executives the old-fashioned way: through intimidation. Let IBM and Xerox breed a bunch of overpaid whiners, Mitchell often argued. Egypt built the pyramids with rye soup and a bullwhip. Rome died in the baths.

"We project it'll go number one next week," Trask said. "*New York Times* and *USA Today*."

Mitchell nodded. *The Trade* outlined a management style he called "asymmetrical dynamics." The whole thing amounted to little more than Napoléon's divide-and-conquer strategy, but his ghostwriters had masked it well with Wall Street jargon and plenty of slash-and-burn war stories. In this now burgeoning economy, everyone was looking for innovative strategies. Mitchell knew this project would sell, and sell big.

"I'm going to hold you to that," he said, wolfing down the last of his breakfast.

"Yes, sir." Trask read nuance as clearly as sans serif print. He stood quietly as Mitchell thumbed through the day's first stack of acquisition prospectuses, marketing reports, and State Department advisories. Both men read to survive — whole pages in a glimpse, books over breakfast, graduate courses on the helicopter ride to the weekend house in the Berkshires.

"Now, what about this new asset we've been cultivating?" Mitchell reached for a separate folder — a personnel dossier marked *CONFIDENTIAL*. The red-and-white-trimmed cover peeled back to reveal virtually every detail of a life that Mitchell had been tracking for more than two years. The subject was a white male, thirty-one years of age, married with three kids. He fit all the profiles, carried all the right credentials, met every criterion. In the lexicon of Mitchell's algorithm-biased market speculators, this man rated one step beneath death and taxes in regard to certainty.

"The seventeenth floor has been watching this closely," Trask replied. Borders Atlantic's corporate security division worked out of a closed-access operations center on the seventeenth floor. Most employees merely speculated about its inner workings. They called it the "Rabbit Hole." "We've been following his every move, monitoring his test scores, tracking his psychological assessments. He still looks very strong."

Good, Mitchell thought. The clock on the wall read 7:10 AM; breakfast was over. Time to begin the day's real work.

"Let's set up a test resolution and see how well he performs."

Trask made a note and nodded. Of all the job openings he'd tried to fill over the years, this was the toughest. Something about a transitional economy made it terribly difficult to find high-grade, dependable killers.

▮

JEREMY DROVE INTO work Monday morning wearing a smile so wide he could barely see the road. Despite his success in the dog-collar competition at Beef's house, no one actually earned the designation "Operator" until they graduated in the traditional HRT initiation ceremony. Today's fete would stand as the culmination of everything he had worked so hard for, and after two weeks of selection and six months of NOTS, the payoff waited less than twenty minutes away.

He slowed at the FBI Academy's main gate, flashed his security badge at a guard, and drove into a wooded, neatly cloistered campus built in the 1970s of brown brick and smoked glass. Though known as one of the world's top training facilities, the FBI Academy had always reminded Jeremy more of a midwestern community college than a law enforcement facility. Deer meandered along its narrow roads. Students wandered the campus deep in thought. Only the sounds of gunfire and squealing car tires gave up its true curriculum. And the barbed wire.

Tucked away in the woods, however, stood facilities that had nothing to do with academia. Just inside the gates, at the east side of the 400-acre campus, stood the Electronics Research Facility, where specially credentialed scientists and technicians developed the Bureau's most sophisticated eavesdropping and surveillance equipment.

Farther down Hoover Road, Jeremy drove by a vast new $130 million forensic sciences laboratory. Inside, agents in vapor-locked hazmat suits worked on nerve agents. Others developed cutting-edge technologies such as recombinant DNA "sniffers," which one day would allow investigators to determine identities just by sampling air in a given environment. Computer specialists searched encrypted databases. Forensic entomologists observed bugs feasting on corpses to learn more about the effects of environment on murder victims.

But just a half mile farther, beyond the classrooms and the new multimillion-dollar indoor firearms complex, stood Jeremy's final destination: the most secure and impenetrable of all FBI cells.

HRT.

Virtually any visitor granted access to the FBI Academy could get close enough for a look-see, but no one — not agents, not tourists, not even family members of the operators themselves — ever knew all the secrets behind these walls. The only way to gain access to HRT was to make the team and earn placement on one of its eight seven-man sniper or assault units.

Jeremy turned into the team's secure parking area, shut down his Suburban, grabbed his team-issued day pack, and walked to the gate, where he ran his security card over the Cypher lock. The sign on the fence read SECURE AREA. HRT PERSONNEL ONLY, but that just added to his smile. An hour from now, Jeremy Waller would no longer be a selectee or a NOThead or one of the "FNGs." When he joined the team in the Kill House for the morning's close-quarter battle, or CQB, session, he would be one of them.

▥

"BETSY! HOLD UP there, Betsy!"

Only one person in the world called Senator Elizabeth Beechum "Betsy," and she couldn't stand the thought of him. Marcellus Parsons ran up behind her in the hallway as she walked toward her office.

"My name is Elizabeth, Marcellus," she said, without breaking stride. "And what is it? I have a very busy morning."

"I want to talk with you about all that nonsense with Jordan Mitchell in committee last Friday."

He held the *New York Times* and the *Washington Post* in his right hand. As expected, word of Jordan Mitchell's testimony had leaked out and made front-page news. Unnamed sources — certainly from Mitchell's camp — had drawn first blood, alleging that the closed-door hearings were being used unfairly to thwart cutting-edge technological advancement.

The strategy of making this issue public seemed risky, Beechum figured, but Mitchell's people desperately wanted to avoid getting branded as profiteers. Terrorism still resonated as a top issue in the presidential race, and Borders Atlantic's status as a multinational corporation made it vulnerable to Democratic challengers trying to stand on nationalism. Beechum had actually *expected* Mitchell to hit first. It was his only chance.

"It's Monday morning, and I haven't even had a cup of coffee," Beechum said. "I read your new partner's little diatribe in the *Post* this morning. I guess he didn't quite understand that part about all our proceedings remaining secret."

She continued down the hallway.

"You don't know who leaked that," Parsons huffed, trying to keep up. "God knows nothing stays hidden behind those doors for long. And I wasn't talking about the *Post* article, anyway. I was talking about the way we handled ourselves in front of the committee."

"You mean the way *I* handled myself in front of the committee," she said. "What you mean, I presume, is that I should have acted more 'presidential'; that I shouldn't have taken such open shots at your newest benefactor."

"Well I . . . no," he stammered. "Look, Betsy . . . Elizabeth, these new factories mean a lot to my state. You know that. Jordan Mitchell is not the scourge of Western civilization you make him out to be; he's just a businessman trying to market a damned fine new product."

"Yeah, like Fritz Haber," she argued, picking up the pace.

"Who?"

"The chemist who invented Zyklon B gas." She pulled out her cell phone but remembered there was no reception in the heavy marble halls. "Mitchell's an opportunist trading national security for private financial gain," she stated. "I'm going to stop him."

"Now wait . . . you and I have worked together for many years, and even though we've had our differences, I'd hate to think that something like this could —"

"*Something like this?*" She stopped dead in her tracks. "We're talking mass producing cell phones that terrorists can use like walkie-talkies during their operations! We're talking about erasing decades of top secret, enormously expensive research that now allows us to eavesdrop on virtually every signals-based communication on Earth! I don't think the American people would call Jordan Mitchell's new toy 'something like this.' In fact, I think that if he had come out with it a couple months earlier, we would not be having this discussion!"

"What do you mean?" Morning sun poured out of an adjacent office, painting Parsons's long, haphazard frame in a particularly uncomplimentary light.

"Don't try to play naive," Beechum said. "Jordan Mitchell is playing you to win favor with the committee. Do you really think he gives a damn about the working people of Montana? He's moving those two factories to your state so he can keep you in his pocket."

"Oh, please!" Parsons snarled. "Nobody has Marcellus Parsons in his pocket. Besides, the intelligence committee is not a regulatory body. We can't tell him what to do. We're not even going to refer this back to the floor. Why in the world would he care?"

Beechum could see in his eyes that he really didn't get it.

"He's invested billions in this product, and he wants to bring it to market with no hint of controversy," she said. "The last thing he needs is full Senate hearings on the national security implications of his new cell phone technology. If we go out claiming that this Quantis phone is a tool for terrorists — particularly in this political climate — it could end up in front of the FCC. It could cripple him."

Parsons quieted long enough that Beechum wondered if he had even considered such a plot. "Why, that's ridiculous," he said. "That's —"

"That's reality." Beechum tried to stop herself, but the momentum of disgust pushed thoughts out of her mouth before she could reel them back in. In an age when people like Jordan Mitchell could amass more wealth than all but seven of the world's industrialized nations, money meant power. It was the engine that propelled the world. Politics was just exhaust.

"You know what the problem is with people like you, Marcellus?" she snipped. "Your sense of political vision ends at the sneeze bar atop the pork trough. It all comes down to money — the public teat — highway projects, hydroelectric farm subsidies, anything that brings jobs and tax dollars and headlines back to your voters."

"Don't try to turn my obligation to the voters of Montana into something nefarious. Of course I represent their interests. That's my job."

"Your job is to represent all Americans," she countered. Even before her new life as a presidential contender, Beechum had felt an allegiance to a larger electorate. "What about the lives Mitchell's phones will cost if they help a single terrorist plan his mission? You've been read in on Matrix 1016 — you know we're talking about a credible and immediate threat."

Parsons stepped into Beechum's face. "What about climbing down off that high horse and talking about the real reason for all of this?" he spat. "You want a campaign issue that gives you and the Democrats some parity with the president. You fought against the Patriot Act, you fought against the Homeland Security Act, and you fought against the war in Iraq. Losers on all counts. Now you need an issue to wrap yourself up in because we have the flag."

Parsons stepped back and started to leave, but changed his mind. "Don't preach to me, Elizabeth. Nothing happens in this building without some underlying motive; you're only thinking about what you have to gain."

The two senators stared at each other, suddenly realizing that staffers had poked their heads out of offices up and down the normally silent halls.

Beechum's voice softened, but only to a hiss. "I believe in this country, Marcellus. I'm not going to sell out the safety of two hundred eighty million Americans so you can bring home a couple new factories. I aim to stop him, and if I have to use the leverage of a national presidential forum, I'll goddamned good and well do it."

Parsons's disproportionately large bottom lip started to vibrate, the way it always did when he got upset.

"You know what I think?" he continued. "I think this is your way of covering up the forty-billion-dollar black hole of off-line appropriations you've fought so hard for over the past few years — all those classified projects no one ever gets to see. You have nothing to show the voters, so you're going after Jordan Mitchell."

Beechum wanted to fight back, but the sheer enormity of Parsons's ignorance stumped her. Yes, the Intelligence Committee had pushed through several so-called black programs, but only because the budget process demanded certain extra layers of secrecy.

"Is that your problem? Black operations?" She shook her head in disbelief. Decorum should have stopped her there, but nothing in *Robert's Rules of Order* dealt with arrogant morons in sea-bass cowboy boots.

"The war on terrorism is a lot more complicated than off-line appropriations, Senator," Beechum growled. "The simplest overseas arrest can fall apart when a country refuses to let our planes fly through their airspace. A highly classified operation can teeter and crumble on a single media exposé. Don't try to paint my support of the intelligence committee as pork barrel slurping."

"He'll find a way to stop you," Parsons said.

Beechum leaned in close enough to smell fresh bacon on the man's breath.

"One word of advice, Senator," she whispered. "Justice. It's on my side."

With that, Senator Marcellus Parsons turned and stormed away. Beechum just stood there and shook her head as the erratic beat of his roping heels faded into echo through the cold marble halls. She truly hated this man, bolo tie and all.

▌

"ALL RIGHT, HEADS up . . . let's get started." HRT Supervisory Special Agent Billy Luther stood at a lectern near the front of a crowded, windowless classroom. Two dry-erase boards covered the front wall; numbered beer mugs rested on shelves along the back. Nearly fifty men sat in between, staring up at him, most wearing green flight suits tied at the waist and white T-shirts bearing the team logo — an eagle with chains in its talons and two Latin words: *Servare vitas* — To save lives.

HRT has many traditions, but one of the oldest is the morning meeting. Each business day at 8:00 AM, the entire team gathers for a combination team muster/intel briefing.

"Hotel?" Luther asked.

Chuck Price cleared his throat and opened a small black ledger. After nearly five years as team leader of Hotel, HRT's aircraft specialist unit, he knew the drill.

"I've got Pipes and Fish at Redstone, Harbaugh has that DT inservice, and Big Jack is taking an RDO for that Khallin rendition."

Translation: Hotel assaulters Mike "Pipes" Sinnott and John Fisher were bolstering their explosive breaching skills at the Army's Redstone Arsenal ordnance school in Huntsville, Alabama. Luke Harbaugh was teaching a defensive tactics course across the street at the FBI Academy, and Jack Morrissey was taking a regular day off, or RDO, the Bureau's equivalent of comp time. He'd returned just the night before from a whirlwind overseas fugitive snatch in Bangkok.

"Echo?" Billy jotted notes in the log and pushed through the roll call of assault teams.

"Echo's up." Ed Damon's voice rose somewhere from the back of the room.

The door opened, and HRT commander Les Mason slipped into a

chair on the inside wall. As HRT's only remaining original member, he commanded respect that went far beyond his official rank as assistant special agent in charge. His personnel folder read like a chronology of America's major law enforcement crises: the Covenant, the Sword, and the Arm of the Lord standoff in 1985; the Sperryville sniper shot in '88; the Fawaz Younis abduction in '87; the Talladega Prison riots; Waco; Ruby Ridge; Kosovo; Yemen; 9/11. He'd seen it all.

"Xray Snipers?"

"We got Bucky and Cox over in Lithuania on that Agency deal," Jesús Smith said. He was the most senior of HRT's team leaders and one of the most respected. He had come to the FBI from the Army's Delta Force, or Combat Applications Group, where he had earned numerous medals for bravery. He wore the intangible quality that lifts natural-born leaders above all others. He had gravity.

"Tiny's gonna be out on maternity . . . paternity . . . he's going to be off for a while."

"I didn't know he was pregnant," someone mumbled. The snickers started. Dave Shellenby, a Charlie Team assaulter, sensed blood in the water and ventured a drive-by.

"I hear he's gonna do all the breast-feeding himself," he said.

Laughter broke out in earnest.

"All right, let's get through this," Billy said, laughing. He ran through the rest of his roster: Charlie and Golf assault teams. Yankee, Whiskey, and Zulu snipers. Everyone present.

"OK, boss," Billy said, turning to Les Mason. "They're all yours."

Luther stepped away from the lectern as Mason walked to the front of the room. The team seized quiet. HRT's five newest members sat along the back wall: Waller, Mike Moss, Jorge Salinas, Will Andrews, and Fritz Lottspeich. As HRT's most recent generation of new operators, they had cleared all the hurdles. It was time to bring them aboard.

"You all know I'm not much on ceremony," Mason said. Eight years as a sniper had left him prone to understatement. "But there are a couple things I need to say."

He rested both hands on the podium, gathering the moment.

"This nation is at war. You can call it a shadow war, a closed-door war — anything you want, but it's a war you may not fully under-

47

stand. We're dealing with an enemy that is stronger, lighter, and faster than anything you have seen. It doesn't wear a uniform, and it doesn't always have a name."

Les cleared his throat.

"A few minutes from now, you're going to accept a mission that may take you places you never thought you'd go to do things you never thought you would. You need to understand, before you ring that bell, that accepting this assignment means commitment. It means sacrifice. It means excellence — excellence as a way of life, from the way you run your CQB routes in the Kill House to the way you raise your kids."

Every heart in the room swelled up with the same pride.

"We have two inviolable rules here. One: mission comes first. We depend on one another for our lives."

No one blinked. They all walked past the McAllister oak every day; a twenty-year-old shade tree planted for the first HRT operator killed in the line of duty. Everyone understood its significance.

"Two: what starts in this room stays in this room." He pointed to a sign above the door. It read, in Greek, the Spartan motto: EXO TES THYRAS OUDEN, or *Out these doors, nothing.*

"I don't care if it's road-trip bar debts or flash traffic from the White House," Les warned. "If you've got an issue, you air it in here and it stays in here. Period. We have no armor but honor."

Shellenby started rapping his knuckles on the table. Others followed in a cadence that swelled, sounding like men pounding breastplates before battle. All eyes focused on the NOTs who sat along the back wall transfixed by this percussive display of solidarity.

"*Servare vitas,*" Mason said, reciting the HRT motto. He nodded to Billy, who walked to the corner of the room and lifted a large brass ship's bell tethered to an oak stanchion. Since the team's inception on January 3, 1983, every new operator had joined in the same manner. Each man walked to the front of the classroom, called out his newly assigned "alpha number," rang the bell, and announced his readiness for duty.

Billy planted the heavy, brilliantly polished bell on the front table. Les cleared his throat. "Special Agent Will T. Andrews," he said. "Charlie Team."

Billy stood up and walked to the front. He could barely conceal his smile.

"HR-27, signing on," he said. He reached down and pulled the clapper, filling the room with a brilliant tone and tolling everyone's recollection of his own first day on the job.

Mason wasted no time on sentiment. "Special Agent Fritz Lottspeich, Xray Snipers."

Fritz walked up front and rang the bell. "HR-78, signing on," he said.

Les went down the list: Special Agent Michael A. Moss, Echo Assaulters; Special Agent Jorge Salinas, Hotel Assaulters. He shook their hand as they rang in, greeting them with the same authoritative nod. When he was done, he looked to the back wall for the last name on his roster.

"Special Agent Jeremy M. Waller, Xray Snipers."

Jeremy got to his feet and started toward the front of the room. Had he been given the chance, he would have chosen the assault side, but HRT seldom considered personal preference. At least he and Fritz would work on the same team. That seldom happened with NOTs.

"HR-28, signing on," Jeremy called out. He pulled the bell's clapper, triggering a wave of emotion that swelled in his windpipe and narrowed his vision. He shook Les's hand and headed back toward his seat, trying to maintain the stoicism these men wore so proudly.

Snipers, he thought. So be it. Mission came first, and like it or not, this was his.

III

———

ELIZABETH BEECHUM DROVE home early on the first Friday in July with her radio tuned, as always, to NPR's *All Things Considered.* Her campaign manager had told her early in the process that despite its sometimes anemic ratings, National Public Radio served as a better barometer of Democratic sentiment than any other mass-market medium. With the Democratic National Convention just three weeks away, the entire country was talking politics, and her name had risen to the top of the list.

"Lists," Beechum mumbled aloud. "So many goddamned lists."

She had begun to obsess over them. Campaign deadlines, speaking appearances, fund-raising events, poll rankings, focus-group summaries, DNC officers, district organizers, electoral vote indices — she made lists of her lists. They piled up on her committee desk, her Dirksen Senate Office Building desk, her campaign headquarters desk, her desk at home. Lists filled her car, her briefcase, her pockets, her dreams.

Beechum sped northwest along the Rock Creek Parkway, hands wrapped tightly around the wheel, flipping through the things she still had to accomplish before tonight's AFL-CIO address at the

Botanic Gardens: a quick trip home to clean up and change clothes, a brief stop by 400 North Capitol for a hit with Chris Matthews, then a CNN phoner. All this with less than two hours to go before a crucial speech to top union officials.

The speech. *Oh, you damned moron, Elizabeth!* she scolded herself. That should have been first on her list of things to remember, yet she'd left it right there atop her Dirksen desk on the way out the door. She pounded her fist on the wheel, drawing a smile from a passing commuter who winked and gave her a thumbs-up. There were no private moments now that she had emerged as one of two potential nominees; no room for emotion. *Someone's always watching,* she reminded herself as she exited the parkway in Georgetown. She'd have to add self-control to the list of things to work on.

Traffic seemed even heavier than normal as she drove east on M Street. Students lined the sidewalks, filling up the bars and shops with an almost effervescent energy. Any other time she might have been thrilled by the sights and sounds of a youthful city waking, but not tonight. Running for president meant forgetting anything spontaneous and capricious. It meant discipline and commitment and strategy and focus. It meant . . . *brrr, brrr, brrr* — her cell phone began to vibrate — it meant distraction.

"Hello?" she answered, checking the caller ID. The number looked as familiar as her own.

"You home yet?" a man answered. It was her administrative assistant, James Hastings.

"Just turning up Wisconsin." She yanked the wheel to avoid a Georgetown coed weaving through traffic on a Segway scooter. Construction had narrowed the thoroughfare to a single lane, turning a normal traffic jam into a parking lot of road rage and wagging fists. "Hey, before I forget, I left tonight's AFL-CIO speech on the . . ."

"Are you listening to NPR?" James interrupted. Beechum could hear a whirling dervish of office voices, machinery, and ringing phones behind him.

"I'm trying!" she barked. Beechum reached down to turn up the radio's volume just in time to hear a familiar voice rise above the jackhammers and thunder-thump stereos raging around her. It was Parsons. *Oh, hell, what's he got to say?* she wondered.

"I have the speech . . . ," James said, trying to catch up with the conversation. "He's going offensive on the Borders Atlantic thing. Better listen to . . . hey, I gotta go. Call me back when he's . . ." The phone clicked off, part of the rude frenzy that now defined her life.

"And I understand that Senator Beechum has an obligation to the citizens of this country," Marcellus Parsons whinnied out of the radio, "but she is wrong in trying to use it as an election-year lightning rod. We have many more important issues to focus on, like straightening out our response to terrorism and getting the FBI, CIA, and NSA dancing on the same sheet of music. We're picking a president in a time of war against terrorism after all, not a CEO."

Beechum flipped off her radio and turned up Prospect Street toward her house. She'd heard enough of Parsons's pathetic attempt at spin. He had nothing new to say, and listening to that moron would only ruin her mood, a less-than-intelligent tack considering the importance of tonight's speech. The AFL-CIO still hadn't offered an endorsement, and this might be her best chance to gain advantage on Venable.

"Sparkle, Elizabeth," she told herself, mimicking her speech coach's enunciation. She tuned thoughts of Parsons out of her mind and cranked the wheel of her Mercedes, turning up N Street toward a row of elegant old brownstones — her capital address of more than two decades. Though she loved her native Carolinas, a politician's life balances on broad roots, and hers had spread in Georgetown, an eclectic community of bureaucrats, artists, and moguls. It sometimes seemed a million miles from the tobacco fields of Berkeley County, but 201 days a year, when the Senate was in session, 173 N Street NW still felt like home.

"Goddammit, Elizabeth, when are you going to call the city about this parking situation?" she barked. The senior senator craned her neck, trying to parallel park the big sedan. Two eccentricities often got her into trouble: a tendency to think out loud and a sailor's tongue. Few women swore in public like Elizabeth Beechum. Even fewer got away with it.

"You're getting too old for this tripe!" She slammed the car into park, slipped her purse strap over one arm, gathered her dry cleaning and her briefcase with the other, then climbed out. Most people would have assumed that an elected official would have someone to take care of things like transportation and the laundry, but with the race so close, she didn't want to risk looking "high maintenance" to voters. Though staffers, campaign workers, and volunteers took care of a few of her mundane chores, she still got up in the morning on the cold side of the bed and put her pants on one leg at a time.

Beechum walked along F Street toward her house, trying to push Parsons, Mitchell, Matrix 1016, and the whole SBT thing from her mind. It was a beautiful if sultry evening in the nation's capital, one of those magic day's ends when the sun flares over the Potomac, painting all that white marble and bronze in deep, iridescent hues of scarlet and pink. *Red weather*, the old-timers called it. Legend held that Abraham Lincoln saw this phenomenon for the first time in the summer of 1861 and considered it an omen of a bloody war.

"*Strugger di gioia di timor mi sento . . . ,*" she sang aloud, trying to reset her mood with a broken contralto rendition of *Adriana Lecouvreur*'s "Ecco il monologo" aria. Maybe today's red weather was an omen of war, too, she guessed. Though the president's crusade against terrorism had gone back into the shadows, his battle against the Democrats was just gathering steam.

Senator Beechum walked quickly, focusing on the last blooms of potted marigolds and the mums and Asian azaleas that peeked out of courtyards and breakfast gardens up and down the street. Her neighborhood had changed a great deal since she'd first arrived in 1982, but this was still her favorite place in Washington. Though most of the old families had moved away, selling out to younger, richer, less-interested people, the buildings and grounds retained their Victorian charm. If not for the Range Rovers, jog strollers, and yoga mats, she would barely have noticed that time had passed since she first moved in.

By the time she arrived at her own front door, the senator had regained herself. *Screw Parsons and Mitchell and their empty justifications*, she thought, turning her attention back to the fund-raiser. There was no point in taking any of this personally; it was politics, pure and simple. She'd learned to accept that over the years.

Beechum slipped her key into the old lock and pushed open the door. The house smelled of worn leather and fresh flowers, two fragrances she'd grown to love. Her father, Ancil Beechum, had raised her up in a man's home, one of those sprawling Southern dynasties the Washington press corps so loved to mock. Tobacco farming had faded as a gentleman's trade in this smoke-averse generation, but she revered its legacy. Tobacco had given her a good life. She never forgot that.

"Hello?" Beechum yelled as she entered the foyer. It was habit, mostly; her housekeeper had the night off.

She dropped her dry cleaning, purse, and briefcase on the library table at the center of the hall and walked back toward the kitchen, savoring the peace of her old house. Something in the day's fading light reminded her of the first time she'd seen the house — a Georgetown landmark that had been built when Washington was a small place where you could still smell the swamp and where slaves were sold on ground now occupied by the Smithsonian.

The senator remembered how the rich glow of mahogany and oak had glittered in her husband's, Paul's, eyes the first time they saw it. As a Georgetown history professor, he had been fascinated to learn that the place had once been owned by Ellington Peach, a respected Washington lawyer exposed after the Civil War as a Confederate spy. Paul had made the house a personal research project and discovered that Peach had built a secret staircase that led from the basement to a hidden second-floor chamber. Members of his treasonous cabal apparently used a tunnel from a nearby garden to sneak into the house and plan their operations. Further investigation with a flashlight and pry bar turned up a musty space above the kitchen and a still-functional escape route into the neighbor's petunia beds.

But those were the old days, before her beloved succumbed to cancer and left her alone to Washington. The secret room sat closed and empty now, as it had for a century or more — stumbling into recollection only on afternoons like this when the light reminded her of simpler times.

"I miss you, sweetheart," she called out to the man she still carried in her heart all these years after his death. Sometimes the mere memory of him sustained her.

Beechum had just passed the door to the back parlor when a noise turned her head — the stairs creaking. It was a common voice in the old house — one she'd heard a thousand times.

"Rosa . . . I thought you had the night off," she called out. Her maid spent nights off with a daughter in Alexandria.

There was no answer.

"Hello! I'm talking to you, Rosa!" the senator yelled. She stepped back to look up the grand staircase, but it was empty. After a moment's pause, she turned back toward the kitchen to get herself a glass of wine. Old houses made noises, she decided, and she was thirsty.

∎

JEREMY WALLER HAD paid little attention to politics in the weeks after graduation. HRT's front office had given him just three days to organize his gear before sending him a mile down the road from the Academy to the U.S. Marine Corps Scout/Sniper School for another month of specialized training. While Andrews, Moss, and Salinas joined their assault teams and began learning their way around the HRT building, Waller and Lottspeich spent their days in rye fields and pine forests learning marksmanship, field craft, ghillie suit construction, range estimation, concealment — everything necessary for mastery of what instructors referred to as the "art of the kill."

"Hawk to Walker One," a voice shouted. "I've got movement at your six."

Today's curriculum centered on "stalking," the process of crawling across open spaces, hiding in plain sight, and executing an enemy target before he executes you. Jeremy lay facedown in a field of goldenrod and loblolly saplings as radio traffic rattled out of a Marine Corps walkie-talkie. The last gasps of afternoon sun beat down on his shoulders. His knees and elbows bled from crawling through the red Virginia clay. He had just happened into the remains of a fox kill, and though he suspected the pile of fur and guts had once been a possum, there was no way to tell. After two days rotting in the sun, all flesh smelled the same.

Art of the kill, my ass, Jeremy thought. If there was any art in this miserable slog, he hadn't found it.

"Stand by, Hawk," a short, stocky marine called out. "I'm on my way." The field quieted as heavy footsteps faded into the distance.

Discipline, Jeremy reminded himself. Although the rules still seemed a little confusing, the objective of this high-stakes game of

55

tag seemed clear: he had four hours to crawl across an open field, ferret out a well-camouflaged target, and engage it with a high-powered rifle. In any other place, that might have seemed simple enough, but nothing at Quantico worked simply. First of all, the "enemy" was a Marine Corps instructor called Pitts who had secreted himself somewhere out in the tree line behind a spotting scope and many years of experience. Students called him Hawk because of his uncanny ability to spot them as they tried to crawl up and beat him at his own game. Pitts was the target's guardian. Officially, he was the prey, but in reality, he turned the tables more often than not.

To make matters worse, students had to clear an increasingly difficult series of hurdles in order to score points. Finding the target and getting a shot off would earn a meager score of five. If still undetected after the first shot — and they fired live ammo, despite the risks — the sniper would lay perfectly still while a "walker" moved to within arm's reach. If still undetected by the Hawk, the sniper would have to fire a second round under direct observation. If he got the shot off without being seen, the walker would literally reach out and touch the sniper, and only then, if he had camouflaged himself perfectly and Hawk still could not see him, would the sniper get a ninth point. Ten came with an invisible escape, an almost impossible feat.

Worst of all for some students, this was the tenth and final exercise of the two-week stalking cycle. Each student had to pass the course with a cumulative score of 80, including at least one perfect 10. Though Jeremy had excelled at this demanding game of cat and mouse, more than a third of the marines had already dropped out. Lottspeich was barely alive with a 70.

"What the hell are we doing out here?" a voice whispered. Jeremy craned his head to the left and saw his HRT partner lying just fifteen feet away, flat as a shadow. Fritz did not sound happy.

"Don't move until I find this prick," Jeremy said. Rules prohibited students from helping each other, but Lottspeich — a Chicago native — had not adapted well to his new assignment. If he didn't come up with a perfect score today, he was out.

"You see him?" Fritz lay perfectly still.

"Not yet." The sun teetered just above the horizon, offering no more than thirty minutes of daylight. Time was running out, and they still had no idea where to find Pitts.

Jeremy lifted his head ever so slightly and considered his options. He knew he'd have no problem with the shot if he could just find his target. Marksmanship came easily to him, and it didn't hurt that he carried a .308 caliber match-grade rifle, handcrafted to his own specifications by FBI gunsmiths: stainless steel Hart barrel with a matte green Birdsong finish mounted in a free-floating McMillan fiberglass stock; a jeweled trigger assembly set precisely to a 2.25-pound break-point then matched to a Remington 700 receiver; a fixed 10x Unertl scope backed by a three-sixteenth-of-an-inch leather cheek pad that provided perfect eye relief.

Day or night, in arctic cold or desert heat, Jeremy's bipod-mounted thunder stick was capable of considerable devastation. In his steady hands, it could drop three consecutive bullets into a hole the size of a hockey puck at nearly half a mile.

Unfortunately, Jeremy couldn't shoot what he couldn't see. To get back into this game, he'd have to find a better observation point and scour the field for his target.

BOOM! A rifle shot echoed across the field. Someone had beaten him to first blood.

No problem, he thought. The Marines gave out no prizes for speed.

"Stay here while I try to find some cover," Jeremy whispered. A mash of tangled deadfall off to his right looked like a decent place to set up an observation post. He knew the game well enough now to realize that when Hawk engaged one shooter, the field was wide open to movement for the others. He wouldn't get a better chance.

"You know I need a ten to pass this thing," Fritz reminded his NOTS mate. Talk of this elusive score filled most of their days.

"Keep your ass down until I get back," Jeremy warned. No HRT sniper had ever failed out of the notoriously difficult school, and Jeremy wasn't about to let his partner be the first. "Do what I tell you, and we'll be drinking beer in an hour. On you."

With that, he slithered off into the grass. Somewhere in this field sat a Marine Corps sergeant with a 40x spotting scope and an attitude. Jeremy meant to kill him.

▌▌

SENATOR BEECHUM PULLED a favorite vintage from a floor rack and poured herself a full glass of wine before turning off the kitchen lights Rosa had absentmindedly left on and heading upstairs for a quick bath. Campaign disclosure statements placed her net worth between $3 and $7 million, but she saw no reason to waste electricity.

Watch the pennies and the dollars will watch themselves, Father always used to say. He had turned forty acres of overgrown ridgeline into one of Charleston's biggest acreages by watching the pennies. She'd never forgotten the virtue of thrift.

The senator grabbed her dry cleaning and briefcase on her way through the foyer, then climbed the stairs and walked down the central hallway to her bedroom — second door on the left. Before turning on the lights, she threw her things on the huge antebellum plantation bed, then closed the shutters on the room's floor-to-ceiling windows. Her room looked out over the street, lending it beautiful sunlight during the day but exposing her to paparazzi cameras, reporters, and nosy neighbors at night. Like all public figures, she'd long ago learned that a modicum of caution could avoid incalculable loss.

Once she had secured herself within the privacy of her own bedroom, she sipped her Merlot and allowed the cool red wine to linger a moment on her tongue. She set the glass on her French secretary's desk and walked through her dressing room and into the bathroom to draw her bath. Within seconds, the sounds of running water and the comfort of the wine had pushed the day's stresses further and further from her mind. All the position papers, guest lists, platform considerations, and polling numbers seemed less important as she stepped back into her dressing room and began to disrobe.

"Names," she said to no one but the image in her full-length mirror. "What's Frank Morgan's wife's name?" Beechum slipped off her Lord & Taylor jacket, reminding herself how important something like a question about one's spouse could be when asking a man to contribute more than $100,000.

"Nancy," she reminded herself. "Sons, Darrell and Jon."

Nancy had organized Democrats in Virginia's horse country — what there were of them — to the tune of $1.7 million, largely through afternoon teas and polo matches. James had placed them at the head table hoping for a little extra bump for the recognition.

"Tom Kolikowsky's daughter just had a baby boy . . . Emmet? Athol? Anders," she mumbled. "Anders. What the hell ever happened to names like Dick and Fred?"

Beechum unbuttoned and removed her shirt before checking her watch. There was just enough time before the speech to gather herself in a moment among the bath salts. She hung her blouse on a padded hanger and turned toward the sounds of running water.

Something caught her eye as she unzipped and slipped out of her skirt, but she paid it no attention. Evening light danced oddly through the old house. Besides, the image she saw in the mirror seemed much more troublesome. *Amazing how the years have begun to take me,* she thought, standing there in her bra and panties. Gravity and the relentless pace of partisan politics had exacted their toll, especially now that the campaign had relegated exercise to the hours she used to reserve for sleep. At fifty-five, she still commanded attention, but now more with rank than looks.

She had just turned toward the bathroom when her cell rang. Beechum walked over to her bed to get it.

"Hello?" she answered, standing alone in her underwear. The cool air felt good against her skin.

"Senator Beechum," a man's voice answered. "This is Andy Peltier at Group. Sorry to bother you at home, but they asked me to call and tell you that the Starfire meeting has been moved up to one PM — president's request."

Beechum shook her head and choked down a loud rebuke. This man was a staffer at the National Security Council's Counterterrorism Security Group. Starfire was a code word — protected National Reconnaissance Office satellite project. This was one of three programs that Jordan Mitchell's SBT phone would place in greatest jeopardy. Just mentioning Starfire over unsecured phone lines violated at least a half dozen security protocols.

"All right," she said. "I'll be there."

She hung up. Reprimanding this careless staffer over the phone would have just sent up even more red flags to anyone listening in. In this case, it would make better sense to file a formal complaint in writing. That way, the NSC wouldn't be able to ignore it.

"We'll see how much you have to say once I get your clearance yanked," Beechum said. She would never get used to the attitudes of White House staffers, particularly Republicans. Like their boss, most of them carried Texas-sized egos and showed no interest in rules meant to govern lesser men.

Beechum walked back into the bathroom, punching numbers into her phone. If she could get ahold of James before he left, he would at least start the paperwork. With all the other things on her mind, this wasn't something she felt comfortable adding to a list.

◼

IT TOOK JEREMY ten minutes to crawl thirty feet and roll into the root cluster of a fallen oak. His neck ached. His eyes burned. Thirst begged him to stand up and call it a day. But he pushed all that out of his mind. Pain was weakness leaving the body, HRT had told him — it should never cloud the mission.

"All right, you son of a bitch," he whispered to Pitts a little too loudly, "where the hell are you?"

Jeremy pulled a set of binoculars out of the rifle bag he dragged behind him and carefully pushed himself up to the edge of his new hide. He scanned the field, starting with the tallest pine on the horizon and moving left to right in five-degree increments. If he could just find the target he might have time to move Fritz into position and get him the points he needed to pass.

If he got really lucky, he might squeak out a ten himself. That would feel particularly sweet today because of the rivalry that had developed between the Marines and HRT. One of the devil dogs named Nakamura had bet tonight's bar tab that he would get to Hawk first and exfil with another ten on his scalp belt. Jeremy had no intention of quenching fourteen thirsty jarheads with money out of his own wallet.

Think like your prey, Jeremy remembered his instructors telling him. *Get inside his head and beat him at his own game.*

60

He searched slowly and methodically, fighting the urge to hurry against the dying light. *Where would I hide from a class full of wannabe snipers?* he wondered. First, Pitts would have to find a protected corner with the sun at his back. That way, the light would blind approaching stalkers and increase the odds of generating telltale "scope flash." Next, he would use topography to his advantage. Since this field swept downward toward a narrow valley at the northwestern corner, he'd hide on high ground, just inside the wood line. Anyone coming down that narrow swale would have to make themselves damned near invisible to get through. Finally, he'd have to pick some landmark so his walkers could orient themselves and know where to face when he called them in to bust a student. Because of the terrain and distance, he'd have to use something high and prominent like a fork in a tree trunk or a large broken branch.

Jeremy swept the horizon with his tiny binoculars, searching until he found just what he'd imagined. *That's it. That's where I'd be,* Jeremy decided, locking on to a hundred-year-old larch. The weather-beaten tree stood out above anything around it with a double-masted crest unlike anything on the horizon. He scoured the ground around its base until he found his target: Staff Sergeant Emory Pitts sitting bigger than life with an eight-inch "head plate" target just above his left shoulder.

Jeremy set a back azimuth of 187 degrees to mark the position, then considered his options. The sun dangled just above the horizon, offering less than twenty minutes of light. He knew from the sound of previous shots that no one had yet spotted Pitts. They were shooting at shadows, fruitlessly trying to gather points. He still had a chance to win.

"Enough dicking around, Waller," he whispered, just for the sake of conversation. "Time to get to work."

▍▌

BEECHUM WALKED INTO her bathroom punching numbers into her cell phone and fuming over the security breach that had pushed Jordan Mitchell back among her thoughts. Matrix 1016 outlined specific and credible evidence that his efforts to develop the new Quantis phone would jeopardize national security, but there was nothing she could do at this point to make the report public. As long as Mitchell had Parsons in his pocket, the full Senate would never allow floor debate.

She stopped dialing to bend down and turn off the almost over-flowing water. *Amazing,* she thought. It didn't matter that both the CIA and DIA had independently come up with intelligence regarding an attack on the nation's banking system. To Marcellus Parsons and his cronies, factories in Montana — like the highly lucrative SBT technology behind them — meant dollars, jobs, votes. They were tangibles. Classified reports offered little more than speculation.

Beechum tested the water with a finger but judged it too hot to step into immediately, so she finished dialing the number, unfastened her bra, draped it over the towel rack, and stepped out of her panties. And that's when she saw it — just a shadow at first, but then a body moving quickly past the hallway door, a human shape. She recoiled, backing away toward her dressing room.

"Who's there?" she demanded.

The thought of an intruder didn't immediately occur to her. This had to be something else. Rosa. James. A flickering wall sconce. Seniority in the United States Senate brought a certain sense of immunity, after all. She'd lived in this house — this city — for more than two decades with never a moment's trouble.

"Who's there?"

Then she heard him. The heart-pine flooring creaked behind her, and she suddenly understood that she was naked and not alone.

"What . . . ?" Beechum started to call out, but the words caught in her throat. A hand reached out for her, from behind. She spun toward a tall white man in his midforties, but he turned her back before she could get a good look at his face.

"Sorry, Senator," the man said. No emotion. No particular accent or inflection. "This ain't personal."

She almost believed him for a moment — a victim's denial. Irrational thoughts flashed through her mind as the intruder grabbed her by the hair — *she'd left her wineglass in the bedroom. Her car needed a tune-up. Parsons's breath always smelled of bacon.*

The intruder wrapped her neck in the crook of his arm. Images flashed past her eyes. The shower curtain. A cobalt-blue pitcher on the sink. A brightly colored tattoo of rolling dice on the man's forearm. She felt the rough fabric of his shirt against her back. He wore gloves — latex surgeon's gloves like the men who had come in the ambulance to take her husband away all those years ago. The rubbery grip stuck to her skin when she tried to wrench free.

"Please . . . ," she started to beg, but the man's arms scissored around her neck, and she felt herself falling backward into him, slipping on the steam-slick tile, fumbling with her hands, trying to cover her breasts and her pubis.

"Please . . . don't . . ." *Not like this*, she thought. Not tonight.

Fear swelled into anger as she imagined fighting back, but it was too late. The grip around her throat tightened as the man spoke words that muddled together through the adrenaline and her fading consciousness. The last thing Beechum remembered was how much she'd miss her bath.

▮

JEREMY SLITHERED OFF to his left, back toward Lottspeich. Winning this thing would have been easy from his position in the deadfall, but it wouldn't have got his partner through the course. He had to go back and get him.

"Fritz!" he whispered once he'd crossed the open stretch of field. Grass lay crumpled where the man had lain, but all other sign of him had vanished.

What the hell? Jeremy wondered, trying not to lift his head and give away his position. Rifle shots sounded off around him as other students fired out of desperation. They came from the left and the right and behind, but one had fired from the valley. Nakamura still hadn't found Hawk.

Jeremy lay quietly for a moment, trying to come up with options. Fritz had obviously grown tired of waiting in the dying light and struck off in hopes of finding the target. His "slug trail" tracked off to the left, away from the valley, but from Jeremy's ground-hugging vantage, there was no way to see how far he had strayed. *Was there still time to follow him?*

SNAP! The sound of a broken tree branch seized Jeremy's attention. There, just off to the right, perhaps three body lengths away, a ghillie-clad sniper slithered down into the valley.

Waller stared at the passing lump of Cordura and burlap long enough to make out the telltale characteristics of the man inside. Marine snipers pushed their rifles ahead of themselves; this man dragged his behind in a padded case. He wore suede ranger boots, a ghillie suit built on an infrared camo smock, and a veil of unbraided hemp. He might as well have worn a name tag, too. It was Lottspeich — no doubt about it.

"Walker Two, betta get over heah," Pitts called out over the walker's radio. "Got me a shooter twenty meters off your six o'clock."

Jeremy waited until he was sure the walker had passed, then dived down into the channel, chasing after his impatient teammate. Things were moving fast now; no time for caution.

BOOM! Another rifle shot — this time, straight ahead.

"Shit," Jeremy hissed. Someone else had found his way down ahead of them.

"Where are you?" a walker called out, trying to find the shooter. Jeremy stopped and lay perfectly still, listening for what he knew would be a valuable commentary through the walker's radio. Pitts would have his spotting scope welded to the field at this point. There were still a dozen snipers among the weeds, and he wanted to bust as many as possible before the bell sounded.

"I got nothing," Pitts relented. "Tell him ta take his second . . ."

BOOM! Tink!

Jeremy heard the head plate ring out as someone claimed an eighth point.

"I got nothing," Hawk growled again. He hated to lose. "Who is it?"

"Nakamura," the walker announced loudly enough for everyone in the field to hear.

Jeremy felt blood pulse in his temples. He had just a few minutes left in the contest, and he hadn't taken his first shot. If Nakamura made it back to the bus undetected, the whole class would be drinking while Jeremy ate crow and emptied his wallet.

"You ain't got it yet," he whispered.

As Lottspeich disappeared ahead of him, Jeremy took his bearings and scurried forward. A small cleft of brush and roots lay off to the right. The path toward it looked dangerously exposed, but there was no time to seek better haunts. It was this or nothing.

Jeremy virtually levitated the last ten feet into position. He held whisper-still for a moment, then rolled onto his binoculars and assessed his view. Perfect. The whole valley spread out in front of him, and he could see Lottspeich rooting around behind a spruce sapling, just off to the left, trying to set up a firing position. Nakamura lay closer, just slightly ahead, at the mouth of the swale, no more than fifteen feet away. The cocky marine had wisely stopped on his way out to wait for Pitts to zero in on some other victim.

Jeremy considered his options. There were no more than four or five minutes of light remaining. Lottspeich seemed to have found his target and discovered a decent hide, but he wasn't ready to fire. If Jeremy waited for him, there wouldn't be enough time for both HRT snipers to shoot and get away with perfect scores. At this point, it was save Lottspeich or beat Nakamura — only two choices.

His only option seemed obvious. Jeremy carefully slipped his rifle out of its drag bag and then arranged the vegetation around him to eliminate backlight and silhouette. He made certain there were no obstructions to deflect his bullet, then carefully used gardener's scissors to clip an avenue through the tall grass that would mask his muzzle flash. He set his bullet-drop compensator to one and a half clicks, then dialed a quarter minute of wind to ensure a perfect shot. Finally, he slipped a cartridge into battery and closed the bolt. One pull of the trigger and Nakamura would know this wasn't over.

Jeremy laid his finger on the trigger, quartered the head plate behind Pitts with the rifle's crosshairs, and exhaled in the cleansing breath snipers give up just before they kill. Every muscle in his body ached. His tongue swelled with thirst. Time was running out.

Jeremy gently caressed the hair trigger and waited until Nakamura started to move. It was almost dark now, and the cagey marine wanted out. All he had to do was crawl back up through the valley and escape. His lust for victory was about to overcome his discipline to wait.

"Hold . . . hold . . . hold . . . ," Jeremy cautioned as Nakamura crawled right up next to him, no more than an arm's reach away yet oblivious to Jeremy's presence. Lottspeich looked almost ready; thirty seconds more and he'd be ready to shoot.

Not today, jarhead, Jeremy thought. HRT's deadliest new protégé drew the killing breath . . . and fired.

◼

BEECHUM WOKE UP in a pool of blood. She regained her senses instantly, like after one of those half-sleep dreams, when you bolt up in bed wondering if you're alive. But, just as quickly, she sank backward into the hazy bewilderment that comes with trauma. Her head hurt deep at the base of her spine, but there was no sharp pain to justify what she saw around her. Blood. Puddles and splotches in different shades of red and black where it stuck or smeared or pooled.

She reached down between her legs, praying he hadn't raped her, wondering if she could tell. But she just felt numb there, everywhere. Her body felt distant, as if she'd lost it and couldn't quite figure out how to get it back.

Beechum managed to pull herself to her knees, using the edge of the tub for support. Steam rolled off the water. The faucet dripped, cracking the impossible gravity around her — *poink . . . poink . . . poink . . .*

"Oh, Elizabeth . . . ," she gasped. The room, her beautiful bathroom, looked like something out of a horror movie. Blood everywhere. On the walls in handprints and streaks. All over the shower curtains, which hung from the halo rod, broken and torn. A long, ragged trail led out into the hallway, where a ghost form marked the floor — a silhouette in gore, as if some horribly injured body had fallen there and then slithered off.

"Stay away from me!" Beechum yelled, suspecting the man might have hidden around the corner. She stumbled backward, trying to gain her feet, slipping on the slimy red tile. She fell against the sink, then to the floor, landing on something sharp — her cell phone. Next to it lay a pistol — the Colt .45 semiautomatic Father had given her when she first moved to Washington.

A city's a city, he'd told her. *No different from New York for all the crime it's got.*

She yanked the gun up off the floor and grappled for the handle, trying to find the trigger through the viscous, slippery gore that dripped off its barrel and grip. *Gun?* she wondered, stumbling from one thought to another with no rational logic. *Why were all the lights on? When would the city do something about illegal parking outside? Had she replaced the cork in the wine bottle?* There was no time to wonder how the gun had ended up beside her. Reason had left her.

"Don't you move, you sonofabitch!" she hollered. But no one answered.

Careful! Careful! her mind echoed, but there was anger, too, with the fear. She inched toward the open door, gulping air, pointing the big steel automatic ahead of her like a probe. She knew how to shoot. Guns were a common part of growing up on the farm, tools her father taught her to use, whether culling varmints or bringing home dinner. She'd never needed one for protection. Until now.

Beechum waved the gun back toward her dressing room, then back toward the door. It made an odd, whispering sound as she spun, conjuring up the noise that had turned her head to begin with. She waved the thing back and forth, unsure of which direction to face. But there was no one there. No noise except for her breathing and the staccato drip of a leaky faucet.

"Who are you?" Beechum yelled. Vignettes appeared to her over-whelmed mind. Two empty shell casings at the base of the sink. A shattered mirror by the door. A man's shoe beside the toilet. Emotions boiled in her head. Someone had broken into her house, attacked her. He was still out there, but she had the gun now and had to stop him.

She stepped into the doorway, standing directly above where someone had obviously fallen. *Where could he be?* she wondered.

"I don't want to shoot, but I will!" she yelled.

Without warning, she began to laugh out loud, then cry in gushing sobs, then shiver with fear so overwhelming, she could barely hold the gun. Emotions rippled through her in waves, disingenuous and wrong. She choked on words, trying to get them out, and then began to tremble, bewildered by the cold and the horror around her.

Beechum inched around the corner out into the center hallway — sliding her feet more than stepping — toward the stairs. Sirens rose loudly enough to break into the dark and sparkling tunnel that seemed to pulse around her. The gun wandered in her hands, but she pushed it ahead of her and pointed it downstairs toward the front door. The blood trail leading down. The shadows.

She started to call out another warning, but then she saw lights outside — flashing blue and red. The gun fell to her side. Her arms went limp and her mind wandered, again, back into the empty misgivings that come with falling victim to violence.

How could this be? she wondered, staring down in dismay. The front door was open. Her attacker was gone.

▐▌

BOOM!

Jeremy watched Hawk flinch behind his spotting scope as two HRT bullets — one from his rifle, the other from Fritz's — pinged the head plate behind him. It's just what he'd waited for — that resonant voice of a clean kill. The two couldn't have been timed better with a metronome.

He turned toward Lottspeich just as his partner cycled his bolt, chambering a second shot.

Pitts instantly focused his spotting scope toward the sound of the shots. Three snipers lay there, but only one lay out in the open, exposed to Hawk's now rigid gaze: Nakamura.

Jeremy turned his eyes from his scope just long enough to enjoy the look of realization on his adversary's camouflaged face. "Fuck you, Waller," the marine called out.

"What do you got?" Walker Two asked as he ran up and stood over Nakamura with a radio in his hand.

"Sniper at your feet," was the reply. Nakamura was busted. No 10 today.

"Tell those last two shooters we've only got enough light left for one of them," Pitts radioed.

"Give it to Lottspeich," Jeremy said, smiling. His partner had secreted himself well this time. No way Hawk would see him now.

BOOM! Fritz cranked off his second round as Jeremy gathered his gear and headed back to the bus knowing Fritz would pass with his perfect 10. Maybe Jeremy Waller hadn't beaten the Marine Corps to-day, but he had surely won.

■

THE CHIEF OF the DC Metro Police responded to the Beechum crime scene himself. Half a dozen FBI and Secret Service agents were there when he arrived, along with two ambulances, assorted fire trucks, and the Senate physician. The president had already phoned from a state visit to China to make sure she was all right — an astute political move tinged with some genuine personal concern. CNN, FOX, and all three network affiliates had parked satellite trucks outside and gone live with bulletins. All of F Street had emptied out to gawk.

"I know this is tough for you, ma'am," a man said. One of the DC homicide investigators — a short, bald man in his late forties — leaned toward Beechum, trying to comfort her. She had always considered herself a strong woman, but she began to cry at the violation, the gruesome attack, the utter confusion of what had happened.

"I don't remember . . . I just don't remember . . . ," she wept.

Images flittered through her mind, but they still made no sense. There was a man with gloves. The vise grip of his arm around her throat, the tattoo, and then the blood. The gun . . .

"I never saw his face," she said, referring to the attacker. "What about my dinner? Someone should call and tell them I won't be there for the dinner." She looked around the room at people, strange faces, ambling about her grand home. "And turn off all these lights. You're wasting electricity. Make them stop," she demanded. "This is my home. Won't you make them stop?"

Someone handed her a piece of paper, asking for permission to search the house. She signed it without looking. Of course they could search her house.

"Yes, ma'am, we'll check on your dinner for you," the detective said. He waved at a passing uniform and told him to turn off some of the lights, comforting Beechum for a moment. "You never saw him?" he asked. "Then why did you have a gun?"

The detective had investigated hundreds of homicides — domestics, exotics, serials, sprees, gangland, contracts, robberies — but none of them had been as high-profile as this. Beechum was one of the U.S. Senate's biggest personalities, a leading presidential candidate and perhaps the best-known woman in Washington. The cable channels had already gone wall to wall with pundits and bullet-point graphics. Reporters were flowing in by the cabful. The chief himself was planning a press conference. If he played his cards right, the detective mused, he might even get his face on TV. His kids would get a kick out of that.

"A gun?" Beechum answered. She looked around the room as if the solution to all this confusion lay among the antique furniture or the oil paintings. "I didn't," she mumbled. "I didn't get my gun. I just woke up and it was there beside me."

"You don't remember picking up the gun?" the detective asked, one of his hands wrapped around a small notebook. The other clicked away at a black mechanical pencil. A forensic photographer pushed past them, toward the shower curtains. Flashbulbs and voices swelled in the house. The senator wiped tears out of her eyes.

"I keep it in my top drawer," she told him. "I never had the chance to get to it." The tears came in earnest now, surprising her, choking out any further response.

"Elizabeth! Are you all right, dear?" Another arm draped around her. "Can't you see this woman has been traumatized?" a voice demanded.

"Yes, sir, and who are you?" the detective asked. The newest face in the room wore a $2,500 suit with a hand-stitched shirt and a pocket hanky. No badge or credentials.

"I'm Phillip Matthews," the man said. "I'm her lawyer, and this interview is over."

IV

JORDAN MITCHELL HAD never married. It wasn't that he frowned on the institution. On the contrary. Marriage struck him as a noble bond, forged of trust and mutual respect. Those were the best elements of any relationship. Or so they said. Life had moved him in other directions.

"Do they have any children?"

He sat in a folding chaise on the lawn of his South Egremont, Massachusetts, country home, a sprawling sanctuary in limestone and spruce. The last clouds of a summer squall rolled out over Mount Greylock, opening the skies to a brilliant midday sun. His chief of staff, Trask, poured Pellegrino into a hand-blown Simon Pearce goblet and handed him a manila folder.

"Three," Trask answered. "Two boys and a girl."

Mitchell opened the file and squinted through sunglasses at a thick stack of pages. The seventeenth floor had given him a half dozen personnel dossiers, each representing a prospective human cog in his Quantis project.

"All right, people! Let's get into position. This man doesn't have all day!"

America's second-wealthiest citizen shook his head and marveled at the odd scene growing around him. Tents, lighting equipment, makeup stations, and catering vans had transformed his idyllic gardens into what looked like a motion picture location shoot. Production assistants, gaffers, stylists, and actors hurried about, trying to fit eight hours' work into the two hours Mitchell had allotted them.

"Places, places, places!" a very tall, very thin production assistant yelled at no one in particular. He wore red sailcloth pants and a rhinestone-studded tank top.

Mitchell never would have allowed such an invasion of his Berkshires retreat, particularly on a business day, but prospective clients had so often asked why he had no family photographs in his office that he decided to have some made up. Trask had approached a New York theatrical agency about casting suitable children, siblings, parents — a faux lineage that Mitchell could frame for his credenza. *Vanity Fair*'s most celebrated photographer had agreed, as a personal favor, to make it look real. Mitchell had cleared his schedule and flown up just for the afternoon shoot.

"What about his wife?" Mitchell asked, trying to ignore the chaos. He pulled a surveillance photo from dossier number seven and ran his finger over a determined, middle-class face. "What does she do?"

Wives fascinated him. Women in general, really, though not in an entirely healthy way. Other than a mother he knew only through ceremony and a series of officious nannies, women hadn't played much of a role in his life. Adolescence had come late, during his sophomore year at Andover, and life at an all-male boarding school had presented few opportunities for dating. His only experience with women had come through two older brothers who taught him the facts of life at expensive Manhattan hotels with even more expensive hookers.

College hadn't been much better. He remembered his freshman year at all-male Dartmouth when the Vermont Transit buses would pull up in front of the Hanover Inn filled with ingenues from Colby-Sawyer and Skidmore and Pine Manor. He and his buddies would charge out of class on Friday afternoons and run down to the "cattle call."

Most times, they had to fall in behind the frat boys and wait for a shot at the second or third tier. That never really bothered him because the best-looking girls seldom did the special things he learned from the pros in New York.

"His wife's name is Caroline; an administrator . . . works for a social service agency," Trask said. "Earns thirty-six thousand a year."

Mitchell stared at the wife's photo. She looked simple but pretty, with that wholesome quality that almost never comes with money.

"Protestant. Master's in psychology from Cal State Long Beach. Subscriptions to *McCall's, Redbook,* and . . ."

"I can read," Mitchell snapped.

Suddenly, a bespectacled photographer and a small army of assistants emerged from the pool cabana and crossed toward him.

"I think we're ready, Mr. Mitchell," the photographer said. "We won't keep this light for very long." The domineering woman, a celebrity in her own right, yelled directions at one of her lackeys and took a light reading near the tip of Mitchell's nose. "Let's get a couple Polaroids first," she barked. "Give me the Leica with the B-back."

Mitchell ignored her, turning to a contact sheet full of candids: kids on a swing set, smiles from a bathtub, a first day of school. He ran his finger over their smooth, matte-finish faces. *What would it be like to have a son of my own?* he wondered — not a fake photograph for his trophy case, but someone to whom he could hand down his life's work.

He flipped through the pages as if they were some spare novel, constructing personas without prose. Résumés. Grade point averages. Foreign Service Exam scores. Mitchell had seen literally hundreds of personnel files over the years, but something about the stolid, middle-class truth of dossier number seven fascinated him. These weren't applicants or new hires sent in by head-hunting firms; they were real lives captured in candid photographs and psychological assessments and behavioral profiles. In Mitchell's world — a corporate charnel house devoid of any true intimacy — the connection felt almost spiritual.

When he was through, Mitchell laid dossier number seven on the table beside him and picked up one marked number three. Sirad Ames Malneaux. Unlike most of the other candidates, this woman already worked for Borders Atlantic. She held a midlevel IT management position in the Atlanta office.

"How about this one?" he asked. "Malneaux? What is she, French?"

"Lebanese," Trask said. "Adopted by a French couple when she was twelve. Grew up in Louisiana."

"Have we done a workup?"

"Basic background. She came in right out of grad school, so she's got to be clean."

"Thirty-one years old. Impressive education. Single. What's the downside?"

As a junior vice president, this woman had already proven herself in a company that chewed up and spit out Ivy League graduates like untrimmed gristle. Her personnel folder bulged with glowing performance appraisals, incentive awards, and bonus recommendations.

"None that we can find," Trask said. "That's why we're looking at her."

"Places! Places!" the production assistant shouted. Mitchell looked up for a moment, wondering how anyone could get so totally overwrought with matters so pedestrian.

"This is the grandpa shot!" The almost comically affected man whistled. "Grandpa! Grandpa! Could we have some grandkids, for Chrisakes, please?"

Suddenly, eight children, ranging in age from three to twelve, filed out of the tent and knelt around Mitchell. They wore white linen pants and blue cashmere blazers, sundresses cut from bolts of muslin, and pastel madras prints in Cambodian silk. Their hair looked sun bleached, perfectly mussed as if they'd just strolled in from an afternoon on the catamarans.

"Yes." Mitchell nodded as they crowded around him, oblivious to his intentions. "Children. This is just what they'd look like."

The photographer bounced back and forth among them, arranging, haranguing, infusing the whole scene with some bizarre sense of family reunion. Mitchell's faux wife, his faux parents, three faux children, and their faux spouses stared on, awaiting their turn.

"Just a couple Polaroids first, Mr. Mitchell," the photographer said. She stepped behind a camera that had been loaded, aimed, focused, and set by one of her assistants. "Chins down, eyes up, everyone. Smiles. Teeth. This is grandpa's house, you rich, preppy fucking cherubs. Smile!"

The children summoned warmth. The gaffers summoned light, shuffling their screens and buffer sheets to add just the right color. Mitchell's face came alive with a grandfatherly smile.

"Hold that," she said, and the flashes popped. Mitchell waited for the photographer to back away from her camera; then he picked up the Malneaux file and turned to his chief of staff.

"All right," he said. "Bring her in. Let's see how well this woman can lie."

◫

SIRAD MALNEAUX ARRIVED in New York on a Thursday. She didn't care that the Northeast had suffered miserably all week under a heat wave that stained fashions from Buffalo to Montauk. Growing up in New Orleans had given her a taste for heat, she told people, from the stultifying musk of the Garden District to the sauce on her jambalaya.

Today, it wasn't the air that bothered her. In the three years she'd worked for Borders Atlantic, Sirad had never stepped foot in the famed Albemarle Building. In fact, she'd never even come to New York. After three months of management training in San Francisco, she'd served yearlong tours in Memphis and Dallas before settling into Atlanta. She'd traveled to seven foreign countries on three continents. But, odd as it seemed, nothing in her corporate or personal agenda had ever steered her through the Big Apple.

Not that she hadn't heard the stories. Everyone who worked for Borders Atlantic knew about Jordan Mitchell's quicksilver temper and impossible expectations. *Time* magazine may have dubbed him "America's CEO," but those who worked for him called him de Sade. Escaping his vitriol all these years struck Sirad as good fortune, but now it seemed that it was coming to an end. She'd been summoned.

"Good morning, Ms. Malneaux." A well-dressed male receptionist greeted her just outside the elevators on the twenty-seventh floor. He pointed Sirad toward an elegant waiting area appointed with teak Zen benches and a twelve-foot glass waterfall. Special lighting gave the room a peaceful, almost hypnotic air.

"I took the liberty of preparing you a chai latte with brown sugar," the receptionist said. A hand-thrown cup sat next to the current issue of *Aviation Daily* magazine.

Impressive, Sirad thought. Checking on her preference for a morning beverage would have been easy enough. But how did they know she'd just received her private pilot's license?

She checked her watch: 8:00 AM. Precisely.

"Good morning." A gentle, refined woman walked up from behind and offered a handshake. "My name is Greta," she announced in a porcelain voice. "Welcome to corporate. I understand this is your first trip to New York."

"Yes," Sirad answered. "Thank you for the wonderful accommodations." Her room at the Mercer Hotel had been sparse but cool.

"Oh, you're welcome," the assistant said. "They're all ready for you. If you'll come this way."

Sirad couldn't help noticing how Greta's Chanel suit clung to her high, pointed hips as she led the way through a maze of corridors. After a minute, they stopped at an unmarked door, which felt strangely akin to the one she'd entered through in Dr. Hernandez's supposed office. Greta opened it and showed Sirad into a paneled office with a panoramic view of Midtown Manhattan. All furniture had been removed from the room except for two chairs and a small wooden table. A large, bald man with unusually hairy hands busied himself with what Sirad immediately recognized as a polygraph. He looked up for a moment, then pointed toward the chair closest to him.

"Have a seat, Ms. Malneaux," he said. "And we'll get started."

◼

SENATOR BEECHUM SAT in her committee office on the second floor of the Capitol staring out the window at her own panoramic view of the Federal Mall. Ordinarily the scene alone would have inspired her to another day of hearings, luncheons, phone calls, campaign appearances, focus group evaluations, strategy meetings, and speech lessons, but today it might as well have been a painting. Nothing seemed real. The week since the attack had moved slowly across her life like some morning mist that refused to lift.

The emotional impact of the assault had surprised her. She'd always considered herself an intrepid soul, a survivor strong enough to bounce quickly back from her father's death, two miscarriages, even her husband's tragic early passing to cancer. She had endured partisan attacks, vicious campaign smears, dozens of crushing ideological defeats on the Senate floor. But nothing had affected her quite like this.

DC Metro's initial homicide report had come out within 72 hours of the attack. "Crime of Misadventure," the jacket read — just another in a long list of home invasions gone bad. No one seemed particularly worried that the police hadn't found a body. A canvass of local hospitals had turned up no gunshot victims or mysterious traumas. No John Does. No leads. This was a high-profile crime, but Beechum hadn't been badly injured and nothing had been stolen. Besides, Washington DC had one of the highest crime rates in the nation. There were plenty of crackheads, thugs, and reprobates to blame it on. One of them had probably wedged open a window, spent a little too long admiring the premises, and been shocked to find the lady of the house was not only a fighter but armed.

"Helluva good shot for an old dame, if you ask me," the detective assigned to the case said. "The mayor ought to give her some kind of community service award."

The DA's office looked for half a second at bringing illegal weapons possession charges against Beechum but quickly dropped the matter. True, Beechum's handgun was not registered, but she was a fifty-five-year-old woman defending herself against a violent home invasion. More important, she was a long-standing member of the United States Senate and a front-running contender for the Democratic presidential nomination. No one had any interest in marching this before a jury.

Official Washington had reacted with predictable accolades. The president made a point of riding up to the Hill for sixty seconds of consolation and a photo op with his potential rival. The full Senate quickly passed a resolution condemning urban violence and calling for renewed support of neighborhood watch programs. Everyone from the National Center for the Advocacy of Women's Welfare to the Council on Domestic Violence to the AFL-CIO, whose speech she missed, called press conferences to praise her and pledge support. Even Marcellus Parsons was quoted in the *Post*, calling Beechum "brave and forceful" in her actions.

It was all part of the game, of course. While Beechum racked up countless hours of positive and completely free news coverage — focusing virtually every political discussion on the importance of her attack and recovery — Republicans and her Democratic rival, David Venable, cursed her luck for walking into such a publicity bonanza. The incident had defined her as the kind of fight-back-and-survive victim people hoped they could be. In fact, this single episode had once and for all destroyed any hopes Beechum's rivals had of milking public doubts about a female commander in chief. How could anyone question her ability to wage war on terrorists when she had apparently gunned down a thug in her own house with a Colt .45? It was perfect — too perfect, some argued, but then Washington was no stranger to cynicism.

"You seen this?" James asked, bounding into her office and snapping her out of a dark-blue funk. He carried several sheets of colored paper — an Internet printout. "It's an AP story I just got off the wires."

"I don't think so," she answered. "What's it say?"

"Newest voter survey. Gallup/*USA Today*."

The smile on James's face betrayed any suspense. The numbers were good.

"The race is now a twelve-delegate lead, according to their analysis," he teased, trying to choke down a howl of excitement.

"Twelve?" she asked. "A week ago we were only down four. How the hell is that good news?"

"This time . . . the twelve delegates are ours!" he yelled. Beechum heard the rest of the office erupt in a cacophony of cheers, whistles, and pounding fists. This was the surreal kind of dream sequence that keeps underdogs in the fight.

"A sixteen-delegate swing with only two weeks left until the convention!" James exclaimed. "I just got a call from a buddy at *U.S. News;* he said their new numbers show even bigger swings in New York and California. We're out front, boss, with seventeen days until Boston. This is really happening!"

Beechum tried to jump up and join in the celebration, but her knees felt too weak to stand on. All her life she'd wondered about the possibility of a female president. She had dreamed of a moment like this, a moment forged of not just her own ambition but the ambitions of millions of other women who had bounced off glass ceilings and swallowed lives of chauvinistic injustice.

"Oh my God." Beechum sighed. Though she swore like a trooper, she almost never took the Lord's name in vain. This exclamation she meant spiritually. "What do we do?"

"What do we do?" James asked. "This has been the closest primary season in decades, and you have just emerged a hero. Screw the president's war on terror — we're giving voters something to cheer about instead of something to hide from. It's a media nuke you're riding, Elizabeth, and if we play this thing right, you're going to ride it all the way to the convention. I'll tell you what we do — we get our asses out on the street and shake this thing around for all it's worth!"

"Senator, I have a call for you on line one . . . ," her receptionist said over the intercom.

James poked his head out of Beechum's office.

"Hold all press calls!" he said. He turned back to Beechum. "Everybody is going to want you on air tonight, but I say we act like this is just another poll, just another number. Doesn't affect us. We're in this thing for the long haul, concentrating on issues that matter to all Americans, same old bullshit until . . ."

"I'm sorry, Senator, but this isn't a press call," the receptionist interrupted. "It's the police. They say it's important."

Beechum shrugged her shoulders, now beaming with excitement. The full promise of James's announcement was beginning to sink in. It didn't matter why voters were turning to her in unprecedented numbers. All that mattered was that they were pushing her into the kind of limelight that terrified primary opponents and incumbent presidents alike.

"You know it's about time somebody brought a little color to the Oval Office," she said. "A palette that includes a few pastels. I think my first official act after inauguration will be to outlaw colonial-blue carpets and bronze statues of horses."

Beechum tossed aside decorum as she reached for her phone and threw her administrative assistant a good old-fashioned high five. The pall of victimization was lifting from her mind. This was a day she would remember.

"Hello?" she asked, almost before yanking the phone to her ear.

"Good morning, Senator," a man's voice replied. Beechum recognized him as the detective in charge of the investigation. "I'm afraid I have some bad news."

■■

SIRAD PULLED AN oak mission chair from the table and sat, just as instructed. The room crowded hot around her, filled with stale smells, all menthol cigarettes and coffee.

"How are you today?" he asked, fidgeting with two thin, suitcase-sized boxes sprouting various plastic-coated wires.

"I'm well, thank you." Sirad folded her hands in her lap.

"Good. I assume they told you about what we're here for this morning."

Sirad nodded. She'd anticipated this for months.

"Regardless of what you've heard, a polygraph exam is a means of identifying deception." He finished setting up the device, making small adjustments and calibrations. "It's not magic or voodoo or mind reading. It simply allows us to measure physiological responses to stress. When you lie, your body reacts. These machines measure those reactions. They tell us when you're lying."

Like most Borders Atlantic employees, Sirad had taken polygraph examinations before. A clause in her contract allowed for periodic testing because of security or promotional concerns, and there was the initial test that came as a condition of employment. She understood. Corporate espionage and the quest for business intelligence cost companies tens of billions of dollars each year. Tests like this seemed a reasonable precaution.

"This shouldn't take more than an hour," the man with the hairy hands told her. He nodded, apparently satisfied with his preparations, then pulled his chair close to hers and sat. "Now, why don't you tell me a little about yourself," he said, crossing his legs just the way she did. "I understand you like to fly."

"Fly? Yes, I just got my license, actually. How did you know that?"

The copy of *Aviation Daily* magazine had already told her that they were aware of her new hobby, but Sirad saw no harm in feeling out her interrogator. On cue, the polygraph examiner reached into his case and produced a personnel file, thick as a Yellow Pages directory.

"I ask the questions in here, Ms. Malneaux. Not you." He thumbed through the folder, pausing at certain passages. "Married?"

"No. I was engaged once, but . . . well, you know."

Sirad wondered why he would know about the flying and not her marital status. Perhaps he was already evaluating her responses.

"Actually, I don't know." He showed her his wedding ring. "I've been married twenty-four years to the former Betty Jean Tufts of Alton Park, Tennessee. High school sweetheart. Only woman I ever dated. You have no children, I presume."

"No."

"Are you presently on any medications?" he asked.

"No."

"Do you have a history of high blood pressure, heart disease, or diabetes?"

"No."

"Kidney problems? Neurological disorders? Depression?" He jotted answers to the questionnaire in the appropriate boxes.

"No."

"Within the past twelve hours, have you taken any nonprescription drugs, pain killers, or other analgesics?"

"No."

"Do you smoke?"

"No."

"Alcohol or nicotine within the past twelve hours?"

"No."

The man stood up from his chair and moved around the table toward Sirad.

"Do you think you can beat a polygraph?" he asked.

"Yes," she said. "I believe I can, but I have no reason to. I have nothing to hide."

"All right then." He sat beside her. "If you'll roll up your sleeves, we'll see."

JORDAN MITCHELL HURRIED up three flights of stairs, from the Office of General Counsel to a suite of conference rooms. He read as he walked, trying to work a little exercise into his relentless schedule. A strong heart made for a clear mind, he always said. Elevators turned people soft.

"Where are we on this?" he asked.

Trask struggled to keep ahead of Mitchell as the boss thumbed through R & D assessments of a promising Boston-based Internet software developer.

"They're waiting for you, sir. You have Dr. Schilling, the Israeli voice stress analyst . . . be sure to mention his speech in Geneva last month. We also have that neurolinguistic programming analyst, Katherine Hillock. And the two former FBI profilers."

Trask had learned to navigate the shallow waters of his boss's attentions with the skill of a bone-fishing guide. He could have recited volumes of information about neurolinguistic programming, a physiological means of assessing veracity. He could have answered virtually any question about the nascent field of voice stress analysis and sloughed off one of Mitchell's impromptu interrogations about the validity of profiling. But he didn't. The toughest part of dealing with Jordan Mitchell was knowing how much information to mete out.

Always prepare for war, Trask reminded himself, silently modeling Mitchell's refined articulation, *but expend just enough to win the battle at hand.*

Trask opened the door to the twenty-seventh floor and walked down a hallway of doors.

"In here, Mr. Mitchell," he said, turning a knob and leading his boss into a dimly lit interview/observation room. Mitchell handed Trask the prospectus as he turned to the four other people in the room.

"Dr. Schilling . . . ," Mitchell said, extending his hand to a slight, bearded man in jeans and a mock turtleneck sweater. "I am so fascinated by your work." Mitchell summoned his politician charm. He could transform himself from ogre to prince with the turn of a doorknob.

"Really," the Israeli said, swelling with ego. "I didn't expect you'd know my writings."

"Oh, yes," Mitchell lied. "I enjoyed your paper in the *Journal of*

American Psychology, and I had the good fortune of seeing your presentation before the UNESCO conference last month in Geneva."

The doctor stared back with a befuddled grin as Mitchell turned to America's foremost expert on neurolinguistic programming. "And it's so nice to meet you, Katherine," he said, shaking hands with the tall, thin woman in blue pinstripes. "I simply loved your last book."

It was another lie. He'd skimmed the first few chapters, enough to see that she wrote with the plowshare arrogance common to academics. Her theories seemed pedestrian, and there had been no point in finishing. Still, he needed her today.

"By the way, I talked to an old friend of yours the other day."

"Oh?" she asked, nodding to cover surprise. "Who is that?"

"John Hagmeier," Mitchell said. She stepped back in complete surprise that a man of Jordan Mitchell's reputation and worth would bother himself with such esoterica, particularly such classified esoterica. Hagmeier ran a little-known unit of the NSA's Security Affairs Support Association. Only a man obsessed with detail and connected to excellent sources would have known the name.

Mitchell greeted the two former FBI profilers with the same familiarity — common friends, professional praise, mention of projects no one else would have named or even known.

"Now," he said, after primping his panel of experts. He pulled up a chair close to the two-way mirror. "I want you to watch closely. They tell me this woman is good."

▮

SENATOR BEECHUM DROVE herself to the DC police station. The detective had offered to come to her office and discuss the situation, but she told him no. This *situation* had invaded her personal life; it would not weigh further on her obligation to the people of South Carolina or to all those registered Democrats across the country who now seemed hell-bent on electing her president. The assault had occurred in her personal life, and that's where she'd keep it.

"Thank you for coming down," the detective said, holding the door as she entered the chief's personal conference room. Chief Splude himself had insisted on this, the detective noted. Washington DC's top cop was a political appointee, after all, and he fully understood the potential indignity to both parties if word leaked out that he had relegated a lead presidential contender to some graffiti-strewn inter-rogation chamber with a hanging lightbulb and a two-way mirror.

"So, what's the big secret?" Beechum asked, once he had closed the door. The detective looked uneasy — more official than he had been in previous conversations.

"I'm afraid we have identified the unsub male wounded in your house on the night in question," he said.

Unsub male? Night in question? she thought, pulling out a chair across the table from him. *Why did these people always talk as if a badge made English their second language?*

She leaned forward in expectation. "Well? Who the hell is he? Was he? How'd you find him?"

The questions leaped from her mind. This bastard's identity had gnawed at her ever since that terrible night. Just knowing he was still out there — healing, perhaps waiting to come back and finish what he'd started — nauseated her.

"His name is Craig S. Slater, ma'am. Do you know him?"

Know him? she wondered. *Why the hell would I know him?*

"Of course not. I've never heard that . . ." She stopped midsen-tence. Her lawyer had advised her not to talk about details of the case without conferring with him first. "I don't recall ever hearing that name before."

"You don't recall, or you never have?" the detective asked. He seemed to perk up the way detectives do when they smell a lie.

"I meet a lot of people in my job, Detective," she said. "I'd hate to say I never heard the name before . . . I don't recall hearing it. Who is he? How did you find him? Does he have a criminal record?"

The detective stared at her as if disappointed that she had asked.

"Senator Beechum, this is very difficult for me." He looked at her with a real sense of regret, almost like a child who'd caught his par-ents stealing toys from Wal-Mart. "I mean, we both know the deal here. You're a United States senator — running for president and all, and I'm just a homicide detective. I'm sure you could get me fired if you wanted to, but the bottom line is that we have to get this thing straightened out before it goes any further. I'm just doing my job."

"Any further?" Beechum felt a deep pain in her gut. It was the same overwhelming panic that swelled in her every time she walked past her bathroom. "What do you mean any further? You're confusing me."

He looked at her for a long moment, then nodded.

"Bernie!" he called out, and the door opened.

"What the hell is going on here?" Senator Beechum asked. All those years in the Senate had steeled her to subterfuge.

"This is Detective Morrison, ma'am," he said. "At this point I think we'd better advise you of your Miranda rights. Bernie is my witness."

▐

SIRAD SAT QUIETLY in her chair, trying to look bored.

"If you'll lift your arms, I'm going to fasten this around your chest," the polygrapher instructed. He stood next to two machines. One looked like the standard lie detector Sirad had seen numerous times before — thin wire arms and pink graph paper with surgical rubber accessories that had cracked and frayed. The other machine surprised her. It was similar in size but appeared brand new, elegant and much more sophisticated.

Though she didn't know it, this device had just recently been developed by the Johns Hopkins University's Applied Physics Laboratory for particularly difficult subjects. It was called the Polygraph Assisted Scoring System, or PASS, and it was attached to an Axciton computer, which provided a statistical analysis of her physiological reactions to stress. Unlike the slower analog system beside it, this totally automated system issued results in a fraction of the time and removed all human prejudice. This was the first time Sirad had seen the art and science of lie detection married in a single application.

The stoic subject rolled up her sleeves as instructed and lifted her arms as the polygrapher pulled a cord around her chest, beneath the bra line, and fastened it. Next, he clipped electrodes to Sirad's right index finger and fastened a blood pressure cuff around her left biceps. When he was done, he checked the lead insertions and returned to his machines to tinker with the dials a little more and type some data into the Axciton's keyboard. If he felt at all intimidated by her beauty, he didn't show it.

"OK, then," he said, looking out the window behind Sirad to a stunning view of Midtown Manhattan. "I'm going to hand you a list of the questions that I will ask you during the exam." The polygrapher gave Sirad a two-page document, typewritten, with brief, numbered lines. "Read them over and let me know if anything bothers you."

She skimmed over the questionnaire.

"Some of these are kind of vague. I mean, like number seventeen: 'Have you ever stolen company property?' Does theft include things like taking home a pen or making personal calls or stuff like that? I mean, I don't want to look like I'm lying, but . . ."

She fidgeted in her seat. It was all part of her act.

"No, nothing like that. Everyone picks up a pen from time to time. I've got your complete personnel folder here, and it's obvious that you aren't the kind of person who would steal. I just need to verify what we already know: that you have never taken anything substantial from Borders Atlantic. Money, trade secrets, financial reports — that sort of thing. Understand?"

Sirad nodded her head.

"Good. I'm going to ask you these questions out loud. All you have to do is respond with a simple yes or no answer. Do you understand?"

"Yes." Sirad nodded. The polygrapher scratched a pen across the printout.

"Good. Is your name Sirad Ames Malneaux?" he asked.

"Yes."

"Do you live at 1542 Marbridge Street, Atlanta, Georgia?"

"Yes."

Sirad measured her breathing, steadied her heartbeat, and focused on the scene outside.

"Have you ever stolen property from Borders Atlantic?"

"No."

"Have you ever offered information obtained during your official duties to another corporation or government agency?"

Sirad held her answer a moment.

"Like what? I mean, I've given out employment information to credit card companies . . . stuff like that."

The polygrapher jotted a brief notation on the graph paper as it rolled through the older machine.

"There are no trick questions, here, Miss Malneaux," he said. "I need a simple yes or no answer. Tell you what — just to make certain we don't show an indication of deception, why don't you write down any instances in which you have given out company-related information. We'll say for purposes of the test, that your answer excludes all this."

Sirad took a pen and notepad from the polygrapher and wrote down three bullet points: credit card applications, a reference check for her co-op committee, and employment information for her car loan.

"All right then." The polygrapher cleared his throat. "Let's start over. Other than those instances which you just wrote down, have you ever offered information obtained during your duties to another corporation or government agency?"

"No."

"Have you ever worked for any federal law enforcement, regulatory, or intelligence agency?"

"No."

"Have you ever traveled to or lived in the Middle East?"

"No."

Sirad stared at the wall and concentrated on her breathing. The cocktail of meprobamate, diazepam, and methylphenidate coursing through her system made the wallpaper dance and move in front of her, just like she had been cautioned, but it accomplished its purpose. Lying credibly had never been particularly hard for Sirad, but this stuff made it easy.

▐▌

"I WANT TO know what in hell this is all about!" Senator Beechum bellowed. Her attorney, Phillip Matthews, motioned with his hands to calm down and ushered her to a Victorian parlor settee that had hosted many similarly bewildered clients. A green library lamp illuminated his office, reminding both of them that official Washington had long since retired for the night.

"Now, Elizabeth, we can take care of this," he said. "I need you to calm down before . . ."

"Calm down? Calm down? They read me my goddamned rights, Phillip, like I was some kind of criminal!"

Beechum jumped up from the settee and began to pace. Her life was quickly drifting from power and respectability to complete chaos. What would the media make of this?

"What happened today was irresponsible," he said. "They should have called me first so I could have gone down there with you. I have already called the chief and demanded that he reprimand the officers involved in the interrogation."

"For what?" she demanded. "For doing their job?"

"For interrogating a member of the United States Senate without benefit of counsel, which they knew you already had," he said. "We have a Constitution in this country; it's designed to prevent this sort of thing."

"I know about the Constitution," Beechum said. She sat back down on the couch and rubbed a deeply tanned hand across her forehead. She still wore her wedding ring all these years after losing her husband. "You told me this man would turn out to be some street hoodlum, probably a drug addict trying to rob me. You told me not to worry about it, that it was all just going away."

The anger in her voice was beginning to fade. She had vented. This was a rational woman, a veteran of national politics.

"Well, Elizabeth, that's not exactly what I said. You have been under a great deal of stress this past week and . . ." Matthews stopped himself, trying to avoid another tirade. "These have been difficult times for you, dear," he continued. "We simply don't know what happened that night. At least I don't."

"I don't either, Phillip! I have told you that."

"And I believe you," he said. "I sympathize with all you have suffered. But things have changed, and as your attorney, I have to be frank."

He reached out and took her hand in his.

"The police claim that this man you apparently shot, Slater, was a White House staffer. More than that, Elizabeth, he was a National

Security Council attorney, personally appointed by the president. He'd worked with your committee staff. You must have known him."

"How the hell would I know him?" she wailed. "Even if I'd met him through the NSC, I wouldn't have recognized him that night! He had me from behind . . . and who said I shot him?"

"Well, it was your gun, Elizabeth," Phillip said, "and though I know what you told the police, they have found evidence to the contrary. Yours are the only fingerprints on the gun, there are no signs of forced entry, and ballistics evidence shows gunpowder residue on the sink near where you fell." He stood up and began to pace. "The DNA in the blood in your apartment matched Slater's. He had to have been there."

Beechum shook her head, trying to make sense of things. The National Security Council had a bevy of attorneys; lawyers clogged the halls of every building in Washington. If she spent all her time memorizing their names, she'd never get anything done.

"There's something else," Phillip added. He handed her a white sheet of paper.

"Do you remember signing this?"

Beechum looked over what appeared to be a form letter. At the top, she saw an FBI seal, the words *Consent to Search,* and a Bureau form number, FD-26. Her signature stood out in half-inch letters along a line near the bottom.

"They must have given it to you before I arrived, because I assure you they never would have gotten it past me."

"Yes, I remember," she said, reading the document. "Why shouldn't I have let them search the house? I had nothing to hide. This man broke in and attacked me. Why wouldn't I cooperate with the people trying to catch him?"

"I don't question your justification, Elizabeth; I'm just telling you that they found things during the search that will prove troublesome for us."

"Troublesome? Like what?"

"Like this." He presented her with a detailed inventory of items taken from her house: a wallet found in a garbage can outside, a man's shoe — size 12 E — a Palm Pilot with personal information about the senator, including her unlisted phone number, birth date, and clothing sizes.

"You're saying what . . . that these things belonged to him? Why did it take all this time to match it all up?"

"It seems that this Slater is some kind of archaeology buff — went off on one of those special-interest vacations in Turkey. No one reported him missing until he failed to return and his parents got worried," the lawyer explained. "Apparently, though, he never left — or at least that's what it looks like."

"None of this means I knew the man. I mean, come on, lots of people have my unlisted number. And who knows how he got my clothing sizes; maybe he was some kind of stalker or something. The police should be investigating him!" She tried to calm herself again.

"You don't have to defend yourself to me, Elizabeth," Phillip said. "I'm simply outlining the police case against you as I understand it."

Beechum stared at her attorney and friend of twenty years with a look of profound bewilderment. "If you are saying that I knew this man, Phillip, you are mistaken. I did not."

Matthews paused, considered his words, and spoke softly. "There's something else. They searched your computer, including your private e-mail account. My contacts wouldn't disclose the nature of the information, but it is apparently quite damaging. They told me it indicates motive."

"Motive for what?" Beechum asked.

Phillip took a deep breath. There obviously was more bad news.

"They found his car this morning at Dulles Airport. Your fingerprints were all over it. And though they haven't yet found a body, the coroner is prepared to testify that the amount of blood found at your house indicates a nonsurvivable wound."

"My God," Beechum mumbled. "This is insane. I have never even . . ." Words fled from her mind. Everything slowed, then went blank.

Phillip moved closer and reached out to clasp her hands between his.

"Out of courtesy to your current . . . situation, they have agreed not to make a public announcement. The papers will find out soon enough, though. We can't stop that."

"Find out what?" Beechum barked.

"Elizabeth," Matthews said calmly, "they think you and Slater were having an affair, and that when you tried to break it off for the presidential campaign he threatened to go public. They speculate that there was a fight and that you . . ." Phillip sat next to his client and friend. "They have already sent this to a grand jury."

He draped an arm around her shoulders as she began to weep.

"I'm sorry, dear," he whispered. "They plan to indict you for murder."

V

——

JEREMY RETURNED TO HRT after sniper school believing he had died and gone to heaven. Though training would continue as an integral part of the job, he was no longer just a student; he was part of the team, an operator. The men who had sat and watched as he rang the bell that first day now joked and prodded him as an equal. They respected him as a peer.

The transformation went beyond acceptance. The rigors of NOTS and sniper school had hardened Jeremy's body like a professional athlete's. His mind raced with trip-hammer efficiency, allowing him to play out complex sequences in his head, weighing variability, identifying solutions, and making split-second decisions, all under extraordinary stress. He moved with a confidence that felt every bit as bulletproof as the body armor he strapped on before entering the Kill House. He felt capable of attaining anything.

And he loved it. While his college buddies began their days focused on market share and stock options, Jeremy and his teammates would gear up for a little quality time honing their combat shooting skills on the firearms ranges or waging close-quarter battle, or CQB — the cornerstone of hostage rescue assaults — in the Tactical Firearms Training Center. Though he would never end up with a corner office and his own secretary, Jeremy much preferred that his "workstation" often hovered ninety feet above the ground in the load bay of a Bell 412 helicopter. There were no executive development or partnership tracks at HRT, but everyone aspired to one of eight team leader slots, and Jeremy knew he'd one day have a chance. And there were other bonuses, such as the thrill that came with "fast roping" down to a terrorist stronghold, or chasing a fireball through a door breach.

If that wasn't exciting enough, he got to spend Tuesdays and Thursdays stalking through Quantico's forests and perfecting his marksmanship skills at distances up to one thousand yards. Two or three times a week he got to scuba dive, rock climb, spar, blow things up, wander off on land navigation exercises, race around the Academy's Tactical and Emergency Vehicle Operators Course in tricked-out stock cars — the list ran on and on in this Neverland for adrenaline junkies.

What most inspired Jeremy, however, had nothing to do with the weapons at hand or the thrill of a job. What drove him through the physical exhaustion and personal sacrifice was the gold badge in his pocket that said Federal Bureau of Investigation and stood for the finest traditions of American justice. He knew by HRT creed that all fifty-five of his teammates would throw down their lives for him if necessary, and he swelled with pride knowing that when the President of the United States needed help freeing hostages or arresting international terrorists, he would call Quantico with the ticket.

Fortunately, things were going well on the home front, too. Caroline had already won a promotion at work. The kids liked their new school. Hampton Oaks now felt like home — a closely knit neighborhood full of Big Wheels and basketball hoops and backyard get-togethers. Virtually everyone in the subdivision worked for one government agency or another: a U.S. Navy master chief next door, a Marine Corps major down the street, a Secret Service agent behind them. Government employment gave them a common bond. They understood the same pressures.

Most important of all, Jeremy's three children still worshipped the ground he walked on. Maybe Maddy, Chris, and Patrick would never tour Europe on a big trust fund, but they'd go to college on money he'd set aside, and when they came home on weekends it wouldn't be just to drop off the laundry. They loved him with the same big-eyed awe Jeremy had felt for his own dad — a career firefighter — while growing up in the White Mountains of northern New Hampshire. HRT may not have had a garage full of bright-red fire trucks like the station where his dad worked, but it supplied the same proving grounds for sacrifice, character, and heroism. Every time Jeremy mentioned the FBI or HRT, his kids lit up with excitement. Even to them, it meant promise.

Like any job, HRT came with days off, and at this time of year that meant baseball. Jeremy had always loved the game, and though his hopes for the big leagues hadn't worked out, he still followed the Red Sox with an almost religious fervor. When Maddy signed up for Little League, he volunteered to coach. On Saturday mornings like this there was no talk of the office. Once the umpire yelled, "Play ball!" it was just Jeremy and his band of toothless sluggers.

"Daddy!" Chris Waller's voice squealed above the low murmur of parents and fans in the bleachers. "I want you to get me a doggie!"

Jeremy glanced at the scoreboard, which read HOME 7, VISITORS 8, and turned to check on his five-year-old terror. His second child had swiped one of the team's bats and was attempting to train a playful Irish setter pup not to mess with his shiny new glove.

"Caroline!" Jeremy yelled, pointing toward the imminent clubbing. "Could you deal with that?"

Caroline leaped down from the bleachers as Jeremy turned his gaze back to the pitcher's mound. Marshall Baldwin, the seven-year-old son of a Hampton Oaks ATF agent, turned toward the bench for his signal.

A sudden yelp from out behind the bleachers told Jeremy that Caroline hadn't reached Chris in time. Luckily, no one seemed to notice. Jeremy's Marlins were down by one run in the bottom of the final inning, and all eyes had focused squarely on the skinny right arm of his number one pitcher.

"Two outs!" Jeremy yelled to his players.

He touched the brim of his hat, tapped his chin, and wiped the front of his shirt.

"Play's at first."

At three feet six and seventy-two pounds, Marshall Baldwin didn't look very intimidating. His teal-blue T-shirt hung loosely from his shoulders. His hat dipped precariously over his eyes every time he started his windup. And the object in his throwing hand looked more like a volleyball than a baseball. But to rival batters, this pint-sized hurler must have looked like Satan himself. Despite his gangly appearance, he possessed a weapon of destruction few Stafford Little League batters had ever before seen — a curveball.

"Here we go, Marshall! Do him!" Jeremy tried to control his HRT-inspired aggression, but sniper jargon invariably trickled into conversation during times of stress.

The visiting batter took a couple of tentative chops, then banged his rubber cleats. Forty sets of home-team eyes stared at the mound as Marshall nodded to the catcher, adjusted his fingers on the ball's stitching, and leaned back into his windup. The stands quieted almost to silence.

The ball flew, curved right on cue, parted the strike zone, and hit its target with a *thump!* Jeremy rose to his feet before the umpire even called strike three. Something about the sound of a curveball finding a catcher's mitt always moved him. The parents cheered, covering the sounds of Christopher's protests as Caroline pulled him away from the puppy.

"All right, listen up," Jeremy said, gathering his team around him near the helmet pile. "This is our last ups, and we need two runs. Three outs to get two runs. Piece of cake, right?"

"Right!" they yelled in unison. Richie McCauley already had a helmet on his head and the warm-up doughnut on his bat. Even as a bunch of second- and third-graders, these kids understood the situation. Two runs would mean a perfect 7–0 record.

Richie took the plate just as someone from the opposing stands yelled, "Batter's a pussy!"

Jeremy bristled. Sometimes kids and parents shouldn't be allowed to mix. But Richie McCauley never even flinched. He leered at the pitcher just like his coach had taught him and spit a loogie across the plate as if challenging for some heat.

"Ball one," the ump mumbled after the first pitch. Easy call — it bounced on the plate.

The next pitch sailed over Richie's head. He swung at the third and missed. The fourth could have gone either way, but the ump erred toward time constraints and judged it a strike.

"Take your time, now. Pick your pitch," Jeremy urged his batter. He touched the tip of his nose, tapped his stomach, and shook his head, offering the universal sign language for the bunt. Richie was fast, and this pitcher looked tired.

The stands quieted during the windup, then the ball sailed toward the plate, and *whack!* Richie either missed the sign language for the bunt or decided to go this one on his own. His hit dribbled to short, where a fat girl with braces scooped it up and made the toss for out number one.

Rachel Bumgartner tagged the next pitch for a double. Billy Shellenby, Dave's son, laid down a bunt that ended up putting him safe on first and getting Rachel to third. Brian Gladman struck out without lifting the bat off his shoulder. That left the Marlins one out shy of dead, with batters at the corners. A base hit would tie. A clean double might win it.

Jeremy's gut tightened with consequence. Competition was more than recreation to him. From pickup basketball to sniper comps, his heart beat for victory.

He turned to his batting lineup and almost choked. Batter number nine was a cuter-than-average seven-year-old girl named Maddy Waller. Maddy had claimed that she wanted to play baseball, but she had discovered that staring down fastballs ranked just below the dentist on her list of favorite things. She may have been the coach's daughter, but she certainly hadn't inherited much of his competitive nature.

Jeremy turned toward the on-deck circle and looked straight into the watery eyes of his little girl. This was not exactly what he'd hoped to hang the season on. Sometimes, the line between being a dad and a coach felt a mile wide. He desperately wanted to run over and wrap her up in his arms with a big kiss and a few words of encouragement, but this was a Little League game. Kissing players, no matter how cute, was not allowed.

"OK, Maddy, just make contact, huh?" he said. Jeremy was just about to toss out an additional morsel of support when an all-too-familiar sound erupted from his belt line.

BEEP BEEP BEEP.

His pager. Another in the stands. One across the way in the visitors' bleachers.

Maddy, who had started the thousand-mile walk to the batter's box, froze in her tracks. Jeremy had explained to his kids that when his pager beeped, it meant he had to leave right away, and that he might not be back for a week or two. Any other day and that would have been bearable for Maddy. Right now it would not.

"Shit," he mumbled, loudly enough that a couple kids heard him. An 888 page was like a fireman's whistle to HRT members. There was no time to wait for a second-grader to hit.

"Nice timing, huh?" Shellenby said, joining him at the bench. "Come on, I'll give you a ride. Vicki can go home with Caroline."

With five years on HRT, Dave Shellenby had already sacrificed his share of birthdays, holidays, and Little League games. He even missed the birth of his last child during a deployment to Indonesia in 2001.

Jeremy stared at his wife just long enough to explain that he had no choice. They wouldn't have beeped him unless something dire had happened. She'd understand one day. And with that, he loped after Shellenby, who had already fired up his 1968 GTO.

Jeremy was just about to close the door when — *CRACK!* — the sound of an Easton steel bat connecting with a twenty-two-mile-an-hour fastball rose across the parking lot. A cheer rose out of the bleachers.

"Clutch player," Shellenby said.

Jeremy smiled and pulled out the custom-made Les Baer .45 caliber handgun that he carried under the flap of his untucked baseball jersey. He pulled back the slide and checked to make sure it carried a round in the chamber. Habit.

"Easy, big fella," Shellenby said, turning up the radio.

What the hell, Jeremy wanted to answer. This was his first mission. There was no harm in putting his mind right.

▉

JORDAN MITCHELL SAT at the head of his monstrous War Room conference table and clasped his meticulously manicured hands in front of him. Three men and two women stared back at him from their preassigned seats — the Israeli voice stress analyst, two former FBI profilers, the neurolinguistic programming expert, and the polygrapher. It had been just over a week since they'd witnessed Sirad Malneaux's performance: plenty of time to prepare their findings.

"So, tell me, people; you're the experts," Mitchell challenged. "What does all this mean?"

He could tell from their expressions that his choice of surroundings had gained its intended effect. The room's heavy walnut paneling, incandescent light, and rows of glassed-in weaponry seemed to distract the guests even from the magnificent day that had framed New York in the windows behind him. Virtually everyone Mitchell had ever summoned to the War Room wore the same blanched look of intimidation. It was all a consequence of the planning he put into all his ventures — the time, place, and content equation he relied on like religion. Everything Jordan Mitchell said or did involved reason, from the way he'd dialed up the air-conditioning to make these people shiver to the way he'd scheduled this meeting for a Saturday morning. He wanted them to feel his power, his intimidation. Here, he was the only expert.

"I don't mind going first," the polygrapher said. He adjusted his glasses. "My charts look good; both the analog printouts and the PASS scores. I challenged her in three areas, just to see how she handled accusation, but she never flinched. This woman is telling the truth, or she's the best damned bullshit artist I have ever seen." He leaned back and folded his arms as if challenging the others to contradict him.

The Israeli voice stress analyst ran a pencil over his notes. "You're a bright and accomplished man, Mr. Mitchell," he said. "I don't blame you for reaching outside traditional polygraphy for a final determination."

The man with the hairy knuckles shot him a look of total disgust.

"We're here to make a determination, not debate the merits of each other's field of inquiry," Mitchell intervened. He would have crippled his own executives if they'd chopped at each other like this. "Is this woman truthful or is she making it up?"

"Voice stress analysis discerns differentiation from norm," Dr. Schilling said. "Her voice shows trepidation on a level commensurate with stress that we would expect of a truthful woman of her background and education. If her vita rings true, this woman keenly knows the difference between right and wrong. In fact, I'd say she embraces it. We would certainly expect more oscillation if she were lying."

Mitchell turned toward the expert in neurolinguistics, a little-known and slightly alchemic process of reading veracity via eye movement and facial gestures.

"And you, Katherine? Do you see truth in this woman's eyes?"

"Truth?" the small, erudite woman asked. Thin, graying hair framed her pale face as she shifted in her seat and pointed to a television monitor. "I don't know much about truth, Mr. Mitchell. What I can tell you is that this woman certainly believes what she has said. Look here."

She pointed a remote control at a big-screen television and pushed Play. A close-up of Sirad's face appeared, part of a montage of scenes taped during the polygraph interview.

"Neurolinguistic programming focuses on subtle changes in eye movement as it relates to cognitive function. Human beings tend to look back to the part of the brain where they gather function. Because recall is formed in the left cerebral cortex, we look there when we try to remember," she said. "I'll use this question as a sort of calibration. When asked if her mother's maiden name is Hawthorne, we can see her eyes look up and left."

Mitchell stared at the screen, feigning interest in this frail woman's observations.

"And there, when asked if she grew up in Louisiana, she looks up to the left. Do you see?"

The others in the room listened patiently as she made her case. In a field like this, everyone looked on everyone else as a sort of tarot reader. Hers was just another opinion.

"That's where she finds recollection. Neurosympathetic recall.

People look toward that part of the brain where they reconstruct past events or long-term memory. When they construct fiction, they look to the part of the brain that offers creativity. Once we determine a baseline for nondeceptive behavior with test questions, we can measure differentiation and thus extrapolate deception."

"Well, how do you know she's not lying about everything?" Mitchell asked. "How do you know she hasn't constructed this whole life for herself? Maybe it's all a lie, even the baseline."

"Look at this." She rewound the tape. "Before the interview, when she first sat down, your polygrapher asked her if she had a good night's sleep. She answered *yes*."

The woman stopped the machine and replayed a close-up of Sirad's face. She looked down and right — the opposite of where she'd summoned recollection moments earlier.

"That's not where she looked when he asked her name," Mitchell noted. "Why would she lie about a good night's sleep?"

"I'm not in the *why* business, Mr. Mitchell. I can tell you from the surveillance report that this woman left her room just after nine o'clock and didn't return until almost two. She arose twice before getting up to shower at six. I would not call that a good night's sleep."

Jordan Mitchell nodded his head thoughtfully.

"That's very interesting. So in your opinion, she told just one lie, prior to the polygraph." He turned to his FBI profilers, who listened patiently, used to this sort of analysis. "Please tell us what would prompt a woman to lie about something as simple as a good night's sleep."

"We don't try to tell truth from deception," one of the FBI profilers said. She was a stern-looking woman of about fifty-five. Heavyset. Well dressed. Among all the experts in the room, she was the only one smoking. "But we do understand motivation. From what we saw in that polygraph, we see no reason to suspect she manufactured any of this."

Her partner nodded in agreement.

"The most difficult liars to spot are psychopaths, and this woman exhibited none of the characteristics we normally associate with psychopathy, such as childhood trauma, betrayal, or lack of foundation in social responsibility. Everything in this woman's file shows the contrary. Sirad Malneaux seems well adjusted. Our report says she's just what she purports to be."

"So, what I hear from all five of you," Mitchell asked, "is that she is telling the truth?"

No one argued.

"Just so you'll know," he said, "I took the precaution of hiring private investigators to check out this woman's background. They found that the life she described to you is a complete fabrication. Virtually all the substantive answers she offered were lies."

He could have given them the private dossier, but that wouldn't have been fair to Sirad. She'd started this charade of a life long before the polygraph; she deserved the benefit of her planning.

Jordan Mitchell stood up to leave. He'd found what he wanted.

▍

SHELLENBY WHEELED HIS GTO into the HRT compound to find half the team already knee deep in the mount-out. Jeremy felt a surge of adrenaline rising in his gut at the prospect of responding to his first real mission.

Most teams had already begun loading program gear by the time Jeremy arrived. Three Golf Team assaulters had backed the stake-bed Dodge up to the dive shed loading dock and were neatly stacking scuba tanks and Dräger rebreathers. Two members of Hotel Team were reconfiguring ladder packages atop specially built Chevy Suburbans. Whiskey and Zulu Snipers were stuffing expedition rucks with tropical survival gear. The tech crew was scrambling around, trying to cram a ton and a half of electronics gear into stainless-steel Halliburton cases.

To the uneducated eye, an HRT mount-out would look like a poorly orchestrated frat house moving day. But to the seasoned operators behind the forklifts and leather gloves, every detail was carefully planned out with meticulous efficiency.

"What we got?" Jeremy asked as he rounded the corner of the Xray Sniper "hooch." Fritz and Johnny Langdon were shoveling canned ravioli and boxes of Cracker Jack into their day packs.

"Puerto Rico," he said. "Pack your ghillie, jungle gear, and all your night shit. We're wheels up from Andrews at thirteen thirty."

Jeremy started to ask for details but decided against it. The other guys were already outside in the cage, prepping their gear. He was just one of the grunts, and an FNG to boot. Somebody would tell him what he needed to know when he needed to know it.

▮

"HI, YOU'VE REACHED 643-9623," Sirad's voice chimed over the answering machine. "Leave a message and I'll call you back."

She kicked the door closed behind her and entered apartment 29F, a spacious two-bedroom in Atlanta's Buckhead section. Sunshine flowed in through floor-to-ceiling windows, washing the richly decorated space with sharp, accusing light. She breathed deeply, wiping sweat from her eyes and trying to cool down from a much-needed seven-mile run. Though her fast metabolism kept the weight off, Sirad relied on a strict exercise regimen to stay focused.

"Phew," she muttered, scrunching up her eyes. The air felt stiflingly hot and made her momentarily think of when she was a small child, of sitting in a tent and being almost unable to inhale because of the heat. "Fix my air-conditioning!" she yelled to no one in particular. It was just another thing she hadn't had time to follow up on with the long hours at the office.

"Yes, uh . . . hi, Ms. Malneaux," the caller said. "This is Roland down at Buckhead BMW. I just wanted to check on that . . . I mean, *your* new 540. You know, to see if you have any questions or anything. I guess, uh . . . just call me anytime if I can be of any assistance." He sounded like some high school kid trying to get up the courage to ask her out.

Sirad tossed her keys into a shallow ceramic bowl on a Kaj Gottlob library table and thumbed quickly through two weeks' worth of mail. Bills. Legal documents. Publishers Clearing House come-ons, the typical pile. She tossed most of it into the trash unopened as the call ended, then pulled her jog bra over her head, kicked off her shoes, and stepped out of her sweat-soaked shorts. She'd had to finish a report earlier in the morning, postponing the run and making it a blistering plod through Georgia's midday heat.

Sirad grabbed a towel out of the guest bathroom and walked

naked into a small den just off the living room, where a bright new iMac computer rested atop a mahogany desk. She wiped the sweat out of her eyes and reached down to boot it up. Sirad paused while the hard drive began to whir, admiring the machine's sleek chrome-and-ivory casing. She loved material objects, anything rare and compelling, from those of great beauty to remonstrations of unbridled disgust. A Barnett Newman acrylic hung over a bowl of Yanomami loin gourds; a triptych of Robert Mapplethorpe mutilation photographs rested atop a pristine Jean Pascaud buffet. It was the contrast between aesthetics and disgust that guided her acquisitions, the stark embrace of pleasure exaggerated by the hint of pain.

Sirad leaned forward to stretch her hamstrings as the computer screen jumped to life, then sat in a leather chair made by Alfred Porteneuve. The cool upholstery felt coarse and dry on her bare thighs — a scintillating contrast to the apartment's hot, stagnant air. She reached out for her answering machine and pressed Play.

"Hi, Sirad." A male voice filled the room. "Just calling to say I can't wait to see you next week. I, uh . . . I hope you're well." *Click.*

Hamid, she thought. Her newest suitor — a senior VP in charge of Borders Atlantic's corporate finance subsidiary — seemed more sure of himself than most men, but still a little timid. She'd met him during the polygraph trip to New York, and things had gone well enough that he'd asked her out to dinner Thursday, here in Atlanta.

Sirad ran her mouse over a list of e-mails. Her mother. Her boss. An outbid notice on a vintage fountain pen she'd tried to buy on eBay. Lately, she felt as if she lived in front of a computer monitor. Her job at Borders Atlantic had so little to do with human interaction — it was all spreadsheets, minable databases, market surveys, and cost-benefit analyses. It seemed as if she spent entire days in an alternate reality, trying to forge a career out of pixels, projection graphics, and FORTRAN algorithms.

She scrolled down the list of messages until something caught her eye.

Hotbody69@yahoo.com — Adventure awaits.

She ignored the virus alerts and double-clicked the cursor.

"Hi, Sirad," the phone machine continued. "Look, I hate to do this to you, but I'm going to need those Miami projections after all. First thing Monday." It was her supervisor, and he didn't hate doing this to her. He rather enjoyed it.

Sirad watched as a porno site filled her screen with thumbnails and teasers of people in various approximations of sex play. Men with huge phalluses stood over women who looked like they were being paid to seem impressed. Girls in Catholic school skirts. Fat girls. Skinny girls. Gay men. Something called the "Forbidden Zone."

She clicked on a graphic that read "Naughty but Nice," drawing up a members-only advisory and prompting a password. She typed in APT29F and waited for the screen to erupt in a display of bondage, S & M, and fetish thumbnails — everything from mild latex and rubber fantasies to hard-core dungeon steel.

Sirad shifted in her seat a little, then pulled the cursor to a particularly grotesque image of a man in a Hannibal Lecter mask holding a bullwhip over a naked supplicant who wore nothing but handcuffs and a rubber dog ball in his mouth. She double-clicked again, then downloaded the photograph as an mpeg file onto her hard drive.

"Ms. Malneaux, this is Dieter Planck in New York," her phone machine continued. "I just wanted to call and tell you that your application for the Quantis position looks very strong. If you get this message before seven thirty, could you please call me in the office?"

Sirad transferred the mpeg to a program listed on her desktop as *DEtox*. She pulled what appeared to be an old Iggy Pop CD off a shelf, inserted the disc into her D drive, and waited as the machine began to whir and hum. Seconds later, the computer quieted, and a seemingly endless series of numbers popped up on her screen. The digital stream-analysis technology in the DEtox program had just dissected the binary computer language that turned DOS gibberish into 8 x 10 S & M glossies.

Steganography, the analysts called it, adopting a fancy name to disguise an age-old magician's technique — using sleight of hand to hide something in plain sight. Simply put, this computer software allowed people to encode and transmit text messages within digital photographs — porno pics in this case. Until Jordan Mitchell marketed his new SBT technology, steganography remained a state-of-the-art version of lemon juice and invisible ink.

104

Sirad pushed Ctrl+F7, and the screen suddenly went blank, then flickered on with one brief message: *Approved for Hamid dinner Monday. Borders Atlantic peripheral transactions to $7.2 billion this month. Time to move. Let's do lunch. Hoch.*

She smiled at the message and hit Esc, tripping the screen back to the porno site and forever erasing the transmission. Sirad ejected the CD and replaced it on the shelf.

"Seven point two billion?" she whispered. "I guess that's worth lunch."

With that, she walked into the kitchen, opened the refrigerator, and retrieved its only contents: a liter bottle of Pellegrino mineral water. She picked up the cordless and sat cross-legged in the middle of her living room floor.

"Yes, Sirad Malneaux calling for Mr. Planck," she spoke into the phone. Sirad wrenched herself into a Lhan position and began to stretch. The lithe muscles along the back of her legs began to release as she tolerated a brief silence, then nodded, unconsciously affirming Dieter's voice.

"Hello, Sirad," he said. "How are you?"

"Well, thank you." She tried to sound calm, though her heart had begun to race. A great deal more than a paycheck rested on this Quantis gig. "I appreciate the hospitality. You made my first trip to New York very enjoyable."

"You're kind for saying so." He paused a moment, then cut to the chase. "I'm calling to apologize, actually, for taking so long to get back to you. Mr. Mitchell decides all overseas appointments himself, and due to scheduling difficulties, he's been unavailable. He would like to meet with you, though. I was hoping to arrange a dinner meeting . . . tonight. In Washington."

"Tonight?" she asked. It was almost noon, and she'd counted on taking the weekend off. "Of course . . . yes, if I can catch a flight."

"Oh, don't worry about that, Ms. Malneaux." Dieter laughed. "We'll fly you up in one of the corporate jets. I just wanted to call and make sure you had no conflicting plans."

"No, I'm completely free," she said, wondering how she'd prepare those Miami projections by Monday. But then a smile broke out across her face. Dieter, she now knew, ran Borders Atlantic's expansive security division. She had passed the polygraph. They would not have called otherwise.

"Wonderful," Dieter said. "I'll have a plane waiting for you this afternoon at four. Civil aviation terminal at Atlanta International. We'll take care of things from there."

"Sure. Right . . . I mean, thank you." She fought the urge to yell out loud. This job meant everything to her. Of course she'd fly to Washington for dinner with Jordan Mitchell.

"Auf Wiedersehen."

"Auf Wiedersehen," she replied.

Sirad clicked off the phone and laid her chin atop her naked darkly tanned thighs. First the Borders Atlantic news, now this. Things were shaping up better than she'd dared hope.

"Auf Wiedersehen." She smiled, remembering how foolish the chubby German had looked during that charade in the doctor's office. She hadn't spoken German in years.

▌

HRT IS DESIGNED to be air mobile within four hours, so once FBI headquarters decided to deploy its elite counterterrorism unit, the ball rolled quickly. Jeremy helped load Xray sniper gear into one of their vans, then raced north under lights and siren to Andrews Air Force Base, where team load masters had already prepped two mission-dedicated C-17 cargo planes. He arrived at the loading dock in one of the lead vehicles with his new team leader, Jesús Smith.

"Jesus! You guys are on the first plane out," the logistics officer yelled. Like most of the guys on the team, he pronounced Smith's first name with a hard *J*, like the Savior, not the Chicago Cub.

"You stay with me when we get down there, Waller," Jesús barked.

Jeremy knew that team leaders usually partnered up with new guys on their first mission, and he welcomed the association. Before joining the FBI, Jesús had served as an A-squadron assaulter with Delta Force. He had seen combat around the world, from outright war in Kuwait and Mogadishu to black-bag jobs in Indonesia, South America, and Lebanon — where rumor held that he once shot a Hezbollah sentry at 1,300 meters. Jesús kept a Silver Star in his desk drawer under a stack of Bass Pro Shops catalogs, and though he never talked about his past, everyone knew his pedigree. No one questioned his orders.

Jeremy dived into the task, savoring the excitement of his first mount-out. Members of a violent Puerto Rican independence group called the Macheteros had kidnapped the island governor's seven-year-old daughter, according to the initial briefing. They had threatened to kill her if their demands were not met within specific deadlines. This was the same group that once attacked the local FBI office with Light Anti-tank Weapons (LAW rockets) and used homemade explosives to destroy an Air National Guard fighter jet.

Fortunately, the San Juan office's informant network had provided several promising leads, and agents quickly located a likely safe house. The SWAT and Special Operations Group teams had surrounded the place without getting compromised, but the special agent in charge of the San Juan field office realized her limitations. With a little girl's life and a Puerto Rican political meltdown on the line, she very prudently requested backup.

Within minutes of her call, the Bureau's Strategic Information and Operations Center, or SIOC, had geared up for the response. The assistant director in charge, or ADIC, of the Counterterrorism Division called the assistant director of the Investigative Support Division, who in turn called the special agent in charge of the Critical Incident Response Group (CIRG) in Quantico to prepare for deployment. Twenty minutes later, at 1:37 PM Eastern, nineteen hours after the kidnapping occurred, more than two hundred twenty tactical, negotiations, and logistical experts lifted off.

Jeremy Waller sat among them, riding sideways on a canvas bench seat with a four-ton communications van bouncing up and down against his knees. His T-shirt dripped with sweat from the load-out, which included enough gear, food, weapons, ammo, and vehicles to maintain operations for at least seven days. This was his first time aboard a military aircraft, and he marveled at how anything so big and heavy could get off the ground.

"Hearts?" a voice called out. Fritz Lottspeich walked a narrow alley through the gear. He wore a green flight suit and yellow foam earplugs. The C-17s were more dependable than the old C-5 and C-141 workhorses that had lugged HRT around the world for the past twenty years, but they were loud.

"I'm in," Jeremy called out above the high-pitched whine of jet turbines. Anything to pass the time. Flying had never been one of his favorite things, and this was no commercial hop. Something about riding along at 500 miles per hour in a cylindrical warehouse with no windows made him a little edgy. It didn't help that they had packed an MD-530 helicopter and one of Golf Team's rigid-hull inflatable boats.

"You ever fly one of these things?" Jeremy yelled to the man next to him. Walt Hellier ran HRT's Tactical Helicopter Program. He'd flown Blackhawks for the Army's elite Task Force 160 and knew as much about aviation as anyone alive.

"Not my style," Walt yelled back. "Driving a C-seventeen is like sitting on your toilet, trying to fly your house."

"Let's go, Waller!" Lottspeich called out, summoning the card-players.

Jeremy stared at the MD-530 for a moment, then unbuckled his belt and started toward the game. The only good thing about flying in a plane with no windows was that in a crash, you'd never see the ground coming up to get you.

VI

_____

THE WILLARD HOTEL at 1401 Pennsylvania Avenue is better known for its filigree and mahogany appointments than its cuisine, but Washington's true cognoscenti have no trouble finding reasons to be seen in its grand dining room. Thirty-two incoming American presidents have rested at the Willard since its construction in 1850, and true insiders regularly grace its opulent halls. Jordan Mitchell understood this enchantment; he appreciated pedigree.

Unfortunately for Sirad, Mitchell also understood the power of anticipation. He kept her waiting there twenty minutes past their seven o'clock reservation. *Another silly game,* she thought, trading salacious glances with all the wealthy, married men ogling her from around the room. Sirad teased them, licking gin from her fingers after fishing olives out of her martini. She exaggerated the movement, tempting them to sneak a look past their wives as they reached for a slice of bread or a salad fork. Sirad loved the attention. It made her strong.

"Ms. Malneaux . . ." The voice startled her. "I'm so sorry to keep you."

Sirad turned to greet a tall, imposing figure, a man not handsome so much as striking. He wore long straight hair in a sort of Edwardian shag, faded pure white to stage eyes the color of stainless steel. His jacket hung perfectly along the angular, upright lines of a man ill suited to excess.

"Mr. Mitchell." She smiled, squeezing her knees together. She suddenly felt short of breath. "How nice to meet you."

Jordan Mitchell held out his hand, flashing a smile that shot right down her freshly tanned back to where her black slip of a dress pressed against the outside of her thighs. His hand felt hot in hers, slightly moist, as if he'd just rushed in from the street. This man exuded power, from the long slope of his Greenwich forehead to the family crest on his signet ring.

"I apologize for the delay," he said, accepting a waiter's help with his chair. "They say Washington is a city of Southern efficiency and Northern charm. I'm afraid I sometimes underestimate its challenges."

Sirad smiled through the light of a two-candle centerpiece. The half dozen men she'd toyed with earlier stared jealously in unison, wondering what this older man offered such a stunning dinner companion. Washington, like other power centers, spins on fear — fear that someone else may have more influence, more wealth, more anything. But then they saw Mitchell's face and understood.

"That's quite all right," she said, adjusting herself in the seat. He wore a two-button blazer in cashmere, John Lobb shoes, and the light scent of vetiver. "It was kind of you to invite me."

"The pleasure is all mine, Ms. Malneaux," he said, opening the wine list as the steward and headwaiter hung on his every nuance. He quickly selected a Bâtard-Montrachet, pointed to it, and initiated a rumble of activity among the staff.

"I understand you have done quite a job for us in Atlanta. Tell me about yourself." Jordan Mitchell leaned onto his elbows and transfixed Sirad with his eyes. They glowed blue-gray. Alarmingly so.

"Myself?" she asked. "Let's see. You probably know that I oversee mid-Atlantic . . ."

"No . . . you; I want to learn about Sirad Malneaux," he interrupted. "I understand you spent a year after college traveling in India and Nepal, that you went to Everest. How fascinating."

He guessed at her scent — not a perfume. Less. Just an herb, probably saffron cut with lilac. It emanated from her body, near where her breasts fell into the line of her dress.

"I grew up in New Orleans, mostly, but my dad was a professor. My family used to take me to the spas along the Dead Sea in the winters when I was a little girl. I figured that since I'd spent so much time in the lowest place on Earth, it only made sense that I'd also go to the highest."

"But you didn't climb it?" Mitchell inquired.

"I was raised in Louisiana, Mr. Mitchell. I didn't know much about climbing."

"It seems you're learning," he said as the waiter arrived with the wine, which Mitchell inspected, approved, and sipped.

"Lovely," he said, staring at her the whole time. What a rare woman — less interested in framing her beauty than embracing it. She wore black pearl earrings and a platinum choker with a solitaire pendant, a design he'd admired himself at Harry Winston just the week before. Impressive, he decided, yet more than she could afford.

"To mountains yet to be climbed," Mitchell toasted.

Sirad lifted her glass, modeling Mitchell's every move. "Cheers." She nodded. "One has to save some things for later."

■

"HR-28 TO TOC."

Jeremy leaned into the objective lens of a 40x Burris spotting scope as he called down to the Tactical Operations Center. The air hung around him like a hair shirt soaked in marmalade. Starlight offered 7 percent illumination. Very dark.

"Go for TOC," the soft female voice of a San Juan dispatcher replied through the radio transponder in Jeremy's left ear.

"Sierra Three has eyes on target," he whispered, signifying his operational status at what had been designated as Sniper Position Three. "Mark us one hundred twenty-seven yards from the white/red corner at a back azimuth of two hundred twenty-five degrees."

Jeremy peeked out of a mangrove thicket, across a wide lawn reaching up to a dilapidated plantation house. Light streamed from

111

tall windows on two stories. A stone balustrade stretched all the way across the front, with federal-style dormers rising out of a low-pitched roof.

A short, nervous-looking man with a thick beard hid near the edge of the building, smoking a cigarette. A couple of goats grazed in a small pen just off to his left. A donkey shuffled around the gravel parking circle, unfettered.

"Copy, Sierra Three. I have you with eyes on target at twenty-one twenty-seven."

A light maritime breeze ruffled the leaves above Jeremy's head as he checked the magnetic declination on his compass just to make certain he had called in the proper coordinates. Most of the other snipers used the new GPS devices, but growing up in the northern New Hampshire woods had given Jeremy a strong sense of direction, particularly with a compass. Technology looked good in catalogs, but he'd never trusted batteries.

"I got a long gun outside Red Bravo One," Jesús advised. Jeremy's team leader lay no more than a foot from him. Jesús stared through his rifle scope, sweeping the twenty-two-inch barrel back and forth across the building's front wall. A giant banyan stood between them and the building's rear door, its enormous root system obscuring their view of the veranda.

A lone sentry leaned into the tree, nearly hidden by its sprawling trunk.

"Got him," Jeremy whispered. He keyed his radio mike and relayed the information to the Tactical Operations Center back at Roosevelt Roads. "Sierra Three to TOC . . . have male subject with rifle outside Red Bravo One. Hispanic, twenty-five to thirty years, black crew cut, mustache, glasses." He paused to think up a nickname. "Call him Hector."

"Copy," the radio operator called back. "You have Hector in Red Bravo One."

Jeremy used his spotting scope to scour the grounds for other threats. Initial investigation by the San Juan office had determined that at least five armed men had snatched the governor's daughter off the playground at her private Catholic school. One of the gunmen simply walked up, shot the sole member of her security detail, and whisked her away as two dozen classmates stared on in disbelief.

It didn't take long to find them. Puerto Rico is a small island, and the FBI had cultivated a rich informant base. Agents quickly pinpointed the terrorists at this abandoned cane plantation seven miles east of Ponce, at the edge of El Junke, the Puerto Rican national rain forest. The site's isolated location made visual surveillance risky, but once the Bureau's ultrasophisticated Night Stalker surveillance plane verified human activity with its forward-looking infrared radar, or FLIR, the special agent in charge sent HRT snipers in for a closer look.

"So, what do you think?" Jesús asked. The son of a Mexican mother and a Chicago steelworker didn't talk a lot.

"Think?" Jeremy spotted a man moving across a window but couldn't make out details.

"Yeah, it's your first gig, right? How do you like it so far?"

"Beats the hell out of sniper school," Jeremy whispered.

What he meant to say was that he'd never felt so animated in his life. It wasn't the excitement of holding a man's life in the balance of a trigger pull that thrilled him. It was the sense that he lived among a small group of men who were called in to do a job no one else in the world could do. Sure, the military had special operations teams trained to handle bigger missions than this, but not under these circumstances. The Navy's Surface Warfare Development Group, formerly SEAL Team Six, and the Army's Combat Applications Group, which most people knew as Delta Force, included the most capable warriors on Earth. But they were prohibited by federal law from working in civilian law enforcement without special presidential authority. On top of that, they had no powers of arrest or training in rules of criminal procedure. Military teams excelled at the business of killing bad guys, but they had no way to deal with survivors. In cases like this, HRT always got the ticket.

Jesús said nothing. He spit a wad of Beechnut chewing tobacco on the ground and continued to sweep for targets.

"TOC to all units . . . ," the female dispatcher called out. "Prepare to copy."

Jeremy adjusted his earpiece and waited.

"Be advised we have swimmers two Mikes out," she said. "Hotel and Echo moving to phase line yellow. Break."

Dispatchers often used the term *break* to give other callers a chance to interject with emergency traffic. Unlike cell phones, encrypted radios did not offer simultaneous conversation.

"Please advise when clear for insertion."

Each of the Sierra positions verified in sequence, signaling that the FBI dragnet around this old plantation was complete. Snipers surrounded the building, dividing its four sides like pieces of some big, ugly pie. Each two-man unit focused on a fifteen-degree slice, narrowing the number of variables and reducing the chance of oversight.

"Check, White Bravo Three," Jesús whispered. "Looks like an AK."

Jeremy verified his call. There in the third window from the left on the second floor of the front wall stood a sentry with a 7.62mm assault rifle.

"Chinese, SKS," Jeremy said. "Check the stock." The terrorist turned straight toward him, but Jeremy knew it was just coincidence. He and Jesús had properly tucked themselves into a root pocket and disappeared from the outside world.

Jeremy trained the crosshairs of his rifle scope on the Machetero's forehead, silently calculating all the variables. Humidity: 95 percent. Angle of incidence: two degrees. Wind: zero to three miles per hour out of the south at quarter value. No apparent risk of bullet deflection, no disruptive glare, no reason to miss.

"Sierra Three to TOC, we have another armed male in White Bravo Three." He paused to think up a nickname. The man looked like a detective he'd seen on TV. "Call him Sipowicz."

A light-green gecko scampered down the length of Jeremy's rifle barrel.

"You want this guy or Hector?" Jesús asked. Made no difference to him.

"Hector," Jeremy said. He adjusted the bipod of his rifle between two root shoulders and rested his cheek on the stock. The rifle barrel tracked to the edge of the building and quartered the sentry with the razor-thin crosshairs of its scope.

"Sierra Three to TOC," Jeremy spoke into his radio. "Bring in the swimmers."

114

BY THE TIME they'd ordered their meal, Jordan Mitchell knew he'd found the right person for the job. This woman collected the attentions of everyone around her as gracefully as her skin collected candlelight. In the course of a dinner conversation, she had energized the entire room without uttering a word loud enough for anyone but her boss to hear.

Mitchell relished items as beautiful as this. Sirad possessed charms he'd only seen in rock stars and fashion designers.

"I have to say, you intrigue me," he said, pouring her more wine. "Never married?"

Sirad didn't flinch at the question. This dinner wasn't about sexism or glass ceilings or improper hiring practices; it was about mutual benefit. She wanted the Quantis gig, and he wanted her talent. To hell with the equal employment brochures and complaints about Jordan Mitchell's Edwardian chauvinism; this was business. How things got done.

"I'm a very independent woman," she said.

Mitchell nodded, trying not to stare. Little flakes of candlelight danced on her skin.

"Is that why you applied for the Quantis position?"

"I applied because it seemed like such an incredible opportunity. From what I know about the new SBT project, it will pretty much revolutionize the personal communications industry. If getting in on the ground floor of something like this means moving out of Atlanta for a couple years, I have no problem with that."

"But you like living in Atlanta?" he said, trying to sound engaged. He was not accustomed to lapses of thought, but this woman seized all his faculties. "You do know that you will have to move to New York? And we anticipate market entry by the end of August, so there will be lots of travel back and forth to Riyadh even before you actually relocate."

"Atlanta's a nice city," Sirad said. "But it's not home. I'm ready for a change."

Mitchell lowered his hands to his lap as the waiter served appetizers. He surreptitiously pressed a button on his pager, signaling Trask that he had seen enough. As delightful as this woman seemed, he couldn't bear the thought of watching her eat a single bite. She probably chewed slowly, thoroughly, with her mouth closed and without uttering the slightest noise, but this was one of the quirks he'd carried since childhood. Meals with his father meant enduring a constant barrage of ridicule over manners and etiquette. Eating was an intensely personal matter for Mitchell, more so than sex.

His cell phone rang.

"Please excuse me," he apologized, answering. "I told you not to bother me with . . . no, I . . . yes, all right. Tell him I'll be there in . . ." — he checked his watch, a vintage Rolex Prince with the jumping hour. Sirad noticed. She had never seen one in white gold. "Twenty minutes."

He hung up the phone and motioned to three men sitting at a table on the other side of the room. Two of the men stood and disappeared outside.

"This seems to be my night for apologies," Mitchell said. "Members of Congress have the oddest habit of scheduling meetings after chambers close. I think it's a power thing."

She smiled, but only at the absurdity of his ruse. Jordan Mitchell could get the president on the phone using speed dial. World leaders appealed to him for audiences. Very few politicians from either party would deign to tell him when or where they should meet.

"You're a busy man, Mr. Mitchell," Sirad said. "I fully understand." She started to rise.

"No. Please, finish your dinner," he insisted. Mitchell waved his hand, summoning a tall, strongly built assistant. "This is my chief of staff, John Trask." Sirad shook Trask's hand. "He needs to get a few administrative matters out of the way before we make this official. Also, we have a short lead time on this project; you'll be pretty busy in the next few weeks. Can I count on you for our Quantis initiative?"

"If you'll have me," she teased. Mitchell smiled at the entendre.

"I so enjoyed meeting you, Sirad." He shook her hand, holding it a moment longer than appropriate. "I hope to see you again soon."

With that, Mitchell hurried out to his car and climbed inside. He allowed himself a moment's fancy as images of Sirad filled his head, but then his cell phone rang, distracting him long enough to re-member why he had hired this woman in the first place. The very qualities that made her valuable to him made it impossible ever to fully trust her. She was beautiful, bright, and seductive, but she had history, too.

▥

BY 11:00 PM, the air had stilled to angel's breath. Jeremy could hear the sound of water dripping off Golf Team divers as they rose out of the glassy estuary behind him and crept ashore. The frogmen low-crawled like amphibious vipers and gathered in a bamboo thicket just behind Jeremy's forward firing position, or FFP. He glanced over his shoulder as they stripped off their Dräger rebreathers and wet suits. Out came the swim bags full of weapons, night-vision equipment, and flashbang grenades.

"Golf One at yellow," the team leader, a Boston Irishman named Sean Devlin, radioed to the TOC. "Request compromise authority and permission to move to green."

"Copy, Golf One," the dispatcher radioed back. "You have permission to move to green."

Devlin sneaked up behind them, just to Jesús' right. He looked resolute in the low light, as impenetrable as the mangrove jungle around him.

"What you got?" Devlin whispered. The six other members of his team scanned for threats.

"Two crows with AKs on the black/red corner," Jesús reported. "You're going to have to hit the west entrance."

Their operations order called for three potential insertion points: a trapdoor on the flat roof and level-one doors on the west and east sides. Coming in from the west would give Golf assaulters their best chance of avoiding the sentries, but they'd trade cover for the element of surprise.

"Gimme ten minutes to get up there," Devlin whispered.

Jeremy rested his sights on Hector's forehead, watching for signs that the man might react to Golf Team's movement. The crosshairs of his rifle held a living, breathing human being in their grip. No matter what the Marines had taught him about marksmanship, there was no way to practice for this.

He tucked the rifle stock into his shoulder and shrugged the outside world into subconscious. Lives hung in the balance. Jeremy caressed the trigger.

▌

MARCELLUS PARSONS WAS waiting in the sitting room of Jordan Mitchell's hotel suite when the CEO returned after dinner.

"Good evening, Senator," Mitchell greeted him. "I hope I haven't kept you long."

"No, no . . . just got here." The senator from Montana stumbled while rising from his chair and almost knocked over a tall Ming vase. "Hardly been waiting at all. That A.A. of yours really runs a tight ship."

Trask had gone to great lengths to cover this meeting, making sure that Parsons stopped in just briefly on his way from a Republican fund-raiser to a state function at the Italian ambassador's residence. Senator Beechum had drawn battle lines over the Quantis initiative, and every reporter in town knew it. Neither Mitchell nor Parsons wanted to hand her any ammunition by acting carelessly.

"What are you drinking?" Mitchell asked, leading his guest into the main salon. He walked to a fully stocked bar and selected a thirty-year-old bottle of bourbon.

"Uh, that looks good; whatever you're having." Parsons tried to appear comfortable, but Mitchell's presence clearly challenged him.

"You know, I just had dinner with the most fascinating woman." Mitchell poured two glasses of thin amber liquid. "I'm promoting her to run overseas marketing for the Quantis project. I've got to tell you, she's smart, capable . . . highly motivated."

"Same thing I look for in my staffers." Parsons smiled, taking his bourbon and swirling it around in the glass. He imagined that they now had something in common. "That, a tight little ass, and the ability to keep her mouth shut."

Mitchell frowned at the man's haggard laugh. "I hire competence, Marcellus," he snapped. "This woman's charms are a commodity that will help us in Middle Eastern and Asian markets. Nothing more."

Some people would counsel the CEO of a major corporation not to dine with midlevel management — especially the opposite sex — but then again few people fully understood Jordan Mitchell. Those who did knew about his almost pathological commitment to detail and his fundamental mistrust in subordinates. He wanted to make sure Sirad was right for the job. Physical attraction was nothing more than curiosity.

"Of course . . . ," Parsons chirped. "I just meant . . ."

"What do you have for me?" Mitchell walked to a French provincial couch, sat, and crossed his legs.

"What do I have? I . . . uh, oh, yes. I have talked to leadership, and I think we've come to a clear understanding on the Quantis initiative. This will not go to the floor. This will not end up in any do-gooder resolution or red-flag memo to the FCC. As far as the Senate is concerned, it's a dead issue."

"Good, good." Mitchell smiled, clearly pleased. "Because, you know, I may be a capitalist, but I'm also a patriot, Senator. I really am. Unapologetic . . ."

Parsons shifted back and forth on the heels of his Lucchese cowboy boots, then sat in an armchair opposite his host.

"I couldn't agree more," Parsons said, sipping his bourbon. "Now, about those two plants we're building: I've got the Ways and Means Committee looking into . . ."

There was a knock on the door. Trask entered.

"Continue," Mitchell told Parsons, staring all the while at his chief of staff.

"I've got lawyers on Ways and Means researching tax advantages. The Montana legislature has already offered generous incentives, as you know. I think this is going to make sense on a lot of levels."

"What about the Intelligence Committee?" Trask asked. "Beechum won't let this go quietly."

"No, she won't. In fact, she's trying to tie this all up with Matrix 1016. From what I understand, it lays out a plan by an al Qaeda cell to somehow infiltrate the Federal . . ."

"Yes, I know all about Matrix 1016," Mitchell interrupted. "Does she have enough to use it against us?"

"No, she doesn't," Parsons said. "Besides, she has troubles of her own."

"What do you mean?" Mitchell asked, pretending he didn't know. Parsons judged him a lousy actor.

"From what I hear, this whole thing in her bathroom didn't go down quite the way everyone thought," Parsons said. "They found evidence in her house that links her to a man that disappeared right around the time of her supposed assault — an NSC lawyer."

"And?" Mitchell asked in a calm voice.

Parsons held his answer for a moment, trying to read the subtle glances passing between Trask and Mitchell. The Borders Atlantic CEO showed no expression; Parsons wondered if he had ever seen the man blink.

"What I'm saying is that Senator Beechum's newfound momentum is about to hit a major speed bump," he answered.

Trask took his boss's now empty glass to the bar for a refill.

"That could mean an Ethics Committee inquiry, couldn't it?" the chief of staff asked. "Charges, perhaps. Does that mean there's a possibility that she would have to recuse herself from classified Intelligence Committee hearings pending legal action?"

"It's . . . possible . . . sure," Parsons sputtered. "But . . ."

"And that would mean the Senate leadership — your Republican leadership — might second-guess their crossparty generosity and replace her with some senior, more appropriate member as chairman," Mitchell suggested. "You, perhaps?"

Parsons's expression shifted with possibility. "Well, yes, I suppose," he said. The corners of his mouth rose to something approximating a shit-eating grin.

"Interesting." Mitchell nodded. "We hope you'll keep us up to speed on any new developments." With that, Mitchell picked up a coffee-table book of Helmut Newton nudes. The meeting was over.

"Yes, yes, of course," Parsons said. "Well, I have to get to the . . ." He stood up and started for the door. "I guess that means we're all set to break ground, then. Right? I mean, we should be ready to . . ."

"It was nice of you to come by, Senator," Trask said, walking Parsons to the door. "I want to thank you for everything you are doing for us. You go back to Montana and tell all those backhoe operators and ditchdiggers of yours that Christmas is going to be a good one this year. If everything continues to go like this, Borders Atlantic is coming to Montana."

▌▌▌

GOLF TEAM BEGAN moving out of "yellow," their last position of cover and concealment, just after midnight. They had compromise authority, meaning there was no turning back.

"You ready?" Jesús asked his partner. This was in their hands now. Once Golf Team moved out of the jungle, they would become vulnerable to Hector and his compadres.

"I'm watching him," Jeremy replied. The sentry shuffled through the crosshairs of Jeremy's 10x Unertl scope; he was smoking a cigarette.

"Just keep eyeballing." Jesús keyed his radio. "Sierra Three, clear," he said.

Jeremy checked the dial of his watch. Most of the bad guys were asleep, and those on duty sure as hell wanted to be. If there was any time to launch an assault, it was now.

"Hotel One to TOC, request compromise authority and permission to move to green," Chuck Price whispered. His seven-man assault team would approach from the other side of the house, under cover of Yankee and Zulu Snipers.

"Copy, I have Hotel and Golf at yellow . . ."

Jeremy concentrated on slowing his heart rate, just as the marksmanship instructors had taught. *Take muscle out of the equation and rest bone on bone,* they'd said. Soft tissue swells and flinches with blood or adrenaline or a mosquito bite. Bone seldom waivers.

He squinted fatigue out of his eyes and rested his cheek against the sweat-stained pad. A rifle shoots where it's pointed. The rest is human.

"Don't screw up, don't screw up . . . ," Jeremy murmured under his breath. He'd been lying in position for more than eight hours. He was getting anxious.

"TAC-AIR One to TOC, at yellow, request permission to move to green."

Walt Hellier's voice rattled in Jeremy's earphone, behind the rough chatter of twin Bell 412 jet turbines. Moments from now, two of the blacked-out choppers would flash in just behind the tree line and jettison Charlie and Echo assaulters onto the roof. The bilevel assault plan was designed to shock the Macheteros into confusion. Hotel and Golf would fight up, and Charlie and Echo would fight down until someone found the girl and cleared her for extraction.

"Copy, TAC-AIR One, I have you at yellow. All units stand by . . ."

Holy shit, Jeremy thought, squeezing his hand around the pistol grip of his rifle. This thing was going to happen. No more training. No more lectures or dry fire runs in the Kill House. He swept his sector and settled his crosshairs back on Hector, whose cigarette burned bright red in the scope barrel. Though 150 yards away, Jeremy somehow felt connected to this man, as if he had his hand on an errant child who badly needed a spanking.

"You clear?" Jesús asked.

"Clear," Jeremy whispered. The ground between Sierra Two and the crisis site glistened in the light of a rising moon. He swept his sector one last time, just to make . . .

SNAP!

Just off to their right, thirty yards at the edge of the jungle, something stilled Jeremy's heart. He instinctively turned his head, leaving his scope to scan the steaming darkness. Up ahead, one of the Golf Team assaulters fell to a knee, stumbling under the crack of a broken cypress branch.

"Jesus," Jeremy hissed.

"What?" his partner asked.

"No, not you . . . I'm swearing," he said. "I meant *shit.*" He started to explain, but the words caught in his throat. In the half breath he'd looked up from his scope, Hector had disappeared.

"HR One to all units . . . ," Mason suddenly called into fifty HRT earpieces. "You have compromise authority and permission to move to green."

No! Jeremy called out in the privacy of his own head. Hector had heard the errant footstep. He was hiding now. Golf Team was about to walk right into a trap.

"I'm down, I'm down . . . ," Jeremy whispered urgently to his partner and team leader.

"Down? What's that mean?" Jesús responded. He had plenty of his own issues to worry about.

"He's gone. Hector. I can't find him . . ." Jeremy swept his scope back and forth, but the ten-power magnification made it impossible to gather perspective. Thirty yards ahead of them, the first Golf Team assaulter emerged cautiously from the jungle, working his way toward the breach point. His teammates followed quickly, weapons searching for threats.

The muffled *thump, thump, thump* of helicopter rotors rose over the water, foreign in the empty night. Echo and Charlie Teams were inbound. They were going to war. There was nothing anyone could do to stop this now.

Jeremy scanned the lawn with his naked eye, hoping for some glimpse of Hector. His body felt like a live wire, surging with imperative. He had to do something, but what?

"Find the motherfucker!" Jesús ordered, holding crosshairs on his own target.

Something caught Jeremy's eye. Smoke — just a lungful — rose from the edge of a mangy bougainvillea hedge. Jeremy found Hector's cloudy reflection in the sagging leaded glass of a twelve-pane window. The Machetero sentry exhaled a last breath of cigarette smoke and raised his AK-47 to eye level, waiting for Golf Team. This was going bad in a hurry.

"TAC-AIR One to TOC . . . ," a voice rang out in Jeremy's earpiece. "Thirty seconds . . ."

"Shit! I can't get him," Jeremy announced. He couldn't shoot a reflection.

The roar of helicopter turbines swelled behind him. Jeremy saw their shadows on the horizon, moving 120 knots with fourteen assaulters per bird, fast ropes at the ready. He had to warn Golf without alerting the Macheteros inside. They'd kill the girl before anyone could get to her.

"Cover me," Jeremy said, springing to his feet in less time than it took Jesús to wonder what the hell was going on. Jeremy snatched up his MP-5SD submachine gun as he rose, scurrying along the tree line, right past Jesús' gun barrel. If his team leader called after him,

Jeremy couldn't hear it. He had only one thought in his mind, and that was stopping Hector.

"Stand by, I have control . . . ," Mason called out to all units.

Jeremy bent over to cut his profile against the jungle shadows and moved as quickly as his ragged ghillie suit would allow. He looked like some hybrid swamp creature emerging from the jungle — equal parts shadow, flora, and man.

"Five . . ."

Jeremy raced through the jungle of hanging vines and palm fronds, morphing into the shadows. A branch caught his ghillie veil, pulling it off, exposing sweat-matted hair and a camouflaged face marked by blind obsession.

He raised his gun as he crossed the narrow lawn, moving toward the corner of the house. The chopper rotors pummeled the air behind him. *WHOMP. WHOMP. WHOMP.*

"Four . . ."

Golf Team moved alongside the building. Their breacher pulled a strip charge from his sack of explosives and crouched beside the door.

Where the hell are you? Jeremy screamed to himself as he ran, finally reaching the manor house. Everything looked different up close. The gutters sagged; the stucco was peeling off in large, bowing panels. The goats stared at him, still chewing.

He ducked behind the banyan tree, which provided his only cover.

"Three . . ."

He fought to slow his breathing, to quiet his heart. He leaned into the tree, trying to spot Hector's reflection again in the windows. There, just an arm's reach to his right, the sentry crouched behind a big black rifle barrel. Jeremy didn't think, he simply leaned forward and slipped the muzzle of his MP-5 into Hector's sweaty right ear.

"Two . . ."

"*No más,*" Jeremy whispered. "*No más.*"

Hector froze.

Suddenly, the roar of helicopters drowned out the launch sequence as Hellier's airborne coaches flared over Jeremy's head. Prop wash buffeted the ground around the house. Fast ropes slid to the roof. The powerful choppers kicked up a hailstorm of beer cans, palm fronds, dirt, goat shit, anything loose enough to fly. The whole world seemed to disappear into a roiling chaos of noise and confusion.

Jeremy had been trained to key on weapons, but he couldn't help staring at Hector's eyes, which glowed like Lonsdale embers. He didn't want to shoot the sentry, but at this range, there would be very little reaction time.

BOOOOOOOM!

Golf Team's breach obliterated the French doors leading into the plantation house, and Devlin's crew disappeared inside. Jeremy staggered backward at the overpressure, which knocked the unsuspecting Hector to the ground. The disheveled Machetero groveled in the dust cloud for his gun, but Jeremy had already kicked it clear. Hector reached frantically into his shirt pocket and pulled out a small black box. A bright red LED flashed in the darkness.

What the hell is that? Jeremy wondered.

The sounds of combat erupted behind him. Flashbang grenades fractured the night. Gunfire. Screaming women. Men shouting in English and Puerto Rican Spanish. Breaking glass. More gunfire. The utter magnitude of violence shocked Jeremy. It was different when he was in the shooting house, practicing for CQB. Here, the targets were shooting back.

"Freeze! Freeze!" Jeremy demanded, jamming the barrel of his submachine gun into Hector's face. The terrified man dropped the little box.

Thoughts of finding the little girl hostage held Jeremy's concentration, but the blinking light on the LCD box on the ground demanded attention. Hector stared at it, too, terrified.

"Cómo está?" Jeremy yelled. "What is that?" He reached down and picked up what looked like a common garage-door opener.

Hector sprang to his feet and started to run, but Jeremy kicked the man's legs out from under him before he could escape. He jammed his knee down on the man's throat, shoved the tiny box into Hector's face, and screamed, "What is it?"

"Petrol, petrol . . . ," Hector gurgled. "Is gas."

Light from flashbang grenades exploding inside the building mirrored Jeremy's sudden illumination. The possibility of an assault like this must have occurred to them. Gasoline was cheap and still the most effective firebomb short of Thermit. HRT was fighting its way into a giant Molotov cocktail.

"Sierra Three to TOC!" Jeremy yelled into his mike, but he might as well have been spitting into a hurricane. The rage of combat swallowed his voice.

Without thinking, he snatched Hector off the ground and forced the man through Golf's door breach, into the plantation. This flew in the face of every rule they'd taught him, but then again so did dying.

Two bodies lay just inside the front door, one wearing only half a face. The man's single remaining eye stared up from pallid skin and a ghastly wound. Jeremy pushed his own hostage over the bodies, through the dull light leaking from other rooms.

"La muchacha!" Jeremy screamed in stress-diluted Spanish. "Where's the girl?"

"*Vámonos!*" Hector yelled, fighting him, trying to escape. "Out, out!"

Jeremy drove his knee into the man's common peroneal nerve, just above and outside his right knee. "Show me the fucking girl!"

Hector stumbled forward, bewildered by the pain and the storm of violence that had descended on the Machetero safe house. Flashbangs, "slap" charges, automatic gunfire. A strobe of muzzle flash danced from room to room as HRT fought its way toward the hostage.

"Freeze!" someone yelled above the din. Jeremy turned, holding Hector in front of him like a human shield. Dave Shellenby stood in the corner, leaning into his MP-5. Backlight from his Aimpoint cast his face in a hellish orange glow.

"It's Waller!" Jeremy yelled back. He thrust his own weapon above his head, just in case. Assaulters train to key on weapons, not faces. "This guy can take us to the girl!"

Shellenby blinked in recognition, then turned his weapon on Hector. He stepped closer, through the flashbang smoke and burning furniture, like a demon in the shadows.

"Where is she?" he yelled.

Jeremy realized that he had no body armor, nothing but a sniper ghillie and face paint. He might as well have been naked.

"Where is she?"

Hector just stared.

Shellenby rested the muzzle of his sub gun right between Hector's eyes and fingered the trigger. "Fuck it," he said.

"Downstairs!" Hector blurted out. Terror distorted his face. Whatever he had imagined of the government's response looked nothing like this. "In the cellar!"

He pointed right, to a hallway reaching back toward the kitchen, and Jeremy crossed the space in the time it took Hector to start his *avemaría*. Shellenby swept the room with his barrel-mounted flashlight. No doors. No access to stairs.

"Where?" the assaulter demanded. Hector pointed down at the floor, to a rug, and Jeremy kicked it with his foot, revealing a trapdoor. The initial assault had stormed right over it.

"Bang it," Shellenby said. He covered the hatch with his boot and tossed Jeremy an Ensign-Bickford diversionary grenade. One million candlepower flash, 180-decibel bang.

"No, no, no . . . gas!" Hector shook his head. "Gas!"

They had no time to work out a plan. If the kidnappers hadn't killed the girl already, they would surely do it soon. Jeremy searched for something, anything to give them a moment's diversion — dirty dishes, empty beer bottles, scattered groceries. There, on the shelf, next to the propane stove stood a five-pound bag of tortilla flour. Jeremy snatched it.

"On three . . . ," he said, nodding to the door. Shellenby had no time for explanations. Once that door opened, he was going in, regardless of what Jeremy did with the flour.

"One . . . two . . ."

Hector seized the opportunity and bolted for the door. Jeremy didn't even notice.

"Three . . ."

Shellenby yanked open the trapdoor and backed away from the hail of automatic weapons fire that exploded from the dark space below. Jeremy lobbed the flour bag down into the hole, letting the bullets shred it, vaporizing the flour into a giant white cloud.

"Ahhh!" the Machetero yelled, thinking he'd been gassed. His shooting stopped for just a millisecond — long enough for Jeremy and Shellenby to hang their muzzles into the void and wash it with light. It all happened so fast that the images barely registered with either operator — a gun muzzle, a terrorist's panic-stricken face, air thick with flour and fractured light.

Pop! Pop! Jeremy's "double tap" caught the terrorist between the eyes. The back of his head came right off.

"Go!" Shellenby yelled, but Jeremy had already committed. He hit the cellar floor almost as soon as the dead man, spinning right and left, whipping his light through the underground room. The filthy hole was filled with canning jars, broken furniture, and a dozen jerricans linked by old military detonation cord. The smell of gasoline almost overpowered him.

"There!" Shellenby yelled. Amid the cans, in a torn wicker chair, Jeremy found a terrified little girl not much older than Maddy. They had duct-taped her at the wrists, ankles, and mouth. Tears rolled out of her eyes as she slowly shook her head.

"Easy, sweetheart," Jeremy whispered. "We've come to take you home."

PHASE II

The rabbit-hole went straight on like a tunnel for some way, and then dipped suddenly down, so suddenly that Alice had not a moment to think about stopping herself before she found herself falling down what seemed to be a very deep well.

— *Lewis Carroll,* Alice's Adventures in Wonderland

VII

THE SIGN ON the door read AREA 51 — NO TRESPASSING. Jerry Patterson barely noticed the humor anymore. It all seemed so clever when one of his engineers hung it the first time, twenty-seven years earlier. But the company had been much smaller then, in the industrial park over behind Winchell's Donuts. Now they had grown into an impressive electronics firm, developing products that graced the shelves of major retailers from Radio Shack and the Sharper Image to Wal-Mart. What had started with a simple patent in the 1980s had blossomed into personal fortunes for all the early believers.

"How we looking on the interface?" Patterson asked.

This project had become Patterson's personal favorite. Even at the age of forty-seven, twenty years past prime for most mathematicians, he still got up every morning with a genuine thirst for the work.

"Quite good, actually." His lead designer, Dr. Ilene Proust, smiled. She looked more like a graduate student than an accomplished engineer, but her refined Oxford accent imparted an almost instant credibility. "We seem to have perfected the reverberation sequencing. Nothing will be certain until we complete field tests, but computer simulations look most promising."

"Cool." Patterson smiled. The system sitting in front of him had taken more than five years to develop. Though simple in concept, the principles behind its practical application had required huge effort and money. "How about the stabilization framework and trigger?"

"We went with standard digital European cell phone bandwidths — eighteen hundred megahertz — programmable through an ESN call signature," she said. "Everything mounts nicely to the Steadicam gyro on an aircraft aluminium substrate. It looks a little industrial at this point, but we can sex it up a bit on the way to market."

"Al-u-min-ium." He enunciated each syllable, trying to ape her accent. "You Brits have your own language, you know that?"

"Yes, we do." She smiled. "We call it English."

Ten years ago, he might have found her attractive. Though blondes never particularly thrilled him, she did carry herself with a certain sense of adventure. Fortunately for Patterson, the prospect of romancing a younger woman had lost its thrill. Three marriages and gruesome alimony payments had a way of taming the healthiest libido.

Patterson and his chief engineer moved through twin security doors into the sterile research-and-development lab. Half a dozen men and women worked earnestly on several different high-tech gadgets as Frank Zappa's *Lumpy Gravy* chirped out of vintage Klipsch Cornwall speakers.

Ilene led him toward a side room, designated KINESIOLOGY, where a slight man in hospital scrubs and rubber gloves doted over a strange-looking polymer box.

"Morning, Marty."

"F-f-f-fuck off," he stuttered. The man wore a "Disco Sucks" T-shirt inside out. He'd drawn some arcane physics equations on it in red Magic Marker.

"Ilene tells me you're nearly finished."

Patterson usually tried to ignore Marty, but there was no way around him today. Eccentricity came with the turf here, and Marty served as poster child for Neveu Acoustical Engineering's cadre of mad scientists. Patterson understood the business but hated that his company sometimes functioned more like a nursery school than an applied physics lab. Hiring the country's top mathematicians and physicists away from major corporations and the National Security Agency required a willingness to accommodate quirks.

"Who . . . who . . . who . . ." The man fought for words as he turned a small screw. "Who the fuck's your d-d-d-daddy?" He detached an alligator clip and backed away from what he clearly regarded as a masterpiece. "B-b-b-b-beautiful, huh?"

Marty, a self-proclaimed "wave theorist," dug a Mountain Dew out from a stack of line drawings and fired up a Pall Mall 100. He carried separate Caltech doctorates in electrical engineering and kinesiology, but he had come to Neveu as a soundman. This seemed like a significant step up from his previous job dissecting magnetic passport signatures for the CIA.

"We've got f-f-field tests set up for next we . . . we . . . week in Tucson," Marty said. "You g-g-g-gonna come?"

Patterson hated cigarette smoke, but it covered Marty's particularly acrid BO.

"Yes." He nodded. "I think I will."

Something about acoustics had always thrilled Patterson. Maybe it was his audiophile father's collection of Macintosh tube amplifiers, all those turntable counterweights and monolithic 1970s speakers. It wasn't the music he loved as much as the delivery systems. Something about tossing sound waves around at hypervolume just seemed so damned empowering.

"S-s-stand by f-f-f-f-for incoming," Marty said, pulling ski goggles over his eyes and climbing into a formfitting plastic chair. He pulled a seat belt around his waist and flipped a toggle switch, which raised the two-by-three-foot platform several feet off the lab floor.

"Hand me that ce-ce-cell phone, will y-y-ya?" he yelled over the sound of whirring motors. The platform began to shake like a badly tuned Volkswagen.

Ilene grabbed a thin, credit card–sized phone off the counter and handed it up.

"Now, wa-wa-watch this! And r-r-remember, I n-n-n-n-never shot a gun in my life."

Nothing about Marty's new invention resembled a gun, but they all knew it would be just as deadly. To the uneducated eye, it looked more like one of those half-dome security cameras you might see in a theater lobby than an instrument of destruction. In fact, that's where the whole project began — in the movies. A client had come up with the idea in 1979 while watching the aerial assault scenes from *Apocalypse Now*. The theater's sound system pumped out "Ride of the Valkyries" so loudly that it hurt his ears, he said. It made his whole body shake. He felt as if he was going to have a heart attack.

That literal earthquake of sound, combined with Francis Ford Coppola's imagery of death and destruction, had triggered a moment of revelation. Why not use sound as a weapon? If a jet could shatter windows with a sonic boom, why not find a way to rend flesh with the same physics? It had taken more than two decades to bring this idea to fruition, but like all great inventions, it was worth the wait. Neveu Acoustical Engineering's new "wave cannon" could very well revolutionize conventional battlefield engagement.

"O-k-k-kay," Marty yelled out. "Better s-s-s-stand behind me, just in c-c-case!"

He sat in the small seat on a perforated aluminum shelf attached to the left skid of a simulated MD-530 helicopter. A four-foot industrial exhaust fan blew air down on him from the ceiling, simulating rotor wash. The whole contraption bounced, whirred, and vibrated eight feet off the ground as if the roof had opened and a small attack helicopter had dropped in for a brief hello.

"We're simulating a fifty-foot hover in an urban setting with a ten-knot crosswind and downdrafts off surrounding buildings," Dr. Proust hollered. "We've got no ground effect. It's piss-poor flying. Worst-case scenario for a sniper."

Patterson knew that Marty's simulated helicopter ride had little to do with sniping. Contract specifications called for close contact and remote delivery (0 to 300 meters) of a "wave path" capable of inducing "disruptive sympathetic vibration in bio-organic gelatinous tissue." Though project parameters were written in terms of sine wave modulation, composite frequency responses, and megahertz and vortex decibels, everyone knew the true objective: someone — and contract sources were always obscured in ventures like these — had hired Neveu to build a viable means of wounding and killing human beings with sound.

As with most physics, the broad strokes of theory had been easier to solve than the practical application. Once the team harnessed the concept, it had been relatively easy to load the requisite electrical power and amplification equipment into a helicopter, for example, but producing the same effect with something as small as a cell phone, as the contract stipulated, proved bewilderingly difficult. Dr. Proust's true genius had shown through when she found a way to combine cutting-edge microbattery and capacitor technology with a magnesium/ceramic frequency generator or "speaker." According to lab tests, it worked with devastating efficiency.

"Now, if you watch the computer screen, you'll see what we're dealing with here," the British scientist said. "We have two adult male targets moving left to right across a rooftop. One is carrying a conventional cell phone with a GPS transmitter and a galvanic response trigger. The other is using one of the Borders Atlantic Quantis phones with our HyperSonic Sound package."

Patterson tried to concentrate on the computer simulation as Marty bounced up and down on the helicopter skid in his hospital scrubs, still wearing his rubber gloves. His long, stringy hair danced wildly in the downdraft.

"In this scenario, the phones have been sent in by hostage negotiators," Proust continued. "The first man you see will be using his Quantis phone to talk with police; the other will have his turned off in his pocket."

"But that doesn't matter, right?" Patterson asked. Contract specifications also required that the phones have a dormant feature allowing target identification up to a one-meter standoff even with power down.

"Correct." Proust nodded. "We can tell through space-based telemetry when it is being held by the designated user even with the switch turned off."

"W-watch this!"

Marty hit a button and remotely triggered a projector, which beamed a prerecorded set of movie images at a twelve-by-twelve-foot blue-screen backdrop. Generated by sophisticated software and a high-speed mainframe computer, this scenario played out through a bifurcating logic program. To the casual viewer it looked like a movie, but in reality it was more like a video game designed to read Marty's input and react with lifelike variability.

"B-b-bravo Three to C-C-CP, I have target acquisition. Request g-g-green light!"

"Where the hell is he getting all this lingo?" Patterson asked. Nothing in Marty's personnel folder suggested any knowledge of SWAT operations. The closest he'd ever come to police tactics was the time his roommate got busted for growing hydroponic sinsemilla in the Caltech life sciences garden.

"Come on, m-m-m-man, you're the C-C-CP. I need a friggin' g-g-g-green light!"

Dr. Proust nodded to Patterson, who shrugged his shoulders and yelled back.

"OK, yeah, this is CP," he pretended. "You've got the green light."

All eyes focused on a huge computer monitor as two bad guys dashed across the roof, holding a terrified-looking woman between them. As the figures moved past various obstructions on the roof, it became obvious that one of the men had a small child taped to his back. Their heads were no more than six inches apart.

"My God," Patterson wondered aloud, "how could anyone make a shot like that?"

Marty seemed less than intimidated by the challenge. He simply dialed a number into a thin gray cell phone and pressed the Send button.

Nothing happened. No recoil. No muzzle flash. No noise. No hint that a sophisticated weapon had just discharged a highly concentrated "bolt" of sound and induced sympathetic vibration in the hostage takers' flesh. Patterson nodded knowingly as the lead bad guy suddenly fell to the ground, bleeding profusely from his now disfigured ears, nose, and mouth. Everyone in the room knew that this computer-generated effect — cribbed from violent video games — would look just as impressive in real life. It looked as if a bomb had gone off inside his skull.

"Contestant n-n-n-n-n-n-number two! C-c-come on down!" Marty called out. He again pressed his Quantis phone's Send button, drop-ping the second hostage taker — same instantaneous trauma, same total lack of weapon signature.

"G-g-goddammit, I'm good!" Marty yelled. He flipped a series of switches and rode the platform back to the lab floor.

"Well, what do you think?" Proust asked. Patterson smiled broadly as the computer program's black-suited SWAT team raced out to whisk the woman and her child to safety.

"Awesome." Patterson beamed. The fan slowed, the noisy simula-tor quieted, and the computer screen hibernated to a Britney Spears screen saver. "Looks like we're ready for field trials — on budget, on time, and on spec. The only thing I don't get is why no one thought of this sooner."

"It m-m-m-may be s-s-s-s-simple, but it ain't e-e-e-easy, boss," Marty said, climbing out of the chair and pulling off his ski goggles. "Hey, y-y-you think the L . . . L . . . LAPD could use a N-n-n-new Age, high-tech s-s-sniper?"

"Maybe," Patterson answered, shaking his head. "But you'd hate the haircut."

❚❚❚

ELIZABETH BEECHUM'S LIFE sank from a platform of national adoration to a miasma of shock and despair in the time it took for the grand jury to return a true bill. A reporter from the *Washington Times* had called for a comment on the indictment before her own lawyer notified her of the horrible news.

"How did the damned newspaper know about this before I did?" Beechum had yelled, but the answer was obvious. Washington is a town fueled by leaks and rumor. All the recent success in the polls had painted a fluorescent orange target on Beechum's chest. This was going to get ugly fast, and she knew it.

Early Monday morning, exactly one week before the Democratic National Convention — the same convention that everyone ex-pected to nominate her — Phillip Matthews picked her up at her home and drove her to the police station, where she turned herself in for booking. A jailhouse matron had fingerprinted her, placed her in a holding cell pending arraignment, and made her change into jail-issue greens. She had even taken the drawstring from Beechum's pants to prevent any suicide attempts.

It was all for show, of course. Two hours later, after a hell storm of protest from her attorney, a judge had posted bail on personal recognizance. He saw no risk of flight, the judge said. Despite the apparent severity of the crime, this was a United States senator, after all — an internationally recognizable face and a front-running presidential candidate. Where could she go?

The story had leaped off newsstands around the country. The wires ran it as a news alert. CNN and the cable channels yanked in every pundit, violent crime expert, and behavioral analyst they could find. This was the biggest political scandal in years, and the whole Fourth Estate emptied its closets looking for ratings. They staked out her home, her office building, her every public sighting with the bloodlust that now accompanies any politician's opprobrious fall.

Word spread through the Capitol like wildfire. *Is it possible?* staffers gasped. The mere thought of a woman like Beechum resorting to murder seemed preposterous. How could a doyenne renowned for social conscience and respect for all manner of law have committed such a heinous crime?

Early reviews looked mixed. Some of the senator's closest friends went public to support her, arguing that her years of service to the country should at least lend her the benefit of the doubt. They appealed for patience and to let the justice system work its course. One was still innocent until proven guilty, they argued, even if the accused was running for president. A few even pointed fingers at the Republicans, saying it might not be a coincidence that all of this happened to the front-running challenger so close to the convention. But even those who deeply hated the current administration had a hard time believing that it would stoop so low.

Others whispered that they'd seen it coming all along. Perhaps she had been attempting to cover up some salacious past, protecting herself in the run for the White House. She had always led an intensely private personal life, they said. The fact that she spent most of her time wandering the secret world of black projects and classified operations didn't help. Maybe she too had a secret life that included lies, double-cross, and violence. It just stunk of subterfuge — some Forsyth plotline — a powerful woman with her hands on all the secrets trying to eliminate a young National Security Council lover. What might he know, personally or professionally, that could bring her down?

No one offered a shred of evidence, of course. This was idle, baseless speculation — rumor and innuendo. Unfortunately, rumor and innuendo were the only two things that moved through Congress with any speed these days.

As the story grew, Beechum found herself more and more isolated from the Senate she had served for most of her adult life. Washington crept away from her the way a dog slithers off from a chewed shoe. Intelligence Committee members she had worked with for years shunned reporters' questions for fear of having to defend her. The notoriously political Ethics Committee cloistered themselves behind closed doors, trying to honor a long-standing reluctance to finger its own while still playing to its Republican president's political wishes. The Senate had no precedent for allegations this grave, the Republican chairman said. No member had ever been charged with a crime this foul.

Folks back in the district seemed stunned. They had always thought her a genteel woman bred to calm demeanor and refined sensibilities. But once the media began to stir the pot, the voters came at her with the whetted appetite of a lynch mob.

Only one thing in all of this surprised Beechum: Marcellus Parsons's silence. This was the man who had gone national with his dislike for her politics and his intentions to damage her presidential bid. He was the same man who had once begged her for sponsorship of a military funding bill that benefited Montana, only to turn around and accuse her, personally, of partisan duplicity when other Democrats voted it down.

Parsons had shown again and again that he felt no remorse in kicking a man when he was down, yet he had remained uncharacteristically quiet, at least in public. "Betsy, I just don't know how to say this," he had mumbled during their first postindictment encounter, mustering a semblance of sincerity. "But out of fairness to the committee, I have to ask if you feel mentally competent to continue with your duties. I mean, we deal with some pretty sensitive issues, and the membership is beginning to wonder how this . . . situation is going to affect your judgment."

"I'm fine, Marcellus, but I appreciate your concern." She smiled. "And for the record, my name is still Elizabeth."

For days, she fought the crowds of reporters assembled outside her brownstone and tried to go on with her life as if nothing had happened. Rosa tried to shoo the cameras away from the front of the house, but they closed in around her with questions. *Did the senator sleep with this man? Did you know him? Were there others? How many? Did the senator have female lovers? Did she ever beat you?*

Beechum continued to drive herself to work, despite the protesters who swarmed around her car each day. Most of them came from the radical left and wrapped themselves in antiwar, pro–civil liberties righteousness. "Stop the cover-up!" they chanted in the evening when she came home from work, convinced that the murder had been committed to prevent Slater from exposing the truth — whatever that was. "No more secrets, no more lies! Get the truth from Senate spies!"

The only place she felt safe, at first, was in her Dirksen office — the bunker she'd used to wage so many battles. It had become a refuge over the years, an edifice she could fall back into whenever it seemed necessary to borrow the weight and dignity of the U.S. Senate. But as the story swelled, her office became a big marble grave. Staffers walked on eggshells, unsure how to react, whether they'd have jobs in a month, whether their friends in South Carolina would turn from them. The halls emptied of other senators when she walked through. Pages and interns avoided her eyes. Security guards cast wary glances. Even the lobbyists ran away. No one called, except for reporters.

Almost no one. Early Thursday morning, as the rest of the Democratic party packed its bags for the convention in Boston, her private line rang.

"Yes?" Beechum answered. Only friends and close colleagues knew this number.

"I don't mean to bother you at work," a woman's voice responded. "But this is the only line they haven't tapped yet. We need to talk. Can you meet me?"

The voice sounded midwestern and young.

"Who is this?" Beechum demanded. Washington is a town built on informants, and the head of the Intelligence Committee had plenty, but this wasn't one of them.

"I know about the man with the dice on his arm," the woman said. "I think we should talk."

∎

"DADDY! DADDY!"

Jeremy woke up in his own bed and rolled over just in time to avoid the forty-eight-pound body slam Maddy had learned watching the Rock on WWE's Thursday night *Smack Down!* Christopher was right behind her swinging a Wiffle ball bat.

"You can't defeat me!" Jeremy bellowed, scooping the two children into his arms and rolling them into the tussled sheets. They screamed with delight as he plowed his nose into their ribs, tickling and rooting his way to a bear hug.

"What did you bring us, Daddy?" Christopher asked between giggles. He smelled warm and clean in his Pokémon pajamas. Jeremy tried to lose himself in the moment, wondering if he could ever wash off the smell of mangrove rot.

"How about a conch shell?" he asked, letting the kids up for air. "Puerto Rico has really nice conch shells."

"Conch shell?" Christopher asked, wrinkling his face. "What's that?"

"I want a present, Daddy!" Maddy called out.

"Hey, hey . . . give your dad a break," Caroline interrupted. She entered with two cups of coffee and the morning paper. She'd already been out for her morning jog. "Go brush your teeth and wash up for school. Go!"

Christopher looked to his dad for direction. Mom made the rules, but Dad could break them.

"Brush your teeth." He smiled, plugging a tickle. "I'll get your presents while you're gone."

Maddy led Christopher, at a run, into the bathroom down the hall, and the room settled back into quiet.

"OK, so I want to hear all about it. Don't I? Do I?" Caroline asked. She offered him his coffee and started to peel off her running clothes for a shower. "I mean, the papers said some of the terrorists were killed."

Gorgeous, Jeremy thought, watching his wife undress. After seven years of marriage, she still struck him as the most beautiful woman in the world. Three children had tugged at her athletic figure in places, but the lines just added to her character — her appeal. She was his best friend, yet at moments like this, she still made him itch with lust.

"Need some help with that?" he asked as she attempted to pull her jog bra over her head.

"Sure, if you want to lock the kids in their room." She smiled. Caroline flashed him, then scurried into the bathroom, giggling.

Jeremy lay back in bed and stared at the ceiling. He'd slipped in during the middle of the night, long after Caroline and the kids had gone to bed. The signs and balloons they'd left for him still dangled about the house, remnants of yet another party he'd missed because of the FBI. He remembered sitting there in the kitchen as they slept, eating cookies they'd baked and reading the handmade cards in the dim green glow of the microwave clock.

The whole Puerto Rico incident seemed like a thousand years ago, though it had been just four days.

"You killed a man," Jeremy said out loud, lying there in the warm bedsheets. He addressed himself like a stranger. Perhaps if he said the words enough, it would feel real.

It all seemed so different from what he'd imagined. The enemy hadn't appeared and died in the crosshairs of his sniper rifle, like all the training targets. There had been no official authorization to take the shot. No green light. No official nod from the command element. He'd simply reacted . . . assessed the situation and fired.

Now he was home — a place far from war. This was a place where Daddy was the man who read bedtime stories and gave hugs in the morning. Bad guys were limited to cartoons. Guns were made out of wood and plastic.

"You killed a man," Jeremy said a little louder. He felt guilty for bringing the whole thing into the house with him, as if he had stepped in something and forgotten to wipe it off his boot. He wanted to walk into the bathroom and hug his wife, tell her everything that had happened. But something deeper kept him away, some strange fear of spilling emotion out over a series of events he still hadn't fully processed. *How does a man tell his wife he's killed another human being?* Jeremy wondered. Where the hell was the FBI manual for that?

"So, what time are you going in?" Caroline yelled above the sound of the shower.

"They gave us today as an RDO," he yelled back. "I don't have to go in until tomorrow."

Jeremy looked forward to having a little time to gather his thoughts before meeting the Bureau's Shooting Review Board Tuesday morning. FBI headquarters had already scheduled a series of interviews to officially investigate the whole Puerto Rico operation, and he wanted to make sure his answers lined up with documented events. This was all part of the process any time an agent discharged his or her firearm, of course, but there was no sense in showing up unprepared.

Jeremy climbed out of bed and pulled on a pair of jeans.

Deadly force may not be used except to protect the life of an agent or another person from the threat of death or serious bodily harm. He knew the Bureau's deadly force policy by heart. It was the first thing they would ask him about.

He remembered instructors back at the Academy who told him the average FBI agent makes no more than one arrest a year. *One* arrest. The odds of ever pulling a gun in the line of duty ranked right behind lightning strikes for most G-men, but HRT was different. Jeremy could count on one hand the operators who had *not* been involved in some kind of violent altercation.

Don't worry, it was a good shoot, they'd all told him in the aftermath. *You never should have left your post, and that shit with the flour was a little weird, but it was a good shoot.*

Fact was, in an era when the slightest FBI controversy ended up in congressional hearings, this mission had turned out magnificently.

The governor had got his little girl back; two of the terrorists had been taken alive, giving the politicians someone to blame during a very public trial; and no operators had been injured.

Jeremy pulled a T-shirt out of his bottom drawer just as his wife emerged from the shower. He loved the smell of Prell in her hair.

"Well, I'm glad you'll have a little time home with the kids," Caroline said. "So the news said four of the terrorists were killed." She wrapped herself in a white terry-cloth towel and wiped water droplets out of her eyes. "Who did the shooting?"

"Two Charlie guys," he said. "Albert Kraus and Jimmy Keefer?" Jeremy stepped into their bathroom and grabbed his toothbrush. "They took a lot of fire right after we went in."

Caroline reached for her hair dryer. "*We?* I thought you were out in the woods." He hadn't told her much over the phone. She rarely asked about his job anyway. It was enough to know he hadn't been hurt.

"Jungle, honey; it was a jungle."

Jeremy squeezed toothpaste onto his brush and stared at her in the mirror. They stood no more than two feet apart, but he felt a million miles away.

"I went in, Caroline. I shot a man. I killed him."

VIII

————

SIRAD HURRIED TO finish buttoning her new Catherine Malandrino blouse, put on simple diamond studs, and stepped into a pair of floral cutout Jimmy Choo sling backs that she had bought just for tonight. Though she seldom went out on Thursday nights, her new friend Hamid Mirhadi had flown into Atlanta for the evening, and she wanted to look her best.

She'd first met the Borders Atlantic money manager during her polygraph trip to New York. A mutual friend had introduced her to the handsome executive in the elevator and casually mentioned that several people were getting together for drinks later that night in SoHo. Sirad had already tipped a couple martinis by the time Hamid arrived, and conversation led on to dinner, which turned into more drinks, and then some late-night dancing. Though things had ended innocently enough that first night, Sirad had seen him again in Washington after her dinner with Jordan Mitchell, and by the time Hamid left her hotel room the next day, Sirad knew this would end up being more than a one-night romp.

Hamid agreed. He sent flowers while she waited at the airport. He had flowers waiting when she returned to her apartment. She tried to remain aloof at first, but he called repeatedly, dialing her home, her cell, and, finally, her office. That this man managed institutional capital worth more than $30 billion, including the retirement accounts of virtually all Borders Atlantic employees, was lost on no one. Once Hamid reached out to Sirad's boss, she called back within the hour.

Easy, girl, you don't want to kill him, Sirad cautioned herself, turning left then right to check herself in the mirror on the way out of her apartment. Ordinarily, she wouldn't have placed time constraints on seduction, but Hamid struck her as a man she'd have to cultivate carefully — especially in light of her pending transfer. Long-distance relationships often presented serious obstacles, but Mitchell had said this job would bring her back to New York a couple times each month. There was no harm in giving Hamid a little taste of what he could expect during reunions.

Sirad hurried down to the parking garage and drove herself to the restaurant, smiling all the way about her new beau. Though ten years her senior, Hamid kept himself fit, stood tall enough to back up his boyish good looks, and carried both an MBA from Stanford and a law degree from Harvard. Like Sirad, he spoke several languages, including Arabic, but unlike Sirad, who had domestic roots, he had spent his youth in the Middle East — he escaped from Iran with the Pahlavi family as the shah fell in 1979.

What most intrigued Sirad, however, was Hamid's life among the shadows of international finance. Thanks to several in-house sources and a few too many glasses of wine, Sirad had learned that this Ivy League Midas had pioneered a complicated and very closely held type of securities trading known as "peripherals." Even in a world conditioned to junk bonds, derivatives, and hedge funds, this venture stood out as a crapshoot, but the potential for profits seemed staggering.

The concept, which traced its origins to the Defense Advanced Research Projects Agency's (DARPA) Terrorism Futures Project, sounded fairly simple: Third World countries accumulate debt — huge debt — from industrialized nations like the United States and its G8 allies. The more debt they incur, the more interest they pay, and the more they pay, the more they have to borrow. It's a downward spiral that has driven many impoverished nations into civil war and economic collapse. Yet, once a particular country demonstrates strategic value to the West, it often finds itself flush with debt relief, including upgraded lending status, loan guarantees, or even outright grants. The Soviet Union gleaned more than $20 billion between 1989 and 1999. Other countries have made more.

The war on terrorism had increased this calculated generosity dramatically. Since 9/11, countries like Somalia, Sudan, and Yemen had suddenly found themselves in position to trade terrorists for millions of dollars in "aid." Even stable countries like Turkey, Cameroon, Poland, and Kuwait had parlayed the situation into major loan packages. Offering Third World governments money for "humanitarian aid and international goodwill" made sound financial sense for the United States: backroom payoffs beat troops in body bags any day.

Jordan Mitchell agreed, especially once Mirhadi showed him how to make money on America's largesse. Hamid discovered that for a relatively small investment, venture capitalists could "option" foreign debt in exchange for tangible government assets. For pennies on the dollar, investors could speculate on international monetary policy in return for cash, land, natural resources, or infrastructure. It was just like buying mortgage and consumer debt, only with greater risk and significantly bigger rewards.

With Mitchell's blessing, Mirhadi carefully masked his new market and began looking for clients. He set up a Cayman-based subsidiary as cover, then approached wealthy speculators — mostly Arab oil sheiks — who were tired of turning 2 percent in money markets or losing their shirts on dot-com scams. Hamid's Iranian heritage and Middle Eastern connections helped during start-up, but by the end of the fourth month, this peripherals trading literally took off on its own.

The World Bank and the Securities and Exchange Commission look unkindly on such transactions, of course, so secrecy became an important issue — particularly once Hamid discovered that the U.S. government used the Federal Reserve system to move its share of the payoffs. If Borders Atlantic could tunnel into Fed Wire, the organization's complex and highly secure transfer system, Hamid pointed out, they would be able to anticipate and manipulate the market for even bigger profits.

According to the encrypted e-mail Sirad had received, that may already have begun. During the past three years, Hamid had secretly leveraged an extraordinary series of transactions — $7.2 billion in the previous month alone.

"Park it where I can see it, will you?" Sirad asked the valet as she pulled up in front of Felig, Atlanta's hottest new eatery. She tossed the man a ten and a loaded smile, then hurried inside to a packed bar. Thursday nights weren't ordinarily a problem, but Felig had become a scene.

"Hello, Sirad. You look absolutely lovely." Hamid smiled, stepping away from the bar and leaning in for a kiss.

"Thanks." Sirad nodded. "You, too." He did, actually. The athletic cut of his suit lent presence to his six-foot-one frame, and he wore his hair in a traditional style that spoke of old money and refinement. He dressed tastefully in expensive though conservative clothes, from the Hermès tie around his neck to the Patek Philippe watch on his left wrist. Hamid had the thick black hair of his Iranian father, intoxicating eyes, and a French accent common to Swiss boarding schools — traits that only added to his considerable charms.

"So, how's your appetite?" he asked.

"Depends on what you have in mind," Sirad answered. She reached out, grabbed his tie, and pulled him close enough to trace his lips with her tongue.

"Mmmm . . . what's that, single malt? Macallan?"

"It's so nice to see you, Sirad," Hamid said. It was Lagavulin, but why wreck a moment?

█

"JUST A COUPLE of minutes until we start our descent, Mr. Mitchell," the flight attendant announced in her most ingratiating voice. "You might want to buckle up."

Jordan Mitchell sat on a fawn leather couch in a luxuriously appointed Gulfstream G-V with an aviation phone welded to his right ear. He had spent most of the four-hour flight talking to his office of general counsel, trying to finalize delivery arrangements with the

Saudis. Everything had gone wonderfully to date — from launch of the SBT's low-earth orbit satellite network to repeater station and infrastructure installations throughout the Persian Gulf — but the Saudis now wanted to move up the announcement to coincide with an OPEC summit.

"Tell the pilots to do something about this damned turbulence!" Mitchell growled, holding his hand over the mouthpiece. His mood really had begun to sour. "This is the roughest flight I've had in weeks."

The flight attendant nodded officiously and disappeared down the corridor leading to the flight deck. There was nothing she or anyone else could do about the rough air, but that didn't matter; when the boss gave orders, the troops tried to follow them.

"Look, I don't care about how this affects our tax status with the state of Montana," Mitchell yelled into his phone. Lawyers had never been his favorite class of people, particularly when they confused paperwork with the bottom line. "This is the biggest single venture Borders Atlantic has ever undertaken, and I'm not going to tell the Saudis we can't meet production schedules because you are having trouble with a tax stamp. Deal with it!"

With that, he hung up and turned toward the back of the plane.

"Trask!" he yelled, loudly enough that the flight attendant poked her head around the corner to see if there was a problem. Trask immediately put down his own cell phone and walked over to attend to his boss.

"General counsel is having trouble pushing production to meet the Saudis' new deadlines," Mitchell said. "Can I assume that you will take care of this before it becomes a problem?"

Trask checked his watch, which read 9:40 PM, eastern standard time. He'd already set his internal clock back three hours to work in Arizona, but the shining sun still felt a little odd. He dreaded trips like this because they always meant adding three hours to an already interminably long workday. Tonight would drag on forever.

"Of course, Mr. Mitchell," Trask said, jotting a note in his PDA. "I'll make sure we have everything set by tomorrow morning. By the way, I just got off the phone with our people in Qatar; they're in position and ready for early activation. We still have a couple technological issues to deal with, but I assure you they will be ironed out before delivery."

Mitchell nodded affirmation. He knew that engineers had already tested the SBT system throughout the Persian Gulf and used individual Quantis phones as far away as Pakistan. Though most of the ground-based infrastructure remained in Saudi Arabia, satellites still provided worldwide coverage.

"What about the . . . contractors?"

"Confirmed. We have reset to the new operational constraints — including arrangements with the Yemeni government. Funds have been transferred. Both electronic and human intelligence verify time and location, right down to OPFOR coordination, exfil agreements, and offshore medevac capabilities. We plan to move our insertion team in-country contemporaneous with the OPEC summit. It all comes down to target acquisition, but everything looks good to go."

Trask occasionally lapsed back into military speak during briefings like this. He had organized enough five-paragraph orders, logistical annexes, and operations plans to do them in his sleep.

"Sirad?" Mitchell asked.

"We haven't talked to her about the new time line yet. She'll get the briefing, of course, but due to operational security . . ." — he paused a moment as the jet bounced a couple times over clear-air turbulence — "we think it best to wait."

"I agree," Mitchell responded. "As of now, she should be given the date and enough information to handle the show-and-tell. I still have a couple issues to resolve before we fully read her in. Make sure you move up her flight, though, and take care of all the tech issues. I want to make certain there are no problems when we hand everything over to the Saudis."

The pilot throttled back the engines, and the jet slumped into initial descent, prompting Mitchell to glance out his window at a spiderweb of broken mountains glittering in the sunlight below. The airspace they had just entered stretched over an isolated plot of land owned since World War II by the Department of Defense. To passersby, this barren stretch of Arizona rock and cactus looked like any other southwestern landscape, but to those in the intelligence community it was better known as Castella Air Base, Delta Force's west coast jump zone and home to Conifer Air, one of the CIA's covert airlines.

150

"How do we look for the demonstration?" Mitchell asked. He stared down at the desert floor, suddenly filled with excitement for what lay ahead.

"I hear it's amazing," Trask said. "We're on for nine tomorrow morning."

Mitchell nodded, offering the slightest hint of a smile. He had been waiting more than a year for this trip — a field trial that represented the culmination of one fascinating initiative and the beginning of another. Borders Atlantic juggled dozens of R & D programs, held countless companies in their sights, and constantly sought out new markets, but this enterprise was different. During the next twenty-four hours, he would see technology he only could have dreamed about even three years earlier — technology that would help him realize his greatest ambition.

"Good, good." Mitchell nodded. He pulled a pad of paper out of his case and jotted down a note. "Any word on the Beechum situation?"

"Her candidacy is over. Our sources on the Ethics Committee tell me there is a strong sentiment that she should be suspended as committee chair pending results of the investigation. Should know something by next week."

Mitchell said nothing in response. He simply stared out the window and smiled at the rising horizon. He'd harbored a fondness for the Southwest ever since his father — a die-hard hunter — had taken him and his brothers there a half century earlier to shoot pheasants. Mitchell well remembered the brilliant desert light and Arizona's dry, fragrant air.

"Better buckle up, gentlemen," the flight attendant warned, belting herself into a jump seat. "We should be on the ground shortly."

America's best-known CEO barely flinched as the pilot nosed the plane down and dropped rapidly into an FAA-prohibited descent. This was restricted airspace, and in order to escape the watchful eye of air traffic controllers, the private jet would have to duck quickly into the 10,000-acre facility. The pain in his ears and queasy feeling in his stomach barely bothered him; what he'd accomplish in the next couple of days would be well worth the discomfort.

■

"LIE BACK, BABY . . . this might take awhile."

Sirad pushed Hamid down on the couch in his hotel room, pulled up her skirt, and straddled him.

"Dinner was great, huh?" he said, fumbling with the buttons on her blouse.

"Dinner?" she asked. "Don't tell me you flew all the way down here for dinner." She ran a finger down the outside of Hamid's neck, tracing the line he shaved just forward of his earlobe.

"You know," she said, "there's a spot just above the collarbone called the brachial plexus." She pushed lightly with her finger to mark it. "If I press hard enough, I can disrupt blood flow to your brain and cause instantaneous death. But if I lick or suck on it like this . . ." She demonstrated with the skill of a seasoned instructor.

"My God," Hamid moaned. "Where the hell . . . did you learn something like that?"

"You don't want to know," she whispered. She sucked on the special spot, moving slowly back and forth above him.

"You're killing me," he moaned, trying to finish with the buttons on her shirt.

Sirad pulled back, shaking her head. "Not yet," she scolded, pressing him between her legs. This wasn't about release. It was about suspense — the sweet anticipation inherent in fine lingerie, the scent of chocolate with raspberries, an ice cube melting. Sirad understood the poetry of foreplay, how to bait a man into senseless indenture.

"I was wondering . . . ," she whispered, leaning back into her work, "what you think about when you're all alone in that big office of yours and I'm all the way down in Atlanta." She pulled off her blouse and bra, then pressed herself against his chest.

"I think you know."

"Tell me," she demanded, grabbing his hands and using them to cup her breasts.

"You drive me crazy," he said. The tone in his voice sounded urgent, almost pathetic, like a boy whining over a scraped knee.

"Tell me you think about this when you're alone," she said. Sirad lifted herself onto her knees and pulled her skirt high enough for him to see the red lace panties she had shopped all afternoon to find just for this moment.

"My God . . . ," he groaned again.

"Tell me what you'd do to have me." Sirad pulled his hand up between her thighs to show him she was ready, too. She leaned in to kiss him with the tongue that had tortured him just enough. And finally she reached down for the zipper that almost tore as she pulled it down.

"I think of you," he said.

"Tell me what you'd do to have me."

"I'd do anything, Sirad," he said. Hamid sounded more like a broker closing a deal than a lover. For a man who controlled every aspect of his life, this was a moment on the edge.

"Promise," Sirad told him.

Hamid tore open his shirt and pressed against her, fumbling with the button to his pants, groping for her, pulling her panties aside, then reaching inside, desperate for her.

"I promise . . . ," he mumbled, grinding himself against Sirad, twisting on the damask couch, trying to gain all of her with the same wanton lunge.

And she relented, giving herself to the great climax she felt growing down from her stomach, then up through her thighs. It was the power she loved, the seduction, the sense that she could win, from this man or any other, things no one else could pry.

"I promise . . . ," he said, yet again, and she knew he wouldn't lie. Sirad pushed her face back down onto his neck, sucking on that magic spot, opening herself to Hamid's desperation. She lowered herself over him, guiding him inside, and then she came and came and came.

▐█▌

THE RESEARCH AND development team from Neveu Acoustical Engineering had already been on-site at the Arizona testing facility for a day when Mitchell touched down. Patterson had booked the whole crew into the Embassy Suites in Tucson, hoping a nice swim and the free happy hour would put his people in top form for the demonstrations. Unfortunately, Marty had developed an unexpected interest in the physics of two-stepping and got way too drunk at a local haunt called the Cactus Moon. He called from jail just after three o'clock the next morning claiming police had arrested him for taking on the bouncer at a gentlemen's club called TD's West.

"What the hell were you doing at a strip joint?" Patterson demanded, driving the still-intoxicated engineer back to his room. Neveu was a small company that made most of its money working on classified projects. If his acoustics wizard lost his security clearance because of something as stupid as this, it could cost them dearly.

"B-b-b-bitch set me up," Marty said. Then he threw up all over the rental car.

When Patterson checked on him six hours later, the eccentric mathematician claimed he had been drugged by some guy in a cowboy hat who didn't want him moving in on his date. He was far too sick to ride out into the desert, Marty said, refusing to discuss the fact that he had a black eye and his pants were on backward.

After considerable prodding and various threats, Marty finally got out into the car, but no one was happy about the dismal turn of events. Patterson held his temper, knowing all too well that this was Marty's project and that he was the only one who really knew how to make it dance. With the clients already on-scene for today's final shakedown, he'd have to get things together in a hurry.

"Give him some coffee and he'll be all right," Dr. Proust said as they drove north of town along Highway 15. Patterson held a test protocol in his lap, checking to make sure they'd thought of everything. Marty lay across the backseat, mumbling something about Egg McMuffins.

"Let's go over this one more time," Patterson said. "We've got the chopper flying in with the mounts attached."

"Same bird we used yesterday," Proust added. "Same target system, same firing sequences and coordinates." Everything had gone perfectly the day before, but engineers obsessed about details, particularly Patterson's engineers.

"That's it up there." Patterson pointed to exit 37. A small sign at the side of the highway read CASTELLA AIRPORT, NEXT RIGHT.

Ten minutes later, Dr. Proust shut down the engine and climbed out into a dusty parking lot. A small shed stood in the middle of an otherwise open expanse of sand, rock, and scrub. An MD-530 helicopter waited just beyond the shed with two pilots aboard.

"Name's Earl Carbonough," one of the pilots said, climbing out of the left seat and crossing to the Neveu crew. He wore Wal-Mart jeans, Sha Na Na sideburns, and a green satin Southside Johnny and the Asbury Jukes tour jacket.

"Jerry Patterson. This is Dr. Proust. Where are the pilots we had yesterday?" Patterson asked. He had taken great precaution in making sure every detail of the test could be re-created here for the client demonstration. Changing pilots did not strike him as a good thing.

"Don't worry," Earl said. "I been flying weapons systems since Tet. You bolt it on, and I'll make sure we hit the target."

"All right," Patterson agreed. There was no sense in arguing at this point. "We'll be set to go in just a minute; one of our associates is feeling a bit under the weather."

"Well, wire his ass to his brain housing group," the pilot barked. "Winds really rile up early out here, and I ain't got time for malingering."

▥

TRASK DROVE NORTH on Highway 15 on Tuesday morning, sipping on a giant cup of coffee and trying to function on three hours of sleep. He turned off the two-lane highway at exit 37, at an empty circle on his AAA map, then followed a dirt road to an abandoned aircraft hangar.

Mitchell bounced around in the back of the big SUV, reading a four-year-old issue of *American Rifleman*. One of his scouts had found a particularly interesting Henry rifle in the estate of a New Mexico banker. According to the article, a prominent Texas rancher had ordered the rifle for his son's wedding, but it had been stolen by one of Pancho Villa's top lieutenants during a cattle raid in 1910. The rancher was so incensed, he hired a private army to get it back, but his son was killed in the effort. The rifle had remained in the family for five generations and was known as the Dorado Henry, after its original bridegroom owner.

"Beautiful, isn't it?"

155

"Yes, sir," Trask answered. "Have you decided to buy it?"

"I meant the light," Mitchell snapped. "Why can't we have light like this in New York?"

Trask shrugged, wondering if the boss was talking to him or directly to the Almighty. He turned left at the hangar and drove down into the desert, silently grousing about how the dry air cracked his skin and hurt his eyes. The Marines had sent him to Twentynine Palms in the 1980s, and he had never forgotten how this environment could bite a hundred different ways.

"I believe this is it, Mr. Mitchell," he said, pulling up to a cluster of newly erected structures that looked out on a broad expanse of desert. More than a dozen cars sat in a single-file line at the side of the one-lane dirt road. Dust had already caked them the color of adobe.

Trask parked near the front and jumped out of the big 4 x 4 to hurry around and get his boss's door. The first thing he noticed, other than the heat, was a semihidden cadre of armed guards all around them — some inside vehicles, some standing at the edge of buildings, others in a wider perimeter out among the cacti. These were not run-of-the-mill checkpoint sentries but bearded men wearing civilian clothes and an air of utter superiority.

"My God, it gets hot early," Trask remarked as Mitchell climbed out of the truck, adjusted his sunglasses, and pulled on a wide-brimmed hat. The two men walked a short distance to a wooden platform that looked like a press box from some high school football field. An army sergeant in crisp green BDUs met them at the base of the stairs.

"Good morning, sirs." The soldier nodded with military formality. "If you'll follow me, the general is expecting you."

The sergeant led them up to a crowded room. Someone had carefully arranged cheap foldout chairs in one corner and stocked a table with pastries and coffee. Combat engineers had faced the front wall with darkly tinted Plexiglas, which would afford a clear view of the mile-wide proving ground but protect guests from the sun and shrapnel.

"Good morning, Jordan!" someone called out. Trask turned to his right as a four-star general in Class A's motioned for Mitchell to join him. The CEO waded in among the uniforms like a commander himself, smiling and shaking hands as if he had a West Point ring of his own to knock.

"Still kissing ass and taking names, huh, Trask?" someone asked. Trask turned back to his left and came eye to eye with a face he hadn't seen in three years.

"Well, I'll be a son of a bitch." Trask shook his head as the two men grabbed each other around the shoulders in one of those hugs only old soldiers ever get quite right.

"How the hell you been?" they asked simultaneously. Trask stood there, admiring the full bird insignia on his old friend's lapel. "Looks like you been moving up in the world," Trask said. He'd known "Chinch" Wollerton since their Academy days.

"I can see that you've been doing pretty well yourself," the colonel said. "My car probably didn't cost as much as that suit."

Trask started to respond, but a louder voice interrupted. "If I could have your attention," a major suddenly called out. "Fire control has secured for testing. We should have ordnance headed down-range any second now."

"Where's the target, General?" Mitchell asked loudly enough for everyone to hear. He looked out over a barren stretch of sand, rock, and cacti that ran twenty miles all the way to the Mexican border.

"Right here, sirs," Colonel Wollerton answered, pulling a room divider aside to reveal two storefront mannequins propped side by side. "If you'll stand right here, Mr. Mitchell, we're going to . . ."

Suddenly, a chaos of noise and vibration grabbed everyone's attention. Mitchell spun left as a four-seat MD-530 helicopter settled into a hover just outside the front window.

"We have target acquisition," the pilot's voice barked out of a loudspeaker.

"Just press the Pound button, sir," the major directed. He pointed to the Quantis cell phone in Mitchell's hand and nodded. The CEO did as instructed and almost instantly recoiled as one of the plastic dummies' heads exploded with a sharp crack and a shower of viscous green sludge.

"Ho-ly . . . ," Mitchell sputtered. The speed and violence of the attack caught him completely off guard. Before he could gather himself, the second dummy exploded. Its head tumbled in pieces onto the plywood floor.

"Charlie Two-eight to OB One," the pilot called out over his radio. "Targets acquired and eliminated. Returning to base, copy?"

"Copy, Charlie Two-eight; nice run," the general spoke into the radio. The smile on his face suggested that the mission had been a complete success. "Now, gentlemen, if we could . . ."

"Wait a minute," Mitchell interrupted. "What just happened here?" If Borders Atlantic's CEO felt conspicuous asking questions at such a demonstration, he didn't show it.

"What you just witnessed," Colonel Wollerton explained, "is a whole new generation of warfare."

"These devices work outside the audible spectrum, sir," one of the aides added. "They induce vibration through frequency modulation. Even the target never hears a thing."

"And it shoots through walls?" Mitchell asked.

"Yes, sir — through walls, glass, most building materials. And we can lock on, within three hundred meters, to a specific electromagnetic frequency generation — as low as thirty hertz. Standing still or moving at Mach one, as long as we can pick up a frequency to target, we can take it out one hundred percent of the time with zero footprint and no collateral damage."

"Zero footprint?" Mitchell asked. He reached down and swept two fingers full of goo off the floor.

"No sign of mechanism," a new voice interjected. Everyone turned toward the door as Patterson entered with Dr. Proust and a pale-green Marty.

"Zero footprint means no one will know how, where, or by whom they were hit. Whether mounted on a helicopter skid or installed in a cell phone, this system will offer deadly force applications with virtually no traceable signature."

"Damn, that's some gun, gentlemen." The general whistled.

Mitchell shook his head without correcting him. The Dorado Henry he would buy at auction later that afternoon was a gun. This was something more — a whole new application of justice.

IX

"GOOD MORNING, AGENT Waller, I'm Supervisory Special Agent Jack Oushiski." Jeremy shook the man's hand as he produced FBI credentials verifying his identity. "This is SSA Melissa Kennedy; SSA John Lee," he said. "We're with OPR . . . handling the Villa Davila incident."

Those three letters — *OPR* — sent shivers up the spine of most FBI agents, particularly if associated with a shooting. When the Office of Professional Responsibility showed up with a microscope in one hand and a Manual of Investigative and Operational Guidelines in the other, it almost always meant trouble.

"Where do we start?" Jeremy asked. He sat behind the front-row table in one of the seats reserved for team leaders during the morning meeting. The supervisors sat across from him, three abreast.

"First, we have to read you your rights," the lead investigator said. Jeremy had already forgotten the man's name.

"This is still just an administrative inquiry," the woman explained, handing Jeremy an FD-395 Waiver and Advice of Rights form. "But we have to advise you that this could potentially end up a criminal matter, so anything you say can be used against you in court. You

159

aren't obligated to talk to us without a lawyer. Do you understand your rights?"

Of course he understood his rights; there were none. Jeremy carried personal liability insurance and could eventually get legal representation through the FBI Agents Association, but he knew that once inside the Shooting Review Board, he was on his own. He picked up a Skilcraft Bureau-issue pen and signed the FD-395.

"Fire away," Jeremy said, instantly regretting his aphorism.

For more than an hour they asked him questions about the shooting itself and about events leading up to it. What weapon was he carrying? How many rounds in the magazine? How many fired? Date of last qualification? Was he taking any medication? Had he been adequately briefed on mission-specific rules of engagement? Why had he handcuffed the Machetero as he lay dying on the floor? Had he offered the victim first aid?

All the answers came easily except the last two. *First aid?* he thought. *The son of a bitch was trying to kill me. Why would I want to give him first aid?*

"We handcuff everyone," Jeremy explained, trying to sound professional. "We didn't have time to do a medical assessment — we wanted to get the girl out of there as fast as possible."

The female supervisor took notes, occasionally asking him to repeat details or spell out tricky names like *Heckler* and *Koch* or *defilade* or *ghillie suit*. She nodded, accepting his answers as if this was just a formality. She was a white-collar crime investigator, after all — the only thing she knew about Jeremy and HRT was that their actions sounded heroic.

When they were done, the lead interviewer asked if Jeremy could think of anything they had forgotten to ask or if he wanted to make some kind of statement. "No, that's about it," Jeremy said. He'd written the requisite FD-302 immediately after the incident, but those Results of Investigation forms were notoriously vague. No one wanted to put into writing the intimate details of a once-in-a-lifetime crisis. Adrenaline adversely affected recall; it was better just to highlight the major events and let the mind settle a couple days before committing to minutiae.

"Thank you for your cooperation," Oushiski said, standing to leave. "We'll advise you of the results of our investigation."

When? might have been a good question, but Jeremy didn't ask it. He wanted out of that room as soon as possible.

Oushiski and the others shook Jeremy's hand again, gathered their Bureau forms, and left him alone in the HRT classroom, staring at the brass bell. He sat there for a moment, trying to slow the speed with which his life seemed to be spinning. Three days earlier, he'd been coaching his daughter's Little League game; now he was facing an OPR investigation for killing a man.

Killed a man? He could hear Caroline's words as he stood next to her in the bathroom. *I'm so sorry*, she'd said. Her voice had sounded distant, removed, almost uninterested.

Yeah, he had told her. *What did Maddy say when she knocked in the winning run?*

The winning run . . . Caroline had stopped toweling her hair and stared at the man she thought she knew. *Don't you want to talk about Puerto Rico?*

Jeremy remembered putting down his toothbrush and splashing water on his face as she talked, images popping into his head: the sound of Marshall Baldwin's fastball hitting the catcher's mitt, racking a round into his .45, Maddy's bat ringing out across the field. Suddenly, he was right there again — inside the Machetero house fighting through the violence. The visions flashed back so hard, he flinched.

It was like this all the time now. The memories came when he least expected them, like waves of a migraine building and receding without reason, leaving him tired, almost hungover. The whole thing played out like some slow dream in which he was trying to run, but his feet wouldn't move fast enough. A white cloud of shifting light, followed by two giant black holes, flashing reds and yellows, then something slippery underfoot. Blood. Pooling, oozing from the man's head. The man. No name, no identity other than the "terrorist" handle he'd adopted when he and his asshole buddies kidnapped that little girl.

Did he have kids? Jeremy wondered, standing up to leave the HRT classroom. *Did he have a wife? Where did he live?* The thoughts came

161

without provocation. They flashed through his mind without any conscious summons. Jeremy knew there was something bizarre about not being able to let it go. If he hadn't killed that man, Jeremy could have been killed himself.

"Hey, Doughboy!" someone called out, passing the now open classroom door. Jeremy turned toward the voice, but there was no one behind it.

Everything is different now, Jeremy thought. He'd first noticed the change during the "hotwash" in the officers' club at Roosevelt Roads after the mission. First there were tentative stares from his team-mates, then a couple free beers, then the shots of tequila. Everyone wanted to know how he felt, what it was like in there, whether the little girl had said anything to him. They'd gathered around him in circles, nodding as he and Shellenby talked about finding the trapdoor and deciding how to breach it. At times, the only sounds in the bar had been Jeremy's voice and a George Strait song in the background.

Days had passed, yet sometimes it felt as if Puerto Rico had been years ago. Other times, it felt as if he were still there.

Jeremy stood up from his seat in the HRT classroom and tried to push the whole thing from his mind. He walked across the hallway to the mail slots in the front office.

"Don't forget to sign your time card," the secretary said, tapping the "three register."

"He doesn't sign in anymore," Lottspeich joked, elbowing Jeremy out of the way to check his own mail. "He's a war hero."

"Yeah, well, this is the FBI, not the Marines. War heroes don't get paid unless they sign their time cards." The secretary tossed him a pen.

Jeremy did as he was told, then picked up his daily shipment of form letters and interoffice "cheesy" envelopes and walked back toward the squad room. Lottspeich caught up with him halfway down the hall.

"Hey, fuck the three register, OK?" He smiled. "You want anything, you just let me know. Everything all right at home?"

"Yeah. Fine," Jeremy said, walking down the main hallway. He nodded to Jimmy Gagliano, the number one man on Golf Team, who would have walked into the sentry had Jeremy not intervened. The veteran operator nodded with a curious smile Jeremy hadn't seen since the dog-collar competition. For better or worse, he was no longer the FNG on Xray Snipers. He had become a member of that uneasy fraternity of men who'd pulled the trigger in the line of duty. He'd earned his bones, and everyone was watching to see how he'd carry them.

Jeremy smiled and nodded back, settling the whole issue through suggestion.

"How you think Albert and Keefer are doing?" Lottspeich asked. Two other operators who'd engaged targets in other parts of the house were still in their interviews with the Shooting Review Board.

"Just tell the truth, right?" Jeremy asked. "It was a good shoot. There's nothing to hide."

A couple of passing teammates slapped him on the shoulder.

"Of course it was a good shoot, man," Lottspeich said. "You know that."

Jeremy noticed a photo on the wall — an 8 x 10 of the Talladega Prison rescue in '91. It was one of dozens of pictures recording twenty-one years of HRT missions around the world. Once OPR settled things, the Villa Davila rescue would glow prominently among them.

Jeremy turned left halfway down the hall and stepped into the blue snipers' "hooch," a large room crammed full of six-foot-high work cubicles, sweaty clothes, and war gear.

"Hey, Waller, I'm thinking about buying the wife a bread maker . . . got any recommendations?" Manny Salinas stopped at the sniper deli, just around the corner from Jeremy's desk, to pick up a morning snack. Whiskey Team hustled everything from Power-Bars to Beechnut chewing tobacco and used the money to fund team functions like the NOTS barbecue.

"Kiss my ass," Jeremy said, wishing he'd come up with something clever. Salinas had brought his bones to the team from the Gulf War, where he'd killed his share of "indigenous personnel" as a Marine Corps tank commander.

"They teach you the powder toss at sniper school?" Manny asked, selecting a box of Jujubes. "Or did you think that up all by yourself?"

Jeremy started to respond, but someone yelled, "Incoming!" and lobbed a Baggie of flour over the cubicle divider. It landed on Jeremy's desk and burst in a big white cloud.

"Hey, fuck you guys!" Jeremy called out. He grabbed what was left of the bag, jumped up, and lunged around the corner, but whoever threw it was already gone.

"Easy, brother," Lottspeich said, wiping Gold Medal off Jeremy's flight suit. "It's all part of the process. Things are going to be like this for a while."

▮

SIRAD LEFT HAMID'S hotel room just after eight Friday morning and took a cab back to her apartment. The knowing grin on her doorman's face might have bothered her after some less well-planned tryst, but not today. Everything was falling quickly into place, and she had no time to worry about something as trivial as returning home in yesterday's clothes.

"Gonna be a hot one, huh, Jimmy?" she'd asked, hurrying past him with a wink and a smile. What she'd gained in a wild night with Hamid would outweigh any lustful presumption from the hired help.

Once upstairs, she stripped off her wrinkled, musky outfit and hurried into the shower. Important clients expected her downtown at a business breakfast in a little more than an hour, and she still hadn't studied their prospectus. Hamid called twice while she was dressing, but Sirad saw no need to answer. He was already helplessly tangled in her charms; keeping him on the hook now depended more on what she promised than what she delivered.

Sirad called the office to check messages, then grabbed her case, hurried down to her car, and twenty minutes later pulled into the Buckhead Four Seasons. Borders Atlantic owned more than thirty thousand square feet of office space in Atlanta, but these clients had specifically requested conference in their favorite hotel. With almost $40 million on the table, her boss had complied. She valet parked her BMW and had just walked into the lobby when the concierge approached her with something in his hand.

"Ms. Malneaux?" he asked in a thick eastern European accent.

"Yes." She looked around, wondering how he had identified her.

"You have a phone call, please."

The man handed her a wireless phone.

"Hello?" Sirad half expected to hear Hamid's voice but knew

164

within the first two syllables that this call had nothing to do with pleasure.

"I thought we were going to do lunch," a voice answered. It was a man's voice, erudite, double basso, with suggestions of an inner-city youth.

"You're not exactly the kind of person I can keep on my speed dial." Sirad smiled at the surprise. She had a contact number for him, but she'd only used it twice. "Let me guess: you're in town, but just for the day."

That's the way he worked. Mr. Hoch would appear out of nowhere — always when she least expected it — and then disappear, sometimes in the middle of a sentence. He wasted nothing on tact or sentiment.

"How'd you know I was here?" Sirad asked.

"Please," he answered with deadpan confidence. For the past three years, he had been her controller, the lifeline that tethered her to a dark world few people even guessed at. Of course he knew.

"I need to talk with you," he said. "In person."

"When? Now?" She checked her watch. The clients had scheduled a nine o'clock briefing, and she was already running late.

"This won't take long. Meet me in the hotel restaurant."

Sirad nodded to no one in particular and handed the phone back to the concierge. She looked around the lobby, immediately suspicious that someone had followed her, then hurried down broad stairs to a dining room full of business travelers and tourists. Mr. Hoch sat at a small table near the kitchen door.

"You look well." Hoch talked softly with a voice that resonated even at idle. He wore a cashmere blazer, gray flannel slacks, and that offhand gravity she had always admired in certain men of color.

"You look well yourself." Sirad sat opposite him and the plate of eggs Benedict he'd begun to dice with his fork. Hoch reached out to shake her hand and passed something rectangular and stiff. Sirad tucked the object into her purse without looking.

"That's a room key: number three twenty-seven," he said, munching on a side order of wheat toast. "You'll find an envelope on the bed; inside is a software package that you'll need to load into Hamid's PDA before your trip to the Middle East."

"Middle East?" she asked. "What are you talking about?"

"The Saudis have moved up the delivery date. They want to introduce your Quantis phones early."

"Wait a minute," Sirad said. "I thought we were looking at fall. I haven't even been fully reassigned to this project."

"Two weeks from now, you will be summoned to New York and briefed on new plans for the Quantis project. Shortly afterward, you will fly from New York to Dubai for the formal launch of operations with the Saudis."

"Dubai? Why not Riyadh?"

"The Saudis want to announce the agreement at an OPEC summit. It's a strategic move that they think will give them negotiations leverage on production quotas."

Sirad scowled at the news.

"What about *our* time line?"

"We have to move it up." Hoch ate a bite of his breakfast. "I see no problem with that."

"Why now? They've told me all along that this was set for fall release."

"Things change. You know that."

Sirad shook her head. "Don't you think someone should have told me about this?" she asked. "I mean, there's something wrong when I hear about a move this big from you before I hear it from my own company."

"Let's not forget who you really work for, Sirad," Hoch admonished, summoning history neither wanted to discuss in public.

Sirad looked down into her empty plate. Though her résumé would have grabbed the attentions of virtually any Fortune 500 human resources department, her true curriculum vitae began right after college with recruitment to the Central Intelligence Agency. Two weeks into the paramilitary aspect of her training at Harvey Point, North Carolina, Sirad had been singled out for a shadow cell of promising young case officers who were being placed in junior executive slots at major multinational corporations. Code-named "Stagehand," this new and deeply firewalled Office of Nonofficial Cover project operated under the premise that the best way to gather intelligence is to follow the money behind it.

For the past three years, Hoch had orchestrated virtually every aspect of her life, from the men she dated to the clothes she wore. He decided when she traveled, where she vacationed, even what car she drove. The CIA, not Borders Atlantic, determined her destiny; Sirad's promotion — even the overseas transfer — was nothing but a cover. Beneath it all, she was an NOC.

"Don't worry about Mitchell," Hoch said. "He controls the Quantis initiative very closely; you'll get word just as soon as he satisfies his curiosity about your new love interest."

"He knows about Hamid?"

"It's his business to know."

"How much?"

"Enough that he has people surveilling you. Your office, your phones, your apartment."

Sirad shook her head. "Well, they must have gotten an eyeful last night," she groused. "Did they follow me here this morning?"

Hock spread raspberry preserves on a crust of wheat toast as Sirad tried to look around without appearing obvious. "Second table from the door," he said. "I'll deal with them while you go upstairs and get the software."

"You should have told me . . . ," Sirad started to object, but Hoch stilled her with a glance.

"I'm sorry." Sirad nodded, realizing that she had overstepped her authority. "I shouldn't have said anything, but my personal life . . . I thought it was private."

"Private? From whom?" Hoch motioned to the waiter for more coffee, then pushed his plate aside and leaned close to Sirad. "Understand this: Jordan Mitchell is a businessman. His only goal is to make money. If he ever ties you and Hamid in anything more than a love knot, we have significant problems."

Sirad stared into his bloodshot eyes. They were the only clue she'd ever seen that he felt stress in this life.

"What do I do in Dubai?" she asked.

"Don't worry about Dubai. All you need to worry about right now is that key in your pocket. Take it upstairs, pick up the software, and load it onto Hamid's PDA. Whatever Mitchell wants you to do in Dubai is secondary to our goals at this point."

Hoch leaned back in his chair, glanced at the surveillance team by the door, and finished his coffee. "I'd love to stay and chat," he said, signing for the meal, "but you're late for your meeting."

He stood and bent over to kiss her good-bye. "Lots of people are paying attention to this account, Sirad," he whispered into her ear. "I don't need to emphasize its importance."

He stood back up and left, but Sirad didn't bother watching him go. She just stared into the eggs he'd left half eaten and considered her options.

"Dammit," she mumbled finally, checking her watch. Her clients would be wondering about her by now.

■

INFORMANTS ARE THE cornerstone of any intelligence-gathering operation, and like the agencies she oversaw, Senator Beechum had plenty. Serving as chairman of the government's chief oversight committee meant knowing more than anyone else about who was chasing whom, what they were after, and, most important, why it mattered.

Beechum walked boldly out of her house, past the media cameras, screaming reporters, and protesters. She calmly opened her car door, climbed inside, and drove east on the Rock Creek Parkway toward her Capitol Hill office. Instead of turning off at Memorial Bridge, however, she took the I-395 exit and headed south toward Virginia. She'd always prided herself on being able to dig beneath Washington's layers of subterfuge, but the events of the past three weeks had completely baffled her. How had an NSC attorney's blood shown up on the floor of her house? How had his personal effects shown up in her garbage? This was the first time in decades she couldn't find anywhere to turn for answers.

Until now. The woman who had called her office the previous day had asked to meet at the Silver City Diner in Potomac Mills, a shopping mall thirty minutes away. There were a million reasons why Beechum should have declined the meeting, but none outweighed her desperate need to know. Someone had deliberately decided to ruin her career — her life — and she needed to find out why.

"Listen and nod, old girl," Beechum told herself, turning off the highway. This was the first advice she had been given on coming to Washington, and it had served her well on many occasions. "Ask the questions, don't answer them."

She spotted the diner a quarter mile down the road, pulled into the lot, and parked her car. Beechum looked around for anything unusual without knowing exactly what that meant. When the National Security Agency came to brief her on al Qaeda intercepts out of Kashmir, she knew how they got them. When the National Imagery and Mapping Agency came to explain its latest generation of 3-D interactive terrain modeling technology, she knew who designed it. When it came to looking for a suspicious car, however, she had no idea what to do.

Elizabeth walked into the diner and seated herself by a window overlooking the road. A couple families of I-95 vacationers occupied booths on both sides of her. Across the aisle sat a half dozen members of a blue-haired Mall Walkers Club. No one seemed to recognize her.

"Hello ma'am," a woman said, startling Beechum. She wasn't used to feeling nervous like this. "My name is Ruth."

"Good morning, Ruth. Sit down, please." Beechum was a politician with a politician's knack for names and faces, but she knew two things immediately: (1) she'd never seen this woman before, and (2) Ruth was not her real name.

"I appreciate you coming," Ruth said.

Beechum nodded. "I'm glad you called. You must know how much this means to me."

The waitress came, and they ordered coffee.

"You have helped a lot of people in this town," Ruth said. "I couldn't just sit back and let this happen without trying to return the favor."

Beechum's behind-the-scenes clairvoyance had earned her a sort of cult status among the true believers. Whenever people didn't like the smell of a certain project or operation, they came to her. They always knew where she stood, and in the wilderness of mirrors known as the "wet side," she never changed faces. Perhaps this woman was a fan.

"Let what happen?" Beechum asked. "This is damned hard to talk about because I don't have the goddamnest idea what is going on here. One minute my life makes perfect sense and the next, I'm . . ." The senator remembered her surroundings. She didn't need to draw an audience.

"Look, I don't know how to do something like this," Ruth said. She looked over her shoulder so often, Beechum thought the waitress was going to suspect a robbery. "Could we go for a drive, maybe. Talk in the car?"

"Sure," the senator said. She didn't understand why Ruth had insisted on so public a place to begin with. Beechum dropped a five-dollar bill on the table and followed the woman out to a late-model Mustang.

"Now we can talk," Ruth said when they were inside. She started her car and drove west along the Prince William Parkway. "Let's quit beating around the bush. You're getting screwed here, and we both know it. I have something that can help you."

"All right," Beechum prodded. She would have listened to anything at this point. "What do you have?"

Ruth pulled out a microcassette, the kind Beechum had in her home answering machine.

"What's this?" Beechum asked.

"This doesn't have to happen, Senator," Ruth responded, checking her mirror and turning left into a subdivision of two-story homes. "People are trying to send you a message. That's what this is all about. They want you to know that you don't have the power anymore. They want you to go away."

"The power? What's this got to do with power? One day I've got Tim Russert and Dan Rather begging me for interviews, and the next I'm riding around northern Virginia with a total stranger begging for answers. Where's the goddamned power?"

Ruth held out the tape for Beechum, but the senator just stared. "The world's been through a lot the past couple of years," Ruth said. "We're beginning to look at war in different terms. You know what I'm talking about?"

"Who are you?"

"You may not believe this, but I'm on your side. I don't want to see you get hurt."

The woman turned left again.

"Hurt? What's that supposed to mean?"

"I'm asking you on behalf of people who care about you to step down from the Intelligence Committee and bow out of the presidential race. The war on terrorism is moving in a new direction, and a lot of people think you won't let that happen. If you don't take yourself out of the picture, they will do it for you."

Beechum shook her head.

"Take this." The woman pushed the cassette into Beechum's hand. "It might change your mind."

Beechum took the tape and threw it right out her window. This woman was with the people who so badly wanted to hurt her. Nothing on that tape could do her any good.

"It's Parsons, isn't it?" She'd known in the back of her mind all along. "You go back to that sorry son of a bitch and tell him I will not lie down for this," she said. "Secrets don't last in this town. I will fight him, and I will win."

"I'm sorry you feel that way," Ruth said, tapping her brakes twice and pulling over to the side of the road. Beechum noticed something flashing in her side mirror and turned to see an unmarked police car pulling up behind them. "I thought you were smarter than this."

"What the hell are you doing?" Beechum asked.

Ruth stopped the car and shifted into Park. Two men in suits approached the passenger-side window.

"Good morning, ma'am," one of the men said. "Did you throw this out of your window?"

He held the microcassette at the end of a government pen. Beechum looked at Ruth and then straight through the windshield. There was no sick feeling of despair this time, just an overwhelming urge to fight.

"I'm Special Agent Weatherby with the Federal Bureau of Investigation, Senator," he said. His partner opened her door. "We're going to have to ask you to step out of the car."

X

JEREMY WAITED TWO weeks for headquarters to issue its preliminary findings in the Villa Davila investigation. Ordinarily this kind of speed would have shocked anyone familiar with FBI procedures, but then again, HRT had performed brilliantly in a high-profile case. No one on the seventh floor of the J. Edgar Hoover Building saw any point in delaying a well-deserved slap on the back.

"In consideration of exigent circumstances, including the known presence of heavy armament, hostage imperative, and demonstrated proclivity toward violence," their letterhead memorandum read, "we have ascertained no alleged or actual impropriety on the part of any Hostage Rescue Team personnel." This was as close to vindication as one could get in the Justice Department, Jeremy's boss told him. It was a good shoot, just like the guys had said.

That didn't make things easier for Jeremy. Small things upset him. Spilled milk. Christopher's refusal to pick up his toys. Maddy's cartoons. Caroline tried to keep the kids at a distance, thinking Jeremy simply needed time and space to deal with the stress, but after a couple weeks, she realized that Jeremy was growing more and more distant. He seldom talked at the dinner table, rarely tucked the kids into bed, and erupted at the smallest irritation. She'd reach out to touch him when he woke up in the middle of the night, only to find the sheets soaked with sweat. He'd pull away every time she tried to hold him. They hadn't made love since he'd got back. He seemed to have one emotion now: rage.

Fortunately, Mason had noticed, too. He called the division's Employee Assistance Program coordinator, and within twenty-four hours, a crisis intervention specialist sat down with Jeremy to explain that the FBI now offered post–critical incident counseling to all agents involved in shootings. What Jeremy was going through was not unique, the specialist explained, just a natural human reaction to an overwhelming experience.

But it wasn't as easy as that. The motto above the classroom door — "Out these doors, nothing" — meant just what it said. HRT operators were expected to hold themselves to a hard line on outside intervention from wives, headquarters suits, or loose-lipped "shrinks."

Take it like a man, several of the older veterans had told Jeremy, which meant taking it alone, so he sat through the counseling sessions without saying a word. Caroline said nothing about his obvious lack of progress until he one day blew up over new curtains she had just bought.

"This isn't just you anymore, Jeremy!" she cried in an emotional outburst that was long overdue. "We're a family. We're all suffering. You have to deal with this before it destroys everything we've worked so hard to build."

It worked. The next morning, while the rest of the team was out training, Jeremy climbed into his Suburban and drove to Snowden Psychiatric Associates in Fredericksburg. It was a small practice on the second floor of an elegant antebellum mansion along the banks of the Rappahannock River. The practice maintained separate entrances and exits so clients would have the least chance of seeing anyone else during their visit.

"You're not crazy," his doctor told him the first time they were alone. The pedantic wraith of a man wore wide-wale corduroys and a polo shirt. "This anger is your mind's way of reacting to something totally outside its experience. It's like getting lost and reaching into your pack for a map. Think of me as that map."

Jeremy knew this man had never used a map in his life, but after that first therapy session, things began to improve. Dr. Scarloni offered no answers. He simply listened and restated the occasional phrase as a question, spinning Jeremy into some new corner of self-doubt. *Had he wanted this all along? Had he gone into this line of work hoping to experience this ultimate confrontation, to test himself against other men capable of the same thing?*

It all seemed so unclear at first, so gray. *What's the big deal?* Jeremy wondered. *Men have been killing other men ever since Cain and Abel. This happened in the line of duty.*

Finally, he accepted that he didn't need answers just yet. It was OK to bleed.

"You killed a man," he said out loud to himself one morning while brushing his teeth. "Big fucking deal." Toothpaste dripped from the corner of his mouth. Water dripped down between his eyes where the shower fog had condensed, and tears might have fallen if he could have mustered them.

It was almost like a switch had flipped, shining light back to his life, framing the whole Puerto Rico incident as if it were just another one of those photos on the HRT trophy wall.

The voices faded. Christopher left his toys around the house without chastisement. Maddy turned up her cartoons. Jeremy even got used to the drapes in the living room. Life returned to him in ways he remembered enjoying it.

∎

UNITED FLIGHT 2134 from Atlanta touched down at JFK in New York just after eight on Thursday evening, and Sirad emerged from the gate carrying a Louis Vuitton weekend bag with a matching attaché. Just as Hoch had predicted, Dieter had called and summoned her to New York for a briefing on what he called "pressing developments" in the Quantis program. He offered no details over the phone — purposely, Sirad decided, keeping her from preparing for the Saudi trip she now knew was coming.

Sirad met her car outside the airport and rode to Hamid's apartment, where she planned to spend the night. She arrived just before dinner and was met at the door with roses.

"Wow," was all Hamid could say. And he was right. Sirad had spent considerable time preparing for this trip, making certain that she looked just as good in clothes as out of them.

"Aren't you going to invite me in?" she asked.

Hamid leaned forward for a hug, looking absolutely weak with lust.

"Of course. Please," he beckoned, showing the way with his outstretched hand. He motioned to a uniformed maid, who scooped up Sirad's bags and disappeared down a hall.

"What a beautiful apartment," Sirad said the moment she stepped through the door. She had not expected such magnificence. The artwork in the living room alone would have bought a sizable estate in Atlanta's finest neighborhoods. "Is that a Renoir?"

"William Merritt Chase," Hamid answered, finally able to focus on something familiar. "I have a Renoir in the dining room."

"A William Merritt Chase in the living room. A Renoir in the dining room. What am I going to find in the bedroom?" Sirad unbuttoned a cashmere cardigan and tossed it on the sofa, then kicked off her shoes and paraded her own sculpted form around the room, wearing a Burberry skirt cut just above her knees and a white linen blouse. She feigned interest in a Chinese vase, ran a finger over the heavy brushstroke of a darkly shaded Degas.

"Such a fan of the Impressionists, huh?" She stopped at the edge of the couch and ran the same finger admiringly down the side of Hamid's face. "You know the woman who waxed my bikini line this morning is an artist, too. She asked me if I wanted any special design . . . you know, down there."

Hamid had trouble thinking of anything to say. Planning dinner so soon after his new girlfriend's arrival had been a complete miscalculation.

"So? What did you tell her?"

Sirad bent over from the waist, letting her blouse fall open just enough. "I told her my new boyfriend was a conservative man of considerable wealth and refinement. A practical man." She touched his lips with her finger. "I told her to leave a postage stamp, in case you needed to scratch your upper lip."

Hamid shook his head. He'd never met a woman so innately sexual as Sirad. She talked with the base vigor of a Victorian parlor whore, but she moved with the bearing of a Southampton debutante. In every manner of grace and intention, this woman absolutely entranced him.

"Will you excuse me for just a minute?" Sirad asked. "It was a long trip. I need to freshen up."

"Your bag is in my room." Hamid nodded. "Last door on the right."

With that, she disappeared down the hallway and entered Hamid's most personal space. She closed the door and locked it, suddenly tingling with proximity to another person's secrets. She'd always loved the intimacy of moments like this — from the first time she'd stolen a peek at her mother's journal to field craft practicals during CIA training at Camp Peary. There was something unabashedly wrong about betraying a confidence, but it gave her a pure, unadulterated thrill.

That's the primary reason she hadn't lived with anyone since her freshman year in college. Her first and only roommate had petitioned the school for relocation midway through the first semester after she came home one day after class to find the dorm proctor handcuffed to the springs of the bunk beds with Sirad riding him like a merry-go-round pony.

She's a complete psycho, the roommate wrote in her petition to the Student Living Advisory Board. *She steals my shampoo, reads my boyfriend's letters, and keeps conning me out of my physics notes.*

The advisory board had asked Sirad to come in for a little chat, thinking they might have to mark her for expulsion, but by the time she left, they felt small and guilty for ever doubting her in the first place. *What a lovely young woman,* the dean of student affairs had said.

Sirad searched Hamid's drawers. Socks in one. Boxers in another. Sweaters and pajamas moving down. "Pajamas?" Sirad whispered, shaking her head. This guy was forty-one years old and lived alone. Why would he need pajamas?

A box on top of his dresser held three watches: an IWC chronograph, the Patek she'd seen in Atlanta, and a Cartier Tank Américaine in eighteen-karat gold. There were assorted cuff links, a signet ring, and what appeared to be some kind of fraternity pin.

"Where the hell are you?" she whispered. Sirad quickly tossed his closet, rifled through the nightstands, and checked the drawers in his armoire. Nothing. Finally, she noticed his suit coat resting on the arm of a carved Federal armchair. Sirad reached into the right breast pocket and pulled out his Palm Pilot. She'd seen him use it during previous dates and paid particular attention to the access code.

"Open sesame." She smiled. She pressed the power save, pulled what looked like an MP3 player out of her purse, and attached it to Hamid's PDA. The software inside — the package Hoch had left her in Atlanta — represented the latest evolution in data-mining and encryption intrusion technology. Originally developed at the FBI's Electronic Research Facility in Quantico, Virginia, then enhanced by a National Security Agency contractor outside Houston, this program allowed analysts to recover and track every mouse click, every keystroke. Civil libertarians would shriek at the ramifications of this Big Brother device if they knew about it, but like much of what the intelligence community had developed since 9/11, this black technology would never show up in any published report.

Sirad worked quickly, pausing only to strip off her blouse and skirt in case Hamid came down the hall. The sight of her standing there in her bra and panties would certainly distract him long enough to cover her real intentions.

"I've been waiting for you," she'd say, moving closer to pay off all that anticipation she'd built coming into his apartment. Lots of people wouldn't understand why someone would do a job like this, she thought. They wouldn't understand how she could set up a relationship just to betray it, or how she could have sex with a man just to get information. But most people lived small, hypocritical lives with no real idea of what it took to keep them safe. *So what if sex helps me do my job,* she reassured herself. It was just a tool. Everyone used it for something.

Sirad opened the device Hoch had left in the Four Seasons hotel room and pressed two buttons. Within seconds, it began to whir as the tiny disc inside uploaded a completely transparent program, created specifically to break down commercial intrusion firewalls. Minutes from now, this software would give her access to every memo, spreadsheet, and e-mail in Hamid's system. It would lay bare every transaction, trade, and collection he'd ever made, and it would burrow itself into other hardware he docked with, providing real-time tracking of all Web-based communications.

"Come on, baby," she murmured, realizing that she'd soon own this man in ways that reached far beyond sex. "Make me a star."

Sirad sat down in an overstuffed armchair while the machine worked its magic. Sometimes this job thrilled her so much that she needed to rest for fear of losing her balance.

▥

MITCHELL RETURNED HOME from a fund-raising dinner at the Kennedy Center only to find Trask waiting in his library. Though his chief of staff often worked long into the night, he almost never showed up unannounced.

"Sirad is here in New York," Trask said. He paced back and forth in front of the window, the way Mitchell often did. "She's staying with Hamid."

Mitchell's jaw clenched shut. It wasn't Sirad's choice of men that incensed him; it was the increasing risk that she might have used her considerable skills to uncover Hamid's extracurricular financial dealings. Borders Atlantic was a telecommunications conglomerate, already stepping into very dangerous territory with Saudi partnership on its SBT system. Public exposure of illegal financial transactions with some of the same Middle Eastern investors would prove devastating.

"We don't know whether or not she knows about the peripherals trading," Trask ventured, correctly reading his boss's now sanguine humors. Despite physical surveillance of all Sirad's travels, taps on her phones, and extensive use of eavesdropping devices, Borders Atlantic's security department still understood painfully little about her underlying intentions with Hamid.

"Of course she knows," Mitchell hissed. "Why else would she go after this guy?"

"Yes, sir," Trask agreed. He'd served on General Schwarzkopf's

178

staff during the Gulf War and knew that great leaders often suffered violent tempers. Better just to nod and answer.

"All right, where's Dieter?" Mitchell asked.

"He's still in his office working on security issues."

"Get him," Mitchell directed. "Tell him I want Sirad in his office right now. Not tomorrow morning — right now!"

"Yes, sir," Trask agreed, reaching for his cell phone. "What do you want him to do with her?"

"I don't care, as long as he keeps her occupied. I want all of our elements in position by Thursday night, which means a full rewrite, from the media annex to medevac support and exfiltration ops. Also, I want you to get a sweep team over to Hamid's apartment to clear it for bugs; I want a full rundown on every piece of hardware he has that interfaces with our databases."

Mitchell started poking his finger in the air like a battle warden aligning assets.

"As for Sirad, I want to know everything she does between now and tomorrow's flight. I mean everything, you understand? I want to know whom she talks to, where she goes, what she says on the phone, which goddamned side of the bed she sleeps on!"

"I'll take care of it, Mr. Mitchell," Trask said. "But I think we're all right on Sirad. She met Hamid by accident in an elevator. Besides, Hamid fully understands our downside on this. I can't imagine he'd compromise opsec."

Mitchell slammed a fist into his open palm. "You don't get it, do you?" Mitchell asked. "This woman sees everything. If you think for a moment that she doesn't know precisely what she's doing, you're too naive to work for me. I want Sirad in Dieter's office within the hour. I want her watched."

Mitchell walked to his window and stared out over the lights of New York. "Who's handling security on this trip?"

"Bartholomew."

"Who?"

"Chris Bartholomew. The former Delta Force guy."

Mitchell couldn't place the name but trusted his provenance. Everyone working corporate, financial, and IT security operations from the seventeenth floor had been carefully screened and tested.

Though their expanse of electronically shielded offices had no windows, the seventeenth floor kept watch over virtually all of Borders Atlantic's secrets.

"I want you to brief him personally," Mitchell ordered. "You understand me? He gives Sirad nothing until they get in-country. He is to let me know immediately if he thinks something is wrong. We've got a hell of a lot riding on this little excursion, and I don't want you to screw it up because of what you *think* Sirad knows."

"I understand, sir," Trask said. He breathed a sigh of relief as Mitchell walked to the bar and poured himself a drink. The boss had chosen his battle and engaged. That usually made him tolerable.

▮▮▮

"ANYBODY SEEN MY NVGs?" Jeremy asked, ambling into the Xray equipment cage Friday afternoon. The training coordinator had scheduled a "night shoot," and Jeremy needed the high-tech optics in order to test the new infrared laser on his patrolling rifle. "I left 'em in my locker yesterday, and they're gone."

"Oh, yeah, I forgot to tell you," Cox said. "Bucky needed them last night. His are broken."

"Last night?" Jeremy asked. He spoke loudly, over the sounds of Guns N' Roses' "Welcome to the Jungle," which blared out of the Echo Team cage next door. "What was last night?"

"Low-light harvest," Lottspeich said.

Jeremy shook his head. Bucky liked to kill animals — deer, bear, hogs, woodchucks, anything with legs and fur. He often bragged about never having to pay for meat.

"You mean he was jacking," Cox said. He made no bones about being a tree hugger, from the vegetarian meals he and his family lived on to the Greenpeace bumper sticker on his highly efficient Honda Insight. "Shooting animals at night is illegal in Virginia, isn't it?"

"Hey, you on that antikilling shit again?" Tiny joined in, arriving late and throwing his rucksack on a shelf stacked with black Cordura tactical bags. "The man's got to eat."

"I ain't antikilling," Cox said, defending himself. "I'm just anti killing animals. People deserve a good whacking every once in a while, but why the hell sneak up on some defenseless animal in the middle of the night and shoot him dead?"

"Because they taste good barbecued!" Bucky walked in on the debate. "Don't tell me you're back on that PETA bullshit, Cox." He laughed, tossing Jeremy his NVGs. "Where the fuck you think the leather on your boots came from?"

"Yeah, how come you always gotta be such a wimp?" Tiny challenged. At five foot six, Tiny was HRT's smallest operator by several inches, but the chip on his shoulder made up for it.

"Wimp? I got no problem kicking your ass." Cox smiled. Rivalry never died here.

"Bring it on," Tiny responded, jokingly pushing Cox against the wall.

"Hey, hey, hey . . . ," Lottspeich protested, stepping in between them. "Quit dicking around. I want to know how he did."

"Four-point buck at four hundred thirty yards," Bucky said, tossing Cox a flank steak packaged in freezer wrap.

"Get that shit away from me," Cox said.

"Four hundred thirty yards at night? No way," Tiny said. He prided himself on being Xray's top shooter, despite the fact that Jeremy plowed him under nearly every day. "Nightscopes are only good to two hundred."

"Gut pile's still there to prove it," Bucky said. "Which means I'm now the man to beat."

He reached up on the wall between two stand-up lockers and wrote his name on a hand-drawn chart. Xray snipers bet on everything from daily shooting competitions to how many times Mason would spit tobacco juice during a morning meeting. The latest pool pitted each of the Xray snipers in a contest of distance and difficulty. Rules stipulated only that the target start out alive and end up dead. After that, it was up to team members to agree on who demonstrated the most refined and remarkable application of surgical shooting skills.

"Looks like you're out, Waller," Lottspeich announced. As chartmaster, he had final say in the event of contested findings.

"Good! I never wanted to be up there anyway." Jeremy checked the lot number on a box of match-grade .308 ammunition and stuffed it into his shooting bag. His name had been added to the list because of the Puerto Rico shooting, which met all criteria except good taste. Jeremy shivered at the thought of the Office of Professional Responsibility finding out that he might win an office pool for taking another man's life.

"Everybody buck up," Lottspeich demanded. The pool had started with a ten-dollar buy-in, with a five-dollar kicker each time someone new topped the list. Whoever sat atop the chart at the end of the training quarter — now just two weeks away — won the pot, which was up to $125.

Jeremy had initially tried to duck out of the pool, thinking it was in extremely poor taste, but he eventually realized that HRT was no Harvard social club. These men worked a violent business, putting their lives on the line every day, even in training, and this was just a way of blowing off steam, of maintaining their competitive edge. They may have been lawyers and accountants in the outside world, but here they were warriors.

"I still don't buy it," Tiny said, shaking his head. "I mean, don't we have to check the gut pile first? How do we know where you took the shot?"

"You calling him a liar?" Langdon asked. He was Xray's man of fewest words, but in here a man's word was good.

"No, I'm just saying . . . we shoot on the range; we got rules. I just don't see how he could have made a shot like that. My nightscope just won't see that far."

"I used an IR laser with the NVGs," Bucky said. "One shot. You want to go out and sniff the gut pile, be my guest. That's why I left it there."

"What's the big deal, man?" Langdon asked. "You want to beat him, get your ass out there and dream up a better shot."

"Hey, you think they'll write up dialogue like this when they make the movie?" Cox asked. He was always talking about the HRT feature he figured someone would make one day. "I mean, don't you think this would be kind of embarrassing? You remember that bathroom scene in *Full Metal Jacket*? Now that was some dialogue."

"What the hell are you talking about?" Lottspeich asked. "Waller, gimme five bucks."

Jeremy reached into his locker for his wallet. "Who's the wiseass?" he asked, pulling out a small plastic bag full of flour. "Cox?"

"Why you got to blame everything on me, man?" Cox smiled.

"Because you're the only asshole on the team who won't hunt," Jesús interrupted. The Xray team leader strode into the cage looking a little edgy. "Get your shit together. We got work to do." Jesús yanked his rifle box off the floor and disappeared outside.

"Who the hell put a bug up his ass?" Tiny asked.

Lottspeich shrugged. They all knew Jesús ran a little hot at times. "Hey, Waller, you still owe me five bucks," he prodded again. Jeremy paid up and followed his team leader out to the range.

■

"SO, WHAT'S THE big emergency?" Sirad asked, knocking on the half-open door to Dieter's office. The heavyset German stood on the other side of a thin steel desk covered with meticulously arranged piles of paper. Black-and-white photos of Weimaraners covered most of two walls. "Please don't tell me you brought me all the way to New York just to tell me about this little trip to Dubai."

The German slouched visibly, obviously disappointed that he hadn't been the only person entrusted with this secret. He sat in his chair and pretended to take added interest in one of the paper piles.

"Who told you about Dubai?" Dieter asked.

Sirad closed the door behind her and walked toward him. "I have my sources, too." She smiled.

"Yes, well, did your sources tell you that you leave today?"

Sirad stared at him. "I can't leave today. I haven't packed . . . I don't even . . ."

"You leave today. A car will take you to the airport at three, where you will meet one of our security specialists. The G-IV will fly you to Dubai for a conference with some of our Middle Eastern clients. You'll be home by Thursday night."

"And what exactly am I supposed to do when I get there?" she asked. It seemed like a reasonable question considering that her new promotion was supposed to make her vice president in charge of all Quantis operations overseas.

"We've had some difficulties in the last twenty-four hours," Dieter said, happy to hold Sirad at slightly more than arm's length. She bothered him on a personal level. "You'll get a briefing once you land in Dubai."

"Difficulties? What kind of difficulties?"

"Security issues. I'm sure you understand the sensitive nature of the Quantis project."

"No, I don't understand the sensitive nature of the Quantis project. In fact, I apparently don't know much of anything." She stared long enough to make him feel uncomfortable. "Jordan Mitchell picked me for this assignment himself, yet I haven't received even the most rudimentary information about how I'm supposed to support it. How do you expect me to do my job when you won't even tell me what it is?"

She picked up a report off Dieter's desk. The German stared at Sirad with utter contempt. He hated her physical beauty — the way she used it to manipulate men.

"If you have any complaints, I suggest that you take them upstairs yourself," Dieter said with a half sigh, as if to show how little he cared. "If this assignment bothers you so much, I'm sure Mr. Mitchell will find another candidate to take your place."

She propped her hands on her hips with appropriate drama. "What the hell is the matter with you anyway?" she asked. "The very fact that Jordan Mitchell gave me this project should demonstrate his trust in me."

"You'll get your briefing in Dubai," Dieter replied. "And as for trust, don't forget this: as far as I'm concerned you're a mildly talented midlevel administrator leaning way too much on that cute little ass of yours. I told Mr. Mitchell that you weren't right for this assignment, but he went with you just the same."

He stood and waddled to the door.

"I can accept that," Dieter added, "but success, here, is more commitment than you understand. Passing the striptease and the polygraph get you in the door, but credibility is a whole different matter. You've got to earn that."

Sirad stared at him, considering how much she should push the issue. Dieter obviously knew more about this trip than she did. So did Hoch. Something about her role at Borders Atlantic had suddenly changed, and she needed to know why. Sirad turned toward the door.

"I'm not the enemy, Dieter," she said, hoping Mitchell could hear her through one of the microphones she knew he had planted around the building. "If we're ever going to realize the full potential of the Quantis project, you're going to have to accept that."

"Don't be late," Dieter warned her. "The plane will leave without you."

Sirad paused at the door before opening it. Snapping back at him would have been easy, but she'd made her point already. Turning this into a personal matter would only lead to trouble down the line.

XI

———

"SENATOR! YOU CAN'T go in there!" The towel attendant stood out of the way as Elizabeth Beechum stormed through the lobby and into the Senate locker room. There was no sign on the door that read MEN, because there was no women's facility to confuse it with; even thirty years after the first woman took a seat in Congress's higher chamber, the boys' club hadn't gotten around to adding a proper ladies' lounge.

"Marcellus!" she bellowed. It was late on a Friday afternoon and the locker room was nearly empty, but several faces blanched white as she rummaged from room to room looking for a man she hated to call Senator.

"Elizabeth, you can't come in here!" Bertram Mathers, a Republican from Maine, stood in the mirror, shaving. He sounded as if he were shooing away an errant bird dog.

"Where is he?" she yelled. There weren't many places to hide.

"In the steam room," another colleague said. Two other senators poked their heads out of showers, wondering what all the yelling was about. They saw Beechum striding toward them and wondered if she'd finally lost her mind.

"Marcellus! I know you're in here!" She marched down the carpeted hallway, turned left, and yanked open the door to a white-tiled steamer. A stiflingly hot fog filled the room, making it impossible to see more than a few inches.

"Marcellus, you son of a bitch. Are you in here?"

"Betsy, close the damned door," a small voice said. "You're letting all the heat out."

She stepped forward until she could see him sitting on the top row, naked as the eyes of a clown.

"You may think you're going to get away with this, but I can sure as hell tell you that you aren't." The anger rose up in her throat to a point where she couldn't tell if it was the steam or the rage that made her dizzy.

"Could we do this outside?" Parsons asked. He sat with his legs open, a potbellied bald man covered in sweat, gray hair, and splotches of red. "I'm naked here."

"Now you know how I felt when your goons came for me. And don't flatter yourself, Marcellus. I've seen those damn things before. They're usually a whole lot bigger."

Suddenly the door burst open, and two uniformed Capitol police officers entered the room.

"My God, haven't you people ever been in a steam room before?" Parsons bellowed. "Shut the damned door!"

The officers tried to find him through the fog. "Senator Beechum, are you in here, ma'am?" The taller of the two bumped into her. "Excuse me, Senator. I didn't mean to . . ."

"This is official business of the Senate, gentlemen," she shouted. "We don't need any help."

"Ma'am, this is the men's locker room. You can't just walk in . . ."

"Please, fellas," Marcellus said. He pulled his towel out from under himself and laid it over his midsection. "This isn't the first woman to take care of business in here, and it probably won't be the last. You just leave us be for a minute, and everything will work out fine."

The Capitol police officers paused for a moment to consider the paperwork involved in forcibly removing a female senator from the men's locker room and the way the steam was making their polyester uniforms stick to their skin.

"We'll be waiting outside," one of them said. The door opened again, and they were gone.

"Now, what seems to be the problem, Betsy?"

She didn't even bother responding to the name. Parsons was doing it just to piss her off. "Problem? If *you* had problems with the way I ran my committee, why didn't you just say so?"

The fact that David Ray Venable had won the Democratic presidential nomination in Boston the week before hardly seemed worth mentioning.

"I don't think I've ever been coy with my distaste for your leadership," he said. The thermostat kicked in, sending up a new batch of steam in one big hiss. "But that doesn't matter now, does it? I have the chair, and by the end of the day you will no longer have the security clearances necessary to remain a member."

Beechum sat down on the soaking-wet bench.

"That's what this is all about." She felt stupid for not seeing it earlier. "This isn't just about politics, is it? It's not even about disgrace. You want to take away my ability to chase you."

"Betsy, I'm sorry to see you like this. I really am. The stress of this whole situation has clouded your reasoning."

She shook her head back and forth.

"That's what you want them to believe, isn't it? You bastard. You want them to think I've gone nuts . . . that I really killed that poor man."

Marcellus stood up, wrapped a towel around his waist, and stepped past her to the floor. He pulled the cold rinse over his head and wiped the water out of his eyes with shriveled fingers.

"This is about seeing the bigger picture," he said, "which you clearly don't. You had a chance to back off yesterday, and you threw it out the window. Literally. So now you've got problems nobody can fix."

He started toward the door.

"You won't get away with it," she said.

Marcellus turned back toward her. She could just see his face through the steam.

"Look at yourself," he said. "If there was a single member of this august body who believed in you, they'll change their minds by the time this little stunt hits the papers."

Marcellus opened the door and motioned for the police officers to go in and retrieve a broken, sopping-wet woman from the Senate locker room — a woman who had once looked like the Democratic nominee for president, but now was done.

▥

"SO, WHAT DO you think about this G8 gig up in New York?" Lottspeich asked as Jeremy parked his Chevy Suburban in the lot behind Range Four, a Marine Corps tactical rifle course less than a mile from the HRT complex. Billy Luther had mentioned a training trip to the CIA's Camp Peary facility to prepare for the upcoming economic summit in New York. HRT had been given a high-risk dignitary protection responsibility for finance ministers from Afghanistan and Iraq's new coalition government. The two leaders had been invited as a sign that the world was ready to embrace their emerging economies.

"I think it would be great," Jeremy answered. "But I'm not all that wound up about the possibility of taking a bullet for some Third World puppet." He opened his door and climbed out into the bright sunshine. The 100-acre shooting range rolled out in front of them, bordered with lush Virginia hardwoods.

"I don't plan on taking bullets for anybody," Lottspeich agreed. "As long as the State Department does its job, our inner perimeter won't be anything but window dressing. Besides, I'm looking forward to seeing Camp Peary. I hear they have a great track."

Fritz reached into the back of Jeremy's Ford Expedition and pulled out a Halliburton rifle case as other HRT snipers began to roll in for a morning of training.

"Yeah, they say you can shoot out of cars down there," Jeremy replied. "Perfect spot to warm up for a dignitary protection gig." He saw to his own equipment, ignoring the convoy of vehicles until one pulled up playing music blared so loudly that both men looked to see who was coming.

"What the hell is that?" Jeremy asked.

Langdon pulled up and parked next to him in an Expedition with smoked windows and a big brush guard on the front. Jeremy could see the doors rattling.

"Kerfor," Lottspeich said.

"What?" Jeremy could barely hear him over the sounds of industrial speed metal.

"Kerfor. Some German band he discovered on an overseas gig last year. It's all he listens to now."

Jeremy pulled out his rifle case and shooting ruck as Langdon pounded an earthquake rhythm on his steering wheel and stared devilishly through his windshield.

"Thank God he's on our side," Jeremy said. Langdon had come to HRT the year before with impressive credentials — a law degree from Northwestern and a number three ranking in two national competitive shooting federations — but lately, he seemed to have bought into the war on terrorism just a little too seriously.

"Yeah," Lottspeich said, sucking on a ball of Levi Garrett. He pulled a camouflaged rucksack out of his partner's truck and opened his shooting kit to make sure he had everything he needed for a morning on the range. The standard load included a beanbag stock support, a spotting scope, a Therm-a-Rest ground cover, and 100 rounds of match-grade Federal 168-grain boat-tail hollow-point ammunition. All snipers carried pretty much the same thing.

"You ever spend much time in New York?" Lottspeich asked as the two men walked across the parking lot to a concrete shooting deck that looked out over a 300-yard rifle range.

"I went there a couple times when I was in college," Jeremy said. He picked a spot near the middle of the deck, then laid down his shooting kit. He rolled out his mat, removed his rifle from its case, and extended the bipod, positioning it downrange with the bolt back and the chamber open. "If this gig goes, I don't think we're going to have much time for sightseeing."

Langdon arrived at the deck as Jeremy set up his firing position. He moved in next to Lottspeich, beating a dozen other HRT snipers to the best remaining spot, and quickly arranged his gear. Training started precisely at nine o'clock, and everyone was running a little late.

"We betting?" Jeremy asked. He opened a box of ammunition and arranged two red plastic bullet holders alongside his rifle.

"The usual," Lottspeich said. The two men had bet a dollar on every training session since sniper school. Jeremy was up more than forty bucks.

"Stand by for targets," the range master called out from the control tower. Jeremy adjusted his body over the stock of his rifle and laid his finger on the trigger. He sighted his 10x Unertl scope on a distant tree, then scanned the field until it erupted with little green plastic men painted to look like Chinese soldiers. The three-dimensional targets raced forward and back, left and right, like players on a giant floor-hockey table. Jeremy sighted his rifle and fired as the whole deck erupted in a wall of sound and pale gray smoke.

BOOM! Reload. *BOOM!* Reload.

Jeremy slipped into a rhythm, sighting his targets in tactical order and engaging them as they appeared, from close to far. That's the way it works in combat, the instructors had trained him: address the immediate threats first, then move back as they fall. Seize every advantage, even if it's just distance.

Jeremy pulled his trigger, watched a green man drop, then cycled his bolt, scanning for new targets. *BOOM!* Reload. *BOOM!* The rifle lurched under him as he worked at calculating distance, estimating leads, killing. Targets ran, then fell in the field. Brass shell casings glistened in the morning sun. Small clouds of smoke drifted out of the muzzles as two dozen guns coughed and bucked under their heavy loads.

Perhaps each jolt of recoil should have brought him back to that Puerto Rican kitchen, but it didn't. Jeremy's mind focused intently on measuring each shot, and his hands did the shooting; he was a well-conditioned and now properly tested killing machine.

"That's your course!" A horn sounded, and they were done. "Range is cold."

The lineup of HRT snipers rolled off their rifles and reached into their rifle cases for logbooks in which they would record every shot. The logbooks provided a detailed history of performance in all kinds of heat, cold, elevation, wind, and humidity.

"So?" Lottspeich asked, recording a perfect score in his logbook. "What about that bag of flour?"

"What about it?" Jeremy asked. He'd heard enough ribbing about the Puerto Rico assault.

"I mean, it sounds so goofy, you know? Why would you throw a bag of flour at the guy?"

Jeremy smiled and shook his head. "It was the first thing I could find. The cellar was full of gasoline, and I knew a flashbang would set it off, so we needed some other kind of diversion. It was either flour or a couple empty beer bottles."

Lottspeich looked at him, undecided about Jeremy's judgment. "What the hell. It worked, huh?"

"Stand by for movers!" the range master called out from the tower.

Jeremy settled over his rifle again. The sun felt hot on his back. He looked out over the empty field, concentrating, waiting for targets to pop up and run . . . then something hit him in the sole of his boot. Again. Someone was kicking him.

"Waller . . . ," Jesús said. Jeremy's team leader stood above him, motioning for him to stand.

The targets popped up and *BOOM!* a chorus of rifles rendered any conversation futile. Jeremy climbed to his feet and followed Jesús back to his truck, which was still running.

"What's up?" Jeremy asked.

"Grab your shit and stow it in the cage," Jesús said. He looked stern, preoccupied with other details. "Leave your gun and creds in your desk. Badge, too."

"Something wrong?" Jeremy asked. The first thing that came to mind was Puerto Rico.

"Meet me in the parking lot in twenty minutes with an overnight bag," he said, climbing back into his SUV. Jeremy heard Howard Stern on the radio as he leaned in through the window.

"What for? We got a mission or something?" His pager hadn't sounded with the traditional 888 call-out code. None of the other guys seemed to be leaving.

"Just get your shit!" Jesús yelled over the din of rifle fire. He dropped the shifter into drive. "And no calls home. This is a private gig."

With that, he stepped on the gas and disappeared in a cloud of exhaust and gravel dust.

Gun and creds in my desk? FBI agents didn't go to the bathroom without their gun and creds. Where the hell were they going?

▉

SIRAD ARRIVED AT New Jersey's Teeterborough Airport pulling a garment bag filled with the fruits of a last-minute shopping spree. She'd packed light, coming to New York without the appropriate business attire for Jordan Mitchell's Middle East excursion but caught up during a quick trip to Bergdorf's.

"The pilot is inside waiting for you," her driver said. He had pulled around to the civil aviation hangar, where Borders Atlantic always picked up its corporate fliers. Sirad thanked the man and walked inside, where she found a uniformed captain sitting on a couch, reviewing his flight plan.

"You waiting on me?" she asked. It was a beautiful day outside; she was eager to go.

"Good morning, Ms. Malneaux," he said. He stood to shake her hand. "I'm Frank."

Sirad smiled politely but looked beyond the pilot to another man studying a black-and-white photo exhibit of old DC-3s and Grumman Otters. He looked just a little too square cut for corporate America. His face seemed familiar, but she couldn't place it.

"We're all set if you want to head out to the plane," Frank said. "Here, let me help you with that." He reached for her bag.

"I'll get it," the other man said, crossing toward her. "Frank, you fly the plane. I'll carry the luggage." He threw a black Cordura day pack over his shoulder, shook Sirad's hand, and grabbed her bags.

"Hi. Chris Bartholomew," he said. She made him for a player right off the bat.

"Nice to meet you. My name is Sirad."

"Nice to meet you, too." Bartholomew studied her with eyes that she imagined had seen less pretty things. He nodded toward the door and followed the pilot out to a sparkling white Gulfstream G-IV, which sat with its auxiliary power unit turning, ready to go.

"You work in New York?" Sirad yelled above the sound of the APU. She could feel his eyes on her ass as she walked.

"Yeah, security." He leaned over her shoulder as they arrived at the plane. "Overseas stuff, mostly. I'm setting things up for you in Dubai."

"Oh, so you're one of those Rabbit Hole guys nobody is supposed to talk about," she said.

He smiled. "Ever been to the Gulf?"

"First time," she lied, leading the way onto the private jet. Sirad selected a reclining leather chaise next to the window. Bartholomew ignored eleven other empty seats and sat right next to her.

"Hope you don't mind a little company," he said. Sirad smiled at his insouciance.

"Not at all." She pulled a pillow out from under her seat. "You don't snore, do you?"

"No." Bartholomew laughed. "Guys I sleep with on the road would kill me."

"Guys?" She pouted. "And I had such high hopes."

Bartholomew pulled out a novel and leaned back in his seat, suddenly realizing that this might be a whole lot more fun than he'd hoped. The pilot goosed the engines, and they taxied out to the runway. Fifteen minutes later, a Gulfstream G-IV bearing a tail number registered to a small import/export company in Antigua lifted off from runway 27 West.

Sirad watched New Jersey disappear beneath her, prickling with the excitement that comes with a new adventure. It no longer seemed to matter that she was traveling blind in an operation that everyone talked about with shaded awe. After three and a half years of laboring on the sidelines, it appeared that she was finally getting into the game.

▌

MANASSAS REGIONAL AIRPORT lies thirty miles from Quantico, out the back gate, then northwest toward Dulles International. This proximity to DC and its two major airports makes it a prime alternative for small commercial freight companies and charter services. Immaculately maintained hangars line the main runway, housing everything from gleaming white corporate jets and private helicopters to single-engine hobby craft.

Officially, hangar 7 was leased to Portner Aviation of Burke, Virginia, but everyone at the airport knew that Portner Aviation was an FBI shell company and that hangar 7 housed its most sophisticated fixed-wing aircraft, including two Night Stalkers: Mitsubishi twin-engine prop jets equipped with advanced surveillance electronics and FLIR.

"So, you gonna tell me where we're going?" Jeremy asked Jesús as they drove north along Route 234 from the HRT building toward the airport. Traffic was light, and the hot gray overcast had burned off to reveal one of those brilliant days unique to Virginia in summer. It seemed like a reasonable enough question considering he hadn't even called home to tell Caroline he'd be late for dinner.

"Sorry," Jesús said. "This thing came up so fast I didn't have time to get into many details." He passed a tractor-trailer on the double solid line. The speedometer read eighty-seven and was still climbing when he snaked the big SUV back into its own lane. "We've got a rendition. An Agency deal."

Rendition? Jeremy thought. He'd heard of them but not much more. Guys sometimes talked about quick overseas flights to pick up high-risk fugitives, terrorists, political leaders — anyone bad enough and politically volatile enough to warrant arrest and extradition. Photos of these unsuspecting fugitives lined the HRT halls, all portraying hangdog faces of men who naively thought they'd found refuge in Third World countries.

Jeremy had read about renditions before he even joined the Bureau. Nearly twenty years earlier, the government had gone after a Libyan hijacker turned drug dealer named Fawaz Younis. Undercover agents equipped with bikinis, tans, and champagne lured Younis onto a thirty-foot sloop, then sailed him into international waters. While he was partying on the sundeck, HRT divers swam up, snatched him onto a high-speed cigarette boat, then launched him off an aircraft carrier in what was, at the time, the longest nonstop flight of its kind in history.

HRT had done lots of renditions like this. In fact, during the years right after Waco, it was just about the only work they could get. Overseas grabs were quiet, classified, and just below the radar screen of congressional oversight. HRT went out and brought lots of very unfriendly people back: Ramzi Yousef, Mir Amal Kansi, Ramzi Binalshib, Khalid Sheikh Mohammed; more than three dozen hits in all. Since 9/11, the team had been very busy.

"An overseas gig?" Jeremy asked. He'd never traveled outside the United States.

"I'll give you the warning order once we're airborne," Jesús said.

"Europe? Middle East?" Jeremy asked. HRT usually laid things out in great detail prior to a mission.

"You ask a lot of fucking questions for a new guy," Jesús said. He braked hard enough to bang Jeremy's head against the windshield, then wheeled the truck into an airport access road. "Look, this is the way it works. Somebody from headquarters calls and puts you on a plane. You spend the next twenty-four hours in the air, riding shotgun on some asshole while a bunch of people you don't even know try to get him to talk; then you land at some no-name airport, and the guy disappears in a blacked-out Suburban. It's not rocket science, man. This is the world's most expensive babysitting gig."

Jesús looked tired of conversation. His forehead sagged under what Jeremy imagined to be considerable stress. "You got any chew?"

Jeremy reached into his pocket and pulled out a bag of Levi Garrett. Caroline found the habit disgusting, but the slow, relaxing buzz helped center his aim. Half the team chewed.

"Enjoy the ride, Waller," Jesús said. "Mission's a mission." The big Ford bounced over a set of railroad tracks at double the posted speed limit.

Jeremy nodded, understanding that HRT revealed itself slowly, like this, through moods and strange silences. He tucked some chew inside his cheek and stared out the window at the subdivisions rising out of old dairy farms. There was a time for conversation, he supposed, and a time to ride along.

▐▌

WORD OF ELIZABETH Beechum's locker room romp cascaded through the rumor mill before Marcellus Parsons had dried off and finished his comb-over. Though the Capitol police had simply escorted Beechum to the hall outside, the damage had already been done. As her luck would have it, a particularly venomous *Washington Post* reporter was standing just outside interviewing the new majority leader and two of his committee chairs.

"Good morning, Elizabeth," was all her colleagues could say. They stared at Beechum with slack jaws, wondering why in the world a female member of Congress would emerge from the most sanctified of all Senate chambers with an armed escort.

"A word, Senator?" the reporter asked. It sounded more like advice than a request — the kind of admonishment a teacher offers a failing student.

"I have nothing to say to you," Beechum snipped. She knew the woman's face, and she'd read the *Post*'s torrid stories about her situation. All trash — rumors and leaks from unnamed sources. "Haven't you people written enough drivel about me?"

Beechum wrenched her arm free from one of the guards. She had lost all dignity and authority here. She had been cast out of the circle. Even the journalists knew it.

"I'd love to comment," she added as she walked away, "but my father once told me never to get into pissing contests with people who buy ink by the gallon."

Parsons emerged from the locker room just moments later, still dewy from his steam. It normally would have taken his staff an hour or more to think up a press strategy to maximize the benefit of this political debacle, but not today. He took the reporter aside and addressed the whole "sordid indiscretion" without breaking a smile.

"She's a deeply troubled woman." He sighed. "I have always counted myself among her closest colleagues, but this really shakes my confidence."

This story had legs of its own; there was no point in gloating.

▌

JUST BEFORE 5:00 PM, a Gulfstream G-IV bearing tail number NA5767 flew in from the north. Jeremy was hanging out in the hangar lounge when it touched down.

"You ready?" Jesús asked, emerging from a back room. He had disappeared into the unit chief's office shortly after they'd arrived.

Jeremy nodded. He slung his day pack over his shoulder as Jesús led him out the front door. The plane was waiting outside, already taking on fuel. The sleek corporate jet was painted white with blue and green accents. It looked brand new.

"Beats the hell out of a military hop, huh?" Jeremy said, walking toward the plane. Jesús walked beside him, too distracted for conversation. The Xray team leader pulled a small green notebook from his pocket, checked a handwritten number, and punched it into his cell phone. His Nextel beeped twice and died.

"Shit. You got your cell phone with you?" Jesús asked.

Jeremy handed over the new phone they'd just given him two weeks earlier. Like most FBI offices, CIRG was moving away from the old Motorola encrypted radios to Nextels. The new equipment cost a fraction of the old system, weighed less, gave agents greater range, and provided a paging feature. Most agents bitched that it just gave management greater range in tracking them.

"I'll meet you inside," Jesús said. He walked off to the right, away from the high-pitched wail of the jet's APU. Jeremy nodded to the fuel crew, gave the jet a quick preflight look, and walked up the four steps into the fuselage.

"You got to be kidding me," he mumbled, walking down the aisle toward a pivoting recliner. The cabin looked like something a rock star would enjoy. He'd ridden first class, once, on a United Airlines sympathy upgrade, but this made that seem like slumming. The G-IV's interior was carpeted in a rich Berber and appointed with supple leather couches, teak trim, rich-looking wallpaper, and smoked-glass reading lamps. Phones sat next to each seat. A video screen on the front bulkhead offered live television, DVDs, and a Global Positioning System map that would detail the jet's altitude, location, and exterior temperature throughout the flight.

"You got somebody with you?" a voice called out behind him. "My manifest says two."

Jeremy turned toward the cockpit. The pilot looked about fifty, with military aviator glasses and shaggy, platinum white hair.

"He's outside making a call," Jeremy said. He shook the pilot's hand. "Jeremy Waller."

"Nice to meet you." The pilot offered no name in response. "The galley's fully stocked. We got plenty to eat, so make yourself at home," he said. "Should be about four hours to Gander, then another four into Shannon."

"Gander?" Jeremy asked. This was the first he'd heard about any particular itinerary.

"Newfoundland," the pilot said. He climbed into the left seat and started his preflight checks. "We can't make it all the way to Shannon on one tank of gas."

"Where?" Jeremy asked. The man looked up and stared at him a moment with no particular commitment; then he smiled and continued with his preparations.

Jeremy turned toward the cabin and saw two people sitting midway down the fuselage. The man on the aisle looked like a shooter; Delta maybe, or SEAL Team Six. His haircut and physique would have given him away by themselves, but there was something else — that intangible ease that sticks with guys who've walked in fire.

"Jeremy Waller," he said.

"Chris. This is Sirad."

Jeremy could barely keep from gawking. The woman sitting near the window had long black hair pulled back in a simple ponytail. Her dark skin looked almost luminous; her eyes were a light source all their own. She looked up briefly from a laptop and nodded.

"Nice to meet you," Jeremy said. She smiled obliquely, apparently too busy to bother with a formal introduction.

Jeremy walked past them, dropped his pack on the floor, and sat in a leather recliner. It struck him as odd that Jesús hadn't said anything about these two. But then everything seemed odd about this mission. Why no warning order? Why no briefing?

Jeremy pulled a copy of *Men's Journal* out of the seat back and stole another look at the woman he'd just met. She wore jeans and a sweater and had simple gold studs in her ears. An evening gown wouldn't have made her look any better.

"Sorry for the holdup," Jesús said as he climbed aboard. He pulled the steps closed and locked the hatch. The pilot waved and throttled up the engines as Jesús walked back toward Jeremy.

"You meet the neighbors?" he asked, plopping down across the aisle. Chris reached back over the seat for a familial handshake. The woman continued typing.

"Yeah, you know 'em?" Jeremy pretended to read, holding the magazine so he could stare without getting busted.

"You never know anyone on these gigs," Jesús said. "Remember that." The engines raced, and they began to taxi. "And from now on, a first name will do. If they want anything more than that, have 'em talk to me."

XII

EDGAR VALEZ HAD never heard of Senator Beechum before taking this job. He'd registered to vote when he went into the Army, but moving around all the time made it impossible to keep up with who was running for what. Then he'd got arrested and lost all interest. Felons can't vote.

"Good morning, sir," the doorman said as Valez passed on his way out for a cup of coffee.

"Yeah, whatever," he muttered. He'd lived at the building a little more than two years already but never bothered to learn the doorman's name. Valez was away on travel most of the time, and when it came right down to it, the building's staff were paid well to keep him safe and happy. They were not paid to talk.

Even with the distraction, Valez walked out into a sunny New York afternoon with a slight smile on his face. Today was payday, and a considerable one at that. An hour from now, he would receive a cell phone call directing him to a Sixth Avenue mail drop where his most recent employer had secreted $100,000 in loose diamonds. By dinnertime, he would visit the Deutsche Bank branch at Times

Square and secure them in a safe deposit box along with his cache of other negotiable, yet untraceable, assets.

"Coffee, black," he said to a street vendor at the corner. He'd stopped at the same kiosk for the same thing every day he'd been in New York but never bothered to ask this man his name, either. Names were a liability in Valez's business — and it was a business. Like payment trails, phone records, and legal contracts, names were a nuisance he most often tried to avoid. That's why he had always done business anonymously through word of mouth and a well-disguised personal advertisement in the Internet classifieds section of the *London Times*. With greater regularity each month, he received diverse requests dealing with everything from messy divorce surveillance and intervention to outright murder.

"Nice tattoo," the coffee vendor commented as he rung up Valez's $1.50 purchase. Two brightly colored dice stood out on the regular customer's right forearm. One of them had the number one with an asterisk. The other bore three twos. "Bet you was in the military. Gulf war, huh?"

"Yeah," was all Valez offered in response. Lots of people had tattoos.

▌▌

SIRAD WORKED AWAY at her laptop, trying not to notice the man sitting over her left shoulder. All men stared, but he actually made her feel uncomfortable. Every time she turned to say something to Bartholomew, this guy, Jeremy, would look away or pretend to read his magazine. It wasn't that he was leering at her; he looked as if he knew her from somewhere else. He seemed more interested in what she was up to than what she'd do with him.

"So, when are you going to read me in on this?" she asked Bartholomew once they'd reached cruising altitude again. She'd decided to work him a little, just enough to get some information. She rubbed against him from time to time, excusing herself at first, then making her interest a little more obvious.

"Come on," he smiled. "It's going to take more than a little grab ass to get information out of me." She should have known that this would take more than a casual flirt.

"How about these two new guys?" she asked, feigning embarrassment. "You could at least tell me who they are."

"Well, let's see . . . I used to work with one of them." Bartholomew smiled. "That would be the guy right behind us. My guess is that within five minutes he's gonna drop two tabs of Ambien and crash out listening to Neil Young on a Discman. He's a creature of habit — same as the old days."

"What old days would those be?" Sirad asked. She leaned forward to take something out of her bag. She knew the back of her thong would show and wanted to see his reaction.

"Army days," Bartholomew continued. "Both of us enlisted first, then got our degrees. Had to make some money, so we got out."

"Doesn't look like you got very far out," she said. Sirad caught Jeremy watching again.

"How about you?" Bartholomew asked. "How the hell does a woman who looks like you end up on a plane with three knuckle draggers, not knowing a thing about where she's going or what she's going to do when she gets there?"

"Guess I just love big surprises," she said. "Something tells me you've got one."

There was no pretense in the conversation now. She wasn't going to last a whole trip without sampling this guy, and they both knew it.

"Tell you what," he said. "You bend over and show me that thong every once in a while, and I'll let you in on a little secret about this escapade."

She laughed out loud.

"These guys are private contractors," Bartholomew said. "Best thing you can do is stay the hell away from them."

That piqued her interest, and he knew it. "What if I show this guy, Jeremy, my thong?" she whispered. "Maybe he'll tell me what I want to know."

"I doubt it," Bartholomew whispered back. He paused for a moment to drink in the smell of her skin. "He doesn't know any more than you do."

■

TRASK USED HIS own key to open the door to apartment 12D, a nicely furnished two-bedroom pied-à-terre that Borders Atlantic had purchased years earlier through an offshore import/export subsidiary. The company used it to stage liaisons for out-of-town clients with "particular" interests. Today it would serve a very different purpose.

"Hello?" he called out.

"In h-h-h-here," a man answered. Trask followed the voice to the front bedroom, where he found Neveu's project engineer laboring over a strange-looking device that was only slightly larger than a handheld DV camera. A cloud of blue-gray cigarette smoke filled the room. The bedspread lay in a heap on the floor. The TV was blaring *SpongeBob SquarePants* on Nickelodeon.

Trask ignored the distractions, crossed immediately to the device, and nodded. "So this is it," was all he said. As weapons went, this looked totally unimpressive.

"I g-g-g-got a y-y-y-year of my l-l-l-life in this little b-b-beauty, man," Marty said. He stamped his Pall Mall out on the windowsill and tossed the butt into the corner. "Th-th-th-that's my l-l-little angel."

"I thought it would look . . . bigger," Trask said.

"The b-b-box is just the aiming p-p-package," he said. "Everything e-e-else fits in the cell phone, j-j-just like the specs called for." He twisted a Phillips head screw, squinting through a dull haze of smoke. "You can h-h-h-hide this baby in your p-p-p-pants if you want to."

"Good," Trask said, picking up the small black device and holding it gingerly in his hands. He still found it hard to believe that anything could wound or kill with sound. Sure, he'd seen the demonstration, but that was a field trial. Using it in the real world seemed like an entirely different matter.

"You're certain it will work in our phones?"

"All ab-b-bout the physics," Marty said. "S-s-size may m-matter in the bedroom, but not here."

"And no signature? I never heard a thing in the desert, but we were standing behind bulletproof glass and I couldn't hear anything above the sound of that chopper. Are you sure this won't stand out in a crowded urban setting?"

"N-n-n-no s-s-signature at all." Marty took the device back from Trask and continued to tinker with it. "Unless y-y-you're the t-t-target. And it's amplitude d-d-dependent, just l-l-like your s-s-stereo. Down l-l-low it won't e-e-even b-b-bother the neighbors. T-t-turn it up and it's l-like gettin' b-b-bitch-slapped by God."

Trask let that analogy pass without comment.

Marty finished what he was doing and packed up his tools. He lit up a fresh Pall Mall, downed the last of his Mountain Dew, and checked around the room to make sure he hadn't dropped anything. When he was done, he said good-bye to *SpongeBob SquarePants* and turned off Nickelodeon.

"B-b-best of luck," Marty said, looking one last time around the room before heading for the door. He kind of wished that the device he had just delivered bore some markings, brand name, or serial number that would record his work on this extraordinary endeavor. But then again, anonymity was the trademark of black projects. History recorded names like Colt and Sikorsky, but the real genius behind weapons development would always remain hidden among the shadows.

▮

"HERE," JESÚS SAID, once they had leveled off at 32,000 feet. "This is your ID packet."

He pulled a plain manila folder out of his pack and handed it across the aisle. Inside, Jeremy found a passport, two credit cards, a Wisconsin driver's license, and assorted wallet stuffers. He thumbed past a Blockbuster video pass to an ARCIN Oil employee identification card. The plastic ID read Brian Campbell of Tulsa, Oklahoma. *Nice name,* he thought. His mother was Scottish.

"Make sure everything matches up," he said. Jesús opened an identical folder of his own and began to sort through his own wallet stuffers.

Jeremy opened a billfold and found 160,000 Yemeni rials, worn dark with circulation. The plasticine photo flap held two candids of his wife and kids — someone's wife and kids. He'd never seen them before in his life.

All the cards carried his physical description and photo, but the date of birth, social security number, and home address were all wrong. Everything looked worn, as if it had been riding with him for years.

"Memorize that shit," Jesús said. "Then take this."

He handed Jeremy two small, white oblong pills. "Small one's Ambien. Four hours of sleep per hit. You'll need it."

"What about this one?" Jeremy asked, rolling them around in his palm.

"Chloroquine," Jesús replied. "Prophylaxis treatment for malaria."

"Malaria?" Jeremy recoiled. "What malaria?"

Jesús grabbed his pack and fished around inside for a CD player and a set of headphones. "Yemen is a risk country for malaria," he said. "No sense in taking chances."

Jeremy stared at the two pills a moment, then opened a 7UP, plopped the white pills into his mouth, and washed them down with a long draw.

"Oh, and for future reference, I usually wait till we get out over water before dropping." Jesús smiled. "If we get called back, you're going to end up sleeping that off in the hangar."

Jeremy shrugged his shoulders. "Called back from what?" he asked. "I don't even know what the hell we're doing."

Jesús stretched his legs out on the seat facing him. "Don't worry about it," he said, dropping a Neil Young CD into his Discman. He offered his teammate a package of yellow foam plugs, which Jeremy rolled between his fingers and slipped into his ear canals. "Better get some sleep. Yemen is one helluva commute."

Yemen, Jeremy thought to himself. He stared out his window into a white mist as the plane flew into a high maritime cloud cover. *Second mission in a month — this time in some Third World shithole on a private jet. Probably some terrorist pickup.* To hell with IBM and the rich corporate life. This shit was cool.

▌

EDGAR VALEZ WALKED south on Fifth Avenue toward an address he'd received earlier that day. He had plenty of time before they were scheduled to call with the final drop point, but it was a nice day, and punctuality was one of the reasons clients never balked at his fee. If he was scheduled for a gig at a certain time, you could set your watch by him.

▮

TRASK PICKED UP his boss at the office precisely on schedule. Mitchell had a book signing at Barnes & Noble's Fifth Avenue superstore at seven o'clock and the event organizer had already called to check on them. Mitchell always complained about doing these things, but $10 million contracts come with certain stipulations.

"So, what exactly am I supposed to know about this whole thing?" Mitchell asked. The driver pulled up to the corner of Forty-eighth Street and waited for the light to change.

"Nothing," Trask replied. "When it's time, you'll want to look out the front window and watch, but other than that, you are there for a book signing."

A line of people stretched from the front doors of the bookstore all the way down Forty-eighth Street. Some people already held two or three books apiece.

"Just make sure you have those pens I like," Mitchell said. He reached for his briefcase as the driver pulled over and parked near the side entrance. An entourage of flacks and Barnes & Noble executives waited in their finest suits and smiles.

"All taken care of, Mr. Mitchell," Trask said. "I've got everything all ready to go."

▮

EDGAR VALEZ TURNED east on Forty-eighth Street with fifteen minutes to spare. He stopped at a red light, trying to stand at the edge of the sidewalk to enjoy the sun. His watch read 6:55 PM as he counted the blocks between where he stood and where he needed to go. A good-looking blonde stepped out into the street as the light changed, and he started to follow, but his cell phone rang, pulling him back into the job at hand.

"Yeah," he said. Caller ID was blocked, but he knew who it was.

"Where are you?" a male voice asked him.

"I'm sure you know." Valez craned his neck, looking up to the

high-rise buildings all around him. They were up there watching —
he had no doubts about that.

"There's been a change of plans," the voice stated. "Continue east,
but turn north on Fifth and walk north to the corner of Forty-sixth.
There's a cab on the corner — number 6N76. Your money's in the
trunk."

A smile broke out on Valez's face, and he didn't try to hide it. Some
days were better than others, but the best were always when you got
paid. He walked across the street, following the blonde as she
turned south and walked toward a crowded Barnes & Noble bookstore. A long line of people stood outside, apparently waiting for
some celebrity book signing.

What the hell? he thought, following the woman toward the store.
He had a few minutes to kill and had been meaning to pick up a decent read.

◧

"WE IN NEWFOUNDLAND yet?" Jeremy asked, waking up and rubbing an Ambien haze out of his eyes as a front of thunderstorms
bounced him around in his seat.

"Already been to Newfoundland," Jesús said. Had Jeremy stayed
awake, he would have marveled at the 6,000-foot runway emerging
out of the massive polar ice floe that stretches north all the way to
the arctic circle. He might have liked the fresh-baked cookies that
the lounge kept out front twenty-four hours a day or the photos de-
picting early trans-Atlantic flight. But all that was thousands of
miles in the rearview mirror.

Jeremy stared out the window. It was raining hard, and they hadn't
yet cleared the cloud bank on descent.

"Man, that Ambien shit really hits you hard," he said. Drool
stained the richly carpeted wall where his face had lain. He looked
over to see if the woman had noticed. She was sleeping herself. "So,
you gonna tell me what we're doing, or do I have to figure it out on
my secret decoder ring?"

Jesús smiled for the first time the whole trip.

"Sorry," he said. "Nobody gets much information on gigs like this.
Opsec."

208

A pocket of hard air flipped the plane left, then violently right again. Both backpacks rolled onto the floor, and Jeremy's eyes shot wide open. Jesús barely noticed.

"This is an Agency gig," he said. "You ever work with them before?"

Jeremy nodded, trying not to look like a rookie. "A little," he lied.

"One of their assets located the shithead behind the *Cole* bombing back in 2000. We're going to get him."

"Anybody I'd recognize?" Jeremy asked. He knew most of the faces on the FBI's twenty-one most wanted list.

"No, just some midlevel operations commander. A Saudi named Asam alal-Bin."

"Who's coming with us?" Jeremy asked. It seemed like a logical question. Jeremy counted four bodies in the cabin, and one of them definitely wasn't a shooter. The Puerto Rico gig hadn't sounded as dangerous, and they'd taken the whole team.

"This is the Agency's gig," Jesús said. "We're just here for the warm fuzzy."

"What's in Shannon?"

"Gas," Jesús said, returning to his legal pad. "Just a touch and go. Next stop Luxembourg, then Dubai, where we get off for a commercial hitch. From there, it's into Yemen for insertion."

"Insertion?" Jeremy asked. Guys usually complained that there was nothing to do on these renditions but sleep and read. *Two books and a week of constipation*, they bitched. Most times, the host country had the bad guy waiting in shackles, just begging to get rid of him.

"I hope you like the desert," Jesús said, "because this asshole ain't gonna be waiting at the airport." The plane jumped and shuddered in the rough air. Rain streaked across the windows, obscuring any view of the airport down below. "You got any more chew?"

Jeremy reached for his pack and noticed that the woman had awakened. She looked beautiful even after eight hours in the air.

"We there?" She yawned. Sirad turned and caught Jeremy staring.

"Here," Jeremy said, handing Jesús the tobacco. "Better go easy on it. That's all we got."

The plane touched down ten minutes later, officially handing Jeremy his first overseas visit, but he barely noticed. Something about this woman struck him as wrong. *Screw the tobacco*, he thought. It was a nasty habit anyway.

▌

TRASK TRIED TO look interested in Mitchell's book signing, but the real reason for his presence along Fifth Avenue captured his attention. He felt confident that he had flawlessly backstopped this whole thing, but years in Mitchell's company had taught him the value in obsessing over every detail. There was no point in taking chances. Trask walked over to the table where the boss sat scribbling autographs into hardbacks for his adoring fans.

"Mr. Mitchell, may I interrupt you for one moment, please?" he asked. Trask handed his boss the phone and apologized to the next person in line, saying that it was important and would only take a moment.

Mitchell stood up and walked off to the side, where Trask had found a place with a perfect view of the street.

"Which one is it?" Mitchell asked, looking out the store's broad front window.

"Not sure, sir. I've never seen him in person." He checked his watch. "Just press Send."

Mitchell tried to smile, realizing that everyone within eyesight was watching. He looked outside at a couple dozen pedestrians crossing with the light. Cabs and trucks and bicycle couriers sped along in heavy traffic.

"Now, sir," Trask said. He looked a little anxious.

Mitchell pressed the green button and held the phone to his ear. He heard two rings and a connection. No voice.

SCREEECH!

The sound of skidding tires and honking horns filled the store as dozens of people turned just in time to watch a big blue-and-white transit bus skid right, clip two cabs, and smash into a light pole. A cop standing nearby ran out into the street to assist a man lying in the road and bleeding from his ears and nose.

"Are you all right?" the cop asked. He helped the man to his feet and asked him if he needed an ambulance.

"No! No . . . I'm fine," the man said. Edgar Valez was still conscious, and he was still alive — there was no way he was going to any hospital without the diamonds. "What the hell happened?"

"I don't know, sir," the cop said. "It didn't look like anybody hit you, but you're bleeding. Are you sure you're all right?"

Valez knelt down on unsteady legs and sat in the street long enough to gather his senses. The cop reached down and picked up Valez's cell phone, which had started to ring. He handed it to Valez, then turned to the bus, which was emptying its angry passengers out onto the sidewalk.

"Impressive, huh?" Mitchell said to Trask inside the bookstore, as people in line craned their necks to see what had happened.

"Yes, it was," Trask said. He took the phone from Mitchell's hand and held it to his ear. He could see the cop helping the target to his feet and steering him back to the Fifth Avenue sidewalk.

"Hello?" the target asked. He had pulled a white handkerchief out of his pocket and was dabbing blood from his ears and nose. "Who is this?"

"This is your future," Trask said as Mitchell walked back to the signing table. "And that ringing in your head is a warning. Your payment is waiting in the cab, Mr. Valez, just as promised. But should you ever decide to talk politics, you need to know that there will be a downside."

"Never liked politicians," Valez said as Trask watched him through the Barnes & Noble window. "Can't trust a one of them."

▮

YEMEN APPEARED OUT of the blue-green sparkle of Indian Ocean like some rolling mirage. It was late afternoon when they arrived, and the heat of a desert sun danced across the tarmac. Jeremy stared out his window at the surrounding vista of sand, tidal pools, and oil storage facilities as they landed. Low buildings of bleached clay tile and concrete spread north, out the right side of the plane. A big harbor full of cargo ships and oil tankers stretched out on the other side.

"Holy shit, look at that," Jeremy said. He pointed out his window toward two wrecked planes, which rested along the runway in crumpled balls, as if warning incoming visitors not to bother complaining about Yemeni Air's flight service.

Jeremy heard a loud, screeching noise and looked across the aisle at a traditionally clad Arab carrying a peregrine falcon in a cage on his lap. The bird flipped its head left and right, trying to interpret the thud of touchdown from beneath its leather hood. Jeremy wondered how such a wild and noble animal could handle the thick haze of cigarette smoke that hung about the cabin. He could barely see the end of the fuselage.

"Follow me, keep your mouth shut, and look bored," Jesús said as they walked toward the terminal. The Aden Airport had no Jetways, so the flight emptied out onto a runway softened by the sun to the consistency of well-kneaded Play-Doh. Jeremy followed toward a one-story structure built of rough brick and concrete blocks. It was just the two of them now. The man and woman from the G-IV had stayed in Dubai.

"Holy shit is it hot," Jeremy said. It wasn't a complaint; he simply couldn't believe it.

The two men fell in among the rest of the passengers and walked into the main terminal. Fans hung from the ceiling but failed to provide even the slightest movement of air. Jeremy felt as if they had walked into an oven.

A customs official sat behind a broken table. Right next to him stood a white man in a khaki safari vest and snakeskin cowboy boots. He had short blond hair and wore aviator sunglasses. "He looks a little overt," Jeremy mumbled.

"Just give Skinny your passport and follow me," Jesús said. He didn't sound interested in any of his partner's operational security assessments.

They approached the counter and stood in line until the Yemeni civil servant nodded and reached out for their papers.

"Biness?" he asked Jesús, who stepped up behind the man with the falcon.

"No biness," Jesús replied. "Bacation." He was just being difficult. Jeremy was about to intervene with a little tact, when another voice interjected.

212

"ARCIN Oil," the man said. "They're with me." He spoke some Arabic with a West Texas drawl, like a Berlitz tape on dying batteries. The customs inspector motioned for Jeremy's passport, inspected it thoroughly, and then nodded.

"Biness." The customs inspector stamped the two documents and handed them back. A woman in a black shawl and veil pushed Jeremy out of the way, ending their engagement.

"This way, gentlemen." The Texan motioned with his head and led them across the room and into a doorless closet distinguished by two open sewer holes in the floor and a short length of rubber hose. The stifling bathroom smelled so strongly of human waste and ammonia Jeremy's eyes began to water.

"How's the flight?" the Texan asked as he unzipped his pants. He relieved himself with a grunt, then spat in after it.

"Fine," Jesús said, taking the hole next to him. "We good to go?"

"Last I heard," the Texan said. He finished, zipped up his fly, and turned toward Jeremy, reaching out with the same hand to shake. "Name's Powell — RSO, Sanaa."

Jeremy took the man's hand. He understood that this guy was resident security officer at the American Embassy in Sanaa — at least that was his cover.

Jesús finished, then stepped aside, nodding to Jeremy that it was his turn. But Xray's newest sniper had no interest.

"Pretty bad when you won't even piss on the place, huh?" Powell laughed. "Welcome to Assland."

XIII

———

HAMID LIVED WELL. The view from his Upper East Side apartment encompassed four Manhattan buildings in which he held at least a controlling share. His painting and sculpture collection drew both praise and derision from the New York art world, which referred to it as the finest private catalog "built within the past fifteen minutes." Half the New York Knicks had sipped champagne at one of his homes.

At 41 years of age, the Borders Atlantic financial wiz lived high in a stratosphere of new wealth that seemed to exemplify the American dream. His financial prowess had earned billions and left him with a certain notoriety — everything from his own barstool at O'Flaherty's to a *Wall Street Journal* dot portrait.

No matter what this man accomplished in terms of material gain, however, none of it would ever pass down to heirs. All the Brancusis, the French Impressionists, and the one-off Tiffany pieces looked impressive in his portfolio, but none of them existed on any estate plan. Hamid earned a healthy salary, but Jordan Mitchell owned him.

"Tell me what you know about this woman."

Hamid sat in the lounge of the Mercer Hotel, nestled between a stem vase of calla lilies and Dieter Planck, a stern and humorless man. The director of seventeenth-floor operations tasted a 1982 Château Le Pin and nodded approval.

"What do I know about her? I know she's one of the most exciting women I have ever met," he said. "A friend of mine set us up. Is that a problem?"

"Everything is a problem in this case," Dieter said. "You've gotten very comfortable in this lifestyle we built you, but it could go away in a moment."

Dieter wore black Prada from head to toe. Everything fit, but nothing seemed right.

"You're not going to lecture me, Dieter. No one has ever questioned my loyalties."

"It's not loyalties we're worried about. This woman emerged out of dust and suddenly she's staying at your house. We can't find anything about her before 1989. She just disappears before that."

"What are you doing checking on the women I date?"

"You're sleeping with her. That's more than dating. You know we have guidelines."

"To hell with your guidelines. If I lived within Rabbit Hole rules, I never could have accomplished any of this!" A couple people looked, and he lowered his voice. "I work hard. I meet my obligations. I don't see why you would object to my having a little fun from time to time."

"We're not talking about a little fun. We're talking about a potential threat to one of the most important programs this company has ever undertaken. You want to jeopardize that so you can get laid? I ask that you consider your priorities."

Hamid fought to control his sometimes vitriolic temper.

"I have given everything for this program," he hissed. "Everything I built, thought up, and worked my ass off to make happen ends up being nothing more than a damned incentive award in your paycheck and a lousy promotion. This isn't about getting laid. It's my life." He stared straight into Dieter's eyes and spit out the last words. "Maybe this is the point where your corporate security goals and my mental health run two different ways. I'll date who I damned well like."

"I'm sorry to hear you feel that way," Dieter said.

215

"I know your spiel," Hamid responded. "I know about the political realities behind this project, the part about shaded nationalities and bottom lines. I understand all of it. But money has nothing to do with my new lover. She's an IT executive from Atlanta. Take away her computer and she's no more dangerous to us than this actor over here."

Hamid nodded toward the far wall, where George Clooney tested his big-screen charm on a Thai cocktail waitress. Hamid checked his watch and nodded toward the door.

"It's time to go. Reservations are at eight, and they won't hold the table."

Dieter studied his companion for a moment, trying to decide just how much Hamid had a right to know about his new love interest. Emotion had obviously clouded the financier's judgment in this matter, but no one could question his intentions or his value to Borders Atlantic. It would be quite impossible to replace him.

"You're right," Dieter said. "I hope you'll forgive my overreaction."

"No problem," Hamid said. He checked his watch and motioned for their check. "She's a beautiful and talented woman with aspirations, but other than that, she's harmless. Trust me."

▌

THE RIDE TO the Aden Hotel took five minutes. Jeremy tried not to stare, but he'd never seen anything like this — squalor as far as the eye could see. Filth. Garbage. Dilapidated buildings, goats in the street, potholes that shook Powell's Range Rover as he raced through streets he seemed to know well.

"Who did we piss off to get this gig?" Jeremy asked. He rode in the back, playing with his watch, trying to dial in something close to local time.

"It's not so bad up north in Sanaa," the RSO said. He honked his horn at an old man wearing nothing but shorts and skin that hung off sagging bones. "Aden has been going downhill since the *Cole* bombing."

Powell stopped suddenly for a donkey cart that blocked a crowded intersection. A group of children swarmed around them, pounding on the windows and holding out their hands for anything these rich Westerners might spare.

"Average per capita income here is around eight hundred dollars . . . one of the poorest nations in the world." Powell said. "And the fucking president has his own personal Seven Forty-seven. That tell you anything?"

Powell popped the clutch and yanked the wheel right, sending the kids scurrying away from the front bumper. "Little bastards will break your heart if you let 'em."

Two of the older boys chucked rocks at them as the car sped away in a cloud of white dust.

"Yeah, your head, too," Jeremy said as a rock bounced off the back windshield.

Ten minutes later, the RSO dropped them off outside the hotel and promised to pick them up in an hour for dinner. He told them the ambassador was coming south from the embassy for the weekend and that he had to make sure everything was ready for her regal visit.

The Aden Hotel, an eight-story European-looking building, sat next to a traffic roundabout, halfway between the eastern foothills and the harbor. Compared to the city around it, the place struck Jeremy as fairly pleasant.

"Good day, gentlemen," the desk clerk greeted them. He wasted no time in telling them he had attended the Cornell School of Hotel Management and worked an apprenticeship at the MGM Grand in Las Vegas. His favorite casino show was the *David Cassidy Review*. He had also liked Siegfried and Roy, before the tiger incident.

They checked in using their undercover identities and took the elevator to the sixth floor. On the way up, the elevator stopped at the restaurant level, and two traditionally dressed Arabs walked in, engaged in a heated discussion. They stopped talking at first, studied the two Westerners, and then resumed their conversation.

"They think we're Russian," Jesús said, once they'd got off at the sixth floor.

"You speak Arabic?" Jeremy asked. He had no idea Jesús spoke the language, though the FBI sent lots of agents to the Defense Language Institute south of San Francisco.

"Yeah, while I was in the Army." He never talked much about his time at Delta, though there were lots of rumors.

Jeremy followed his team leader into a typical-looking hotel room. It looked clean, if low rent. Two sagging double beds lay in front of sliding-glass windows. Lots of linoleum furniture in simulated wood grain and cheap carpeting with scuff balls the size of field mice.

"Hey, check this out," Jeremy said. He pointed to a plaque glued at an odd angle to the dresser. There was an arrow, some Arabic writing, and the English spelling of *Mecca*.

"That shows them which direction to face for prayer. Heathen Western baby killers like us don't need to worry about that," he said. Jeremy reached for an apple in the complimentary fruit basket, and Jesús grabbed it out of his hand.

"And leave that shit alone." He tossed it in the trash can. "Don't drink the water or eat anything washed in it." He tossed his pack on the bed. "You haven't lived until you've spent three days in the fetal position, quivering like a dog shitting razor blades and blowing Tabasco sauce out your ass." His mood seemed better, though not particularly cheerful. "I need you healthy tomorrow, Waller, so eat what I eat. That way, if you get sick, I can only blame myself."

No problem, Jeremy thought. The only things he really cared about at this point were a hot shower and a couple hours of sleep. This was a whole new kind of adventure for him. Letting Jesús serve as tour guide made perfect sense.

▮

BEECHUM ARRIVED AT her Dirksen office Friday morning to find a frenzy of activity and wailing phones. It was the same incessant din that had consumed the place when the indictment was announced.

"Damn it, Senator, what the hell were you thinking?" her administrative assistant asked. "The presidential race may be over for us, but you still have this office to think about." The rest of the staff turned and stared.

"I'm afraid I made a stone fool's ass of myself last night, James," she said. "I should have talked to you before . . ." Her voice trailed off as she walked past him toward her office.

During the past twenty-four hours, the Ethics Committee had

censured her, the Intelligence Committee had stripped away her security clearances, and the minority leader had publicly rebuked her, but at least they hadn't taken her seat. The founding fathers had looked after all kinds of inalienable rights in the Constitution, but none more than their own. Kicking a member out of the United States Senate took some doing.

"This whole mess is only going to get worse," Beechum said as her administrative assistant followed close behind. "I'll understand if you want to resign." Administrative assistants run Washington, and the good ones are prized almost like family members. She would have felt proud to call James her son.

"Senator, I told you when you hired me that loyalty was my strongest ambition. I'm staying until you get this behind you, whatever and whenever that may be." He seldom even thought about the presidency anymore. "Besides, these people are beginning to piss me off."

Beechum started to chuckle. "Yeah . . . me too." She stared out her window at the Capitol, the symbol of an institution she loved more than anything in the world.

"You know, my first office was in the basement of the Dirksen Building, in the back, under the kitchen." She wiped something out of her eyes. Tears, fatigue, and sentimentality often overwhelmed her now. "It used to smell like a damned Frialator in there. I lost ten pounds my first year because the smell of food made me nauseous. All I ever wanted to do was take a shower.

"And look at us, now." She folded her arms and nodded at the grand mahogany-paneled space around her. "You know something? I never took it for granted. Not for one moment."

She turned around and sat in her chair. Stacks of paper cluttered her normally meticulously organized desk. Moving boxes filled with the contents of her committee office rose in stacks around the room.

"I used to tell people the only thing that ever frightened me about Washington was that I'd fail her. All the travel back and forth to the District. The long hours. The crap you have to put up with from lobbyists and PACs and reporters and the Republicans . . . it didn't bother me a bit because I was scared to death the whole time that I would screw up and deny this wonderful institution the respect it deserved. I didn't want to betray the faith. And you know what? I never did. Not for a single moment."

"I believe that," James said.

The door opened a crack, and the sounds of the phones filled her office.

"Senator," her receptionist interrupted. "I hate to bother you, but Tom Brokaw is calling for you. I mean, personally. He's on the phone. What do I tell him?"

James turned to the senator. "Elizabeth, I've never known you to back down from anything. You've told me that you had nothing to do with this and that you wanted to fight. Well, now's the time."

"How, James? I want to fight, but dammit, every time we turn around, it's another leak in the press. The judge won't do anything because he's afraid it'll be perceived as a cover-up. Nobody from the party will step in to help because they think I'm guilty. The police won't give up the evidence against me because they claim it will violate national goddamned security."

He moved close to her, closer than appropriate.

"You remember what you told me when I first took this job? That intelligence oversight is easy in this town because bureaucrats can't even conspire where to eat lunch together. You told me that the only way three people can keep a secret in this town is if two of them are dead." He paused so that his words would reach her. "If secrets are all they have, you can beat them."

"You know, you're right," she said. "There are two possibilities here: either we've got a conspiracy waiting to fall apart, or we have a bunch of dead people waitin' to get dug up. Way I see it, it's time to quit whining and start digging."

"Press conference?" James asked.

She shook her head. "Not yet. First we go back to my house and find something we can use for ammo."

"Like what?"

"I don't know, but we've got two law degrees and almost thirty years in Congress between the two of us. If we can't find something those cops overlooked, I deserve to go to jail."

Beechum grabbed her coat and slapped him on the shoulder. Brokaw would have to wait.

"Let's get to work," she said. "Time is money, and you know I hate to waste them both."

░

"OK, YOU'VE GOT me here, now what the hell is with all the secrecy?"

Sirad pulled her garment bag through a long, glittering shopping mall running the length of Dubai Airport's central terminal. A fifty-yard-long row of glass display cases ran down the middle of the walkway, with a giant stack of gold bullion bars at each end and rows of expensive jewelry, Hasselblad cameras, Mercedes convertibles, and French perfumes. The abject poverty television so often depicted in the Middle East was nowhere in sight.

"Not here," Bartholomew said. "Too much risk of overhears."

Sirad looked around at the Middle East's busiest airport, which throbbed with activity and a mixture of nationalities that made American travel hubs look Wonder Bread white. Traditionally attired Arabs and Africans walked alongside Slavic oil workers, Swiss financiers, and Turkish day laborers. Women walked into the bathrooms in black burkas and emerged wearing Chanel suits and diamonds the size of marbles. Everything smelled of Estée Lauder and dark Moroccan cigarette smoke and body odor stained with the indescribable musk of poorly digested curry. It struck her as an amazing scene.

"Are you serious? No one is listening to us. They're too busy shopping for Western imperial decadence." Sirad stopped briefly to ogle a shiny new Porsche dual turbo, which rested on chrome ramps as if caught midjump in suspended animation.

"Close this deal and you'll be able to buy one in every color," Chris said.

He shuffled through a crowd of Japanese tourists, hustling to make their duty-free purchases before catching flights.

Sirad stopped in her tracks. "All right. I've had enough of this. Before I walk another step, I want to know what's going on."

"Cell phones."

"No shit." Jet lag and sixteen hours in a G-IV had soured her sense of humor.

"OPEC's board of ministers begins a weeklong summit tomorrow," Chris said, looking around to make sure no one was listening. "Crown Prince Abdullah of Saudi Arabia will be among them."

"And?"

"And Borders Atlantic has negotiated a deal with the Saudis to introduce the SBT technology here before we go to market with it in the United States. Mitchell wants it certain that we announce the deal before word leaks out to the financial markets."

Bartholomew reached into his briefcase and pulled out a Borders Atlantic SBT phone. It looked identical to the prototype Sirad had seen in the office, except that jewelers had encased this one in platinum and studded it with precious jewels.

"Tomorrow evening, during a break in the OPEC summit — while all the world is watching for the slightest hint of news on production quotas — you are going to present this phone to the Crown Prince as a gift from Borders Atlantic," Chris said. "It will be the first SBT phone put into commercial use anywhere in the world. All you have to do is smile pretty for the cameras, hand Prince Abdullah this phone, and get him to make a call."

"Why deal with the Saudis? Why not Israel?"

"Because Israel doesn't have any money." Bartholomew laughed. "This is business, Sirad, not foreign policy. The Saudis are offering bandwidth control throughout the Persian Gulf. They plan to undercut the market with startup subsidies and three months of free airtime per subscriber. I saw one report that projected more than five hundred thousand units by the end of the first quarter. The Saudis will be powerful partners."

Sirad stared at him in disbelief. Mitchell had to know that putting SBT technology in the hands of these people would make it much harder for the CIA and NSA to spy on would-be terrorists.

"We're not even scheduled to launch in the United States for months," Sirad said, genuinely surprised at the scope of what she still didn't know. "The FCC is going to freak."

"Let them freak," Bartholomew said. "They have no authority in foreign markets. In fact, that's precisely why Mitchell wants to start overseas. By the time word hits Washington, there will be nothing the FCC or anyone else can do to stop us."

He stopped to read her expression.

"This is the single most lucrative deal in the history of the industry," he said. "If you have a problem, I need to know about it right now."

Sirad thought to herself for a moment but said nothing. Hoch had told her to do what she was told and not to worry about Mitchell's intentions. The Agency had to know what it was doing.

"So, do we have a problem?"

"No problem," Sirad said finally. "But I wish they'd told me about this before we left." She tugged on her garment bag and started walking toward the taxi stand outside. "If I'd known I was going to meet a prince, I would have brought pearls."

▐▌

JEREMY FOUND HIS team leader sitting in the hotel lounge in the mezzanine. He had only managed a catnap, but it took the edge off the dull haze that had gathered around him. Yemen was Zulu plus three; eight time zones ahead of Stafford, Virginia. Jeremy's internal clock was lagging just a couple ticks offbeat.

"I got you a beer," Jesús said. He sat near the back of the lobby, next to a giant chess set laid out on the floor. The queen's crown rose almost to Jeremy's shoulder.

"What's with the decor? I got to tell you, man, you don't strike me as a chess player."

"At least this is out of the way. We don't exactly blend, you know?" He pushed a Tuborg toward Jeremy. "This place has changed a lot since the last time I was here. Used to be a lot of tourists, mostly trekkers. This place has a lot of pre-Etruscan ruins."

Jeremy nodded. He'd never thought of Jesús as an archaeologist either, but this guy was turning out to be full of surprises.

"You boys been waiting long?"

The RSO walked up, wiping sweat off his forehead with a Callaway golf towel.

"Just got here," Jesús said. "You all set for Her Majesty?"

"I guess you've heard about her, huh?" Powell said. Barbara Shotte, the U.S. ambassador to Yemen, had earned quite a reputation.

"I got my share of her in Somalia," Jesús said. "I learned everything I needed about the diplomatic corps right there."

The State Department had demoted Shotte after the ill-fated Black Hawk Down debacle in which nineteen American special operations troops were killed. The only hellhole worse than Somalia was Yemen, so they sent her there.

"Don't judge the State Department by one woman," Powell said, motioning to the waiter and holding up Jeremy's Tuborg can, signaling his order. "My man, Rayfa, take care of you?"

"Yeah, just like the Four Seasons," Jesús said. "We got any problems with overhears?"

"They're pretty primitive, but the Russians gave the Yemenis a lot of analog stuff in the eighties." He looked around the room for faces he might recognize or mannerisms he might suspect. "You fellas ever seen a belly dancer?"

Jeremy shook his head. Jesús smiled.

"Come on. Let's go someplace safer."

He led the two FBI agents through the lobby, past the concierge's desk, to a little hallway just inside the hotel's glass front entrance. A tall man at the door welcomed Powell by name and escorted them inside what looked like a typical Western nightclub. Unlike the Holiday Inns of Northern Virginia, though, this place had fuzzy red wallpaper, Arabic filigree, and the sounds of a nine-piece band covering Middle Eastern pop songs.

"We can talk in here," Powell said, settling into his seat along the back wall. There weren't more than twenty patrons in the whole place, all men.

"Check that out," Jeremy said. They turned toward the stage as an attractive white woman in Ali Baba veils slithered out and began undulating her way toward them.

"This is the closest thing you're going to find to pussy in this shithole," Powell said. "They bring the girls down from Belarus, get them to dance a little and hook a little, then rotate them out to some other Casbah. They call it white slavery in the States, but here it's just business."

"How we looking for tomorrow?" Jesús asked. His travels around the world inured him to women shaking their asses for tips.

"We're on. Your escort is staying at the Golden Mahore, just over the mountains. They'll be expecting you tomorrow morning."

Jeremy sat back and wondered which of the recent turns in his life should feel stranger — the belly-dancing hooker in the Casbah or the CIA agent laying out details about an overseas fugitive snatch he still knew almost nothing about. He tried to shoot his team leader a "What the hell is this all about?" look without giving himself away to Powell.

"What do we have for transportation?" Jesús asked.

"ARCIN Oil brought three Bell Jet Rangers over from Dar. They'll fly you into a little town called Anisi, about one hundred fifty clicks from your objective. It's Land Rovers in from there — dirt roads mostly, probably about four hours to grid coordinates in the Hadramawt region. You leave tomorrow at seven o'clock and should be in position by dark."

"Cover?"

"You're geologists, but nobody's going to ask you too many questions. Everyone's on our side. We've got a couple of NSA E-4 field techs with NMARSAT and a sort of half-assed SCIF. There's an Agency doc out of Walter Reed, the two of you, and two civilian seismologists from George Washington University. You've also got a couple armed guards, just in case some local shithead tries to shake you down. We've worked with these guys before; they won't get in the way."

Jeremy listened intently, trying to follow all the jargon. He'd never worked with anyone from the National Security Agency but knew that most of their field guys came from the military. E-4 meant they were sergeants and had done plenty of this before but that they weren't going to be issuing any orders. NMARSATs were battery-powered International Marine Band Satellite phones that would allow them uplink capability from virtually anywhere in the world. He had used one in Puerto Rico during the Machetero raid.

"What's a SCIF?" he asked. It seemed like a reasonable question considering he was about to embark on a mission that sounded more dangerous with each passing beer.

"Secure Compartmented Information Facility," Jesús said. He shot Jeremy one of those "What the fuck is wrong with you?" looks and shook his head to Powell.

"Who's the XO on this?" Jesús asked. From logistics to execution, this was progressing like a military operation. They'd need an executive officer to keep things in line.

"The doc. He's a full bird colonel, former Special Forces. Any problems, he pulls the strings."

Jeremy sat in his chair and said nothing. A million questions streamed through his head, but he'd rather run into a Yemeni machine gun emplacement than embarrass himself in front of Powell again.

"Equipment?"

"Very little. Climate is pretty brutal this time of year, but there is no rain, light winds. You'll need lots of water, two days' rations, and your kit. I got everything on the list you gave me — all commercial purchase. It'll be waiting on the birds in the morning."

"Exfil?"

"Back to the camp and then straight west to Dar. Make it look like a medical emergency to cover for the civilian types. It'll be a night-time extraction via Black Hawk to the USS *Duluth*, which is headed south through the Suez Canal on its regularly scheduled Med cruise right now."

"What about your end? You got all the suits lined up?"

"That's why the ambassador is coming down for the weekend. She thinks this is a straight snatch orchestrated by State, and that the Yemeni president is fully behind this. Washington told her it's a thirty-million-dollar buyout, and she's cool with that. After the deals we made during the war in Iraq, they could tell her it was fucking Martians landing and she wouldn't say shit."

"Good." Jesús nodded. Jeremy nodded too, trying to fit in.

The band finished its song, and Powell waited for them to begin the next one before speaking up.

"I know this is a tough gig for you guys, but I think we've set it up right. Should be a quick in-and-out. Famous last fucking words, huh?"

"Famous last fucking words."

Jesús lifted his beer, toasted the operation, and turned his eyes toward the belly dancer. "Ever wonder what the rest of the world is doing on a night like this?" he asked.

Jeremy shook his head. He'd forgotten the rest of the world somewhere south of Dubai.

XIV

——

ELIZABETH BEECHUM SURPRISED Rosa for lunch, something she hadn't done in ten years. James stood in the doorway behind the senator, threw his jacket on an Empire period love seat, and put his hands on his hips.

"We start here," he said.

Rosa looked at him as if he were crazy, then returned to her cleaning. Fridays were bathrooms and the kitchen; *The Montel Williams Show* had already put her a little behind schedule.

"What do we do?" Beechum asked. The mere thought of reliving that horrible night sent goose bumps up and down her spine, but she knew this was necessary. Someone had gone to great lengths to frame her for a horrific crime. If spending another couple hours traipsing through memories of the attack would coax the person who did this to her out of his viper's nest, so be it.

"Tell me what happened that night. Tell me when you left the office, where you went, how you came home, everything," said James. He looked around, as if clues might be written on the walls in lemon juice, waiting for the flame of inquiry to reveal them.

"Well, I left work just after six o'clock. I got into my car and drove home. I always go the same way, down the Rock Creek to M and straight out. It's the quickest route."

"Any troubles?" He walked through the entry foyer into the first of two parlors. A central hallway ran all the way through the house, linking dual sitting rooms on the right with a library and an office on the left. The kitchen was all the way back. She had decorated the showplace with Southern period furnishings and some of the heirlooms her father had handed down. James had visited many times and was always captivated by its grand elegance and beauty.

"Troubles? What do you mean?"

Beechum looked around, almost afraid to venture after him for fear she might trample evidence. The fact that every cop in DC had already done the same thing didn't bother her. They had failed to convict Marion Barry with a videotape of him smoking crack. Surely they could have missed something.

"I mean, like somebody following you. Somebody cutting you off in traffic. Somebody coming up to you on the street." He rubbed his hands through his short, sandy hair. James had no more an idea about how to proceed with this sort of thing than she did.

"Nothing. I drove up, parked my car down the street . . . you know, the parking is just awful around here, and . . ."

"Senator, was there anything unusual that might indicate men breaking into your house or tracking your movements?"

"No. I don't think anything stood out as unusual."

"Rosa was off that night?"

"She often spends weekends with her daughter in Alexandria."

"OK, so you come up to the door. Did you unlock it?" James walked back to the vestibule, opened the heavy double doors, and waved for the senator to stand beside him.

"Yes. There's just the latch. I've never had a dead bolt."

"And no security system?"

"I've lived here more than twenty years and never needed one." She shook her head. "Sounds kind of stupid now, huh?"

"You stepped inside. Then what?"

She closed her eyes, trying to replay the night as if it were a videotape.

"I came inside and called out for Rosa. Just habit. I knew she had the night off, but sometimes her daughter is out of town or something and she stays here." She stepped forward, reliving that night. "I noticed that she had left the lights on in the kitchen, and it made me angry because she is kind of absentminded sometimes. I hate to waste electricity, you know."

"I know." Everyone knew about her sense of thrift. "Then what?"

"Then I went to the wine rack and picked out a nice Merlot. I . . ."

"Did you do anything on the way, like put down your purse, make any phone calls?"

"Not that I remember."

"OK, you go back to the kitchen and . . ."

"Wait a minute! That's when I heard him the first time. I forgot about it, but I was walking down the hall" — she followed recollection — ". . . and I heard something on the stairs. I called out for Rosa again, but there was no answer. Must have been that son of a bitch getting ready for me."

"What did you do next? Did you go right upstairs?"

"I poured a glass of wine, and . . . I went upstairs for my bath. I'm a creature of habit. You know that. I have my bath every night after work."

"So, you go upstairs. Show me."

She led him to the second floor. There was a sitting room at the top of the stairs, then two bedrooms on the right, the master bath on the left, and her room just beyond it. The guest bath and a fourth bedroom lay farther down the hall, with Paul's secret room accessible through what appeared to be a closet door. A back staircase led down to the kitchen.

"I went into my bedroom first, to lay down my things, had a sip of wine, then went into the bathroom, turned on the water, and sprinkled in my salts." She actually went through the motions. "Then I went into my dressing room to, you know, get ready." She felt uncomfortable saying the word *undress* in front of staff. "I had just taken off my suit when something caught my eye."

"What did you do?"

"I started to turn toward it, but my cell phone rang, so I went in to answer it."

"Where was it?"

"In my briefcase, on my bed." She pointed just off to her left, through the dressing room door to an antique mahogany four-poster. "I picked it up and answered it."

"Did you tell the police?"

"No, I had forgotten until just now. Amazing how things come back over time."

"Who was it? Who was on the phone?"

Beechum thought for a moment. "I think it was the White House. Some staffer saying they'd rescheduled a meeting with the National Security Council, changed the time. It must have been a new kid, because I didn't recognize the voice, and he mentioned Starfire."

"That's a very close-hold program. You sure he mentioned it by name?"

"Yes. Yes, he did. I remember thinking he was going to get his ass chewed for talking over an open line. I'm sure NSA picked up on it right away, but I never heard anything about it."

Wheels started to spin in his head. "What did you do after that?"

"Well, the tub was getting full at that point, so I walked into the bathroom to turn it off."

"Were you still on the phone?"

"No, I hung up on the way in." She retraced her steps, trying to remember just what she had done and when. She mimed the process, starting to feel the nausea that came for her that night. "And then I . . . you know . . . took off my . . ." James nodded, saving her the indignity. "I put my finger in the water to test it."

"What about the phone? Where is the phone at this point? On the bed?"

She thought a moment.

"No, it was still in my hand, I think. It's all so hard to remember now." She thought for a moment. "The water was still too hot, and I wanted to call the office and leave you a message so we wouldn't forget to file a complaint against that NSC staffer."

"Did you call?"

"No, that's when they . . . he attacked me from behind. He came out of the dressing room." She turned quickly around, as if the breath on her neck were still hot. James could see this was getting very difficult, but there was no better option. The clues lay in her recollection.

"And the next thing you knew, you were waking up on the floor."

"Right. That's when everything really got . . ."

"That's when you found the gun?"

"I got up and slipped . . . I fell on something sharp, then saw the gun."

"Fell on something sharp? What was that?"

"It was the phone. I must have dropped it when they attacked me."

James rubbed his lips between his thumb and forefinger.

"Do you have your phone records for that night? You know, your cell phone bill?"

"Sure. It's in my desk. I've already paid it."

"Get it. Get the bill."

He followed her into the bedroom, where she retrieved an envelope stamped with Borders Atlantic's distinctive logo. James pulled it open and ran his finger down the list of numbers.

"It says here, Senator, that you placed a one-minute call to our office at 7:01 PM. I thought you said you didn't call."

"I didn't."

"Did you dial the number while you were testing the water?"

"I could have, I guess. I don't remember. I can't really remember."

James thought a moment. "Let me see your phone. Can I see it?"

"Well, I don't have the actual phone. They took it as evidence . . . it was covered in blood. But I have a new one in the same model."

"Like this?" he asked. He pulled out his own and held the sleek, tiny device in the palm of his hand. Beechum nodded.

"Choke me," he said, quickly punching a number into the keypad. Something had dawned on him. "Choke me from behind, the way he did. Go ahead — as hard as you can!"

At six foot one, Beechum towered four inches above her A.A. She stepped behind him and wrapped her arm around his throat.

"Squeeze, goddammit!" he commanded.

Beechum squeezed, suddenly consumed again with all the rage and fear and helplessness that had taken her that night. She levered her arm against his larynx, lifting him up onto his toes, forcing him to instinctively reach up and fight the pressure. His palm closed around the phone as he clawed at the senator's powerful grip, bang-ing his hands against her arm. Then he slumped down to the floor, pretending to pass out. His arms fell limp, and the phone tumbled out onto the thick Persian rug.

"I'm sorry, James! Are you all right?"

Her A.A. reached out for the phone and lifted it to his ear. "Listen to this," he said.

Senator Beechum took the cell and listened as the recording from her office phone mail played through the receiver.

"That's your sixty-second phone call." James climbed to his feet. "When you fought that man, you must have accidentally pushed the Send button. You did call the office after all."

"How does that help us?" Beechum asked.

A smile broke out across James's face as he fixed his tie where her choke hold had skewed it. "It means you had an open line during the attack. If we can find a record of this call in the office, we just might have a blow-by-blow account of everything that happened."

▉

JEREMY WOKE JESÚS from a restless slumber at five forty-five the next morning. They dressed, packed, and waited downstairs for a car. Powell was scheduled to fly back up to Sanaa, so once they checked out of the hotel, they were on their own.

Jesús said almost nothing to him until they arrived at the Golden Mahore, a beautiful oasis set oddly between the trash-strewn hills around Aden and the cerulean Straits of Yemen.

"See that tent up on the hill?" Jesús mumbled beneath the sound of the clanking diesel engine. Jeremy nodded. Two soldiers sat alongside a road leading up to a mountain ridge 400 feet above the harbor. "SAM battery. Russian made. These assholes locked on to our C-5 with it when we came here in 2000 to work the *Cole* bombing."

"Really?" Jeremy asked. He remembered reading in the papers about how well the Yemeni government had cooperated with investigators. "I thought they were on our side."

"One thing you gotta know about working in a place like this is that everybody is your friend and everybody is your enemy, depending on who's paying the bills. This hotel is the first place alal-Bin ever bombed. His mother is a Yemeni, but allegiance is a Western concept. These guys would fuck their brother if they thought it would get them what they wanted."

Jeremy nodded. Working bank robbers in Springfield, Missouri, had been a whole lot different from this.

"One more thing," Jesús said. "You're a deaf-mute today." The driver pulled up to three ratty-looking vans and a bunch of Westerners packing gear into them. "Use your cover name and whatever shit you want to make up about your life back in the world, but remember, the more you say, the more chance you've got of screwing up. We cool?"

"We're cool." Jeremy nodded.

All that stuff Les Mason said in the classroom during graduation was starting to make sense. His role in this mission was to listen, follow orders, and keep his mouth shut until advised to the contrary. Someone a whole lot farther up the food chain was obviously calling the shots.

SIRAD SLEPT WELL, got up late, and took a full two hours in the spa. Mitchell had booked her and Bartholomew into lavish suites at the Ritz-Carlton, hoping to demonstrate that the telecom slump hadn't affected Borders Atlantic quite as much as the rest of the industry. She took advantage of the gesture, ordering a Dead Sea mud bath and a full facial.

Chris called for her just after noon and escorted her to a car waiting outside. She could tell by the look on the concierge's face that she'd worn the right clothes. This may have been the Middle East, but men were men no matter what religion they hid behind.

Twenty minutes later, they arrived at the Royal Dubai, a five-star hotel steeped so heavily in excess that she wondered if they had somehow landed in Las Vegas. Bentley Continentals and Aston Martins lined the fountained driveway. Discreetly caged Bengal tigers strolled around lush gardens. Security guards in expensive suits and earpieces manned the inner perimeter, leaving the grounds to military men wearing neatly pressed uniforms and carrying submachine guns. Magnetometers and X-ray machines screened all guests. The media were kept at a respectful distance, with pool cameras designated for all press conferences and photo ops.

Everything was gold plated, from the fountain pens at the registration kiosk to the fixtures in the lobby restrooms. This place was rich, and it was locked down. If you weren't on someone's list, you weren't coming in.

"How do you feel?" Bartholomew asked as they walked from the magnetometers toward a predesignated conference room. Sirad wore a silk Hermès skirt with a matching V-neck jacket accented by white lapel striping and a vintage lapis gather brooch. She wore her hair pulled back in a style common to Arab women she had seen in the airport mall. She had applied light makeup and carried a Louis Vuitton clutch that complemented her black leather briefcase.

"Like Cleo-fucking-patra," she said. If there was a single set of male eyes that didn't engage her as she walked, they were gay. "Did you get the other phone to the interior minister?"

"All taken care of. Our tech guys have been here for a month making sure all the mumbo jumbo electronic shit is up and running. You stick to the script, and we'll take care of the logistics."

They found Amoud, the prince's public relations flack, outside the Jahira conference room. His Highness had agreed to meet them for fifteen minutes on his way from the Board of Governors conference to lunch, he said. All the groundwork had been laid. Prince Abdullah would call the interior minister from his new Quantis phone, as scheduled, and then pose for press photos afterward.

Both parties understood the symbolic importance of this meeting. Large sections of the Middle East were isolated without phone service, effectively stifling productivity, education, and cultural awareness. This new Quantis SBT relied on a network of low Earth orbit satellites — not the traditional series of ground-based repeater stations — making SBT cheaper and more reliable than other existing systems. The infrastructure and networking hardware were already in place, and soon Borders Atlantic's new system would establish Saudi Arabia as the communications hub of Islam. It would also hand the Crown Prince proprietary control over secure communications among his very wealthy and highly security-conscious neighbors.

"Please remember to refer to His Highness as Your Majesty,"

Amoud said, leading Sirad and her escort into the conference room. "Prince Abdullah speaks perfect English, but you will communicate through a translator for obvious diplomatic and political reasons."

Sirad nodded her head. Appearances meant everything here.

"His security detail will come in before he arrives," Amoud continued. "Do not move unless they tell you to move. His Majesty will stand there, near the dais, but his security minister will address you by name, in English, and welcome you to Dubai. You will walk only as far as his staff beckons. I don't know exactly how they will arrange for you to pass him this phone. Do you have it with you?"

Sirad nodded and touched her briefcase.

"Good. You may answer questions if he asks any of you, but please don't speak unless he addresses you first. It is highly unusual for a woman to be involved in matters like this here."

Sirad had heard enough of this officious lackey's directives.

"Thank you, but we are investing billions in a sand pit that no one else will touch with a ten-foot goddamned pole." She smiled broadly, nodding her head to gawkers passing by for the second or third peek. "The only prince I would ever suck up to lives in Minneapolis and wears purple Spandex jumpsuits. Unless your buddy can sing R & B, I suggest you try selling this shit to someone else. As far as I'm concerned, this is nothing but a high-dollar ass-sniffing."

Amoud stared at her. In his country, women would barely dare speak to him, let alone throw insults with such audacious disrespect. How dare she?

Sirad turned to Bartholomew, who looked almost as shaken as Abdullah.

"I hope this goes quickly," she whispered. "'Cause I have to pee."

∎

BY THE TIME Jesús and Jeremy arrived at their base camp in Hadramawt, both men had begun to feel the effects of jet lag. Even with Ambien and a night in a decent hotel, this blitz of a mission had worn them to a thin sinew of ambition.

The trip through Anisi had been uneventful. There was some small talk on the way to the airport, but the helicopter ride was too noisy for conversation. The whole scene had played out entirely in character, complete with stage names and props.

"Wonder how the Yankees are doing," was the only reference anyone made to America, and the topic died quickly. Neither Aljazeera nor the BBC carried baseball scores.

They arrived in late afternoon at a high mountain pass overlooking the Bashar Valley. One side of the mountain range sloped down to desolate desert lowlands. The other spilled into the country's only real cropland, a sparse cluster of villages with enough springwater to sustain vegetable fields and citrus groves. Jeremy saw little risk of compromise. Their archaeological expedition had been carefully backstopped with everything from academic credentials to government payoffs. Besides, there was no one around to watch them; with the exception of two Medieval-looking hamlets along the way, Hadramawt looked like the dark side of the moon.

The team unpacked the Land Rovers and set up camp in less than an hour. By midafternoon, Jeremy and Jesús had pitched their tent, helped arrange the cooking equipment, and dug a latrine. While all the others rested in the shade, they gathered what they would need for a night out and prepared for a private excursion.

"We'll be back in a few hours," Jesús said when they were ready. He tapped Jeremy's shoulder and nodded to the guards, who simply shrugged and filled their mouths with another charge of khat. They were paid to ride shotgun and sit at base camp in case bandits wandered in — why worry about a couple overzealous scientists?

Jeremy and his team leader left on foot, carrying water, an MRE, GPS locators, and a small black box that Jesús insisted on lugging himself. It was the latest thing in soil testing equipment, he said, when asked about it by one of the seismologists.

The camp bid them farewell as they trudged off into the mountains. "Dedicated buggers, aren't they," one man observed as they disappeared into the blistering sun.

▌

BY THE TIME Beechum and James got back to the office, Millie, the receptionist, had already found two boxes of the microcassettes used to record off-hour calls. Though most of America had converted to digital systems, Beechum refused to discard perfectly good tape machines at taxpayers' expense. She rummaged through them as the rest of the staff searched frantically for others.

"What do we got?" the senator hollered, bursting through the door. This was the first time in two months that she had entered Dirksen 3612 without a feeling of dread.

The place was a mess. Closet doors lay open, exposing stacks of old boxes, discarded office equipment, and mold-covered coffee cups that hadn't been washed in weeks. File drawers hung on their rails as members of her staff rifled through them, looking for anything with magnetic tape.

"We've found two boxes of tapes," Millie said. She looked overwrought to the point where her hands were flying up and down in wild gesticulation. "But we're missing a few cassettes."

"What few?" James asked. Beechum couldn't bring herself to ask the question. "Do you have it or don't you?"

James knew they had to have the tape. He oversaw every aspect of office operations. Hell, he'd started out as a receptionist almost fifteen years earlier, when he was a college intern. Taking a microcassette tape out of the machine every morning and storing it in a box just didn't seem all that difficult.

"Well, no, not exactly," the receptionist said. You could see the life draining back out of the senator's face. "But I remember it. I remember hearing something that morning and thinking it was some kind of crank call."

"What do you remember?" Beechum asked. She walked toward her receptionist and clutched her flailing hands. Beechum looked as if she wanted to choke the answer out of the woman.

"We're all excited. Calm down and think. What did you do with that tape?"

"Well, we were all so upset that morning with what happened, you know . . ."

James grabbed a cardboard Memorex box off her desk and started thumbing through the tiny plastic boxes. Each had a date marked in pencil and an occasional note, like "Gray Panthers," or "AFL-CIO."

Any caller with an organizational affiliation got highlighted for immediate response.

"I remember coming into the office and seeing that the phone lines were just flooded. You know, everyone wanted information. So I asked some of the kids out back to help answer the calls, and I pulled the recorder tape, like I always do. That's the first thing I do every morning, even before I make the coffee. I thought maybe you had called in, you know . . . sick or something."

She could see that the senator wanted an answer now, and that made her even more nervous. Her hands started flailing again.

"But then I realized that I couldn't listen to the tape if I'd already pulled it, so I put it back in the machine and pressed Play."

Tears started to well up in her eyes as she realized what she had done.

"And I heard these voices, men's voices, like, in the background, you know? And then some yelling and . . . it sounded like loud bangs. And then it went *click,* and there was this reporter from some newspaper. All the calls were from reporters or . . ."

"What did you do with the tape? Where is it?"

"Well, that's just it . . . I thought it was all crank calls and reporters, and I was upset about the senator and mad that everyone was calling, and it was Fourth of July weekend, and then the phone kept ringing and . . ."

"What did you do with the goddamned tape?" James demanded.

The receptionist burst into tears and slumped in the chair behind her desk.

"It's OK, dear," Beechum said. She walked over to the broken woman and wrapped a motherly arm around her shoulder. "Did you throw it away?"

"I must have left it in the machine," she sobbed. "I . . . think . . . we . . . recorded over it."

Beechum reached down to the woman's desk and picked up a microcassette labeled "7/2."

"I'm so sorry, Senator," the woman cried. "You're going to jail, and it's all my fault."

Beechum bristled at the jail statement, but there was no point in causing this woman any more suffering. "It's going to work out just fine," she said. No other words came to her.

She walked into her office and closed the door. Seconds later, there was a knock.

"Can I come in?"

The door cracked open, and James poked his head through. He looked even more devastated than Beechum.

"It's cruel, you know?" Beechum asked. She had got so excited at the prospect of an alibi. The call had been made. At least one person outside that bathroom had heard it.

"Maybe we can get someone to look at the tape. They might be able to uncover the first message. Labs can do amazing things with . . ."

"James. Hope is good. False hope is worse than despair." She didn't mean to sound like a greeting card, but sometimes Father's words just popped into her head. Like all farmers, he'd suffered his share of ups and downs.

"I'm sorry, Elizabeth," he said. "I'm really sorry."

Both of them sank into chairs and stared into the hopeless tangle that their lives had become. Suddenly, a smile appeared on James's face. His eyes swelled wide open. "Echelon."

Beechum heard him, but the word didn't register. The gravity of this disappointment made it difficult to formulate a cogent thought.

"There's another tape."

"What?" she asked.

"Another tape. You told me that the staffer who called you used the word *Starfire*."

Beechum looked up at him. Something deep down had registered.

"Starfire is one of the most highly classified programs before the committee. It's got to be a trigger word. Anybody mentions that in a phone call and Echelon is bound to pick it up."

Beechum felt her heart start to beat again. She should have thought of it earlier. For years, the National Security Agency's Fort Meade computers had sifted the airwaves with a sophisticated program called Echelon. This space-age eavesdropping technology allowed them to identify specific words in phone and radio transmissions, words that might link one of the callers with a country, program, classified operation, or weapon. It was one of the most productive tools in the history of intelligence gathering, and if James was correct, it might save her career.

"What if he called from a landline?" she asked. Echelon worked over open-air transmissions. Most domestic landlines, like those from the White House, wouldn't register.

"He called your cell phone. There had to be an open-air transmission somewhere."

"That would have gotten a hit for the first call, but I hung up. There was nothing in the call I accidentally made here."

The mood swings that followed these logic twists made her light-headed.

"They bracket calls. You know that. Once a call hits, the number becomes a target."

"What about . . ."

"Goddammit, Elizabeth!" James jumped out of his chair. "Are you going to second-guess this thing to death, or are we going to get the hell out to Fort Meade and listen to some tapes?"

He checked his watch: 3:15 PM. "If we hurry, we can beat traffic."

Beechum stood, too, but she looked a little less than excited.

"What I was going to say is that they have taken away my top secret clearance. The NSA isn't going to let me through the damned gate, let alone into one of those analyst's cocoons."

That gave James pause, but only long enough to remember where he'd put his car keys.

"They haven't taken mine. Besides, you're the primary reason they have Echelon." She had fought hard to get the program funded when everyone else claimed it was some Star Wars–era money pit.

"Good point," Beechum agreed. "I want to see the man who has guts enough to tell me I can't listen to my own phone calls."

XV

WALKING PROVED TOUGH the first couple miles. Jesús estimated their altitude at six thousand feet, but the altimeter he carried fixed it closer to seven. The blistering sun sent heat prickles up and down their arms. Crumbling rock and a total lack of landmarks made their GPS navigation a stark and viewless plod.

"We've got three miles to go," Jesús said when they stopped after almost two hours of hiking. He pulled out his map and pointed to a village called Hemphi. "Here's your brief. Six months ago, a Dutch journalist working for the *New York Times* walked up to the U.S. embassy in Islamabad claiming he had just returned from Karachi. He said he had been working on a story about possible complicity by the Inter Services Intelligence Agency in the Danny Pearl kidnapping. Remember him?"

Jeremy nodded.

"This guy from the *Times* claimed to have been taken to some safe house where a bunch of former Taliban soldiers showed him a file. They supposedly had fought alongside al Qaeda forces in Tora Bora. They said they had helped escort alal-Bin out of Afghanistan, into

Pakistan, and down through Baluchistan to Karachi, where he bought his way onto a Liberian freighter. Alal-Bin's protection detail told them he was going to Somalia, but one of the men saw a bill of lading that showed a destination of Aden, Yemen."

"We came all the way out here based on that?" Jeremy asked. Criminal cases sometimes spun on sketchy information, but this sounded very thin.

"The RSO in Islamabad passed the intel on to Langley, which worked up a full press with NSA communications intercepts and National Reconnaissance Office satellite imagery. They make seventy-thirty odds that alal-Bin, two wives, a dozen kids, and a light security element are holed up in a cluster of houses five clicks due east, over that ridge." He pointed off to the right.

"You got to be fucking kidding me." Jeremy looked around. "We've got a hard fix on one of the most wanted men on the face of the Earth, and they sent the two of us to get him? Maybe I'm missing something here, Jesús, but what are you smoking?"

Jeremy had never complained during selection. He had put up with all the FBI's ridiculous paperwork and career ladder–climbing empty suits from headquarters. He hadn't even balked at running into a Puerto Rican firefight without body armor, but this was beginning to stretch his patience.

"We've got no weapons, no night-vision gear, no air support . . . you think they're going to let us walk down there, shake their hands, and invite that asshole back to America for a little ride in the electric chair? What do we do when they start shooting, throw rocks at them?"

Jesús finished his first bottle of water and stood up to leave.

"Grab your shit," Jesús said. "We got an hour to get into position."

❚❚

SIRAD HAD PLENTY of time to reconsider her arrogant attack on Amoud. Crown Prince Abdullah's meeting took longer than expected, which meant that she had to sit inside the huge, empty conference room with Chris, a host of security guards, and one pissed-off public relations rep. There was no doubt that her cracks about the Saudi prelate had soured the diplomatic stew. For a time the room fell so quiet, she could hear the fluorescent lights humming twenty feet above her head.

"I like your shoes," she finally ventured to Amoud.

"Bally," he said, sensing her more conciliatory tone. "They're Swiss."

"How long have you worked for His Majesty?"

"Seven years. I attended Harvard, where I rowed crew; then I returned home to work for the Interior Ministry."

"*You* rowed crew at Harvard?" She smiled. Amoud cocked his head, trying to understand what she meant by the obvious slant. He had received the finest private American education since high school at Phillips Exeter. Why would she . . .

"Attention, please!" someone called out. "His Majesty has just arrived. Please prepare yourselves to attend in his audience."

Just then, a front man, higher up the pecking order than Amoud, broke through the door. He was early to midforties, meticulously groomed, and wore a hand-tailored English suit in cobalt blue. He walked with the measured gait of a cricket player wielding too much bat and too little shoe.

"Ms. Malneaux," he stated. Though they had never met, this man seemed to know his newest business associate intimately. In fact, he had already scoured Borders Atlantic's current prospectus, studied Sirad's security précis, and solicited the comments of numerous trade partners. The prince expected full disclosure.

"How do you do?" Sirad asked, extending her hand. Amoud backed up a step and joined Chris by the audiovisual cart, relegating himself to window dressing. Harvard crew or not, his position in the Interior Ministry apparently didn't rate a speaking role in the Prince's entourage.

"His Majesty will be here momentarily, but I just wanted to run a couple things by you before we begin."

Sirad nodded, summoning her most devastating smile. He ignored it.

"We are running a little late, so let me . . ."

Suddenly the doors opened and a wall of bodyguards, attendants, policy wonks, protocol experts, diplomats, and sundry royal hangers-on descended on the room. The media followed deferentially — more so than any self-respecting journalist would offer in the West — and there amid the crowd stood one rather large and tented prince. His jet-black mustache contrasted brilliantly with the flowing white robes, a dashing Arab sirocco.

"Yes, yes, Ms. Malneaux," he said, streaming toward her like a locomotive at the head of a thirty-car train. He stopped the impossible momentum just an arm's length from her, no longer among the crowd but in front of it.

"I am Prince Sifir bin Adin Faisal Abdullah, a trusted friend of your Jordan Mitchell and an ally of the United States," he said in the perfect English Amoud had claimed he would not stoop to. "Welcome to the land of Allah."

▮

JESÚS STOPPED FIFTY minutes later, just below the crest of a jagged arête where two enormous limestone boulders had collided to form a sheltered arch. He ducked into the shadows, checked his watch, and yanked a water bottle out of his pack.

"We there?" Jeremy asked. His legs burned from the steep ascent. Dehydration and altitude had already taken a toll.

"Let's take a look," Jesús said. He reached into his pack and pulled out a set of Burris binoculars fitted with magnification doublers. Both men were breathing hard against the thin air and the exertion.

"Shoot me a coordinate," he said.

Jeremy punched two buttons, locking his GPS locator into any two of many geosynchronous satellites floating around one hundred miles above their heads. Five years ago, the technology in his hands would have cost $100,000 and carried a Secure Compartmented Information, or SCI, handle. Now you could get it for opening a Christmas account at a local bank.

"Got it," Jeremy said. He took the geological survey maps out of his own pack and marked one of the laminated sheets with a grease pencil.

"Now shoot me a reverse azimuth to that cluster of buildings down there."

Jeremy looked out through the low-hanging rock arch and down a gradual mountainside that stretched out to deep green fields almost a mile below. Halfway between the end of the mountain and the beginning of the fields sat a half dozen crudely constructed huts.

"I've got one hundred eighty-seven degrees magnetic with a seven-degree declination," Jeremy said. Jesús nodded.

"That's it. We're here."

Jeremy pulled out some binoculars and focused them on what appeared to be five mud huts with thatched roofs. Two new-looking Toyota Land Cruisers sat just off to the side. A bunch of kids were playing with sticks near a well. He could just make out some taller figures clustered around a table, probably men. The mirage made it very difficult to see, especially with the high-magnification lenses on the Burris glasses.

"Look, I've been trying not to ask questions and just do my job," Jeremy said, "but I've got to tell you — this whole thing is starting to bother me."

Jesús had pulled the mysterious black box out of his pack and was trying to fashion a level surface out of fallen rock.

"What do you want to know?"

"I want to know what we're doing out here, man, because I'll tell you — there ain't a paycheck big enough to make me sneak down through a mile of open terrain to get this bastard by myself."

Jesús shook his head. "We're not going to bring alal-Bin back to the States. We're going to kill him."

"Kill him? In what fucking reality?" Jeremy regretted questioning his team leader before the words passed his lips, but it was too late to take them back now.

"If you've got a problem with my orders, you can walk your righteous ass back to camp right now," Jesús said. He showed no signs of humor.

"I don't have a problem with your orders," Jeremy said, backpedaling. "I just meant . . . two of us? We don't even have any weapons. And since when does the FBI kill people in foreign countries?"

Jesús reached into the box and pulled out a small tripod-mounted device that looked like a small black lunch box. "Times have changed," he said. "We don't wait for terrorists to target us anymore. We target them. All you have to know is that the people who put you here have already taken care of the politics — and they expect you to do your job."

Jesús held out the small device. "As for weapons, this is all we're going to need. Don't ask me how it works — all I know is that it's silent, accurate, and kills without leaving a ballistic signature. Once it gets dark, we're going to stalk in to within one hundred meters of alal-Bin's hooch and set it up."

He adjusted a dial on the side of the innocuous-looking device.

"Next time that cocksucker bends over to thank Allah for helping him butcher Americans, he's going to get a message from heaven right up his raghead ass."

▍▍

ALSAM ALAL-BIN had never really taken the threat of American ret-ribution seriously, even during the war in Afghanistan. He had used his vast wealth to organize the world's widest-reaching terror net-work and had repeatedly humiliated the United States in spite of its vast military machine. It didn't matter that his health had grown poor and frail at this point in his life; he had accomplished what he set out to do. History honors the true revolutionaries who change the world, and he had certainly secured his position as a chapter heading among the volumes on war.

"Your dinner is ready, husband," Liah called to him.

Despite his notoriety as al Qaeda's heir apparent and one of the world's nastiest terrorists, alal-Bin still rose before dawn to pray, put his pants on one leg at a time, and ate his meals when his wives cooked them. The U.S. government may have tried to paint him as an elusive and devilish mastermind, but alal-Bin knew himself to be just a man. He got sick. He felt fear. He sometimes wept with des-peration. But in the end, he was a warrior, and this was a holy war to preserve all that Allah had promised. His people had been fight-ing together for more than fifteen hundred years. He'd continue this war until they killed him; then he would pass it off to his sons. The infidels would never win, even if they fought another thousand gen-erations.

"Father! Father! Look!" one of his sons yelled. The eight-year-old child ran by him with an AK-74, the smaller carbine version that young warriors found easier to carry. Yassir, one of the senior personal guard, had disabled the gun so the boy couldn't harm himself. This was a boy, after all, and no matter how much his heart raced for battle, it would take three or four years before he was ready to take up jihad.

"Your meal is here, my son!" alal-Bin called out. "Come to the table!"

His men ate by themselves, but his family always gathered around to take their sustenance and give thanks to Allah. It was a brutal and thankless life he had been handed, but God had been good to him and his disciples. He had wealth, fame, millions of devoted followers, and a certain place at heaven's table. How many men could claim such things?

Alal-Bin gathered with his last two wives and what was left of his children — the others had died or been lost in the Afghanistan bombing — around a crude cypress table. He bowed his head and blessed the food; then he began to eat.

"So, tell me, Father," his oldest son asked, "when will we see this new weapon that you say will help us bring down the eagle?"

Muhammad was a tall, powerfully built twenty-one-year-old with bright black eyes like his Saudi mother. Alal-Bin had seen the boy fight in Afghanistan, and it had made him proud. If not for the B-52 bombs and the missiles, al Qaeda and their Taliban hosts would have crushed the Northern Alliance under their boots like rotten pomegranates.

"You can see it now, of course," alal-Bin said, laying down his flat bread and reaching into his pocket. One of his couriers had delivered the remarkable device in a food shipment from Najran just hours earlier.

He pulled out a light-gray, credit card–size cell phone from his shalwar. It had the words *Borders Atlantic* embossed across the top and the word *Quantis* written in the lower right corner.

"What is this?" Muhammad scowled. "Some kind of phone? How will something so small help our fighters carry the jihad?"

"Small?" alal-Bin responded, trying not to raise his voice to a son much stronger than he. "We killed three thousand with box cutters! Jihad is not about doomsday devices, Muhammad; it is about smiting our enemies with weapons they cannot see. They look for nuclear weapons and chemicals and germs — but we give them shadows and air. Shadows and air. You will see."

Alal-Bin ate a few bites, chewing his food and listening for signs that his men had finished outside. Shadows and air were about all he had these days. Sure, he had men in America, but most of them lived in ramshackle apartments and earned their operations money with credit card scams and petty thievery. The intelligence agencies like the FBI and the CIA didn't want to confess that they couldn't stop a loosely aligned band of loners, so they dreamed up grand stories to make him look worthy of their efforts.

The media made it all possible, of course. The smallest attack triggered a chain reaction of terror that spread twenty-four hours a day to places he never could have reached, even with the most intrepid suicide martyr. Television was everywhere, from the poorest neighborhood to the Situation Room at the White House, and it, not bombs, was his greatest weapon. It spread horrifying images over and over again, creating a whole psychological shift in the way people looked at America's dominance.

A pipe bomb was over in seconds, but the footage would last for days. The talking heads — those so-called experts who actually knew nothing about him or his operations — would spread their fear and uncertainty. Then would come the politicians, spending billions of dollars on airport security and intelligence operations and lawsuits filed by citizens against the very government that was trying to protect them. The businessmen would yank back their investments, fearing economic downturn. Ultimately, the West would waste billions that they could have used to build schools and highways and hospitals.

"Never forget that our greatest weapon is the enemy's capitalistic greed." He took the phone back from his son and held it up like a chalice. "The Americans have brought the Saudis a new technology — these cell phones, which work off satellites like our NMARSAT yet are cheap enough for peasants to own."

"So they can spread more Western culture through Islam," Muhammad groused. "Western decadence. Further proof that the House of Saud is really nothing more than a lackey to the American president."

"Wait," alal-Bin cautioned. "Use your mind, not your heart. Remember what I said about shadows and air, and be smarter than your adversary. These new phones allow secure communication — so secure not even the NSA computers can listen to us. They give us the communications system we need to bring our forces back together. The American government has fought very hard to prevent this company from selling its technology. We have strong intelligence about efforts to prevent its release. Many newspaper articles. Many television reports."

Alal-Bin permitted himself a slight grin. This is why he would always enjoy advantage over the infidels. They worshipped greed and profit above all else, selling him what he needed, ignoring the possibility that he would try to use it against their families. Wall Street traders and telecom tycoons and local Chamber of Commerce presidents — these were his associates, whether they knew it or not.

"What if this is true? So how do we use it?" Muhammad asked.

"We have a major operation just about to begin." He smiled. It had been months in the planning. "It will make you very proud. You will see."

FORT MEADE, MARYLAND, claims many distinctions, including the highest concentration of mathematicians in the country, the second-highest electricity bill in the state, and the most sophisticated signals intelligence–gathering operation in the world. The reason was simple, if little known: Fort Meade is home to the National Security Agency, a highly secretive arm of the Defense Department. The NSA accounts for the largest single chunk of money among all agencies funded through the Intelligence Appropriations Bill.

Elizabeth Beechum and her A.A. turned east off the Baltimore-Washington Parkway onto an odd, specially built exit ramp that immediately emptied all traffic into a maze of hydraulic ramp gates, razor wire, and concrete Jersey walls. Security cameras covered their movement as James drove past heavily armed men in black jumpsuits and body armor toward a five-sided guard post.

"Welcome to the Black Hole of Annapolis Junction," James said.

Of all the secure government installations he had visited with Senator Beechum, this one left him most uneasy.

"Careful." Beechum smiled. "You know they're listening."

"Crypto City," as it was known in-house, struck her as something out of one of those 1970s spy shows in which everyone rides around in golf carts pretending to have a name like John or Jane. This entire culture lay hidden from the rest of the world, a walled community unto itself complete with schools, police and fire departments, movie theaters, and hospitals. It even had its own university, National Cryptologic School.

Without exaggeration, everyone on the NSA compound could have been born, lived his or her entire life, and died without ever stepping foot outside.

Beechum knew as much about the National Security Agency as anyone outside the agency ever could. She had visited Crypto City many times during her years on the Intelligence Committee and would probably one day have had a street or gymnasium or building named in her honor had she not fallen onto hard times. No member of Congress had fought harder to secure funding for projects that many considered frivolous. If not for her backroom politicking, programs like the Cray Y-MP EL supercomputer — which enabled NSA analysts to listen in on and translate vast numbers of microwave communciations — would never have got off the draftsman's table.

Today's visit wouldn't bring out the red carpet or VIP passes, however. Beechum had become persona non grata anywhere a special access badge was needed. The only way James could get her through the gate was by calling an old friend, an air force colonel on his way into retirement who had no problem taking a chance on administrative action. Beechum could get in with one of the Escort Only badges marked with a big red *V.* It might feel a little demeaning considering her background, but she understood.

"James Appleton and Elizabeth Beechum."

James spoke into a fast-food-drive-through-style box. He read off their social security numbers and their contact information. Within a few seconds, a voice told them to proceed, and they drove up to the heavily reinforced guard shack, where a uniformed Department of Defense security officer checked their identification. The guard handed James a site map, a temporary parking pass, and printed security regulations. He saluted the senator and waved them through.

Within minutes, they entered the huge eleven-story Headquarters/Operations Building. It looked like any other corporate office high-rise, with its concrete and reflective glass, but Beechum knew better. This centerpiece of NSA's sixty-building complex was actually nothing but an illusory shell. Like some kind of architectural metaphor, the real structure lay behind the facade — a building within a building. The true edifice was wrapped in copper to seal electronic emissions. It had shock-resistant windows that were specially constructed to deaden sound and prevent eavesdropping.

"No matter how many times I come here, I always think we're in some kind of parallel universe," Beechum said as they walked down the entrance corridor. She'd been to Langley, Camp Peary, Harvey Point, and several overseas facilities, but Fort Meade stood out as another world.

"How do you feel?" James asked. He hadn't had such a knot in his stomach since he asked Jenny Siebert to the senior prom.

"I hope you're as smart as I think you are. Because if the *Washington Post* ends up with a story about me trying to infiltrate the National Security Agency and use my official position to coerce the release of top secret intelligence, they're going to lock me up and throw away the key."

Beechum and her top aide walked up to the main entrance turnstiles.

"They've charged you with murder, boss," he said. "I think they've already decided where to throw the key."

▐█▌

SIRAD STEPPED FORWARD to shake the prince's hand.

"What an honor it is to meet you, Your Majesty," she said. Sirad spoke flawless native Arabic in a strong voice. "I bring the warmest regards from Mr. Mitchell and the entire Borders Atlantic family."

The media jostled back and forth from behind a satin-rope cordon, but none of the entourage moved. None of them dared draw a single breath. This was not part of the script.

"What a lovely suit," the prince said, in English again. The pool cameras rolled, cameras flashed, as his advisers turned their eyes toward one another. Prince Abdullah rarely commented on matters best left to the pages of *French Vogue*, especially during photo ops for trade ventures. "One of my wives would absolutely love one like it."

"Why, thank you," Sirad continued in Arabic. The prince tilted his head, admiring her refined Lebanese accent and the way Sirad's eyes glimmered with the energy of everyone around her. They felt almost hypnotic.

"So, please, tell me about this new venture we start this afternoon," he said. The prince reached out a hand from his starched white robes, as if waiting for a gift.

"Yes, of course," Sirad responded. She held herself board straight, realizing full well that what she said here would play on televisions and financial pages around the world by tomorrow morning. "Borders Atlantic's new partnership with the House of Saud will establish Saudi Arabia as the world leader in telecommunications at a time when information technology means power."

Though she had memorized the script Bartholomew had given her, she sounded as if the words came straight from the heart.

"Our Quantis phone runs on a digitally encrypted transmission technology that allows complete voice and image security at about the same cost as existing systems," she explained. "SBT technology works off our own network of satellites so you do not need expensive repeaters like with conventional cells. Less infrastructure means less maintenance, which means greater profits. And since our system offers broadcast and reception between sixteen hundred and nineteen hundred megahertz, these phones will be completely compatible in virtually all international markets."

The prince nodded and smiled. He knew that, like most of his public appearances, this had been scripted, but he did not seem to mind. Though his aides checked their watches and shot impatient looks, the Saudi leader was in no hurry to leave Sirad's company.

"And we are the first nation in the world to get this!" he bellowed.

"First in the world," Sirad agreed.

"How wonderful! Where is this marvel you have brought me?"

Sirad reached slowly into her bag. She could see the hands hover-ing above holsters and loosely hidden submachine guns all around her. There was so much weaponry in this room, she could smell Hoppes gun solvent over the heavy wash of cologne.

"This is the first SBT Quantis telephone ever used outside our labs," Sirad lied. Several top executives had carried them for months, and according to Chris, they were as common as falafel throughout the Middle East.

"Your Majesty, we have a very tight schedule," another man said. He ranked highly enough that the prince did not wave him down.

"Yes, of course." Abdullah took a beautifully made ebony box from Sirad and opened it to find the Quantis phone Chris had shown her. The case was made from platinum, festooned with square-cut diamonds and emeralds. Engravers had carved the Saudi flag into an onyx insert just above the Quantis logo. It was the only cell phone cover Harry Winston's had ever crafted.

"Thank you, Ms. Malneaux," the Crown Prince said. "And I understand that the honor of the world's first commercial SBT call has been bestowed upon me?"

"Yes, Your Highness." Sirad beamed. "Your interior minister has an SBT phone in Riyadh and awaits word of your success. It's speed dial one. Just press Send."

The Crown Prince broke out in a wide smile. This little ceremony meant more than a photo op with new American partners; it represented a leap forward in mobile communications for Arabs throughout the Middle East. Within weeks, camel traders in Jordan would have access to commodities traders in Chicago. Today marked a whole new era and had his name all over it.

"Hello, Ali!" he called into the phone. "Can you hear me now?"

JORDAN MITCHELL HAD already been at his desk for an hour when Trask entered to tell him the satellite feed was ready. They walked down four flights of stairs to the War Room, where two electronics technicians had just finished sweeping for bugs. Mitchell knew all too well the extent to which his competitors would go to learn his secrets.

"Where are we?" he asked.

Trask pointed a remote control toward the far wall. "The seventeenth floor has synced a video feed of our ground element." Two of Mitchell's floor-to-ceiling display cases slid left and right to reveal audiovisual screens, televisions, and white boards. Most days this telecommunications center offered executives interactive conferencing and PowerPoint slides, but this morning, it would light up with a much more interesting show.

"We've got a positive ID," Trask continued. "The shooters have moved into forward firing positions outside the village."

"Sirad?" Mitchell barked.

"The Crown Prince just placed his call to the interior minister. Word of the deal should be hitting the cable news channels at any moment."

"Excellent."

Mitchell watched as video flickered on three HD-TVs — direct-feed imagery intercepted from a National Reconnaissance Office KH-11 spy satellite as it relayed encrypted intelligence through one of Borders Atlantic's geosynchronous communications birds. Though government intelligence agencies regularly contracted down-feed "bounce" from civilian telecom companies, only Borders Atlantic had broken their codes and accessed imagery. Virtually anything processed through the Army's Tactical Exploitation of National Capabilities Program (TENCAP) could be captured by Mitchell's seventeenth-floor command post, including this — a real-time transmission of two men in Yemen as it was being fed to the Onizuka Air Station in Sunnyvale, California, then on to the CIA's National Photographic Interpretation Center in Washington.

One screen showed a fairly broad shot of what appeared to be five earthen shacks on a desert plain. Two others showed more oblique angles of the same scene, with resolution so clear that Mitchell and Trask could tell what the men were wearing, even in the pale green glow of infrared image enhancers. The figures appeared to be hunkered down in the shadows of two large boulders.

"Which one is Waller?" Mitchell asked. He had seen photos of Jeremy in the dossier. He'd read about him in the HRT selection summaries. He even had photos of the man's family. But none of this did him any good with this surveillance shot.

"The one on the right. See? Smith is shorter and has the NMAR-SAT phone."

He checked his watch. It read 8:17. Dubai was Zulu plus five, nine hours ahead of him and an hour past Yemen. This operation now spanned three time zones, across thousands of miles of curved planet and in direct contradiction to everything scientists thought possible just a few years earlier. But here it was in front of him. Who said money couldn't buy everything?

"So, when will it happen?" Mitchell asked. He liked to wait for nothing.

"There's no way to tell precisely, sir. Within the hour, certainly. We've covered every conceivable variable, but unfortunately, there's no way to harness uncertainty."

Mitchell had personally approved every aspect of the plan, but he knew that despite all the preparation, the billions of dollars, the meetings, the research and development, the risk, and the incalculable benefit in success, this enterprise now rested on human performance — a variable he had never learned to fully control.

◼

JESÚS LAY HIDDEN in the moon shadows of an ancient stone wall, slowly applying camouflage greasepaint to his face and waiting for a command to move. He looked warily at Waller. "So, you got bumped off the list, huh?"

"List? What do you mean?" Jeremy replied, checking to make sure he had adequately covered all exposed skin. He was lying within a stone's throw of one of the world's most dangerous men with nothing but the cover of night to protect him.

"The pool, you know . . . top gun."

Jeremy shook his head. The sheer distance between Lottspeich's pool and this rock-strewn hell seemed impenetrable. "Yeah, well, I got until next Friday to beat him. Think we'll be home by then?"

"We'd better be," Jesús said. He pulled an NMARSAT phone out of his backpack and maneuvered the laptop-style cover to try to line up a satellite. "Anything more than three days on sick leave and you got to get a note from the doctor."

"Note from the doctor? What the hell are you talking about?"

"You took Thursday afternoon and Friday for sick leave. We got to be back by the morning meeting on Monday, or we're fucked."

Jeremy thought for a minute as Jesús set up his hypersonic sound whatever-it-was on a flat rock. He didn't want to make a fool of himself by asking more questions, but this whole thing made no sense at all.

"Help me out here, man. You mean we have to take sick leave to do this shit?"

"What do you think, we're just going to disappear, and nobody's going to ask questions? It's either sick or annual leave, and if you put in for annual leave, you got to list a point of contact and answer the beeper if a gig goes down."

"This doesn't count as a mission? Jesus!"

"*Jesus* like my name, or *Jesus* like you're swearing?"

"Huh?"

"I never know what you assholes are saying when you say 'Jesus.' Got to be a goddamned mind reader with you guys."

Jeremy laid his head back on the boulder as Jesús dialed the phone. This was starting to feel like selection all over again. Either he was just too tired to make sense of everything or he was hallucinating.

"You've done this before, haven't you?"

Jesús nodded his head. "Sierra One in position," he spoke into the phone. "Request compromise authority and permission to move to green."

Jeremy waited until his team leader nodded his head, hung up, and tucked the phone back into his pack.

"Don't feel bad, Waller. I remember the first Delta gig I ever went out on. I'd just gotten assigned to A Squadron, back when Iraq was getting ready to invade Kuwait."

Jeremy lifted his head. Jesús almost never talked about his army days.

"We were prestationed with a bunch of marines on this float off Diego Garcia. My XO came up and pulled three of us for what they said was a plainclothes security detail. Thirty-six hours later, we've got this skinny in a bunker just inside the Iraqi border. Forward-intelligence post. I had the same brief you got on this deal: nothing."

Jesús adjusted himself, trying to find a more comfortable lie on the rocky ground.

257

"So we got this Agency spook with us, a linguist. I hadn't been to DLI yet, so I couldn't understand shit of what was being said. But there was a lot of yelling and some blood. The Agency guy was getting pretty pissed. Didn't seem to be making much progress. So my TL goes outside and gets a Coke bottle full of gasoline. He takes the gas and pours it all over this skinny's boots. I'll never forget it, they were Huskies, you know, the kind they sell at Kmart.

"He tells the Agency guy to ask again. The skinny's eyes start to get big, but he still won't talk. So my TL lights him on fire. I mean the fucker goes up like a gas grill. *Whoosh.*

"And this skinny is too fucking surprised to scream. He just stares for a couple seconds until the flames catch his pants on fire and start to eat through those Huskies. And then he starts to scream. I mean he's really hollering.

"My TL holds up a blanket in one hand and the Coke bottle in the other and shrugs his shoulders, like 'What's it going to be?' And I'll never forget it, this guy starts singing 'Billie Jean.' In fucking English. He's singing a Michael Jackson song with his pants on fire. It was absolutely the craziest goddamned thing I had ever seen in my life."

Jesús shook his head as if it was just one of those things.

"First guy I ever saw lit on fire," he said. "Don't worry about the sick leave, Waller. I'm gonna make sure we get back in time. Now let's get this done. We just got our green."

PHASE III

Down, down, down. Would the fall never come to an end! "I wonder how many miles I've fallen by this time?" she said aloud. "I must be getting somewhere near the centre of the earth."

— *Lewis Carroll*, Alice's Adventures in Wonderland

XVI

ASAM ALAL-BIN FINISHED his dinner, delighted with the day. Though his environs had changed considerably in the past year, he had managed to keep the two things that still mattered to him in the world: his family and al Qaeda. American bombs had decimated huge chunks of Afghanistan and killed thousands of men, but few of them were his. Most of the casualties had been Taliban foot soldiers who couldn't have cared less about jihad. They fought because it was the only thing they knew how to do. Most Afghans were crude, brutish men who had never known peace their entire lives. In a country that lost almost an entire generation fighting the Soviets, this was just a skirmish.

The Americans had forced him out; he couldn't deny that, but it had been a hollow and misleading victory. The American bombs had cornered much of the al Qaeda force, but then to everyone's astonishment, they left the back door open and gave everyone a clear exit into Pakistan. It was such an arrogant and stupid mistake that most of his fighters thought it a trap, but the ambushes never came. They streamed out of Tora Bora and into a country the United States couldn't bomb or invade. Pashtun sympathizers in the northwest frontier province sheltered his men and then smuggled them south the way they had smuggled guns and drugs and stolen merchandise for ages.

Alal-Bin remembered sailing out to a freighter in the Port of Karachi, just five days after leaving Afghanistan. Bush and Rumsfeld had wasted billions trying to bomb blood from stone, while he and his top advisers simply walked away.

"Daddy! Daddy! Daddy! Pow! Pow! Pow!"

Another of alal-Bin's sons ran by with a stick in his hands, playing war the way young boys always have and always will.

"Be careful!" his father yelled. Medical supplies were scarce out here. If the boy stumbled and hurt himself with the stick, it could become a serious problem. "Your mother will beat you if you poke yourself!"

He smiled at the way his children had grown. All his life he had dedicated himself more to the war against the West than to his family, and he sometimes regretted it now. At least they were safe here, and he could spend time with them. Yemen served as the perfect hiding place. It was his mother's homeland, a sprawling desert run by tribal authorities outside the control of any central government. These were his people, cousins and uncles and warlords who understood what he had done for Islam. They revered him as a great Arab warrior. They named their children after him. Martyrs took his image in their pockets when they went out with their bombs.

"Asam!" one of his lieutenants called to him. This man had served him well since the early days, after the Great Sacrifice, when his martyrs brought down the World Trade Center towers and dropped America to its knees. "Asam, is time for your call!"

Alal-Bin walked outside to a crude wooden table where documents laid out all but the most closely held details of the next attack. Two of his top advisers and several members of his security detail stood waiting for news of their grand new venture — a plan alal-Bin himself had code-named "the Wedding."

"Are we ready?" he asked.

One of the advisers — a Yemeni shipping merchant — nodded his head. "The Saudis just announced the agreement with Borders Atlantic," he said. "Our top man in Riyadh just called to verify." This man spoke few words, but what he said carried weight. This merchant maintained important sources in Gulf governments and had the power to move the entire group on a single command.

"Tawakilt al allah," alal-Bin said. *I put my faith in God.* Al Qaeda's considerable intelligence network had approved use of the new phone, arguing that their contacts inside the House of Saud believed it safe.

"Allah huakbar . . ." one of the men began praying in a soft, rhythmic chant. The others joined in. *"Allah huakbar, Allah huakbar . . ."*

Alal-Bin waited until they were done, then reached into his pocket and pulled out the wafer-thin phone. He and his men stared at it a moment, understanding the danger. Despite assurances of its safety and its value as a communications tool, this phone also presented a very real threat. Israeli and U.S. intelligence agencies had hidden explosives in cell phones and used them in assassinations — including one attempt on him.

After an uneasy pause, the phone rang — a scheduled call from a Moroccan national now living in Damascus. Alal-Bin, believing incorrectly that any potential phone bomb had to be triggered by an incoming call, handed the cell to one of the more expendable members of his security detail.

"Yes?" the lieutenant answered. If he felt any apprehension, he concealed it well. "He is here. Please wait."

Alal-Bin took the phone and spoke with a firm, clear voice.

"Hello, hello . . . Fawaz!" he spoke into the receiver.

After a deep breath, the Yemeni shipping merchant offered a brief smile. This phone worked just the way his Saudi contacts had said it would.

"Tell us news of the Wedding," alal-Bin continued. He jotted notes on a scrap of paper as the operative talked, swelling with optimism at the positive developments. This bold plot was coming together nicely. Borders Atlantic's new phone was the answer to his prayers.

▌▐

AMONG THE FOURTEEN autonomous intelligence agencies in the United States, the NSA receives 45 percent of all funding, generates 90 percent of signals-based operations data, and bears almost sole responsibility for electronic encryption and code-breaking tech-nologies. Though the CIA and FBI get most of the credit, the NSA brags privately that it has done more to prevent acts of terrorism against this country than all other competitors combined. It may be right.

"This place always gives me the creeps," James said, standing in the main entrance hallway into the Headquarters/Operations Build-ing. The two-story entryway spilled into the Visitor Control Center and a bank of access control terminals. A six-foot-high NSA seal cov-ered most of one wall, with the Agency's logo on the other. All in all, the space around them contained 3 million square feet of locked doors and secrets.

They walked up to a uniformed security guard, who greeted them with an official smile.

"Good afternoon. May I help you?"

A steady stream of employees walked by and stepped through the turnstiles. Everyone wore a badge around his or her neck — blue for secured employees, green for contractors, and a couple dozen other colors for everyone in between.

"That's all right, Fred. They're with me."

An air force colonel in dress uniform carded his way through one of the turnstiles and reached out to shake his guests' hands.

"Colonel Pratt, Senator," he said. "Nice to see you, James."

They exchanged brief pleasantries; then the colonel escorted them through the turnstiles, retrieved their visitors' passes, and walked them to an escalator that led upstairs into the OPS2A building, which houses the Operations Directorate.

The senator had toured most of the campus at one time or an-other, including during an honored appearance at the dedication of the nearby National Security Operations Center. Though they wouldn't have allowed her near room 3E099 in OPS1 now, she re-membered with fascination how an obsession with confidentiality absolutely permeated this place. Goofy-looking posters popped up everywhere, reminding employees not to talk in the halls or bath-rooms or cafeterias. Secrecy still meant something here. She just hoped the colonel had an open mind.

After a lengthy walk, the colonel turned down a corridor that was lined for the first thirty feet with what looked like cheap cubicle dividers laid end to end. Subdued fluorescent light scattered from above and below, lending these odd-looking wall coverings the abstract oddity of avant-garde art.

"I guess I should have asked you to turn off your cell phones and pagers," the colonel said, "but I'm sure you know the drill by now."

Beechum nodded. She remembered when the NSA first developed these odd-looking hallways, or "wave paths," to detect electronic transmission devices.

"Do you people ever end up with extra toes or fingers walking through this every day?" James asked. He was only half kidding.

"Yeah, but they help me type faster." The colonel chuckled.

He stopped at a door marked "3E132," swiped his card, and punched a six-digit access code into a random numerical access pad. The door clicked open, and they entered a cluttered office space that smelled of fresh paint.

"Watch the workmen," the colonel advised. "We've been putting all that new terrorism money to use up here."

They rounded a corner and almost ran into three men laying Sheetrock on walls that apparently hadn't been there when the colonel left to collect his visitors. He shook his head at the confused mess and led his guests down yet another hallway to a room marked "Cryptologic Service Group 4." The colonel swiped his card again and led them onto a platform that looked down on a large room full of civilian personnel, all separated with military precision into dozens of identically spaced cubicles.

The room looked like so many others she had seen on military reservations around the world. A portrait of the president hung on the wall, flanked by slightly smaller mug shots of the secretary of defense and the post commander. The air felt particularly cool and dry. The hum of fluorescent lights, the tapping of keypads, and the whirring of hard drives gave this space the feel of a college computer center.

"Welcome to the Third Eye, Senator," the colonel said. He marched them into a windowed office along the far wall and invited them to have a seat.

"Now, what can I do for you?"

Beechum noticed a copy of *Newsweek* magazine on the man's

desk. Her photo covered the front page, with a headline that read, *MURDER MOST FOUL — WHAT'S BEHIND WASHINGTON'S MOST BIZARRE SCANDAL?*

"I'm sure you know how much this means to us," Beechum said.

The colonel smiled benignly. He well remembered how this senator had secured funding for one of his pet projects despite heavy opposition from rival DIA managers at the Pentagon.

"I'm also sure that what I'm about to tell you will require somewhat of a leap of faith." Beechum had rehearsed this speech a dozen times. "Everything you have read about me is a lie."

She waited for a reaction, but the colonel's face never changed expression. He must have already decided not to believe press reports, or this meeting never could have happened.

"We have discovered that the senator accidentally placed a call from her cell phone the night of the attack," James interrupted. "During the attack, actually. She was in the process of calling our office. The call went through, documenting conversation between at least two men and gunshots. Our receptionist heard the call on her answering machine the next morning but accidentally recorded over it."

"That's extraordinary," the colonel said. He looked pleased. "But I'm not sure how I can help. If you want someone to doctor up that tape, you should go over to the Skunk Works."

"No, that's not it," Beechum said. She couldn't help herself. "I received a call just prior to the attack, from the White House . . . a young Security Council staffer who wanted to tell me about a change in meeting times the next day. He used a particular SCI designator over the phone — the word *Star* . . ." She stopped to consider her own security protocol.

"It's all right, Senator," the colonel replied, nodding. "I have the necessary clearances, I assure you."

"*Starfire,*" she said. "It's an NRO project that is . . ."

"I'm familiar with Starfire," the colonel interrupted. "He used the designator over an open line?"

"That's right," Beechum said. "We need you to check logs and see if it triggered an intercept of his call."

The colonel sat back in his chair and stared at his visitors.

"Senator, I agreed to see you because of what you have done for us for all these years, but you are putting me in one helluva tough spot here. You know federal law prevents us from using Echelon to intercept domestic transmissions. Especially for a member of the United States Senate."

"I know what the law says," Beechum pleaded. "I helped write it. And I know the way things really work. Once the word *Starfire* was uttered, your computers flagged our conversation and recorded it. You marked the electronic serial number on my phone and recorded everything for twenty-four hours afterward. I know that you have a log of my calls and that you can pull up recordings if you want to. If you choose to."

A long silence divided the room. In the ten seconds it took the colonel to answer, he balanced everything he'd been taught about national security with the underlying tenets of right and wrong. Sometimes national security meant more than a manual. Sometimes it meant doing what was just, doing what brought him to the military in the first place.

"I'm not asking for an answer," Beechum said. "I'm just asking you to walk out to any one of those terminals and call up that intercept. Listen to it yourself. Make your own assessment. Someone staged this whole thing to get me off the committee, to get me away from something that has nothing to do with you or NSA or anyone in this building."

The colonel looked straight at her. "You're saying someone framed you."

"No. I'm saying that this is a very complicated issue that I haven't really figured out. All I know is that someone wants me off the Intelligence Committee badly enough to kill a man and put a duly elected member of Congress in prison. You have dedicated your life to protecting this country from abuses like this, Colonel. Help me stop them."

The colonel stared at her a moment, then stood up from his desk.

"If you'll excuse me, I have to use the men's room," he said. "I might be awhile."

Beechum clasped her hands together and bowed her head. She seldom prayed for personal gain, but there was a time for everything.

◼

IT TOOK JEREMY and his team leader a little more than forty-five minutes to cover the rough terrain linking their hiding place to a large boulder sixty meters from the hut cluster. They moved slowly and carefully under 11 percent illumination, right up to where the shadows thinned among man-made light from a white gas lantern and a single generator-powered table lamp.

"This is our rally point," Jesús whispered when they stopped. "If this turns to shit, meet me here."

"What's the exfil?" Jeremy asked. A rally point was fine, but what if he had to get out by himself? Quantico seemed like a long swim.

"The open lot in front of those buildings." Jesús pointed to the east. "We've got birds inbound. If I go down, it's two flashes red to clear the LZ. They'll know where to take you."

Jeremy shook his head as Jesús slipped out of his pack and broke out the odd little box he had shown Jeremy up on the ridge. This trust thing was wearing a little thin.

"What do I do?" Jeremy whispered. He could see alal-Bin — the taller of the men — standing at a table, talking on what appeared to be a cell phone.

"Soon as the last man goes down, we move in, pick up AKs, and move inside to clear the hooch. Remember — we're going in silent to avoid any problems with the neighbors. We don't go loud except as a last resort."

"The last man? I thought we were here for alal-Bin."

"These assholes all look alike to me, Waller. I ain't got time to read fingerprints."

Jesús made a last-minute adjustment to the device and gave Jeremy a thumbs-up. With that, he dialed a number into the NMARSAT, turned toward the men standing around the table, and watched as the little black box did its job. Alal-Bin dropped first, then the man beside him, then the others in rapid succession. Seven of them. No noise. No bullets. No apparent violence at all.

"Holy . . . ," Jeremy started to say, but Jesús was already packing the gear and getting ready to move.

"On me." Jesús jumped up and closed on the dead men with alarming speed. Jeremy ran a half step behind him, reaching down and grabbing an AK off one of the dead men as he moved. He knelt by the table, training his front sight on the hut, waiting for anyone to emerge. It was so quiet that Jeremy could hear someone calling out in Arabic over alal-Bin's cell phone. Women spoke softly inside.

Jesús moved quickly through the bodies, verifying that they were dead, but it seemed obvious. Their faces looked broken and distorted, as if someone had set off bombs in their skulls. Blood pooled in dark splotches around them, draining into the sand.

Jeremy held the corner until Jesús joined him, prickling with adrenaline and fear and a thousand voices screaming in his head that this was the stupidest damned thing he'd ever done in his life. But once Jesús tapped his shoulder, Jeremy quickly lipped the edge of the hut and half a breath later dived into a large common room, muzzle up, finger lightly pressing the trigger. Inside sat four women and a handful of kids. Jeremy didn't bother counting; he was searching for weapons.

No one said a word. Everyone stared.

Then one of the women stood and silently, slowly reached under her burka.

"Do her," Jesús said. He was moving toward one of three doors leading to bedrooms.

"Put your hands up!" Jeremy yelled. "You said we weren't going loud unless . . ."

"Do her, goddammit!" Jesús commanded.

But Jeremy just stared at the faces before him. Women. Children. He couldn't . . .

"*Allah huakbar,*" the woman screamed, violently ripping aside her burka to reveal an AK of her own.

Jesús turned and fired one shot. *BOOM!* It hit the woman under her right eye, pitching her head back and toppling her to the right, into one of the others.

Jeremy recoiled at the sudden burst of violence, but before he could react, movement caught his attention — the muzzle of an

AK-74 poking out from a linen curtain to his right. He spun right, fingering the trigger and shooting all in the same reactive motion.

BOOM! Jeremy's weapon bucked against his shoulder.

The body of a small boy lurched forward from behind the curtain and landed at Jeremy's feet. It skidded up against his leg like one of the ballplayers on his team sliding into second base. The boy's toy rifle — the disabled weapon his father had made him — tumbled forward onto the floor as he dropped and squirted blood.

That's when all reality left them. The room erupted. The other women pulled AKs. More gunshots. *BOOM! BOOM! BOOM!* Screaming. People running. Chaos. Jesús and Jeremy spinning and firing. A black-and-white strobe of muzzle flash and smoke.

Bullets raged through the room, splintering on the wall, dropping bodies, tearing cloth, splattering blood, and severing limbs. Jeremy had no way to tell who was shooting. It was just adrenaline and violence and an overwhelming compulsion to stay alive.

Jesús fired, aimed, fired, aimed. Children ran toward the door, and he shot them. Others fell into the corner. He shot them, too. *BOOM! BOOM! BOOM!* The rifle jumped and breathed fire until everyone was dead. He fired at the corpses anyway, until the weapon was empty and his finger kept slamming against the trigger.

Silence. Everything stopped.

The gas lamps hissed. Flickering light. Jeremy panted for breath.

Jesús stood there heaving, sweat pouring down into his eyes, shaking his head, trying to clear his thinking. The weapons felt blistering hot in their hands. The room reeked of blood and curry and Chanel No. 5 and cordite. Jeremy held the gun at his shoulder for a moment, then dropped it to his waist, watching smoke curl out the end.

Gold chains sparkled in the gaslight. Gold rings and bracelets, sprawled out over the women where they lay. Bright red blood spilled out of the robes onto the earthen floor, still glistening.

"Assholes don't look so dangerous now, do they?" Jesús grunted.

"My God . . . ," Jeremy replied. He didn't recognize his own voice.

Bodies lay all around him. Women and children. Boys and girls. Mothers and daughters and sons.

"Cover the door," Jesús commanded, but Jeremy couldn't move.

The enormity of what he had just done crushed his chest as if a building had fallen upon him.

Jesús crossed to the lamp and shut down the petcock. The mantle died slowly to a dull red glow and then closed them in a horror chamber of black night. Jeremy clamped his hands around his weapon. For the first time in his adult life, he felt afraid of the dark.

■

JORDAN MITCHELL LEANED back in his chair and rubbed his eyes with a trembling hand. He'd waged hostile takeovers of billion-dollar corporations, toppled giants of industry, survived attacks by rivals, but nothing pounded in his chest like the import of what he had just witnessed.

"Well," he said. He stared at the screens, now all dark except for the light-gray IR signatures of dead bodies cooling. No other words came.

Trask shook his head.

"When will they get back?" Mitchell asked.

It took a moment before Trask saw the tiny pinpoints of light in the upper right corners of the blank television screens.

"If everything goes according to schedule, they'll be back by Sunday night." Trask pointed to the heat signatures of jet turbine engines. "That must be the choppers now."

Mitchell knew that every conceivable detail of this plan had been worked out well in advance, including the exfiltration of his ground team, but this day had gone almost impossibly right. Even in his world of meticulous preparation, that made him nervous.

"We've got a lot of money riding on this," he said. He stood and buttoned his suit coat. "I want to know their status every two hours until they hit CONUS."

Then, for the first time in weeks, Jordan Mitchell actually smiled. What he had just witnessed would never appear as an IPO bulletin on CNBC. Though tonight's actions represented one of the loudest market entries in history, this whole thing had played out silently in the two-dimensional distance of black-and-white TV. The irony seemed almost poetic.

▮

SENATOR BEECHUM SAID nothing to her administrative assistant for more than forty minutes. They sat there in the colonel's office staring at mementos of the man's twenty-seven years in the Air Force. He was an Academy graduate and had flown jets, F-14s and -18s, according to large framed photos of his old squadron, the 459th Raptors. Forty-one sorties in Kuwait and Iraq during the Gulf War. A Distinguished Flying Cross in a display case atop a bookshelf, which held row upon row of training and operations manuals for things even Beechum had never heard of.

"Sorry it took so long."

Colonel Pratt stepped back into his office, closed the door behind him, and sat behind his GSA-issued laminated plastic workstation. He folded his hands in front of him and tapped them on the top of his desk a couple times.

"Let's talk hypotheticals here, for a moment." He sighed.

Beechum stared at him like a child in the principal's office.

"Let's say I had a friend who had obviously been done a grievous injustice and I had seen evidence that proved it. The only problem was that divulging the methodology with which I acquired my evidence would cause me significant legal hardships."

Beechum cocked her head, trying to hear the whole thing out before reacting. He was trying to tell her that he had located and reviewed the tape — which cleared her — but that its existence couldn't be admitted.

"Colonel," Beechum interrupted, "I have worked in this business long enough to know the rules and that the rules get broken every day." She let her eyes wander to a file left open on his desk that read "ZARF" — a code word–sensitive classification that was illegal to leave exposed. He noticed and closed the folder.

"I'm listening."

"I'm willing to bet that somewhere among the five trillion pages of information in your database lies the transcript of a sixty-second telephone recording that United States Signals Intelligence Directive Eighteen says never should have been made," said Beechum.

"I'm also willing to bet that the name on that report — my name — has been replaced with an intercept serial number and a generic identifier. If the FBI were to fax a formal request to the U.S. Identities Office, you would be well within your rights to hand over the file."

The colonel thought for a moment, then reached into his drawer and pulled out a thick three-ring binder. He thumbed to a page and read out loud.

"'Intelligence gleaned from domestic communications — even if inadvertent, accidental, or unintentional — shall be promptly destroyed,'" he said.

"Read on," Beechum said. "There's an exception, and you know it."

"'Domestic communications that are reasonably believed to contain foreign intelligence information shall be disseminated to the Federal Bureau of Investigation for possible further dissemination in accordance with minimization procedures.'"

The colonel sat back in his chair. The weight of what she was asking made his shoulders slump. "Senator, I'm retiring at the end of the month. I will do anything I can to help you, but the people on that tape seem willing to go to great lengths in order to hurt you. I don't need much of an imagination to know what they will do to me."

"I don't think you are easily intimidated," she said.

The colonel thought for a minute.

"I haven't lied yet in twenty-seven years of government service," he said. "You get the FBI in this office to ask the right questions, and I'll answer them."

Beechum stood and reached out to shake his hand.

"Thank you, Colonel. I want you to know that I'm going to get through this one of these days; I'll always have an opening for a legislative assistant for military affairs. Pays good. Boss is tough."

"Thanks," he said. "But I've had enough of Washington. I'm going fishing in a place where you and the NSA and the whole damned government will never think of looking."

"So am I," she said. "So am I."

▮

"WHAT THE HELL?" Jeremy yelled over the ringing in his ears. The darkness had closed around him so tightly he could barely move, but the extreme violence made his heart race, made him want to run. "What the fuck was that?"

He could still feel the weight of the little boy who had fallen against his legs.

"Outside," Jesús responded, lowering his AK-47. He pulled a small red-lens Maglite out of his pocket and pointed it toward the door. Jeremy followed the muted beam of his team leader's flashlight as it traced a path back to the where the first pile of bodies lay around the table.

"Help me," Jesús said, pointing toward two of alal-Bin's fallen guards. "Take everything. We can sort it out later."

The senior HRT operator knelt down to rifle through the dead men's pockets, tucking identification papers into a plasticine envelope he had pulled from the thigh pocket of his cargo pants.

Jeremy laid his rifle in the crook of his arm and did as he was told. He used his right hand to remove paper, loose cloth, coins, anything that wasn't sewn in. Blood had turned their camouflage fatigues warm and soggy, but he pushed forward, hoping there was a purpose to all this — that finding something in their pockets might somehow justify the butchery.

"Fuck this!" Jeremy said after a moment. "What the hell are we doing here?"

Jesús stood up and moved over to the table. "You're following orders, Waller. Why do you always seem to have so much trouble with that?"

The team leader used the toe of his boot to roll three bodies out of the way, then knelt down over a face Jeremy had seen a thousand times: Asam alal-Bin, the myth, now just a dead man. His long straggly beard had been cut close. It was still gray.

"Because they don't make orders for shit like this," Jeremy growled. He pulled his bloody hand out of the last pocket and stood to see what had captured his team leader's attention. "I'm entitled to an answer!"

"You ain't entitled to shit." Jesús stood up and ran the beam of his flashlight over the tabletop. Several yellow, dust-covered pieces of paper ruffled in a growing breeze. He picked them up, folded them, and tucked everything into the plastic envelope. "But I'm going to tell you because I know how it feels to hang your ass out over somebody else's agenda. This ain't about whacking alal-Bin. It's about this."

He pushed the envelope up into Jeremy's face.

"We've known for some time about an al Qaeda op called the Wedding. It was first detailed in one of the Agency's daily matrices — October sixteen of last year — so they refer to it as Matrix 1016. Whatever you call it, the Agency thinks it involves the Federal Reserve and that it's action imminent. That's why we're here."

"How imminent?" Jeremy turned toward the sound of helicopter rotors rising through the empty desert night.

"The NSA says this was their last planning session." He bent down and picked up the SBT phone alal-Bin had used to contact his overseas cells. "Unfortunately, these assholes now have secure comms, so no one can listen in. That's why we had to hit this place now."

"Shit, what's that?" Jeremy pointed toward a dark silhouette flying in just above the horizon.

"Russian-made Hind MI-28 with a Yemeni pilot who's making too much money to care about any of this. Just get on and ride, understand?"

Lights appeared on the horizon, but not from aircraft — headlights. Both noticed.

"What about those oil-company people back there? Who's going to get them out?"

"They aren't oil people, and you don't have to worry about them."

Jesús pulled an infrared "firefly" out of his pocket, pressed a button, and held it over his head. The helicopter grew louder in the vast, empty desert night. Jeremy wondered if it could get here before the headlights, which looked to be no more than five hundred yards away.

"Look . . ." — Jesús waited to be sure the helicopter saw the IR beacon, then tucked it back into his pocket — "I've been a soldier since I got out of high school. I never wanted to make the rules . . . just follow them. Why do you think I hide that Silver Star in my desk drawer? My wife and kids think I was a goddamned cook."

Jeremy started to shake. It could have been the cold, dark air or the dehydration.

"This isn't Delta, Jesús." Jeremy could hardly choke out the words. "We're FBI agents. We don't go around killing innocent civilians."

The helicopter flew in hot, low to the ground, totally blacked out. Jeremy never saw it until it flared in a cloud of dust and settled. The spinning rotors ignited flint in the soil, creating a bizarre nimbus of red, yellow, and orange hues.

Jesús pushed his reluctant accomplice toward their ride back to reality. The approaching headlights were no more than two hundred yards from them; there wasn't a moment to spare.

"It's a complicated world," Jesús said. "Grow the fuck up and do your job."

XVII

"DADDY! DADDY! DADDY!"

Jeremy walked through the front door of his house just before bedtime Sunday night to the sounds of Maddy's surprised elation. No matter what he had been through in the past few days, nothing captured his emotions like that little-girl squeal.

"Madster!" Jeremy yelled. He scooped her up in his arms and threw on a patented double-hug with machine-gun kisses. Christopher was right behind her with a SpongeBob doll in one hand and a toilet plunger in the other.

"Two babies, Daddy! Two babies!" That's what he yelled when he wanted Jeremy to carry him and his sister.

"Two babies it is," Jeremy growled. He snatched Christopher off the floor, squeezed him and his sister together, then fell to his knees and rolled them around on the carpet. For a moment, the laughter and the cries of innocence gave him a fleeting sense of belonging.

"Hey, you two! Leave Dad alone long enough for him to get into the house," Caroline called out. She stood in the hallway like a mother waiting up for a son who'd blown off curfew. He was late.

"Where's my present?" Maddy demanded.

"Yeah, where's my present?" Christopher chimed in.

Jeremy's heart sank. He hadn't even thought about a present.

"They're in the family room," Caroline said. She always thought of everything.

Jeremy shooed the kids inside, where his wife handed out the presents he should have bought.

"Thanks," he said later, moving in for a kiss. But she moved tentatively away from him.

"What's that about?" he asked.

"What's that about? You disappear for days and then just roll back in like nothing happened?" She winced. "Christopher had an ear infection; Maddy picked up pink eye at school; I had a major grant application." Tears welled up in her eyes. "You never even called."

"I couldn't . . ." How could he begin to explain this? He still had no handle on it himself. "You know I have to go away sometimes. You should have checked the office."

"I did. They told me you signed out on sick leave."

She waited for an answer. Caroline had already run the course of emotions from fear to anger. Husbands who disappeared for days at a time had to have reasons. Even husbands who worked for HRT.

"I don't know why they told you that. A mission came up . . . overseas. One minute I was over at the Marine Corps ranges and the next minute I'm in Yemen. It was just bizarre."

He realized they were standing in the entrance hall again, with Caroline blocking the door to the kitchen. The house suddenly felt foreign and off limits, as if he were trespassing. It seemed as if she didn't want to let him in.

"Yemen?"

"It's in the Middle . . ."

"I know where Yemen is!" Her sudden turn in expression startled him. "What I don't understand is why the FBI wouldn't tell me you were out of town on a mission. I even called some of the other wives and . . ."

"You called some of the other wives?" He and Caroline had agreed to keep some distance from the so-called support group. Most of the guys on the team complained that it was nothing but a gossip ring among those who had nothing better to do.

"What was I supposed to do? You don't come home for dinner. You don't come home for days — I was scared to death that something had happened to you!"

Maddy and Christopher ran in from the family room. "What's the matter, Mommy?" Maddy asked. She looked scared. Jeremy and Caroline almost never fought.

"Nothing, honey," Jeremy said. Caroline sent them back to play with their new toys.

"I'm sorry. I wish I had a better answer."

He was an FBI agent. He was supposed to have answers.

"All I can tell you is that this was a classified mission." He reached out to touch her, but she pulled back. Tears started to spill out of her eyes. "I've never lied to you, Caroline. It was a mission. You've got to let it go."

He wrapped her in his arms, and she began to cry.

"I worry about you," she wept. "It's so hard not knowing."

"I know, baby," he whispered. "It won't happen again. I promise."

▐▌

SIRAD TOOK A day for herself in Paris before returning to New York, where she walked off an Air France flight feeling rested and pampered, yet anxious. Mitchell's personal message of congratulations — and a dozen roses — had brightened her stay at the Ritz-Carlton, but it was hard to reconcile his lack of trust. There were only two reasons for his hesitance: either he wanted to give her a test run before committing to broad program access, or he knew about her intentions with Hamid. One meant prudent caution; the other could mean disaster.

Borders Atlantic had a car waiting for her at JFK when she touched down early Monday morning. The day's *New York Times* and *Washington Post* sat on the backseat, blaring headlines about the Borders Atlantic deal. The *New York Post* had slipped to the floor, but its banner headline captured her eye first.

DIAL T FOR TRAITOR! it declared over a full-page split screen posing Jordan Mitchell opposite Asam alal-Bin. In sharply worded articles and editorials, the other newspapers added detailed coverage of the Saudi deal, including speculation by "unnamed government sources" that this would seriously disrupt the war on terror. Financial analysis of Borders Atlantic's stock showed a 14 percent increase in two days.

Television had reacted with similar outrage. All the talk shows had branded Jordan Mitchell a shameless profiteer who chose corporate greed over national security interests. Ironically, they pointed to Senator Beechum's lack of leadership in the Intelligence Committee as a reason for his success. Marcellus Parsons himself suggested that as new head of the committee he would immediately look into the matter.

Sirad arrived at Hamid's Eighty-second Street apartment just before 8:00 AM.

"Europe flatters you," he said as she dropped her bags at the door. She didn't bother with a verbal response. By the time her new Gucci suit hit the floor, he couldn't have heard her anyway. The combination of French lace and specially made perfume turned the entryway into a marble-and-mahogany sex chamber, scattered with clothing and filled with groans and those special sounds she knew how to make when it really mattered.

By the time they were through, Hamid found himself lying on his back in the living room, staring at the Degas and wondering why it or any other part of his life had ever mattered.

"So, what have you been up to?" she asked when Hamid returned to his senses. Sirad reached out with her foot and plucked a lisianthus blossom from a coffee-table floral arrangement. She placed the stem right where the cleft of her carefully coifed sex disappeared between her thighs.

Hamid shook his head. This woman had a way of making the world and all its consequences seem trivial. She took him places he'd never dreamed of.

"Not as much as you obviously, but I went shopping," he said. "I bought you a little congratulations gift."

"Oh? What?" She played with the flower, trying to arouse him again.

"You want me to get it?"

"Of course I want you to get it. What girl doesn't want a gift from her lover?"

Hamid stood up and pulled two couch cushions over him. Something about Sirad's beauty always made him feel self-conscious about his own physique.

"Wait here."

She lay there for a moment, wondering if the seventeenth floor had wired the apartment for sound and video. Hoch had said they were surveilling her — perhaps Mitchell had sent his black-bag artists in while she was overseas.

"Don't tell me I shouldn't have, OK?" Hamid said, returning to the living room with a small, beautifully wrapped box in his hand. "That's one thing no woman should ever tell a man."

He knelt next to her and held out the box.

"Why would I tell you that? I love gifts. Especially from you."

She rolled over on her side, reached up, and snatched one of the pillows from his hand. She tucked it between her knees and held out an open hand. The fact that her outstretched fingers rested just below his now exposed groin was not lost on Hamid. He quickly pulled the other pillow in front of himself and handed her a light-blue Tiffany box wrapped with the traditional ribbon.

"My favorite color," she said.

She pulled one of the finely scissored ears and tucked the ribbon between her teeth. Sirad rolled the box between her fingers for a moment longer than he had expected. She knew how to ripen a moment, how to coax him into anticipation, no matter what the setting.

"I was just wondering," she said.

"Wondering? About?"

"About what you do, exactly." She smelled the box, then closed her eyes and pressed it against her chest, between her breasts, where a normal woman's heart would have been.

"You know what I do." Hamid leaned forward and took the box from her. "I trade other people's money and keep a little for myself."

"I think you keep a lot for yourself."

He laughed.

"Does that bother you?" He used the sky-blue Tiffany box to trace the shadows of a Brancusi bronze where they lay across her thighs.

"No. Of course not. It's just that I have objectives of my own. And

I'm never too arrogant to think I can't benefit from another's expertise."

Sirad slowly took the lisianthus from between her legs and used it to trace little hearts on Hamid's thighs. He was already hard by the time she took him in her hand.

"Aren't you going to open it?" he asked.

"What's the hurry?" Sirad leaned toward him with her mouth. "We've got all night."

"Wait," he said. It wasn't that he didn't want to make love to her again, it was just that he had taken most of a day to select the gift. "I wanted you to see it first. To put it on before we . . ."

She moved just so and cut his thought midsentence.

"All right then."

She took the box from him, almost pouting, and stared straight into his eyes as she lifted the top. The sparkle of diamonds gathered in her eyes before she even looked down.

"Well? Do you like it?"

"I love it, Hamid, because you gave it to me. It could be thumbtacks and a Popsicle stick for all I care. It means so much that you picked it out yourself."

Sirad pulled out a magnificent pink-sapphire-and-diamond briolette bracelet. It was absolutely luminous, crafted to shameless weight in platinum and flawless stones.

"I want you to wear it," she said. Sirad looped it over Hamid's wrist and clasped it tight. "I want to see it on you while you're inside me."

Hamid sat back on his heels and stared at how the jewels seemed to dim against her eyes. This woman accepted him for what he showed in his heart, not what he wore on his sleeve. Dieter had been wrong to suspect anything.

She leaned forward and kissed him, not with the raw passion that she had shown on her last trip or even during the first time they had sex. This was something Hamid hadn't felt before. Subtlety. Truth.

No woman could do this without feeling, he thought as Sirad parted her thighs and took him between them. *I can trust her with anything.*

▮

"WHAT DO YOU mean you can't request that kind of information?"

Senator Beechum sat across a cheaply veneered conference table from an FBI agent named Weatherby — the man who had so unceremoniously extracted her from the Ford Mustang the first time she mistakenly trusted an informant.

"First of all, we shouldn't even be having this conversation. You have an attorney, which means you have invoked your Miranda rights and thereby . . ."

"Oh, to hell with Miranda. I'm old enough to be your mother, Agent Weatherby. I know all about Miranda!"

James looked on without comment. He had advised his boss to call her lawyer into the meeting, but she had refused.

"I'm sorry, Senator, but even if you do waive your right to counsel, I can't discuss evidence we have gathered in this case, especially evidence gathered through highly classified methods and sources."

"I'm not talking about evidence you're going to use against me; I'm talking about evidence that will exonerate . . ."

Just then, the door opened. A petite redhead with fire-opal eyes stepped in with a GS-13 lackey in tow.

"Hello, Senator Beechum, I'm Special Agent in Charge Milbank. May I help you?"

Agent Weatherby seemed to sink in her presence like a puppy about to get cuffed by its mother.

"Well, that all depends. Agent Weatherby seems to have no trouble pulling me out of a car and dragging me in front of a federal judge over some ridiculous cassette tape, but he can't make a simple phone call to request information that will exonerate me." Nothing ticked her off like bureaucratic intransigence.

"What phone call?" The SAC scorched Weatherby with a look. What hadn't he told her?

"Ms. Beechum . . . ," Weatherby started to say.

"I'm still a senator, and I'm going to be long after you choke on this so-called case of yours. I'll thank you to address me with some respect."

Weatherby turned toward his boss. "Senator Beechum . . . claims the NSA has an overhear of a phone call she made the night of the attack." His voice dripped with sarcasm.

"Really? Why didn't the initial police reports note that?"

James emerged from the fray.

"The senator didn't remember making the call until long after the attack. It's posttraumatic recall. She was contacted on her cell phone by a staffer on the National Security Council."

The SAC stared at him.

"Who are you?"

"He's my administrative assistant," Beechum barked. "And he's telling you the truth. I received a phone call in which the staffer negligently mentioned a code word–protected project. The NSA flagged it for Echelon intercept. Fort Meade recorded that conversation . . . and we have reason to believe they recorded another call I made a short time afterward. During the attack."

"And how, may I ask, did you get access to an NSA overhear?" The SAC sat down next to Weatherby. "It's my understanding that you have already been charged with unauthorized possession of classified material. In fact, I'm getting concerned that this conversation is lapsing into dangerous Fifth Amendment territory. You have a lawyer."

James answered on her behalf. "The senator was calling her office to leave a message for me when the man attacked her. In the struggle, she accidentally dialed the phone. Our voicemail recorded the whole thing."

"Where's the tape?" Milbank asked. "If you have evidence that directly impacts this investigation, why haven't you given it to us?"

"Because we don't have it."

"You don't have it?"

"No."

"Why not?"

"Because the receptionist inadvertently taped over it. There was a lot of stress . . ."

"NSA has the tape!" Beechum interjected. She'd had enough.

"And how do you know that?" the FBI boss asked. "As former chair of the Intelligence Committee I'm sure you know that the National Security Agency is prohibited by law from eavesdropping on American citizens within the United States. Even if you got access to

their files, they — by law — should not have any domestic intercepts."

"The NSA monitors ether, air, a bunch of electronic vibrations,"
Beechum argued. "How the hell are they supposed to know which
come from Americans and which don't until after they intercept
them?"

Everything stopped. Agent Weatherby looked at SAC Milbank.
Beechum looked at James. Both sides tried to stand behind rank.

"I can't tell you how I know about these tapes," Beechum almost
pleaded, "but I can tell you they exist. You have the legal right to
make an inquiry."

Milbank considered the situation for a moment, then shook her
head. "I'm afraid there's nothing we can do to help you," she said.
"NSA intercepts of domestic communications — if they do exist —
will not be admissible in a court of law."

Beechum slammed her fist on the table.

"If you do your job and check these tapes, there will be no court of
law!" she bellowed. "I was a lawyer before I was a senator, Ms. Milbank, and I'm telling you that during the past weeks we have discovered exculpatory evidence that not only exonerates me but also
proves that someone tried to frame me for a crime I did not commit.
You're supposed to be investigators; what the hell more do you
want?"

"We want justice," the SAC said. She sounded measured, resolute.

Beechum launched to her feet. "How can you say you want justice
when you won't even consider prima-goddamned-facie evidence?"

The SAC said nothing, but the look on her face showed a willingness to listen.

"Doesn't it bother you," Beechum exclaimed, "that you still have
no body? And what about the blood trail, which abruptly ended at
the front door of my house? Nobody saw this supposedly grievously
wounded man leave my house, despite the fact that it was the end of
the workday in a busy neighborhood with dozens of potential witnesses." Beechum recounted the evidence — or lack of it — as
Phillip had laid it out to her. "And not one of this man's fingerprints
anywhere in my house? How did he get in? How did he get out? If

I'd been having an affair with this man, don't you think he would have left something behind — besides a pool of blood?" Beechum rested her case.

"Murder is not a federal crime, Senator," Milbank said. "Those are Metro PD issues. The FBI's involvement is purely national security related. I'm sure you know that."

"National security! You mean that cassette tape? Come on, Agent Milbank . . . you set me up for that meeting and you surveilled it. Is that standard procedure for coverage of a national security risk? And by the way, has your investigation noted that I threw the god-damned tape out the window without even listening to it?"

"I don't have to explain our investigative methods, Senator, and I don't have to help you formulate your defense. I'm confident in my agents and their work." She stood to leave.

"Wait. Please." Beechum summoned one last appeal. "I've always supported the FBI because I respect your objectivity and your professionalism. All I'm asking is that you look beyond the headlines. If you really want justice . . . help me."

"All right, Senator," Milbank said, shocking everyone in the room. "You bring me information that lends credibility to your claims, and I'll consider it."

▉

JORDAN MITCHELL HELICOPTERED in from his house in the Berkshires, feeling elated. Within the last three days, his dream of reinventing the electronic data transfer industry had shown the first signs of life. It didn't matter that the media had branded him a domestic terrorist or that everyone from the FCC and SEC to the Justice Department was threatening investigations. This was no longer just some wooden brainchild dancing on the strings of Mitchell's imagination; this was now a walking, talking creation that within weeks would revolutionize the way organizations around the world did business.

"Good morning," Trask said as Mitchell entered his executive suite.

"Good morning." Mitchell nodded. "Where is she?"

"Waiting outside," Trask said. Mitchell's office complex included public and private entrances, including a reception foyer accessible by a key-access elevator.

"Sirad!" Mitchell exclaimed, stepping into the anteroom where she sat reading a copy of *Town and Country* magazine. "Congratulations!"

He reached out with his right hand to shake and with his left hand to hold her shoulder.

"Thank you, Mr. Mitchell," she said. "I'm glad things worked out so well."

"Come in. Come in." He motioned toward his office, sweeping Sirad up in his enthusiasm and leading her into the sanctum sanctorum that most employees had only heard described in rumors.

What she saw inside surprised her, even by Mitchell's standards. The ceilings in the thirty-by-forty-foot office reached at least two stories high. Windows opened to the west overlooking Central Park. Rows of lever-action rifles and silver-colored revolvers covered the walls. Library shelves surrounded the room and were circled with a broad upper-level walkway. Wrought-iron filigree railings, black oak paneling, and ogee molding punctuated the display cases and paintings by Eakins, Winslow Homer, and Francis A. Silva.

Bloodred Farouk rugs covered parquet floors. All of the furniture was Empire, thick and rugged; dark as night yet rich with ornamental grain and sagging leaded glass. But the feature that struck her most sat at the front of the room near two pristine Lannuier chairs. It was a battleship-size desk hand carved in a lion's-head motif, inlaid with purple heart, tiger maple, and Madagascar rosewood. The top was thick antique English bridal leather, hand tooled at the edges.

A Tiffany parlor lamp stood in one corner of the desk, a leather inbox in the other. There was also a simple Cartier pen set and three framed photographs of children and two young married couples. Sirad would have assumed they were relatives but knew Mitchell had never married and probably couldn't stand the thought of children. They must have been posed.

"What a magnificent space," she said, taking a seat in front of his desk.

Mitchell walked around to his own chair and sat, separating the two of them with six feet of hardwood. "Tell me, are you ready to take the reins on our new initiative?"

"Yes, of course." She measured his face, trying to decide how much to ask. "But I have to wonder if you fully trust me with this project, sir. I mean, I didn't even get briefed until . . ."

"Borders Atlantic works very hard to safeguard its investments." Mitchell reached into his top drawer and pulled out a single brass key. "This all came up very quickly, before we could fully read you in, but I won't apologize for parceling out trust in small increments."

Sirad looked at the key and then into his eyes. She still had no idea what he knew of her plans with Hamid.

"Here," he said, handing Sirad the key.

"What is this?"

"A key to your new apartment. You'll have a place in Riyadh, of course, but we've taken the liberty of arranging for quarters here — something suitable to your new responsibility."

Sirad accepted his gift. "Thank you, I guess."

"I'm sure this seems a bit abrupt," Mitchell said. "But if you want to succeed here, you have to remember one thing: Borders Atlantic is full of secrets, and they're all mine. This project is moving quickly; you'll be given information as you need it."

"Whatever you need, Mr. Mitchell," Sirad said. "I'm ready."

She fought to keep from smiling. The software she'd loaded into Hamid's PDA had already provided Hoch and his CIA analysis unit with huge amounts of information about Borders Atlantic's programs. Hoch believed Hamid kept important additional information on Zip, disk, and CD files at his apartment, but Sirad would have them, too, within the next twenty-four hours.

"Good." Mitchell nodded. "You'll have discretionary use of the corporate jets and authority to make acquisitions up to one million dollars per transaction. Anything more than that and you'll have to clear with Trask or myself. And you'll need this for expenses."

He handed her an American Express black card. She'd seen them but never had one herself. The $150,000 yearly personal expense minimum felt rich for her blood.

"I don't know what to say."

"You don't need to say anything. You need to get to work. Phase two of the Quantis initiative will take you to London next week. Trask has already booked your flight; we'll have a full briefing at two o'clock."

Sirad put the key in her pocket and reached out her hand. "Thank you for this opportunity," she said. "I won't let you down."

"Of course not," Mitchell responded. "I won't let you."

❚❙

JEREMY SHOWED UP at Monday's morning meeting, just as Jesús had promised. Billy Luther was just starting the roll call.

"You look like shit," Lottspeich said as his partner sneaked into his customary seat. Jeremy didn't bother responding; he hadn't slept much since Yemen.

"Where's Jesús?" Jeremy whispered. He looked toward the front of the room, where his team leader's chair sat empty. None of the seats were assigned, but HRT operators were creatures of habit, compulsively so. From the lucky coffee cup to the way they loaded bullets into their magazines, these guys obsessed with detail and order. Once you picked a spot, nobody moved in on your turf.

"Beats me." Lottspeich shrugged.

Jesús had flown with Jeremy from Aden to Nairobi to London, but there he parted company and boarded a flight to New York. Jesús had taken the alal-Bin documents and the strange-looking weapon with him.

"Hey, did Langdon tell you yet?" Lottspeich asked, changing the topic as Luther moved from team to team, recording attendance.

"Tell me what?"

"He knocked Bucky off the pole. Got a woodchuck yesterday at eight hundred meters on range four. Lucky, probably, but you're two men down now with three days to go."

Jeremy shook his head at how ludicrous the contest seemed after what he'd just been through. He started to respond, but something caught his eye. Jesús. The HRT veteran walked through the door, his day pack slung over his shoulder as if this were just another wake-up. He nodded to a couple of the older guys and slapped Luther on the back. All smiles.

"All right, here's the schedule for the Peary trip," Luther announced. "We've got an all hands for Echo and Xray at fourteen hundred hours. Team leaders meet at one-thirty."

Beautiful, Jeremy thought. He'd completely forgotten about the trip to the CIA's Williamsburg training facility — known within the intelligence community as "the Farm." That meant the protection detail was still a go, meaning he'd have to spend another week on the road. Caroline would not be happy.

"We've got Xray scheduled for the shooting house first," Billy said. "Echo on the TEVOC track. We'll rotate at sixteen hundred. Questions?"

There were none.

"All right then." Billy closed his ledger and nodded. "Let's get to work."

The room suddenly erupted with commands, jokes, reminders, and cuts. Jeremy watched his team leader stand and walk out the door. He followed him back to the men's room and stood next to him at one of the two urinals.

"How'd you sleep last night?" Jeremy asked. It was more an accusation than a question.

"Like a baby, why?"

A couple of guys filtered through. Jesús didn't seem to notice.

"You don't look so good, Jeremy. You feeling all right?"

One of the Hotel assaulters stepped into a stall.

"I need to know what's next . . . what I should be ready for," Jeremy whispered. He turned toward Jesús, his hair mussed, his face still bright red from the harsh desert sun. Dark bags hung under his sleep-starved eyes.

"Ready for?" Jesús asked. He looked genuinely confused. "What are you talking about?"

"The shooting. Chain of custody on the evidence we picked up? I mean, there's going to be a Shooting Review Board, right?"

Jesús zipped his pants and turned to his right. "I have no idea what you're talking about." He spoke loudly enough for the man in the stall to hear. "But I'll tell you one thing: you've been acting like an asshole ever since that Puerto Rico gig. You'd better wire your shit together before people start to talk." He punctuated his words with a clenched jaw, then started to walk away.

"Wait a minute . . . ," Jeremy demanded. They were both talking out loud now.

"I ain't waitin' for shit, Waller." Jesús stopped him in his tracks. "We've got a fourteen hundred show-up at the Farm, and you got two options: either get your ass down there or see Luther about a re-assignment. I'm sorry if you have emotional problems, but we've got a detail coming up in New York and Xray needs shooters. The guys need to know who they can count on."

XVIII

————

HAMID WAS SITTING in his office when Dieter entered and closed the door.

"Hello, Dieter," he said. "I'm rather busy right now."

Borders Atlantic's chief security officer walked right up to Hamid's desk, pushed a stack of spreadsheets out of the way, and dropped a filthy, dust-covered pile of documents on Hamid's meticulously ordered Dunhill ink blotter.

"What the hell are you doing?" He recoiled. Desert sand, fine as talcum powder, filtered down toward the floor, staining his blue suit white.

"Look at them." Dieter crossed his arms and tilted his head knowingly. "It's what you've been waiting for."

Hamid used a pencil eraser to separate and arrange two yellow-lined and five type-covered pages. All of them had been folded several times and looked heavily worn.

"Are these the actual documents?" Hamid asked. He leaned forward, suddenly oblivious to the dust. "They're a mess."

"What do you expect from fugitives living in the desert?" he asked. "Read them."

Like Hamid, the German spoke and read Arabic fluently, but several of the pages contained only numbers. That's where he needed translation.

After several minutes, Hamid leaned back from his desk and ran his fingers through his hair. "Amazing." He exhaled. "There must be more than two hundred fifty account numbers here. Transfer instructions, names, Internet café addresses all over Europe. Have you started to run any of these accounts yet?"

"No." Dieter unfolded his arms and moved around to the back of Hamid's desk. He pointed to the laptop sitting quietly near the in-box. "You and Mitchell have the only access to routing schematics and encryption codes."

"Come on." Hamid laughed. "Are you telling me that there is a secret that the mighty Rabbit Hole doesn't possess?"

"Check the accounts," Dieter said.

Hamid thought for a moment, then booted up his laptop and clicked through a quick sequence of mouse movements. He typed passwords to navigate three firewalls, then scrolled to a file any of the world's industrialized nations would have killed to own.

"The first page is a list of Fed Wire routing numbers and transfer sequences originating from the Federal Reserve, New York," Hamid said.

Dieter nodded expectantly. "And?"

"Federal Reserve, Los Angeles . . . Atlanta . . . Chicago . . . Miami . . . Dallas . . . they're all here. Some in-house security codes, individual laptop passwords, but — my God, these account numbers — there's no telling how much money this represents."

"What about routing codes?" Dieter asked. Access to a bunch of individual accounts meant nothing to him. It was the larger plan he most wanted to uncover.

Hamid used his mouse to scroll through a series of polynomial encryption algorithms, which the nation's banking system used to move virtually all of its money supply. It had taken Borders Atlantic three years, millions of dollars, and a fair amount of luck to breach these security measures. Now they had turned up on weathered yellow legal pages that had been found in the deserts of Yemen.

"They're here." Hamid typed furiously into his laptop, flashing through pages that detailed banks and other financial institutions on four continents. Malaysia, Switzerland, Venezuela, United Arab Emirates, Cameroon, Iran — the list extended to dozens more countries.

"This is much more extensive than we anticipated." Hamid shook his head as he typed and pushed the mouse around. "They clearly have someone inside."

"What does that mean? Are they just moving money around or . . ."

"No, it's much more than that. They have tunneled into the process." Hamid scowled. "There's stuff in here that even I haven't seen before."

"What do you mean?" Dieter handled a great number of sensitive matters, but in a company as big and complex as Borders Atlantic, there were things not even he understood.

"Money never sleeps," Hamid explained. "Each night, account and securities holders — everyone from retired auto workers in Detroit to farmers in Kansas to venture capitalists in New York — go to bed thinking their money is lying in some bank vault some place. In fact, their savings moves around the world, playing in international money markets, foreign stock exchanges, commodities speculation. It buys oil, moves up and down in mortgage transfers, pays out insurance settlements, grows and shrinks and multiplies or disappears while they sleep. And virtually all of it moves through twelve regional Federal Reserve banks across the country."

"How much are you talking about?" Dieter asked. "Billions? Tens of billions?"

"We're not talking rational numbers, Dieter; we're talking GDP — Gross Domestic Product. The aggregate wealth of the strongest free-market economy on the face of the Earth."

Hamid double-clicked the mouse and stared at a DOS-style computer screen that blinked white a couple times, then opened into a code prompt.

"We're talking about the financial reason America is the land of the free and the home of the brave."

"That's what they're after?" Dieter asked.

Hamid turned from his computer screen and ran a finger down the first two pages of handwritten Arabic.

"Unfortunately, I still can't tell you what they're after. This demonstrates that they have access to the system and the expertise to manipulate it, but it doesn't show how or where they plan to attack. They could be looking to steal huge sums of money or simply to crash the system and crush the dollar. There's no way to know because when it comes right down to it we've got a blueprint of the lock here but no sense of the key."

Both men gazed down at the filthy pages. In a world where money served as the ultimate weapon, the plot outlined in these documents could prove more damaging than a nuclear bomb.

"But I've got to tell you," Hamid added, "of all the numbers here, one bothers me most."

He pointed to a date written into the first page of script.

"This thing is going down this week."

"GODDAMMIT, YOU SHOULD have come to me first, Elizabeth," Beechum's attorney said. Phillip Matthews paced his office like a wounded dog, rubbing his forehead and trying to absorb the news that his client had gone to the FBI without his counsel to discuss a case that easily could put her in jail for the rest of her life. "You can't just walk in to the people who are trying to destroy you and hand them information on a silver platter."

Beechum sat on a couch with her legs crossed.

"We handed them nothing, Phillip," she said. "James and I have the information we need to prove this is all a malicious hoax. The FBI can prove me innocent."

"The FBI doesn't prove people innocent, Elizabeth. They put people in jail. This is one of the highest-profile cases they have had in years, and they don't want to lose it on a technicality."

"They have an obligation to chase down every lead, even the ones that will exonerate me. I think Agent Milbank is fair-minded and that she will help. I really do."

"Oh, come on! Remember who you're dealing with here. Ask Richard Jewell about fair-mindedness. How about Wen Ho Lee? Here are the facts: the FBI has overwhelming physical and circumstantial evidence that you shot a member of the White House's National Security Council staff and violated federal law."

"They have no body, no fingerprints, a damned poor case on that cassette. From what I have seen, this is very flimsy."

"First of all, they don't need a body. A member of the president's staff is missing, his blood was all over your house, your fingerprints were on the gun, and the police believe they can show motive. Besides, evidence suggests that this man had significant amounts of information on a highly classified weapons system that you and the Intelligence Committee wanted to kill. That's what they found on the cassette. Unless this guy turns up with one hell of an explanation, we're going to have to prove you *didn't* kill him."

"I didn't," was all she could say.

James, who had sat silently listening to this conversation, realized it was time to intervene. "You don't understand, Phillip. This isn't some desperation defense. We really have a tape that proves her innocence. It proves that someone is trying to frame her for a crime she did not commit."

Phillip barely heard a word he said.

"Elizabeth, I'll tell you what we're going to do."

"Are you listening to me?" James demanded. "The key to winning this case is not some insanity defense; it's proving that this woman was framed. If we want to save her life, we have to find a way to get that NSA tape."

"Enough about the goddamned tape already!" the defense attorney erupted. "What do you think that's going to do for us in a court of law? Now that you have told the FBI about it, the prosecution will claim that you planned the whole thing as a cover. Nobody knows all these esoteric eavesdropping technologies and techniques like you do, Elizabeth. Even if we get a jury to buy into this theory of yours, the government will claim it's a highly classified intelligence-gathering technique vital to national security and refuse further cooperation. It's hopeless."

"This is my life. You forget that."

"I know it's your life, Elizabeth. But you've done enormous damage here." He paused a moment. "If you want any chance of living your last years on your father's tobacco plantation, you'd best forget about this nonsense and let *me* handle the defense."

Elizabeth stared at him a moment, then at James.

"I appreciate what you're trying to do for me," she said, attempting to muster some humility. "But James and I have more important things to do than take a butt chewing from the hired help. You can proceed as you like; James and I have work to do."

She and James stood up and left. Just like that. Didn't even say good-bye.

Phillip waited a moment, then went to his phone and dialed a number. A man answered with a simple hello.

"There's a tape," Phillip said, knowing the man would recognize his voice. "A tape of a phone call. It's going to be a problem."

"All right," the voice answered. "Where do I find it?"

"You don't. This one is going to take some thought. Give me a couple hours and I'll call you back. We're going to have to move carefully."

"You know where to get me," the voice answered.

Phillip hung up the phone and rubbed eyes. He'd always prided himself on being a logician, a trial attorney's lawyer capable of seeing six, seven steps ahead of his opponents. Unfortunately, he'd overlooked something this time. Something vital. There was only one way to fix it and little time to act.

∎

JEREMY ARRIVED AT Camp Peary just after noon. The two-hour ride down had given him time to hash out the previous few days but little sense of how to handle his predicament. If he told Caroline the truth, she would demand that he go outside the team to the FBI's Office of Professional Responsibility or even higher within the Justice Department. This was not law enforcement, she would argue. It was murder.

But murder ordered by whom? Approval for something like this would have to come from the top levels of government. Fake passports, a corporate jet, the CIA contact in Aden, military exfil to a naval vessel — Jeremy ran through a mental list of all the strings someone would have to pull in order to get him and Jesús in and out of Yemen. It had to involve at least three Cabinet-level directors and the National Security Council. The president must have known.

And what about the documents Jesús had snatched off that table? Any plot credible and immediate enough to warrant an operation like this had to be a major priority. *Matrix 1016?* he thought. An attack on American targets. Was it an FBI case?

The whole thing baffled him. Whom could he trust? Did other guys on the team know? Had they gone out on similar trips? Jesús apparently had, but maybe that was because he'd come from the Army and knew his way around the "wet side."

Grow up and do your fucking job. Jesús' words rang in Jeremy's ears.

Right, Jeremy told himself. The HRT motto was *Servare vitas* — To save lives. That was his mission. Perhaps he couldn't take this to OPR, but he surely could chase it himself.

"Name?" A guard's question jarred Jeremy back into the day.

"Waller. Jeremy Waller," he said, pulling his FBI credentials out of his pocket and handing them to a uniformed security guard. The man wore camouflage BDUs and had an MP-5 submachine gun.

Though a sign above him read DEPARTMENT OF DEFENSE, Camp Peary's true identity was a poorly kept secret. The 10,000-acre facility was actually a covert operations training center that had served everyone from entry-level CIA operatives and analysts to insurgent Third World armies.

"Yes, sir. Please pull up to the reception center and they'll process you through."

Jeremy thanked the man, took back his credentials, and drove through a series of portable walls to a parking lot outside a one-story glass-walled building. The lot was already crowded with HRT vehicles; half the team stood in line, filling out nondisclosure agreements and getting their access badges. More secrecy.

Just do your fucking job, Jeremy thought, climbing out of his truck and walking in to join them. Somewhere out there, someone had the answers to his questions. At this point, the most important thing seemed to be deciding just whom to ask.

▐█▌

BEECHUM WASTED NO time in launching a personal crusade for the truth. As the rest of her colleagues filed off to committee meetings, lobby luncheons, and fund-raisers, she closeted herself in her Dirksen office and began working the phones. She'd cultivated many sources during her years in Washington — Capitol Hill staffers, intelligence agency analysts, reporters, Pentagon gadflies — and she called them all, trying to find someone who knew Craig Slater, the man she was accused of killing. *What was his connection to all of this?* she wanted to know. *Why would they have chosen this man as a victim?*

Initial results looked discouraging. Those who did know Slater said he was quiet and isolated, an academic who had been selected to the NSC from a CIA billet at the Pentagon. He liked archaeology, chess, and radio talk shows. Never married. No siblings.

Beyond that, his life disappeared into the firewalls and backstops common to most spooks. James tracked down a fingerprint card, several official and candid photos, and a phone number for his parents, whom they both decided not to call. If there was any reason at all why he had been selected for such a tragedy, Beechum just couldn't find it.

James had just started brainstorming other avenues of inquiry when the intercom buzzed.

"Senator, I'm sorry to bother you," her receptionist said, "but I have a woman out here who wants to see you. She says it's urgent. A Major Ellsworth?"

She shrugged her shoulders to a curious James. Never heard of her.

"Send her in."

The door opened almost immediately, and in walked a short, thin military woman with a page-boy haircut and a neatly pressed air force uniform. Beechum recognized her as one of the NSA telecommunications experts she'd called before the committee during the Jordan Mitchell hearings earlier that fall.

"Thank you for seeing me, Senator," the major said. She walked with a formality of purpose and stopped short of the desk at full attention. "I was hoping we could talk in private." She tried not to look at James, but his presence clearly bothered her.

"It's all right, Major. This is my administrative assistant; I'd prefer to have him stay. But please, talk freely."

"Yes, ma'am. I'm sorry to bother you, but I just couldn't sit around any longer and watch you get . . . watch this happen."

The neatly creased officer reached into her military-issue shoulder purse and pulled out a small Memorex cassette. She held it between her thumb and forefinger as if it were some court exhibit.

"You need to hear this, ma'am."

Beechum hesitated for a moment, remembering what had happened the last time someone offered such a gift, then reached out and accepted the major's offering. James raised his eyebrows as Beechum walked over to a small stereo perched on a row of mahogany bookshelves. She inserted the tape and pressed Play.

"Hurry up!" A man's voice erupted out of the speakers. Heavy southern accent.

"That's him." Beechum placed a hand over her mouth. "My God . . . that's the bastard who attacked me. I hear that voice in my sleep."

"Is she out?" Another voice on tape, distant and jumbled.

"Not for long," the first man said. "Give me the gun."

The room fell silent for a moment, then *BOOM! BOOM!*

"Shit, that was loud!" the second man blurted out. "Hurry up, get the blood down before somebody calls the cops. No . . . over there by the door."

There were muffled sounds of people moving, then, barely intelligible, "Come on, man! Over there . . . don't get any of that shit on me!" The southern accent. "Make sure you . . . splatter on . . . the wall . . . there. Make . . . Parsons . . . is . . ."

CLICK. The tape suddenly ended.

Beechum wheeled toward the tape and fumbled over the Rewind button.

She cocked her ear to the high-pitched whine of a cassette in rewind, then "splatter on . . . the wall . . . there. Make . . . Parsons . . . is . . ." Click.

"Did he say *Parsons*?" Beechum asked. She repeated the process, trying to decipher the words.

"Where'd you get this?" James asked.

"I was there the night the call came in," she answered. "I was the officer on duty when one of our analysts got a code-word hit. Eche-lon locked on your number and recorded the outgoing just a couple minutes later. As an INCONUS intercept, I didn't think much about it until all the stories came out, but then I realized that something else happened that night. I couldn't just sit back and say nothing."

There. Make . . . Parsons . . . is . . . Click.

"Will you take this to the FBI?" James asked. "We can't use the tape without some kind of provenance — proof that it's real."

The woman's shoulders fell. She'd already considered this.

"I have two children, Senator. I'm a single mom. This would end my career."

Beechum nodded, satisfied. "It's all right, Major. I understand your situation." She knew this was too much to ask. "We'll take care of things from here."

The senator snatched the tape out of the recorder as James jumped out of his chair.

"Langley, right?" he asked. He already knew what she was thinking.

"We have to call Phillip first," she said. "Then we go out to Lang-ley. Maybe we can't use the tape as evidence, but we damned sure can use it as leverage."

"I'll get the car," James said.

Beechum thanked the brave young major, then reached down for her phone. She dialed a number she knew by heart, then waited for a man to answer. The road back to life would begin at CIA head-quarters with the one person left in Washington who might listen to her. The house of cards Marcellus Parsons had built was now begin-ning to fall.

▌▌

JEREMY DROVE TO Pine Cabin — a World War II–era Quonset hut tucked down into the woods off Parch Road — and dropped off his personal bag before following Cox out to the shooting house. Though the Agency's open-air facility looked crude compared to HRT's state-of-the-art Tactical Firearms Training Center, it provided operators with a new "look," which came as a welcome relief to shooters conditioned to a steady diet of the same old walls and doors.

"Gear up! We got the house in ten minutes!" Jesús called out as Jeremy spread his gear out on a blue tarp with the rest of the guys. The team leader walked inside to check target placements as the rest of Xray busied itself with black Cordura tactical bags full of body armor, radio harnesses, submachine gun magazines, flashbang grenades, and all the rest of the equipment they'd need for two hours of close-quarter battle.

"So, you going to tell us or not?" Cox asked, loud enough for the others to hear.

"Tell you what?"

"Tell us what's up. Your wife called my wife wondering where you were all weekend," Cox said. "You got three kids, man — no business cheating on a gig like that."

"What are you talking about?" Jeremy demanded. "I wasn't screwing around on my wife. I was overseas on a mission." Jeremy regretted the outburst as soon as the words passed his lips.

"A mission?" Bucky turned an incredulous eye.

Jesús had told him to keep his mouth shut, but there was no turning back now.

"What would you say if I told you Jesús and I flew from Manassas Airport to Yemen last week on a corporate jet, snuck into Yemen on fake passports, and whacked Asam alal-Bin?"

Everyone stared at him.

"I'd say the Puerto Rico shoot is fucking up your head," Cox ventured. "Better see somebody. I mean it."

"It's not bullshit. We found several documents that I think lay out an attack on the United States. Jesús recovered them." He shook his head. "I gotta know, guys — is this some part of the war on terrorism and I just missed the briefing?"

Tiny started to laugh.

"Yeah, all the time. Haven't you seen the medal I got for whacking Osama bin Laden?"

Bucky slammed a magazine into his MP-5. "I'll tell you, Jeremy, you better go see someone in EAP before this becomes a real problem. And you keep your goddamned mouth shut. People hear you talking like this and they're going to ship you off to a rubber gun squad."

302

Everyone stared at Jeremy for a moment, wondering what to say.

"Hey, you guys going to talk or train?" Jesús asked, walking up behind them. Jeremy could tell by the look on the man's face that he knew what had happened.

"Full team, full house," Jesús said, ushering them to the front door. "Cox, you're running number one today." That turned some heads. Jeremy usually ran point. "Tiny's using slap charges on any interior breaches. Any questions?"

There weren't any. Normally, a change in assignment would prompt a round of jeers and ribbing, but not today. Something had changed. Something more than assignments.

"OK, let's do it," Jesús said.

Jeremy walked past him on his way to the last spot in line and caught a leer of suspicion. Jeremy said nothing as the rest of the team shouldered their sub guns, clicked off their safeties, and leaned into the wall, but he knew full well that his confession had not been a smart call.

"Stand by, I have control . . . ," Jesús called out, simulating a command-initiated assault. Cox trained his gun on the front door. Jeremy leaned into Lottspeich, who stood just ahead of him. The whole team quieted, preparing for the live-fire exercise.

"Compromise! Compromise! Compromise!" Jesús blurted out.

In they went, guns blazing. Everything moved lightning fast — a standard SAS leapfrog clear with three-man entries in the bigger rooms, two-man entries in the smaller ones. Tiny fixed a "slap shot" breaching charge on one interior door while Bucky opened another with a 12-gauge Hatton round. It was one tumultuous cloud of flash-bang smoke, rattling machine-gun fire, and overwhelming violence.

Jeremy pushed forward, shooting targets where he found them and knocking hostages to the floor to get them out of the line of fire. Within seconds, he found himself at the last door — the "hot zone."

He fell into position at the edge of the closed door, trained the muzzle midway up, and motioned for the number two man in line to "bang" the room. He felt a hand on his shoulder, the signal that he had company to help make the final entry; then he saw his team leader pass to his left, kick open the door, and toss in an Ensign-Bickford diversionary grenade.

BOOM!

Jeremy dived in behind the blast, double tapped a smiling terrorist just to the right, then spun left toward a gaggle of five mannequins loosely arranged on a beat-up old couch. These were clearly the hostages — no guns, no threat.

"Clear!" Jeremy called out. He lowered his weapon and turned back toward Jesús to hook up with the other guys.

When he looked over his shoulder, though, he saw something that sent the chill of death through his adrenaline-charged heart. Jesús stood along the back wall, just ten feet away, with the sights of his MP-5 aligned squarely on the bridge of Jeremy's nose. The red dot from his Aimpoint sight would have marked him like a New Delhi missus had it not been a passive laser.

Pop! Pop!

Two bullets flew past Jeremy's face. Left and right. So close he could feel them against his skin. Had he flinched, they would have killed him.

"What the fuck . . . ," he started to yell, but the look in Jesús' eyes stopped him midsentence. Cox ducked into the door and offered a thumbs-up.

"We're clear in here," he called out.

Jeremy turned toward the hostages on the floor and noticed a target behind them on the couch. He had overlooked it in his haste. The bad guy now wore Jesús' bulletholes in his forehead.

"I told you to get your head wired to your ass," Jesús said, lowering his muzzle and walking close enough that the two men touched shoulders. "You got a problem understanding the bigger picture, but just because you don't see something don't mean it won't kill you."

Jesús wasn't referring to the target on the couch. This was a warning.

XIX

———

SIRAD SNEAKED OUT of work shortly after four o'clock, claiming she needed to buy clothes for her upcoming trip to London, and took the elevator downstairs. She walked out the front door and took three different cabs around the city, using countersurveillance techniques she'd learned at the CIA's Harvey Point, North Carolina, facility to shake any seventeenth-floor stalkers. Once she believed she was clean, Sirad walked into the subway and rode the Six train to within a block of Hamid's Eighty-second Street apartment building.

The doorman welcomed her by name and offered to announce her, but Sirad flashed the key Hamid had given her and took the elevator to Hamid's door.

"Hello?" she called out, letting herself in. The huge apartment looked lonely and sterile, marked with that empty stillness that pervades museums and cancer wards.

When no one answered, she walked quickly to a control panel and disabled the alarm, then she hurried down the main hallway, past the master bedroom where her clothes still hung in the closet, to Hamid's office. Hoch's interception software had mined hundreds of pages of documents — investor lists, routing numbers, transaction schedules, asset rosters, personnel dossiers — but it had also suggested the existence of additional information that appeared in no hard drive. Sirad meant to find it.

Once inside the office, Sirad began to search. As vice president of Borders Atlantic's mid-Atlantic IT operations, she felt confident navigating computer files, but actually going through desk drawers and Hamid's huge collection of Zip drive tapes, disks, and CDs was another matter. Even though many of the files had been marked, Hamid's acronyms, abbreviations, and code words meant nothing to her. The only option was to copy everything onto her laptop — a long, tedious process.

Sirad had just opened her briefcase and pulled out her computer when the sound of a door creaking open made her spin around in her chair.

"You think you're clever, don't you?" A man's voice filled the room. He was standing in the doorway. Backlight from the hallway obscured his face.

"Who are you?" Sirad jumped up from the chair, trying to decide how to act. She clearly had tripped an alarm. Hamid's paintings alone had to be worth $20 million; perhaps she had underestimated his security.

"Oh, I'm sorry." Sirad smiled. "It was the alarm, right? It's OK; I have a key." She held it up as evidence. "Go ahead and call Hamid."

"I'm not calling anyone," the man said. "I know why you're here."

He crossed from the door in three steps and grabbed her by the throat, just the way they'd taught her during hand-to-hand combat training at Camp Peary.

Sirad instinctively pressed her hands together and threw them up between his arms, breaking his grip on her throat. She could see by the smile at the corners of his mouth that he found her challenge humorous.

"They teach you that at the Farm?" he asked.

Sirad knew that none of the stupid defensive tactics lessons they'd taught her would work for long. She only weighed 117 pounds, and this guy moved like a pro.

The intruder assumed a fighting posture and moved forward in half steps, cutting off the door and pressing her into the corner. This thug wasn't from the alarm company. He looked Israeli — Mossad maybe, Shin Bet, or even their assassination unit, Kiton.

Faster than Sirad could react, he dived at her and grabbed her by the hair. She struck out and shoved her fingernails at his eyes.

"You bitch!" he yelled. Blood poured down his cheeks as adrenaline squirted through both of them. No more pretense. Someone was going to die in here.

The man punched Sirad so hard her ears rang, but she struck back instinctively.

Sirad kicked as hard as she could with the heel of her shoe and found the soft spot between his legs, but before she could level another blow, the man threw his shoulder into the attack and knocked her back into the wall. He jammed his forearm up under Sirad's chin, pressing her larynx against her spine and shutting off all air.

Sirad's eyes bulged. Her arms flailed at him. She pumped her knees like a mad bicyclist, kicking and hammering this brutal man to no effect. Her mind flashed full of a lifetime built on pain and betrayal. All the lies, the manipulation, all the wretched things she had done to get what she wanted in life. And this is what it had got her.

After a moment of agony, the pain started to subside. Sirad began to drift past her lungs' burning desire for air. Everything started to fade. The room. Jordan Mitchell. The CIA. Her life.

And then she was lying on the floor, breathing again. Dark figures moved over her. She heard loud voices, sharp blows, and a heavy thud. Then someone reached down and lifted her to her feet.

"Where's the disk?" a voice commanded. She vaguely recognized it. "The CD. Where is it?"

Sirad began to gag as they carried her toward the living room. She sucked air back into her lungs, clawing back toward life. Who were these men, and why had they saved her?

▊

JEREMY HAD JUST pulled his body armor off when Mason drove up. It was not unusual for the HRT commander to check on training, especially on a trip like this, but when he got out of his truck and walked straight toward Xray's staging area, Jeremy felt sick to his stomach.

"Heads up," Cox whispered. "The old man just rolled in."

Mason motioned to Jesús and pulled him aside. They talked in subdued tones for a few minutes; then Mason waved toward Jeremy.

"Waller! Lottspeich!" Jesús hollered.

"What the fuck you got us into now?" Lottspeich asked quietly.

Jeremy shot him a look, unzipped his flight suit, and wrapped the sleeves around his waist. Like his father had told him, *Never let them see you sweat.*

"Hey, boss," he said, walking over to the HRT commander. "What's up?"

"I've got a job for you two." Mason had never been much for conversation. "We just got a call from the State Department: our principal is coming in early. I need you guys to fly up to New York and start the site survey at his hotel."

"What about the rest of the team?" Jeremy knew he had outgrown his FNG status, but this seemed a little advanced for the two newest members of Xray.

"They're staying here to work out vehicle movement with Echo. They'll be up later tonight." Mason seldom felt the need to explain himself. "Why? You got something better to do?"

"No, boss, I'm good to go." Caroline would be furious, but there was no sense in whining. Mason had been married three times. HRT came first, no matter the mission.

"Good. Walt's waiting over at the airstrip. He'll fly you up to Richmond; you can catch a commercial hop from there."

With that, Mason climbed into his Explorer and disappeared down Parch Road.

Three hours later, Jeremy, Lottspeich, and two heavily laden tactical bags lifted off from Richmond International Airport, bound for JFK. He'd got a chance to call home before taking off, but only to leave a message.

"I'll explain when I get there," was all he'd said. Caroline wouldn't have understood anyway.

▐▌

BEECHUM DROVE EAST along Rock Creek Parkway, out the back way along Route 266 to Langley. She'd called ahead and personally scheduled a meeting with the deputy director of counterintelligence, George Sheridan, whom she had known since his days as minority whip in the House. A longtime friend of the president's, Sheridan had earned untouchable status by providing vital intelligence in the hunt for al Qaeda leadership. Though Sheridan was Republican through and through, he and Beechum had been friends. He knew more about the intelligence community than anyone else in Washington; if anyone could help her now, it was him.

The senator parked to the right of the main entrance and walked inside to get a gate pass. Once checked through, she drove a winding route to the top level of the parking garage and found a spot in the front row, beside the shuttle vans. Sheridan had an escort waiting for her inside the new headquarters building. Three minutes later, she was sitting in his seventh-floor office.

"How are you, Elizabeth?" He sounded sincere.

She pulled a small Olympus recorder out of her purse and without further explanation pressed Play. He listened intently as the tape coughed up the entire recording the major had just given her.

"What was that?" he asked when it was over.

"That was the sound of something that never happened."

He leaned back in his chair and ran a hand through his well-oiled hair. "You're going to have to give me a little more than that."

"All right, let's see. It's a little Surreptitious Entry One-oh-one, mixed with some graduate-level paramilitary ops, and a good old-fashioned hit. Black op. A goddamned frame-up."

"I don't understand where you're going with this."

"The night I was attacked, a young staffer at the NSC called to re-arrange that Starfire meeting at the White House. You remember?"

"Sure. You didn't show."

Beechum shook her head. "He used the word *Starfire* over a cell phone. Echelon picked it up, flagged it, and marked my line for twenty-four-hour intercept."

"They wouldn't do that. You're a . . ."

"Don't cite me manual language, George. You know the mentality — capture it all and let God sort it out. They taped two calls; this one clears me."

He looked skeptical.

"That's NSA's download?"

She nodded. "It's a bootleg. I need you to get me a clean one through formal channels."

"You know I can't do that, Elizabeth."

"I've been charged with murder — a murder this tape clearly shows I didn't commit. Listen again." She replayed the ending. "It's Parsons. They said his name."

A smile broke out across his face. "Come on, Elizabeth. That could be anyone's name. You say it's Parsons, but it would take some serious analysis to know for sure."

"That's why I came to you. Your people can find out."

"I'm the deputy director of counterintelligence, Elizabeth. If I send this down to the Skunk Works stapled to some conspiracy theory, they'll laugh me out of the building!"

"You're a political appointee riding herd over nine separate spy agencies handling psy-ops, insurgency campaigns, billions of dollars in black funding, programs so secret you need a hall pass from God just to read the outtakes. Dammit, George, admit it; there's a world out there you aren't supposed to see. Help me prove it."

He said nothing for a moment. Sheridan knew that like many top executives, he was shielded from many of the darker secrets of his own business.

"Let's say you're right. Why would one United States senator try to defame and outright destroy you? And kill a man? An NSC attorney. It's patently absurd."

Beechum could feel righteousness hardening her spine.

"I don't need an explanation. I need a name. Three seconds of audio analysis. Three seconds of truth. You're the only person left who can help me."

He sat there for a minute, considering her request, then jotted down a note.

"Leave the tape. I'll see what I can do."

Beechum nodded. "There's something else. The man who attacked me had a tattoo on his forearm. Military, I'm guessing." She pulled out a drawing she had been working on for some time: a pair of dice with the number one accented with an asterisk on the left die and three twos on the other. "I was hoping you could track it down."

He ran a finger over the image she'd drawn. "I'm willing to try to help you, Elizabeth, because of our years of friendship. But I'll deny this conversation if you or anyone else ever bring it up again," he said. "I want you to know that."

"I understand, George," she said. "And thanks." Plausible deniability was a cornerstone of their business. It was just part of the game.

▌▌▌

"ARE YOU ALL right?"

Sirad lay on Hamid's gold brocade couch as a half dozen men moved deliberately around her. Two of them dragged a limp body past her — the man she'd just fought.

"Can you breathe?" a man asked. It was Jordan Mitchell.

"W-what h-happened?" she struggled to say. "What are you doing here?"

She sat up and immediately clasped a hand to her throat. She could barely swallow. The side of her head hurt like hell. A knot the size of a golf ball rose right above her left ear.

"What happened?" she repeated.

"I think we're the ones entitled to some answers," Mitchell said. He motioned with his hand, and the man who had attacked her disappeared, unconscious, out the front door.

Sirad fought to clear the murky clouds from her head.

"I feel sick . . ." She rolled over and threw up in a trash can. "I'm sorry . . ." She vomited again.

"You probably have a concussion, but he would have killed you if we hadn't broken in."

Sirad looked up and saw Chris, the security officer she'd met on the trip to Dubai.

"What are you doing here?"

"Listen, Sirad," Mitchell said, "security has discovered that ever since you got back from Saudi, someone has been trying to hack into our most sensitive computer files. We don't know who, but it's possible that you walked in on an attempt to steal Hamid's personal files."

Sirad said nothing for a moment. Were they testing her?

311

"Where are you taking him?" she asked.

"Don't worry about him," Chris said. "He won't bother you again. But his people are going to come looking — whoever they are."

Sirad tried to think through the nausea and pain.

"What did he say to you?" Chris asked. "Did you recognize him?"

Sirad shook her head. She'd never seen him before in her life.

"He asked me about a disk," she answered. "He wanted some kind of disk."

Mitchell stood up and began to pace. His top lip tightened. Veins popped out at the sides of his head, drawing his features up in to razor-sharp lines of accusation.

"I told you not to take that damned thing off the seventeenth floor!" he yelled at someone just off to the left. Sirad looked beyond him to see Hamid leaning against the fireplace mantel. He looked distraught, afraid.

"I'm sorry, Mr. Mitchell," he said. "I thought it would be safe here."

Sirad started to retch again but fought the nausea back to a couple hiccups.

"Dammit, clean her up," Mitchell commanded. Chris and two others lifted her to her feet and walked her out of the room, leaving Mitchell with Dieter and Hamid. Trask had flown out of town for the afternoon to take care of another crucial matter.

"Did she download anything?" Mitchell asked when they were alone.

Dieter shook his head. "But she was trying to. We still don't know what — if anything — she knows about the larger operation."

Hamid ventured an opinion. "She couldn't have gotten anything except some account dupes. That's all I have here. The alal-Bin documents have never been copied. They've never left the building."

"That you know of!" Mitchell snapped. He began to pace. "I want her locked down. We have no time to waste on any more problems."

"Mr. Mitchell . . . ," Dieter responded. "Locking her down is only going to create more problems. If she really is trying to steal from us, we need to let her go and continue to follow her. It's the only way we're going to find out who she's working with."

"Hamid?" Mitchell turned to the man most intimately familiar with both Sirad and the peripherals trading.

"I agree. She trusts me, Mr. Mitchell. Let her stay here for a couple days, and I'll find out what she knows." Whatever personal interest Hamid felt toward Sirad paled in comparison to what she could cost him. "If the dates on the alal-Bin documents are accurate, we still have forty-eight hours to turn this to our favor."

Mitchell stopped pacing and nodded. Two days from now the United States would face the most devastating attack in its history — an attack on its money supply, an attack that would hand someone virtual control over the most powerful economy on Earth. He had invested billions to protect himself — to make certain that he profited, even — and though things had gone well in the early stages, they were now spinning quickly out of control. Hamid was correct; there was little time but no cause for panic.

"All right," Mitchell agreed. "But I want a team on her round the clock." Mitchell pointed at Hamid. "And I want your transaction analysis by morning. Waller just arrived in New York, our intercept facilities are picking up significant spikes in SBT chatter, and the Agency is very quiet. We've got to close this."

Dieter nodded his head. Like Mitchell, he knew that business hated nothing more than uncertainty, and when it came right down to it, this was still just business.

▮

"BEAUTIFUL, AREN'T THEY?"

Phillip Matthews stopped near an exhibit of eighteenth-century violins on the third floor of the National Museum of American History. Of all the Smithsonians, this had always been his favorite.

He turned toward a tall, ordinary-looking man dressed in khaki slacks and a dark green blazer. The visitor could have been a tour guide or museum staff. He wore his hair short and stood board straight, as if retired from a career in the military.

"Yes," Phillip responded. "It's a Stradivarius, made in 1762 for a Frenchman named Henri Larouse d'Attansione, whose only claim to fame is that he played this gorgeous instrument at Versailles for Marie Antoinette the night before she was imprisoned. It likely played the last agreeable sound to caress her ears."

"That's nice," the man said, holding his voice low as tour groups of high school students flittered around them. He had just taken the Delta shuttle down from New York and had little time for idle chat. "What's the problem?"

Phillip tried to look as if he was studying the Stradivarius.

"Beechum has a tape."

The man next to him slouched ever so slightly, then regained his posture.

"A tape? What kind of tape?"

"A tape of that night. The night of the attack — she apparently had a cell phone. She recorded the whole thing on her office answering machine."

"What does that prove?" he asked. "She could have doctored something up through dozens of recording studios. No one will believe her now."

"She got a copy from the NSA."

"How the hell . . ."

"I don't know, and I don't care. But there's more. It mentions Parsons by name."

"Parsons? Who the hell mentioned his name? He's not even . . ."

A group of Gray Panthers turned toward him. One of the little old ladies held up a finger and told him to hush.

"You heard the tape?" the man asked.

"Over the phone, yes. She told me she had to make some other arrangements before she took it to the FBI."

"Other arrangements?"

"I have to imagine that she got this thing through unofficial channels. She's probably trying to leverage a paper trail."

"So, she can't use it yet?"

"I don't think so," Phillip said. "Beechum doesn't have the security clearances she'd need to get this kind of information legitimately."

The man tilted his head back and stared at the ceiling.

"I'm her lawyer," Phillip whispered. "I think I can stall things for twenty-four hours, but you need to take care of this."

"No, *you* need to take care of this." The man didn't hesitate. "I'm not going to risk my ass for your screwup. Deal with it, or we'll deal with you."

"Don't threaten me," Phillip spat. "I'm an attorney. I have some experience in these matters."

John Trask, Jordan Mitchell's right-hand man, stared at what now appeared to be the weak link in this enormously complicated, though meticulously planned, operation.

"Don't overestimate the power of the law," Trask warned. "Remember, we have some experience ourselves."

XX

―――――

JEREMY AND LOTTSPEICH touched down at JFK just before dark and were met in the parking lot by a blacked-out Bureau Suburban with a SWAT ladder package, grille cage, and oversized running boards. The fact that this war wagon stood out in a sea of Town Cars didn't seem to faze the driver, who wore a flattop haircut and had biceps like cantaloupes. The third-year FBI agent wanted to try out for HRT and obviously enjoyed the stares he drew from passing motorists. He hammered the two Xray snipers with wannabe questions from the time he picked them up to the time they rolled into an offsite command post just across the Triborough Bridge.

Jeremy sat in the back on the way in and let his partner do most of the talking. The only thing on his mind was what had happened in Yemen, and with each passing moment, he worried more and more about the documents Jesús had taken from the dead men: names, identification, photos, addresses, credit cards — even in the low light Jeremy had seen the things he pulled from their pockets. And what about the papers Jesús had taken from atop the table? Were they the plans Jesús talked about? The Wedding plans, this Matrix 1016?

By the time they arrived at the command post, Jeremy had decided that Jesús' diversion on the way home must have been to drop off the documents with someone in the New York office. That office had handled both World Trade Center bombings, as well as the Blind Sheik's plot to blow up bridges and tunnels, the USS *Cole* attack, and the East Africa embassy bombings in Dar es Salaam and Nairobi. It only made sense that the New York field office would be most interested in alal-Bin and any attack on the Federal Reserve.

"Waller!" a man called out as Jeremy and Lottspeich entered the main room of a large warehouse facility just off the East River. It was a Detroit accent, deep and gruff. "How the hell you been, man?"

Jeremy turned toward a beefy Italian American with thick black hair. His name was Andy Amustifano; they had been roommates during new agent training at the Academy.

"Musto!" Jeremy called back. He shook the man's hand, delighted to see his old friend. "What are you doing out here?"

Musto was an accountant and former banker who, according to their last phone conversation, had been assigned to one of the New York field office's white-collar-crime squads. It struck Jeremy as odd that he would find a bean counter at a protection detail briefing like this, but then again, the war on terrorism had changed everything. Jeremy could see the Glock 10mm pistol hanging off Musto's belt.

"They got me on the JTTF now," Musto said. His new assignment to New York's Joint Terrorism Task Force obviously had him out on the streets. "I've been working forensic accounting on al Qaeda financial transfers for almost a year now — you wouldn't believe the things we're doing out there. But look at you, man — all high-speed HRT and shit. We always said you'd end up there on your way to the director's chair."

Jeremy laughed out loud, scanning the command post around him. Each of the FBI's fifty-six offices now manned a Joint Terrorism Task Force, and it appeared that they had taken over operations for the G8 summit. Dozens of people hurried about the huge room, working computer terminals, STU-II secure telephones, PowerPoint time lines, copiers, television monitors — it was a madhouse of activity.

"Hey, Waller!" Lottspeich yelled. He and the driver with the arms were standing next to a man in black BDUs. All three looked like models for some kind of tactical operations recruiting poster. "Get your ass over here."

Jeremy told Musto he'd catch up with him later, then walked over to meet the New York SWAT team's sniper coordinator, a former HRT operator named Nakamoto. Nakamoto was a bit of a legend on the team, having held the designations of being HRT's only Mormon bishop — their only Mormon ever, for that matter — and the most prolific shooter in the team's twenty-one-year history. The diminutive and constantly smiling Japanese American had shot and killed four men in three different encounters.

"Nice to meet you," Jeremy said during introductions. He wondered for a moment if killing women, children, and terrorists in foreign countries pushed him past Nakamoto on the list of dubious distinctions.

The guy with the arms led everyone into a side room where two dozen men and women sat in folding chairs arranged roughly into rows. A nondescript-looking man in a tie but no jacket stood at the front of the room reading from a piece of paper. He noticed Nakamoto arriving with the two HRT snipers and looked out over the room.

"All right, let's get started!" he called out. The room quieted, and Jeremy took a seat next to Lottspeich along a side wall.

"I'm not going to waste your time with introductions, but let me point out the non-JTTF members here." He pointed to three men in the front row, all white males in their forties. "These are reps from the CIA's Counterterrorism Center, the Naval Investigative Service, and the State Department's INS. I'd tell you their names, but that would probably violate some kind of national security protocol, and I'm sure they're fake anyway."

The room filled with laughter. The atmosphere seemed pretty jovial compared to other operations briefings Jeremy had attended.

"We've also got two HRT snipers who have come up from Quantico to advance their detachment. Welcome, gentlemen." Jeremy and Lottspeich nodded to the room.

"Finally, we've got a medical support element here from the

Army — two trauma surgeons and three medics who will be assigned to the tactical element. Anything goes wrong, I've been assured that these people will get us to Bellevue, which has been designated our principal trauma center."

With that, the assistant special agent in charge of counterterrorism investigations for the New York field office of the FBI laid out a briefing that seemed more detailed and elaborate than anything Jeremy had seen before. In a five-paragraph order, much like what HRT had used in Puerto Rico, he covered everything from individual team assignments to threat assessments, evacuation routes, weather forecasts — complete with moon and sun cycles — radio frequencies, vehicle allocations, and, of course, the major case number so everyone could properly fill out paperwork. Nothing happened in the FBI unless it was recorded on paper.

"There's one other thing I need to brief you on before you take off," the ASAC said. "Most of you have probably heard talk of Matrix 1016 — an al Qaeda op called the Wedding. It involves some sort of attack on the Federal Reserve, though we haven't yet determined what. Could be some sort of WMD threat or a high-tech cybercrime attack."

Jeremy stared at the man, suddenly confused about the whole meeting. Surely an ASAC in charge of protective services for a G8 meeting involving some of the highest-profile financial ministers in the world would know about what he and Jesús had found in Yemen. Based on what Jesús had said, alal-Bin's death had come during the final operational meeting of his inner circle, meaning the documents on that table had to include specific times and details. If the task force hadn't got access to those documents, who had?

"I want to point out that we have no specific threats against any of our principals, but we have to assume that they're targets. Our CIA friend, here, has provided some very close-hold, sole-source information about a technical cell in Malta that may be playing a role in this Wedding. Unfortunately, virtually everyone we have been watching has gone to those new SBT phones, making it impossible to listen in. Chatter that we can track has virtually gone away."

Everyone in the room groaned, swore, or hissed. Borders Atlantic had surpassed Jane Fonda as the most reviled name in the law enforcement and intelligence communities. Mitchell's name had become synonymous with *traitor.*

"At this point," the ASAC continued, "we're flying blind as far as signals intelligence goes. That means that even though we don't have a specific threat, we have to assume the worst."

Jeremy felt a cold chill run down his spine. Within twelve hours, two teams of HRT operators and a couple hundred other members of this multiagency operation were going to stand guard over half the world's money brokers. Information he and Jesús found in Yemen had to have relevance, but the FBI's biggest and best-connected office apparently knew nothing about it.

Once the ASAC finished, Jeremy walked out of the room and found Musto shuffling a stack of leads that had just come in over secure fax from the Counterterrorism Watch at the headquarters-based Strategic Information Operations Center, or SIOC.

"Musto, I need a favor," Jeremy said. He and Lottspeich had to conduct site surveys at two hotels and route reconnaissance for four different midtown convoy movements. The guy with the Popeye arms was already waiting outside. "You can get access to anything, right?"

"Pretty much, yeah. Why? What do you need?"

"Let's say I knew about a specific NMARSAT call, placed on a certain date and time from a specific location overseas, right down to the GPS coordinates. Could you backtrack it? Could you get me origination and terminus information?"

Jeremy had known since leaving Yemen that whoever coordinated the mission took great pains to avoid any trail. He had turned in his fake passport and identity pack to Jesús just before leaving London. Takeoff/landing logs at Manassas would list a fake tail number on the G-IV. There were no credit card purchases, wire transactions, or anything else to trace. Jesús had covered everything except for the phone call. He must have assumed that as long as he kept the hardware, that too would be just another dead end.

"It's possible, sure." Musto shrugged. "But it will raise some red flags."

"It's important," Jeremy said. He hoped that would be enough.

"All right. Give me twenty-four hours, and I'll let you know what I find out, OK?"

"Hey, Waller! Let's go," Lottspeich yelled from the door.

"It was placed out of a remote section in Yemen called Hadramawt," Jeremy said. He wrote down the time, date, and GPS coordinates of Jesús' call. "It lasted less than twenty seconds, but I'm relatively sure it went out to somewhere in the United States." Jeremy moved close to Musto so that no one else could hear him. "And I don't have twenty-four hours, buddy. I've got twelve. Maybe less."

"I'll see what I can do," Musto said. He could tell from the look on his old roommate's face that this was serious.

▮

SIRAD KNEW THEY would follow her every move, but things had degraded to the point where she needed to talk with Hoch. The attack in Hamid's apartment made no sense on any level. Surely Borders Atlantic had wired the space with cameras and microphones, but she had cleaned herself too well prior to entering the apartment; there was no way anyone from the seventeenth floor could have followed her. So who was this man?

She lay in bed for an hour, trying to clear her throbbing head, running through a long list of questions. Had he been there waiting for her? Had he broken in looking for the same things she wanted? How had Mitchell and his goons got there so quickly, even if the alarm had tipped them off?

Once Mitchell, Hamid, and the doctor they'd sent to treat her had gone, Sirad got up and dressed simply in jeans and a cotton sweater. Yes, they would be watching her, but at this point, she had few options.

She took a series of cabs around New York, using the same countersurveillance techniques she had used earlier in the day. This time, she carried only cash — no purse, phone, cards, or anything else security could have rigged with a homing device.

Once she felt she was clean, Sirad walked into a midtown cybercafe, ordered a skinny soy latte, and sat down at a public terminal. By the time her cup had cooled enough to drink, she had accessed a student activities bulletin board on the Indiana State University

Web site and logged on. Within seconds, someone named APEX575 logged on to join her. Though anyone reading the exchange would think it just another coed chitchat, APEX575 was actually the screen name of a CIA safety officer sitting in a Chantilly, Virginia, off-site. The bulletin board was an emergency contact backstop for nonofficial cover agents who found themselves in situations just like this. APEX575 was her ticket out.

Sirad typed in her own screen name.

```
PORTIA27   Life getting confusing. Looking for
           advice.
APEX575    How can I help?
PORTIA27   Need to meet with mentor.
APEX575    Impossible. Needs?
PORTIA27   Direction.
APEX575    Search home base. ASAP. Time urgent.
PORTIA27   Peripherals data?
```

Sirad waited a moment for her answer. She had just asked to meet with Hoch at a predetermined spot and been told that he was not in New York. He had left instructions for her to search Hamid's Borders Atlantic office computers as soon as possible, but she did not know why. Perhaps that was by design.

```
APEX575    Yes. Time urgent. No additional
           information.
```

Sirad checked out of the chat room, looked around for any signs that someone might have followed her, then logged off. She finished her coffee and rode to a travel agency, where she used more of her cash to purchase a first-class, one-way ticket to Belize. The ticket read Marta Rodriguez, an alias she had backstopped herself.

Never jump without a reserve chute, they'd told her at jump school in North Carolina. Things were beginning to spin a little too quickly, even for her taste: Sirad Malneaux wanted to make sure that, if necessary, she could once again become one of those people that never really existed to begin with.

▐▌

ELIZABETH BEECHUM HADN'T even got back to her office when George Sheridan, the DCI, called to say he had traced the rolling dice tattoo to a small special operations unit out of Tooele Army Depot in Utah. Several members of the 62nd Ordnance Company had been assigned to a joint CIA/Defense Department operation called Task Force Medina, which searched for evidence of chemical and biological weapons during the war. Three seven-man teams of chem/bio sleuths, explosive ordnance disposal technicians, and small-weapons specialists had fanned out over Iraq to try to gather evidence of Saddam's WMD programs.

One of the teams had been entirely wiped out in a fedayeen Saddam ambush, the second had died in a helicopter crash, and the third had completed its work, though months of effort had failed to produce a single cache. Of the surviving seven team members, four were scientists and three were Special Forces soldiers who had got tattoos of rolling dice with 1* — a play on the SWAT slogan One ass to risk — and three twos — 32 — to commemorate their unit back in Utah. Two of the soldiers had transferred to 7th Group headquarters in Panama; the third had been disciplined for mistreatment of prisoners near Kirkuk and dishonorably discharged after a year in the brig.

That man's name was Edgar Gene Valez, a master sergeant born July 27, 1962, in Oxford, Mississippi. According to Sheridan, the man's processing-out information listed a forwarding address of 178 79th Street, Fort Lee, New Jersey. No known occupation.

"Hello, James?" Beechum spoke into her cell phone. Though bail provisions restricted her to a twenty-mile area around Washington, there was no way she could sit back and wait for the FBI to step in. Knowing full well the potential consequences, Beechum had jumped on the Delta shuttle to New York.

"Are you nuts?" were his first words. Beechum had left him a voicemail message before she departed, filling him in on the basics and directing him toward something they had both overlooked during the investigation at her home. "How could you just disappear like this? The police are completely blowing this all out of proportion."

"Blowing what out of proportion?"

"Haven't you seen the news?"

"I've been on a plane for the last hour, James," she said. "What happened?"

"What happened is that your lawyer just withdrew from your case. He said it was a disagreement over defense strategy, but someone is leaking reports that you admitted specific national security violations and then tried to hide behind attorney-client privilege. Tomorrow's *Post* will report that Phillip went to the FBI claiming he had a 'moral obligation' to withdraw from the case and turn you in."

"That son of a bitch!" Beechum exclaimed. She'd known Phillip for twenty years.

"The media have surrounded your house, and the DC police are trying to revoke your bond. As soon as they find out you're in New York, I'm sure they will. You need to get back down here as soon as . . ."

"I'm not going anywhere." She scowled. "The only way we're going to stop this madness is to find the man who attacked me."

"How? You think you're just going to walk up to his door and ask him to testify that he tried to frame you for murder? He'll probably try to kill you!"

Beechum dismissed his outburst and hustled up the gangway from the plane to the Marine Terminal.

"Don't worry about me . . . stop trying to boss me around and tell me what you found."

There was a pause as James tried to decide what to say next. He knew there was no point in arguing.

"Well, you were right about the tunnel at least," he finally conceded. "I went back to the house, walked upstairs, and found the secret door, just like you said — followed it all the way out through the basement to the neighbor's garden. I only had a flashlight and it was damned dark in there, but I found clear evidence that the door had been jimmied. By the time I got back upstairs, the private investigators you called were there. They lifted two sets of latent prints. One came back to the guy Sheridan gave you — Edgar Gene Valez, date of birth July 27, 1962, but with a different address: 271 West Ninetieth Street, Apartment 7A, New York, New York. I don't know where he's living, but that's where he's paying utilities."

Beechum broke into a broad smile as she walked out toward the exit doors, dodging a crowd of business commuters. What James had found was hard evidence of how the attackers had got into and out of her house — proof that they had used the same secret tunnel Ellington Peach and his Civil War cabal had sneaked in through 140 years earlier. It also proved that whoever broke in had intimate knowledge of her home. Only Paul's dinner guests and Georgetown students had ever seen the tunnel.

"What about the other?" Beechum asked. Silence.

"James?" she asked again. "You said there were two sets of prints. Did you get a name on the other?"

"Yes, I did," he answered as Beechum climbed into a hired Town Car and headed for New York City.

"Well?"

He changed the subject. "The investigators used spectral analysis to find blood droplets on the stairs leading down and smudges on the door leading outside. It will take time to run the DNA, but I've got to believe that it will come back to Craig Slater."

"What about the second print? You said they found two sets of prints."

James took a deep breath. "The investigators ran it through their sources. It came back to Phillip."

Beechum sat bolt upright in her seat.

"Phillip James Matthews, date of birth January 16, 1942, SSN 003-56-1189, 27 Marshfield Mews, Arlington, Virginia. It's your law-yer, Senator," James said. "Right after you ask him about dropping your case, you might want to ask him why he was sneaking in and out through your basement with blood on his hands."

▮

"ALL RIGHT, WHERE is she?"

Mitchell stood at the end of the War Room's massive conference table. Dieter and Hamid sat to his left; Trask to his right. He looked poised, consigned, prescient, like a field marshal on the eve of combat.

"She left Hamid's apartment shortly after the incident," Trask said. "The surveillance detail lost her in traffic, but she logged on to a computer at a cybercafe in SoHo. We're still trying to capture all her activities, but we're pretty sure she accessed several offshore accounts that she holds under aliases."

"Good."

Mitchell had long suspected Sirad's motives relative to the SBT project. There was no question now that she had planted software in Hamid's PDA, but that brazen willingness to betray any authority was exactly what he prized in her. Besides, the seventeenth floor had detected her intrusions early enough that they hadn't compromised anything but the peripherals trading.

"Where is she now?"

"She entered the building ten minutes ago and went straight to her office," Trask replied. "The last I saw, she was attending to logistical details for her upcoming trip to London. If she has the time line, she's not showing it."

"All right, show me what we've got."

Trask pressed a button, triggering a series of graphs, flowcharts, and time signatures on monitors at the presentation wall.

"Our frequency analyses and flow graphics show several things: the cell managers have not contacted the trigger, but we believe he is some sort of money manager with access to the FedWire, here in New York."

Trask stood and walked to one of the screens, which showed a flowchart representing the top seventeen members of the al Qaeda organization, descending from alal-Bin through cell managers in Sudan, Indonesia, Pakistan, Morocco, and Canada.

"Sometime around four AM, they plan to attack the Federal Reserve system by taking out trunk cache transfers to Asia. Japan goes shortly thereafter, then Europe — a daisy chain of monstrous failures that will bring down banks and securities exchanges."

Mitchell and the others listened as Trask outlined intelligence that Borders Atlantic had intercepted through their SBT phones. The conduit they had set in place worked exactly as they had hoped. Though everyone from al Qaeda operatives to Middle Eastern oil sheiks believed they were immune from NSA intercepts, every word they uttered was now being channeled through the seventeenth floor, where translators and analysts distilled conversations into actionable intelligence and passed it directly on to Mitchell's inner circle.

"Things get kind of complex after that because of the size of the numbers we're dealing with, but the bottom line is that once al Qaeda makes its move, we will insert our own software, essentially taking custody of the whole train wreck. Our involvement will be totally transparent — kind of like a cybermirror — but the impact will be huge. Not only will we seize control of all Hamid's peripheral investments — with plausible deniability for anyone who claims losses — but we estimate that we can skim one to three percent of all diverted funds. By the time regulators sort through the burning wreckage, we'll be long gone."

"Zero footprint," Mitchell said.

"Zero footprint for us, sir," Trask corrected him. "Al Qaeda will claim credit, incur the wrath of an already angry White House, and face all the retribution."

Jordan Mitchell walked to the east-end window and looked out over New York at night.

"What about Beechum?" he asked.

"Progressing well." Trask threw copies of advance Web site stories from the *Washington Post* and *New York Times* on the conference table. "Her lawyer pulled out of the case. Both the FBI and local PDs have asked for revocation of bond. It's only getting worse for her. She hired a private investigative firm to search her house, and they found fingerprints, but we're taking care of that. Once America reads the stories our sources have planted, no one will hear a word she says."

"How about our other elements?" He returned to his desk and picked up one personnel dossier in particular.

"In place. Time line looks good. We feel very confident that our lines to the Yemen action have been protected. Once we get the intercepts, Borders Atlantic will be well positioned for the takedown. Right on schedule."

"Good."

Mitchell walked over to one of the display cases and traced his finger over the glass protecting his rarest and most treasured weapon, a brass-and-nickel Henry in caliber .5440. It had been offered to Crazy Horse as a gesture of goodwill just prior to the Sioux relocation to the Pine Ridge reservation, but Ulysses S. Grant had made his personal gunsmith shave down the firing pin out of concern that the Indian chieftain would use it on American troops.

"How's sales?" he asked. Even with all the public outrage over the SBT deal, the threats of congressional investigation, and reams of FBI subpoenas, his book sales had continued to climb, proving the adage that there is no such thing as bad publicity.

"Eighty thousand, week to date," Trask said. "We just placed two full-page ads in the *New York Times* targeting junior executives in the twenty-one to thirty demographic. I think sales will really take off if we structure this thing properly."

Mitchell nodded. For better or worse, he was a capitalist. Even with less than eight hours left before the high-wire act that could collapse America's economy and the domino effect that would ensue, he had to make sure all his bases were covered. The strong would survive, and when they did, he planned to stand tallest among them.

XXI

JEREMY CHECKED HIS watch as he stepped into the elevator of the Essex House, one of New York's finest Central Park hotels: 11:17 PM. In the four hours since he and Lottspeich left the command post, they had checked every door, corridor, closet, and fire extinguisher on the fourteenth floor. They had secured the elevator shafts, cleared nonpublic access spaces from the roof to the kitchens, cross-referenced the entire guest registry with National Criminal Information Center and Immigration Customs Enforcement warrants, and conducted threat-assessment checks against CIA, Customs, and Secret Service databases.

Everything looked right for the 6:15 AM arrival of their principal — Afghanistan's foreign minister — and his entourage. Jeremy felt good that they had made such quick progress, but all of this seemed secondary to his real imperative: the phone number from Musto.

"What about the route recon?" Lottspeich asked as they rode down in the elevator. Somebody still had to pre-run the security detail's movement from the hotel to the G8 Summit venue on Thirty-second Street.

"Let Jesús and the other guys handle the recon," Jeremy said.

"They haven't done crap yet, and we still have to check the magnetometer calibrations and verify entrance lists."

Jeremy and his teammate had covered nearly every item on the ten-page site survey checklist and done it in half the time normally allowed. With the principal due into the airport in less than seven hours, it only made sense that Jesús would divide the rest of the job among his other team members.

"Look, I've got to make a quick call," Jeremy said as the elevator came to a stop on the ground floor. "Why don't you check on the magnetometers, and I'll try to get ahold of someone in the command post to see how our time line is running."

Lottspeich nodded his head and started toward the main lobby, where a crowd of suit-clad security guards were already gearing up for the next day's events.

"Don't forget to ask about vehicles," he said. "I want to make sure they don't stick us with junk. We need three SUVs."

"Got it." Jeremy split left toward the security office and entered a cluttered, windowless space with a time clock on one wall and a bulletin board full of hotel policy statements on the other.

Jeremy picked up a phone, pressed nine, then dialed the number Musto had given him in the Joint Operations Center.

"Amustifano," a male voice answered over a din of voices and office machinery.

"Musto, it's Jeremy. You got anything yet?"

"I got a 'you owe me,' man. Lots of people wanted to know what in hell I was doing trying to track an NMARSAT call out of Yemen — especially once they logged in and saw the file indicator."

"What do you mean?" Jeremy checked his watch again. Jesús and the others would be there any minute.

"Less than three minutes after your NMARSAT call, NSA tracked an inbound communication from Hamburg, Germany, to coordinates less than one hundred meters from the GPS coordinates you gave me. It was one of those new SBT cell phone calls, so they couldn't listen in — but the timing and proximity of the two communications really raised some flags. People are really wound up about this whole Matrix 1016 thing, Jeremy. I'm getting a lot of pressure to justify my request."

Jeremy thought to himself for a moment.

"Do what you've got to do," he said. "I'm not trying to hide anything."

He was lying of course, but it seemed his only option. Any formal inquiry would start with some midlevel manager at the National Security Agency and have to find its way through an overworked Terror Threat Information Center. By the time they tracked this to Jeremy, he would have found what he needed.

"So, did you get it?" he asked.

Musto lowered his voice to where Jeremy could just hear it above the office noise before reciting the ten digits. "It's a New York number. Comes back to an investment subsidiary of Borders Atlantic. Jeremy, I don't know what the hell you're onto, but you might want to consider bringing it in here. The SAC just got a stack of FISA warrants and national security letters against Jordan Mitchell over that SBT deal with the Saudis. Once NSA does a frequency analysis on these calls of yours, it's going to be flash traffic to the president."

"Borders Atlantic? Are you sure?" Jeremy asked.

"You hearing me, Jeremy?"

"I need to know, Musto — where in Borders Atlantic? Do you have a specific name? A floor? Give me something, goddammit!"

"I'm trying to help you, Jeremy. And I'm telling you to watch your ass. This isn't going to stop here. Someone's going to come looking for you."

"Thanks, Musto," Jeremy said, tracing the number, making sure he could read what he had just jotted down. "I'm not trying to screw you, bud — I'm just looking for some answers myself. Believe me, you'll be the first to know if I get them."

With that, he hung up the phone and took a deep breath. Why would Jesús have called one of America's largest corporations? he wondered — the same company everyone from the *Washington Post* to the President of the United States was vilifying for shamelessly trading national security for corporate profits. Had they bought Jesús, too?

That son of a bitch, Jeremy swore to himself.

He picked up the phone again and dialed nine. Who but someone with Mitchell's money and connections could have pulled off a hit like this? Who but Mitchell had access through the SBT phone alal-

Bin was using? Who would have shown the audacity and shameless lack of respect for the law? But why?

Jeremy had just dialed half the number Musto had given him when the door to the security office opened. In walked Jesús.

"I hear you've been busy," the team leader said. He did not look happy.

Jeremy hung up the phone. "You're early."

Jesús looked around the room to make sure it was empty. "Lottspeich says you're done."

"Except for the route recon. I figured you guys could help with that while we finish up around here."

Jesús walked to within inches of where Jeremy was sitting. He reached down to the table and picked up the piece of paper on which Jeremy had written Musto's office number.

"There's someone here to see you," Jesús said. He stared Jeremy straight in the eyes and shook his head. No words would have had greater impact.

"Special Agent Waller?" a voice said. It was a woman's voice, firm yet almost condescendingly sympathetic. She entered with two SWAT agents, including the guy with the Popeye arms.

"I'm Sheila Reynolds with the New York field office's Employee Assistance Program. I think we should take a few minutes to talk."

Jeremy's stomach rose into his throat. EAP came after people with drug and alcohol problems . . . and agents who had lost their mind.

"We would like you to come with us," the woman said. Her tone may have been soft, but there was no denying her authority.

Jeremy looked to the door, then at the SWAT agents and Jesús. There was no way around them.

"All right," he said. He stood up.

"Wait a minute, Waller." Jesús stopped him. He held out his right hand. "They're going to confine you to a room until we can get you out of here for a fitness-for-duty assessment. Until then, I'm gonna need your gun and creds."

⬛

BEECHUM'S TOWN CAR pulled to the corner of Broadway and Ninetieth Street in a hot August drizzle. The New Jersey address

Sheridan first provided had turned out to be a mail drop; this had to be it.

The senator stared up through her window at a dark brick facade. Only three lights burned in windows. Considering the hour, that didn't strike her as odd.

"Wait here, will you?" Beechum asked the driver.

She climbed out of the car and hurried through the rain toward the building. It wasn't until she reached the front door that she realized she had a problem. A doorman stood between her and the elevators.

"May I help you?" he asked. He looked at her quizzically, as if he recognized her face but couldn't believe that the spy murderess he saw on television all the time would show up at his building near midnight, sodden and cold.

"Yes . . . I . . . Oh, what the hell — you probably already know who I am, don't you?"

The man avoided looking at the *Globe* tabloid that sat on his desk. Beechum's face was plastered across the cover with the words *TRAITOR ON THE RUN.*

"Yeah, I know who you are." He tried to sound casual. Doormen saw lots of things.

"I need to speak with one of your tenants," Beechum said. There was no point in trying a ruse. "You have someone named Valez in 7A," she continued. "I think he is the man who attacked me in my home and that he may be part of a conspiracy to frame me."

The doorman nodded, as if trying to figure out what the hell to do. Then he lifted a clipboard off his table and ran a finger down the entry log.

"Look, Senator Beechum, I got a brother at Rikers Island says he never kilt no one. I got a high school buddy doing time for armed robbery; said he was framed. So most times I would tell you to your face that you're scum for betrayin' the voters trust and killin' that man from the White House, you know? But I seen this Valez guy most every day for the past two and a half years; always treated him decent — Morning, Mr. Valez; Evenin', Mr. Valez. Never got the time of day. Not once did he even say hello."

Beechum tried not to stare as her face appeared on a small television next to the doorman's security monitors. He had it tuned to

MSNBC, and the slug line read *POLICE: BEECHUM BELIEVED TO HAVE SPIED*. Beneath her face, the crawl line reported: *SOURCES SAY DAMAGE TO NATION "DEVASTATING."*

"I'd help you if I could, but you're about . . ." — he ran his finger down the log — "about twenty minutes too late. He moved his things out this afternoon, all of a sudden. I just got him a cab to Grand Central. Sorry, Senator, but he's gone."

▐▌

MOST EMPLOYEES TALKED about the seventeenth floor of the Borders Atlantic headquarters in hushed tones, knowing from rumor and legend that this is where the world's biggest telecommunications corporation kept its secrets. In fact, everything from confidential personnel files to close-hold technology patents, such as the Quantis SBT phone blueprints, was kept there. But the Rabbit Hole also housed corporate intelligence, security and communications operations that few people outside Dieter Planck's immediate circle knew anything about.

"Where are we?" Mitchell asked as Trask led him out of the elevators, into an ordinary-looking reception room. A uniformed security guard sat at a desk off to the left. Twin couches faced each other to the right. Directly ahead stood heavy wooden double doors.

"We have a definite time but still no word on the actual attack," Trask said. He swiped a magnetic pass card through a reader and punched a five-digit random access code into the cipher box. The system monitored all entries and exits. "Traffic intercepts indicate six AM GMT — that's a little more than an hour."

"Good evening, Mr. Mitchell," Dieter said once they were inside. Borders Atlantic's security director wore his customary wire-rimmed glasses and a navy pinstripe with Dresden lapels. He led his two guests down a hallway and into a room that contained a single Lucite desk and one of the new Apple iMac terminals. An unkempt man in a lab coat bearing the name "Russ" stared up from his perch at the keyboard.

"This is it?" Mitchell asked. The scene struck him as a complete anticlimax.

"Oh, don't let it mislead you," Russ said. "This is just the user interface. What you don't see is the series of Cray mainframes that make it work. We call it Oz. It puts anything the NSA has to shame. Runs circles around the Seven Dwarfs."

"The what?"

"CIA's main data-processing center," Russ explained. "Seven series-stable platforms running in concert. This blows it away; Oz is the most sophisticated information-processing center in existence."

Jordan liked this man immediately. He spoke with economy, knew his business, and obviously felt passionately about keeping Borders Atlantic well out in front of the slower world. "Let's see what it can do," he said.

"Yeah. Good." Russ scratched out a series of mouse clicks and brought up a screen full of attractive graphics aimed at simplifying a complicated array of high-speed Internet functions. He clicked on an icon labeled Transfers. The screen changed to reveal a businesslike yet imaginative background and three distinct option buttons: Traffic, Origination, Routing.

"Are we ready?" Mitchell asked.

Russ pointed to the Traffic icon, then clicked on it.

"It'll take awhile before the fireworks start," he said. "There's a delay for accounting purposes and security code accesses. But it's mid-morning in the Middle East. They're watching for signs of trouble."

"We ready for them?" Mitchell asked.

"Oh, yes. Here . . . listen to this."

He clicked on another icon: Origination. This time, a map of the world flashed on the screen. Russ demonstrated the program's ability to isolate regions, countries, cities, and individual financial and government organizations.

"This is our tracking program. It incorporates GPS locator features in the Quantis phones with their electronic serial number indicators, financial transaction updates, and forensic accounting software."

The screen lit up with graphic and text representations of specifically who was using Quantis phones, where they were, and what they were saying.

"Every word, image, or byte of information traveling through our network is accessible at this or any other designated terminal. There . . . look — we have our first bite."

Dieter activated internal speakers, and the electronically shielded room filled with the sounds of men in conversation — Arabic — with a translator's voice in the background. The conversation was casual, two men trying out their new toys.

"Damascus foreign ministry to a Libyan rug merchant in Alexandria, Virginia," Russ said.

"Looks like they can export these things faster than we can," Mitchell noted.

"DHL overnight," Dieter cracked.

"Here we go. It's starting."

Oz calculated, then locked onto cell phone transmissions, Internet servers, and a vast array of civilian and military communications satellites, including those of the NSA and National Reconnaissance Office. Within seconds the screen erupted with information — an entire network of international greed and subterfuge exposed to Mitchell's electronic wizardry.

Mitchell shook his head at how easily he'd breached the government's thickest firewalls. Money. Someone had to build the spy equipment they used to snoop on the world. Who better than the world's largest telecommunications company? Borders Atlantic had simply bid well beneath the competition, knowing that in the long term, they'd gain more profits from information than product development.

Amazing, he thought, that the CIA and NSA obsessed about individual security clearances and cipher locks on doors, but paid little attention to the owners of the corporations they did business with. People like Robert Hanssen and Aldrich Ames were pedestrian in their knowledge compared to major development firms like Ford Aerospace and Rand and SAIC. These companies wrote the software, developed the products, and printed the instruction manuals and administrative protocols used by every spook cell in America. It was like locking the cookie jar but forgetting about the guy with the recipe.

"This is it, Mr. Mitchell," Dieter said. He could barely contain his excitement as he turned up the volume on one particular conversation between the Syrian foreign ministry and the Libyan rug merchant.

"This is the call we've been waiting for. And I know it sounds cliché, but the reality is that in less than an hour from now, Borders Atlantic will quite literally own the world."

▌▌

JEREMY SAT ON one of two queen-size beds in a nicely appointed room on the Essex House's eighth floor. The EAP counselor sat in an overstuffed chair to his right. The guy with the arms stood near the door.

"Is there anything I can get you?" the woman asked. "Some tea? A ginger ale?"

Ginger ale? Jeremy screamed inside his head. His whole world was coming to a screeching halt, and she was treating him as if he had the flu!

"I'm fine, thanks," he said, trying to muster a look that approximated sanity. There was no telling what they had said to her. Irrational behavior, delusions, unexplained disappearances from work. And that bit down at the Farm . . . what a stupid mistake.

Jeremy thought about the looks on his teammates' faces as he walked past them on his way up to the room. Lottspeich had been the only one to wish him well; the others just stared, caught somewhere between sympathy and betrayal. Jeremy sat on his bed wondering if Caroline would look the same.

Jeremy tried to remember the phone number. He had to get out of that room — to find out what Jesús wanted so badly to keep him away from.

"Actually, some hot tea would be great," he said. It had to be something she couldn't pull out of the courtesy bar, something she'd have to call down for. "Excuse me for a minute, OK? I've got to use the men's room."

The woman smiled that same sympathetic grin he'd got from the shrink after the Puerto Rico gig. "You go ahead while I call room service."

Jeremy stood up and started toward the bathroom, moving slowly past his muscle-bound guard. He watched the SWAT agent out of the corner of his eye, hoping to find some sign of weakness, some opportunity to strike and escape.

"Sorry, bud, but I gotta stay with you at all times," the man said. He puffed himself up and followed Jeremy into the bathroom.

"Knock yourself out," Jeremy said. He turned toward the toilet and started to unzip as the man caught himself in the mirror and flexed his left arm just enough to make its cantaloupe biceps wrinkle. A slight smile of approval appeared on his face as he turned away from Jeremy to admire his hard work. Surely all his weight lifting in the gym would earn him a place on HRT, he thought.

The SWAT agent flexed his pectoral muscles, still staring at himself in the mirror as Jeremy took care of business behind him. He barely noticed when the toilet flushed and never even saw the lightning-quick arc of Jeremy's fist as it slammed into the side of his head. Before he knew what hit him, the guard dropped to the marble floor like so much laundry.

By the time he recovered enough to hear the EAP counselor yelling, the man with the arms realized that Jeremy had disappeared. *Son of a bitch!* he scolded himself. Even through the ringing in his ears, he knew his chances of making HRT had just evaporated. He'd never live this down.

▐▌

SIRAD HAD TRIED three times to contact Hoch, all without success. Now she sat at the desk of her new Borders Atlantic office, trapped between Mitchell's surveillance and a gnawing sense that something had gone terribly wrong with the Agency. Hamid was not in his office and would not return her calls.

Sirad tapped the elegantly manicured nail of her right index finger against the touch pad of her phone while trying to decide what to do next. Someone had already attacked her in Hamid's apartment, and she had not ruled out Mitchell's own seventeenth-floor goons. If she didn't find a way out of this in a hurry, the next attack might not end as well.

She stood up and grabbed her purse. Without direction from

Hoch, her only option was to try to take down Mitchell herself. That meant getting access to all those secrets he kept talking about. It meant going down the Rabbit Hole.

▍

TWO MILES SOUTH of Jordan Mitchell's empire, in a sprawling office space now empty but for the hum of fluorescent lights, Theodore Allen Dokes reached down to pick up a wastebasket full of Starbucks coffee cups, handwritten notes, and half-eaten jelly doughnuts.

"Bism Allah al-Rahman, al-Rahman," he murmured beneath his breath, reciting from the Koran, which he'd just one year earlier taken as the word of God. He'd already gone to his mullah for help in picking a Muslim name, a name he had legally changed to reflect his new devotion: Mustafa Ali Muhammad. *Sounds like a jihad warrior,* he thought; it was a tribute to his two favorite fighters, Eddie Mustafa Hamsho and the former Cassius Clay.

Dokes emptied the trash can into his janitor's cart, dusted off a monitor in one of the cubicles, and moved on to the next. He did the same thing every night, cleaning up in the early morning hours after the capitalist Americans who now seemed so arrogant in their imperialist march through Islam. It was the same oppressive white government that had busted him for crack possession five years earlier, destroying any chance he'd ever have to break out of his South Bronx neighborhood. It was the same evil government that had festered in his gut every day of his five-year sentence — until the E-block mullah showed him the true God.

Once he had converted in his heart, everything had changed. He had direction now, a sense of belonging. He no longer looked at himself as a menial laborer. Now he was a holy warrior, an operative, snatching valuable information from trash cans and desktops and Rolodexes, here at one of the most powerful banks in the United States.

"Allah huakbar," Dokes mumbled under his breath, turning briefly toward Mecca and offering a short prayer that his work tonight would equal that of the brethren who had given their lives for Allah. No, this wasn't a suicide mission, but it would distinguish him

among all martyrs, his controller had said. Once he got the phone call, a phone call on this fancy new phone they'd given him, he'd use the financial system's own computers to cripple itself.

"*Allah huakbar.*" Less than an hour from now he'd bring jihad to the Western world in ways that made previous attacks on New York pale by comparison. That's what they told him, anyway.

Dokes emptied another trash can, then double-checked to make sure his new Borders Atlantic Quantis phone was on. He didn't want to miss the biggest opportunity of his otherwise wasted life.

XXII

———

JEREMY RAN THE first ten blocks, west toward the Hudson, then north up Broadway and east to Central Park. Staying out in the streets exposed him to the intervention he knew they'd send, but ducking in among the dark, shadowy forest gave him a sniper's advantage. In there, he could remain invisible, hiding and moving until he was sure they were no longer a threat.

Just after midnight, Jeremy emerged along a joggers' trail at the east side of the park and spotted a sign that read SEVENTY-NINTH STREET. Everything looked dead still, despite the now pouring rain. No pedestrians, only an occasional cab. Water ran off his forehead, clouding his vision as he sucked deep breaths against the exertion.

There, he thought. Across the street, a bank of three phones, almost obsolete in the cell phone age. Jeremy looked both ways for signs that anyone might have tracked him; then he dashed across and leaned into the three-sided shelter and dialed home.

"Caroline, listen to me," he huffed as his wife picked up the phone in Virginia. Except for the message, Jeremy hadn't talked to her since leaving for work that morning.

"Where are you?" she demanded. "Your office called . . . they said they were taking you to Chicago for some kind of psychological evaluation. Jeremy, what is . . ."

"Listen!" he yelled, instantly regretting the emotion. "Listen, baby, I'm sorry I can't explain this right now . . . but I need you to do something for me."

He paused for a response, but there was nothing but the sound of rain.

"I need you to call me a car like you did that time in Washington, remember?" Jeremy squinted, trying to read the street sign down the block. EIGHTY-FIRST STREET. "But this time I'm in New York. Tell them to pick me up at . . ." He stopped himself. This was a pay phone; any operation sophisticated enough to pull off the Yemen gig could be listening. "Take our anniversary and add sixty — got it?"

"The day or the month?" she asked. Jeremy smiled for the first time in weeks.

"The day. The day plus sixty. Tell them to pick me up on that street, at . . ."

He stopped for a minute. What the hell was he going to use for longitude?

"Central Park East. That number and Central Park East," Jeremy said. He assumed the dispatcher would know Caroline meant Fifth Avenue; he had no time for more games. "As fast as you can get them here baby. OK?"

Jeremy scanned for threats as Caroline said she understood.

"I'll call as soon as I can," he said. "And Caroline . . ." He held his breath a moment, trying to decide what to say. "Remember that I love you, OK? Don't believe them, no matter what they tell you."

He hung up and ran back into the park, hoping that he could hide there long enough for the car to come and save him.

▮

GRAND CENTRAL STATION is a huge expanse of marble, concrete, and history, but all Senator Elizabeth Beechum could see as she entered the Forty-second Street entrance was her life flashing before her eyes. Somewhere between the front door and the train tracks stood proof that everything they had said about her, everything that had been alleged, charged, plotted, conspired, and written, was a lie.

Beechum hurried into the terminal, following what little information she had gathered about Valez. The doorman had shown her videotape of the man coming and going at the apartment building, so she had a face. James had given her the identifiers from Valez's driver's license, so she had a physical description. A phone call to the station's information office had given her train schedules and track locations, so she had objectives. The only thing she seemed short of was time.

▐

JEREMY WAITED IN a juniper hedge until the black Cadillac pulled up at the Eighty-first Street intersection, then ran out and jumped in the backseat.

"Phone," was all he said to the driver. "I need your phone."

▐

SIRAD KNEW SHE'D never gain access to the seventeenth floor. There was no point, anyway. All the answers she needed had to be accessible through the computer in Hamid's office.

Just after midnight, she walked away from her desk, took the elevator up to the twentieth floor, and simply walked into Hamid's lushly appointed sanctum. His computer terminal sat quietly to the right of his desk. The laptop she had seen him use for peripherals trading sat off to the left.

"Borders Atlantic is full of secrets, and they're all mine," she whispered, mocking Jordan Mitchell's words to her. His policy of prohibiting employees from locking any door may have discouraged impropriety, but it also made things easier for her tonight.

Sirad sat down without turning on any lights and booted up both machines. The quiet glow of the monitors provided all the illumination she needed.

All right, you bastards, she thought as she typed, *let's see what the hell this is all about.*

343

❚❚❘

MITCHELL STEPPED BACK from Russ's computer terminal, confident that everything he had worked so hard to arrange was finally coming together. The endgame had already begun.

"So we believe the Arabs remain confident in the system?" he asked.

"Yes, sir," Trask said. "The BBC is running a story about how the SBT phones have been found in terrorist safe houses in Cairo, Caracas, and Manila. All three cable channels are carrying stories about FBI plans to serve search warrants tomorrow morning. All three remaining Democratic challengers have issued statements condemning Borders Atlantic — and you, by name — for selling out the United States for financial gain. With the exception of Senator Beechum, you and Borders Atlantic have to rank among the most hated names in America right now."

"Good." Mitchell clasped his hands in front of him the way he did in rare moments of contentment. "What about the threat level?"

"The Department of Homeland Security is preparing to elevate the terror threat level to red over the Matrix 1016 issue. They don't have a time line, though, so we don't know if that will come tomorrow or later in the week. There's speculation that the move could cause significant downward pressure in our stock."

"It won't matter," Mitchell said. "We'll be safe long before it becomes a . . ."

"Wait a minute," Russ interrupted. "I've got a firewall intrusion on the peripherals databases. Just popped up."

"Where?" Mitchell asked. He sounded curious more than surprised, as if he'd expected it.

"Hamid's office. Someone's using his terminal and password."

Mitchell turned to the company's brightest financial mind.

"See what I told you, Hamid?" he said. "This girlfriend of yours is interested in a whole lot more than your smile."

❚❚❘

WITHIN THREE MINUTES of entering Hamid's office, Sirad had accessed the company's peripherals trading schedules, accounts, and routing information — virtually everything Hoch had sent her into Hamid's apartment to find. Sirad duped everything to disks, shaking her head as she went at the extent of Mitchell's dealings and the craft in his deception. Hundreds of billions of dollars, clients throughout the Middle East, Europe, Asia, even inside the United States. If the FCC got their hands on this, Mitchell would be finished.

Sirad watched the reception lobby as she worked, knowing full well that everything she did on Hamid's computer would probably show up on some kind of activity alert. Perhaps the goons up on the seventeenth floor already knew she was there.

"Come on, baby," she said out loud as she typed a final command line and popped the fifth disk of information out of the laptop's A drive. Off went the power. No noise. No pop-up inquiries on the monitor screen.

Sirad stuffed the disks into her suit coat and hurried out of the office. Her Internet contact had made it clear that they needed this information as soon as possible. All she needed now was to use one of the cybercafe computers to arrange a dead drop somewhere in the city.

She walked out of the office suite and punched the elevator's Down button. After what seemed like an eternity, the doors opened, and she started to step inside.

"Working late?" A man's voice startled her.

Jordan Mitchell stood inside the elevator with a knowing grin on his face. Hamid, Trask, and Dieter stood around him.

◼

BEECHUM SPOTTED HIM from fifty feet away, standing at an Au Bon Pain counter, paying for a cup of coffee. He wore a baseball cap, a denim welder's coat, and cowboy boots. The former military man looked heavier than she remembered, but it was him. No question. This was the animal who had attacked her.

"Sorry, Mr. Valez; this isn't personal," she said, walking up behind him. She spoke softly, with a firm confidence, just the way he had last spoken to her.

The man who had haunted her dreams for weeks opened his coffee cup without turning around and stirred in a double shot of half-

and-half. Beechum couldn't see the tattoo through his thick denim jacket, but she remembered the way his arm felt around her throat.

"You've got some balls trying this in person," was all he said.

Beechum stood less than an arm's length behind him, knowing that he could have turned and broken her in half. But he wouldn't. This was a public place, and he was a military man. He understood the stipulations of defeat.

"All I want is a name," Beechum told him. She walked to his side so she could see his face. He had bright blue eyes and a light brow. "I need to know who hired you to do this to me."

Valez looked up from his coffee. He didn't seem to mind looking at her.

"You know I can't tell you that," he said. "Even if I felt bad about what has happened to you, I couldn't give them up."

What he didn't dare say was that he would never forget what had happened to him along Fifth Avenue, that he would never stop thinking that they could reach out and snuff him if they wanted to.

"No one is ever going to know you told me," Beechum promised.

Valez laughed out loud. He looked conspicuously past her to a man standing across the cavernous room: African American, refined. He apparently felt no discomfort in their scrutiny.

"They know everything," Valez said.

"Who are they?" Beechum asked. She started to turn away. "To hell with it, I'll go find out myself!"

Valez stopped her. "You're smarter than that," he said.

"I'm smart enough to put an end to this nonsense!" she barked. "I have your fingerprints in the tunnel you and my lawyer used to get into my house. I have an audio recording of everything you said and did."

"Then what else can I offer you, Senator? Sounds like you've got your case."

"I need you to tell me who's behind all this."

"Let's walk." Valez took a sip of his coffee and led her toward the platform where he still meant to meet his train.

"You know I don't have that kind of information," he said. "That's the way it is on the wet side. Shadows, suggestions, denial. Only the cash is real." He took a deep breath, sizing up what he thought of the path his life had taken. "I'm a subcontractor, ma'am, in a much larger project. I don't get to know every damned thing."

"You must have had some kind of contact," Beechum said. She almost tripped over a stack of newspapers sitting beside a newsstand: *Washington Post, USA Today, New York Times.* The covers were split between shots of Jordan Mitchell and herself.

"They called me," he said. "I never contacted them."

"What about Phillip? Was he your contact? What did he tell you?"

"If you mean the guy I went into your house with, I never knew anything about him, either. He seemed to know his way around. That was the only time I ever saw him."

They stopped at the train platform, and she noticed that the African American had followed them in from the coffee stand. He stood closer now, by half.

"Help me with *something*," Beechum pleaded. The FBI had agreed to listen if she could just bring them a name, but if that name was Marcellus Parsons, she'd need proof.

"There is one thing," he said, reaching into his pocket and pulling out an odd-looking electronic device. Beechum recognized it immediately as one of the SBT Quantis phones she'd tried so hard to keep Borders Atlantic from selling. He handed it to her. "This is how they contacted me . . . but I wouldn't turn it on if I were you. They almost killed me with it."

Jordan Mitchell? she asked herself. Would he have gone that far just to market cell phones?

"I meant it when I said it wasn't personal, Senator," Valez said. The train rolled onto the platform, and the doors opened. "I don't know that I'll ever get away from these people, but I'm going to try. Maybe you ought to try it too."

Valez turned to leave, but Beechum grabbed his arm. "You can't just walk away and leave me to this!" she pleaded.

Valez pulled back his arm as the black man watching them started to move closer. "Good luck," he said. And with that, Beechum saw her last shot at vindication walk onto the train and disappear into a tunnel. The black man moved closer.

▐█▌

JEREMY DISMISSED HIS driver and climbed out of the warm, dark Cadillac at Sixty-seventh and Park. Quick calls to Musto and directory assistance had told him everything he needed to know about what lay ahead this night. According to Musto, the New York office had issued a BOLO — Be On the Lookout — for him, with a written notice circulated through the nation's sixty-six regional Joint Terrorism Task Forces that he was a "credible and immediate threat" to ongoing investigations.

The good news was that Musto had tracked Jesús' NMARSAT call to a hard line at Borders Atlantic's corporate headquarters, less than two blocks away. Jeremy had no idea what he should expect to find at midnight in an empty office building, but at this point there was no place else to go. Something intuitive told him that if he could just get inside, he might be able to cut this Gordian knot that had choked off his life.

▌▌

SIRAD SAT IN a heavy walnut chair near the floor-to-ceiling windows looking out of the War Room into a hanging New York rain. Her hands had been wrenched up and tied between her shoulder blades, forcing her forward in an agonizing posture. Her feet were spread and shackled to the chair legs. They had stripped her to her underwear.

"I'll ask again. Who do you work for?" Mitchell had done all the talking.

"You know who I work for." Sirad tried to sound strong, despite the burning pain in her face where Dieter had slapped her several times already. There was no blood, just the sharp bite of an open hand and the humiliation that came with failing her mission. "I work for you."

WHACK!

Dieter slapped her again. This time hard enough to draw blood on her lower lip.

"Now you know that can't be true, Sirad," Mitchell condescended. "No one who works for me steals the way you have stolen. No one sleeps with my top executives just to get information. No one in my employ would betray my confidences, particularly after all I've done. Isn't that true, Sirad?"

Mitchell moved around Dieter, close enough to run his hand over her face, to let his fingers drift down the elegant lines of her neck, to caress her naked shoulder. Hamid stood just behind him, staring at her with a look of utter betrayal as Mitchell slipped the strap of her bra off her shoulder.

"You may draw a paycheck from Borders Atlantic, Sirad, but you obviously don't work for me. Who sent you here?"

WHACK!

Mitchell himself hit her this time. He stepped back, as if shocked by his own actions. He stared at his palm like a child finding a new and fascinating toy.

"This isn't going to work," Trask said.

"I agree." Dieter tilted his head, studying Sirad like a curious professor. "We are running out of time. If she knows about the peripherals trading, she probably knows about the Matrix. Which means we have a very difficult situation here."

Mitchell agreed. "Let's try the water board," he said. "Maybe that will loosen that pretty little mouth."

▮

JEREMY HAD LITTLE time to formulate a plan. Talking to Musto over the Town Car's cell phone had provided an address and a location for the NMARSAT origination, but it had almost certainly given him away, too. All he could hope for, at this point, was to make enough of a disturbance that Jordan Mitchell would be drawn back to the building. If he could get to Jordan by the time the FBI tracked him down, he might be able to force Jesús' hand. He also might be able to help stop what Jesús had called Matrix 1016 — the Wedding — from happening.

Getting into the building was easy. So was the disturbance. He simply strolled in through the revolving door, walked up to an overweight, underpaid swing-shift guard at the reception desk, and cold-cocked him. One punch to the head.

Jeremy should have regretted the unprovoked attack, but at this point, a clean blow seemed almost kind. He was soaking wet, exhausted to the point where his mind barely worked.

"Mitchell!" Jeremy yelled out loud. He looked up at the forty-foot ceilings, waving to the security cameras, hoping to trigger a rapid response from guards in other parts of the building. "Mitchell! You son of a bitch! I'm here!"

Nothing.

Jeremy stepped behind the desk and pulled out the still-unconscious guard's phone directory. He ran his finger through the hundreds of extensions until he found the one Musto had given him.

Room 3171.

"Fair enough." Jeremy pulled a 10mm Glock pistol from the guard's holster and tucked it into his belt line. "Then I'll force you out."

▌▌

MUSTAFA ALI MUHAMMAD waited until the designated time before switching on the fancy new phone he'd received DHL from Paris. His instructions were simple, but he'd practiced them again and again in his mind. After booting up a computer his controllers had identified through other means, he inserted a CD that had arrived just that morning under separate cover.

He typed commands and executed mouse clicks until the screen he'd been told to expect blinked brightly across his monitor.

"*Allah huakbar,*" he whispered, wondering what it looked like through the cockpit of those jets as his fellow jihadists piloted them into the World Trade Center towers and the Pentagon. He let his mind drift to wonder how bravely his comrades had fought before losing their airliner in a Pennsylvania field. He imagined how it would feel to have the whole world know his name — his Muslim name — and speak it with reverence.

Mustafa Ali Muhammad leaned back in his chair and looked over his shoulder to make sure none of the other janitors walked in on him.

Patience, he told himself. He ran his fingers over the new Borders Atlantic phone that had made this whole operation possible. *The call will come.*

∎

SIRAD STRUGGLED BRAVELY, but Trask was much stronger than he looked. Dieter and Hamid helped too, binding her to the massive conference table and pulling her head back almost perpendicular to her body.

"You're not going to like this much," Dieter said. She understood why he never liked her. Sadists don't like anyone.

He poured seltzer water down her nose, and she began to choke, then gasp, then seize against the restraints as the bubbles erupted in her esophagus, effervesced in her lungs.

"Who do you work for?" Mitchell asked again. He seemed surprised at how awful this whole interrogation business looked in person. The polygraph had been so much cleaner.

Sirad tried to rip her arms and legs free, but there was no escaping. Her eyes searched wildly for the next dose, knowing this or the next would render her unconscious.

"Again?" Dieter looked at Sirad the whole time, wearing a curious expression that Mitchell had never noticed on his face before — something akin to arousal.

"Yes, again." Mitchell nodded.

Dieter lifted the seltzer bottle and began to pour, when . . .

"Back away from the table!"

Mitchell turned nonchalantly toward the massive double doors where a soaking-wet, desperate-looking man stood against the light of the foyer. He held a large-bore pistol at arm's length. He looked willing to use it.

"Ah, Special Agent Waller!" Mitchell exclaimed.

Jeremy just stood there, dripping water all over the antique Oushak rug. The weight of the room amazed him. The light, the wood, the walls of rifles and truncheons. The woman on the table — the woman from the Yemen trip.

Mitchell started toward Jeremy with an outstretched hand. "You took longer than I'd expected," Mitchell said. "Did you have trouble getting in?"

"Stop," Jeremy commanded. He swept the muzzle of his pistol

across the room, letting Dieter and Trask and Hamid know that he was interested in them, too.

"Get away from her," Jeremy demanded. He moved toward Sirad and used his left hand to loosen her restraints. She jumped off the table and stumbled her way toward her clothes.

"I want to know why, you traitorous bastard," Jeremy demanded. "I want to know what you are trying to do with my goddamned life!"

"I've heard that about you, Agent Waller, that you ask a lot of questions. Perhaps it's just natural for a man of your profession." Mitchell motioned toward Trask. "Unfortunately, we don't have a lot of time."

Trask reached out to pick up the remote control for the media center.

"Freeze!" Jeremy called out, but Trask pressed a button anyway. The claro walnut doors slid aside, exposing the same wall of television and audio monitors they had used to follow Jeremy's Yemen expedition.

"I told you to . . ."

Before Jeremy could finish, someone stepped inside the room behind him. He saw the figure out of the corner of his eye and started to turn, but a voice stilled him. It was a man's voice, a voice he'd obeyed before.

"That's enough, Waller. Drop the gun." It was Jesús.

Jeremy blinked twice, trying to clear his vision of the rain dripping out of his hair. *How the hell did Jesús track me here?* he wondered.

"I'm not dropping anything," Jeremy responded. He pointed the weapon right at Mitchell's face, so close that the CEO could smell the gun oil glistening on its barrel. "What are you going to do, shoot one of your team members in the back? You may have gotten away with murder in Yemen, but I don't think it's going to work in here."

Suddenly, a blunt, percussive pain shot through Jeremy's head. It felt like standing in front of a giant loudspeaker, without the sound. He staggered under the pain, then clutched the sides of his head and dropped to his knees. The gun tumbled onto the carpet in front of him.

"Guns belong in collections now — on walls — Mr. Waller," Mitchell said. "Technology has taken us well beyond them." He motioned toward Jeremy's Glock and Jesús shuffled quickly over to snatch it up. Once he did, Jeremy's pain immediately subsided, focus returned to his eyes; a small trickle of blood seeped out of his nose.

"Hoch, bring them in!" Mitchell directed, loudly enough that someone in an outside room could hear.

The handle to a side door rattled and in walked three men and a woman. Sirad was the first to react with astonishment. *My God*, she thought — the first man through the door was Hoch.

"Permit me to introduce our guests," Mitchell said. He clasped his hands in front of him as if convening a board meeting. "This is Charles Hoch, an army colonel assigned to the Central Intelligence Agency."

Hoch stood near the wall of truncheons with no expression on his face. Next to him stood a man Jeremy vaguely recognized from newspaper and television reports of the Beechum scandal.

"This is Craig Slater of the National Security Council," Mitchell continued, moving down the lineup. "You may know him better as the supposed victim of United States Senator Elizabeth Beechum, who I'm certain needs no further introduction."

Jeremy and Sirad stared in disbelief. Beechum stood there in front of them, right next to Slater, who looked healthy and fit despite reports to the contrary. No one else in the room seemed even slightly impressed.

"And last but not least, let me introduce Phillip Matthews — a Washington lawyer of unimpeachable pedigree," Mitchell said. He paused a moment to examine the various faces around the room. "I suppose we're all here now. Nicely done, Mr. Trask."

He nodded to his chief of staff, who pointed the channel changer at the multimedia wall. He clicked a button, and the screens erupted with a grainy, cockeyed image of a man's face. Though no one in the room knew his name, it was Mustafa Ali Muhammad — the janitor about to execute Matrix 1016.

"I know that some of you have a lot of questions," Mitchell continued. "We'll get to them in a minute. First, we have to deal with a little business."

Trask punched up the volume, allowing everyone to listen in on a cell phone conversation between the janitor and an unidentified voice on the other end of the line.

"A brave and industrious hero of al Qaeda," someone said in Arab-accented English. The loudspeakers echoed through the War Room. "It is time, Muhammad. It is time to cripple these rich American pigs."

"That's why they hate us, you know," Mitchell said. "The money. The United States is the greatest empirical power in the history of the world not because of its military might, but because of its wealth."

As if on cue, Hamid moved to a computer terminal and began to type. Everyone else watched the screens, trying to make sense of the events playing out around them.

"This is the reason we have so much trouble fighting al Qaeda," Mitchell explained. "They recruit through ideology — fundamentalism — that has no bounds in geography. They can find otherwise ordinary citizens even inside the United States and sell them on hatred and fear. Call them sleepers or rogue agents, whatever you like; the result is the same. They mean us harm, and it is very difficult for anyone to find them."

"He's starting the process," Hamid said. The money manager sat at a computer terminal, glued to the screen. "I'm tracking his keystrokes, and he's already . . ."

"He just hung up," Dieter interrupted. Everyone turned to the wall of screens, which flickered, then went black. "The camera only works when the line is hot."

"All right, we don't have a lot of time," Mitchell said, dispensing for a moment with his explanations. "Let's intercede."

Jeremy regained his feet but leaned against the wall for fear of falling. He noticed that though Jesús had lowered his pistol, he was more interested in Jeremy than the workings around them.

"Got it!" Hamid called out. He worked his keyboard, pausing to check new information, then working some more. "All international financial transfers through the Fed have been deposited in our accounts. At this moment, you are the wealthiest man in the history of the world, Mr. Mitchell."

"Good. Kill him," Mitchell said.

Without questions or further explanation, Dieter pulled out a

Quantis phone and dialed a number. The screens lit up again as Muhammad the janitor answered his phone.

"Hello?" he said. The integral camera projected his image for all to see as a moment of silence gave way to a thud as Muhammad fell to the floor. The phone tumbled unceremoniously out of his lifeless hand and landed under a desk, its digital camera fortuitously capturing a close-up of Muhammad's now distorted face. Blood dripped from his nose and ears. He was dead.

"Who the hell are you?" Jeremy asked, turning toward Mitchell. He'd seen enough.

"Ah, yes — those answers I've been promising," Mitchell said. "Mr. Hoch, perhaps you can help us out."

Everyone turned to the four people standing at the wall of truncheons.

"Thirty-seven years ago," the CIA operative began, "a young Dartmouth College student applied for employment with the Central Intelligence Agency. We hired him, financed his MBA at Harvard, finished him at the Farm, and cut his teeth with a one-year academic cover in Peru.

"This was 1967, by the way — a point in history when private business and government intelligence agencies were just beginning to work closely together for mutual benefit. In this case, the business was ITT — the world's first multinational corporation. Due to a general strike in Chile — where ITT obtained copper for its telephone wires — and our war on communism, the two parties entered into a mutually beneficial arrangement. They provided money, and we provided operational support in orchestrating the overthrow of Salvador Allende."

Hoch looked around the room to make sure everyone was following, then continued.

"Once the Directorate of Operations reached out for volunteers, this Dartmouth kid jumped at the chance, and within six months, he had turned four hundred thousand dollars in black seed money into a small but profitable business flying copper mining supplies in and intelligence out. Same idea as Air America, only smaller.

"But what started out with a Grumman Goose, two salesmen, and a secretary quickly blossomed into an extensive South American import/export company. Within a year he'd purchased another plane and hired twenty-seven more employees. A year later the company tripled. By the late eighties his company had diversified to include telecommunications, finance, and even Internet technologies; a tremendous success, it seemed, because this new operations officer had as good a nose for business as he did for intelligence work.

"Which turned out well because he gave the U.S. government something every other agency on Earth would die for: access. With one hundred twenty-seven thousand employees; subsidiaries in banking, shipping, manufacturing; and legitimate trade routes in one hundred seventeen countries, his company opened doors we never could have through conventional means."

Hoch turned proudly to his right. "That man is Jordan Mitchell."

Jeremy and Sirad looked on in disbelief.

"You're telling me that one of the biggest corporations in America is a CIA front?" Jeremy asked. "Why the hell would a CIA front sell secure communications to the . . ."

Sirad understood at just about the same time he did. Her face still stung from what they had done to her, but things were beginning to make sense.

"He knew they'd use them," said Sirad.

Beechum nodded. She'd obviously been briefed on her way from the train station.

"It was the only way we could stop them," the senator said. "Al Qaeda spends years plotting attacks. The intelligence community knew from chatter that alal-Bin was plotting an attack on the Fed — what we call Matrix 1016 — but had no idea what. Chemical attack on Wall Street, a dirty nuke inside the New York reserve bank, cybercrime: they had no idea."

Trask stepped in.

"Jordan Mitchell allowed himself to be vilified — hated, really — by the entire country in order to save it."

"What about the money?" Jeremy asked. He still didn't understand all the details. "You just stole the money from the terrorists."

"For moments," Hamid explained. "Once al Qaeda started the transfers, we couldn't stop them all, so we trunked the entire process through our secure servers. Everything is back in place now. No one but us will ever know exactly what happened."

"*Us?*" Jeremy asked. "What do you mean *us?*"

"This is a different world, now, Agent Waller," Mitchell said. "It demands a new approach toward terrorism. What you see in this room represents the foundation of a whole new way of fighting: zero footprint, plausible deniability, immediate response — a black operations unit so secret the president knows about it only in concept."

Jeremy could see by the look in Jesús' eyes that he had been in on this from the start. The others clearly had been brought in somewhere along the way.

"I needed three people out of two hundred eighty million with the skill sets and the positions to make this a possibility," Mitchell said. He stood up and walked toward his newest prospects: Jeremy, Sirad, and Senator Beechum. "Phillip and the others have helped us establish a framework, but we need operatives in law enforcement, the intelligence community, and politics. You three are the survivors. Congratulations."

"This is some kind of selection?" Jeremy exclaimed. "You ruined our lives over some kind of goddamned selection?"

"Ruined!" Mitchell exclaimed. "Hardly, Agent Waller. What has been taken away can be restored by breakfast. Life is odd that way. It all comes down to opportunity and what you choose to do with it."

Mitchell allowed his three candidates to consider their options for a moment. A commitment of this kind would rely more on faith than logic.

"You're patriots. You've proven yourself in every test," he said. "You've seen, tonight, what we can do apart. Imagine what we can do together."

PHASE IV

Suddenly she came upon a little three-legged table, all made of solid glass; there was nothing on it except a tiny golden key. . . . She came upon a low curtain she had not noticed before, and behind it was a little door about fifteen inches high: she tried the little golden key in the lock, and to her great delight it fitted!

— *Lewis Carroll,* Alice's Adventures in Wonderland

XXIII

————

JEREMY WALLER SAT in the back of a late-model Cadillac STS. The newspaper beside him contained two stories of particular interest. On page one, in print large enough to read in the dark, he saw a headline: *BEECHUM FRAMED!* Craig Slater had been found, it seemed, now fully recovered from a bad fall suffered on his archaeological excursion to Turkey. Sources claimed the FBI was investigating an error in DNA mapping that linked Slater to the blood in Beechum's town house, and Washington police admitted that they may never know exactly who was responsible for what everyone now accepted as a real attack on the senator.

Page 3A contained another story about the G8 Summit, which had progressed smoothly without incident despite what intelligence community sources now called a foiled attempt by al Qaeda to take down the Federal Reserve. Though the FBI and CIA tried to take credit, several investigative reporters had uncovered hints that a shadowy new counterterrorism force had played a role.

Jeremy's cell phone rang, and he answered it. "Hello?"

"Daddy, I just wanted to call and say good night." It was Maddy.

"Good night, sweetie," Jeremy said. He hadn't got home in time to

Christopher Whitcomb

tuck her in; he seldom did anymore. HRT's new selection coordinator turned the dome light off and nodded to his driver. A thin Pakistani man pulled away from the curb and drove slowly past the Egyptian embassy. He flashed his lights twice and drove away as if nothing had happened.

"The following is an individual event of indeterminate duration," he whispered. "Your next objective . . ."

You thought you had proven yourself, but you never had.

362

About the Author

Christopher Whitcomb is the author of *Cold Zero*, a memoir of his fifteen-year tenure in the FBI, where he served as a Hostage Rescue Team sniper, an interrogation instructor, and, most recently, the director of intelligence and strategic information for the Critical Incident Response Group. Frequently seen on NBC, MSNBC, and CNBC, he is a recipient of the FBI's Medal of Bravery for exceptional courage in the line of duty. Whitcomb left the FBI in 2002 and is at work on the follow-up to *Black*.